WAIT FOR IT

MARIANA ZAPATA

Book Cover Design by Letitia Hasser, Romantic Book Affairs

Editing by Hot Tree Editing

Formatting by Jeff Senter, Indie Formatting Services

To my true love —
the one person I'd trust to protect me in jail:
my sister, Ale.
I wrote this book imagining
what it would be like
to not have you around…
and it sucked. A lot.
(Obviously.) Luckily for me,
evil never dies
so you're stuck with me forever, biatch.
(And I wouldn't have it
any other way.)

CHAPTER ONE

I WOKE UP SCREAMING.

Or pretty close to screaming, considering I was still getting over a cold I'd caught from Josh two weeks ago that had left me sounding like a chain-smoker going through puberty.

My eyes snapped open at the middle of my *"Ahh!"* to find a mini demon inches away from my face. I jumped. I flinched. I swear my soul left my body for one millionth of a second as the two eyes staring at me blinked.

"Shit!" I shouted as my back hit the headboard, and I sucked in what might have been the last gasp I'd ever take before having my throat slit.

Except...

In the middle of reaching over to grab the pillow next to me to—I didn't know what the hell I was going to do with it, pillow fight Willy Wonka's evil Oompa Loompa or something—I realized it wasn't a travel-sized disciple of Satan about to sacrifice me to the Dark Lord. Camouflaged in the nearly pitch-black room, the little face a few inches away from mine wasn't really the devil's minion; it was a five-year-old. *He* was a five-year-old. My five-year-old.

It was Louie.

"Oh my God, Lou," I wheezed at the realization of who was trying to kill me before I turned thirty. I blinked and clutched the skin over my heart like it was about to dive-bomb out of my chest.

I shouldn't have been surprised to find him on my bed. How many times had he scared the living shit out of me in the exact same way over the last couple of years? One hundred? I should have been used to him sneaking in to my room by now. He was the cutest little boy I'd ever seen—*in the daylight*—but somehow he didn't understand that staring at someone while they were sleeping was pretty damn creepy. *Really* creepy.

"Jesus Ch—" I started to say before going with "cheese and crackers." I could still hear my mom's voice a year ago ripping me a new one for teaching the boys to use the Lord's name in vain. "You scared the hell—" I groaned, realizing I messed up again. I really had been trying to get better about using bad words in front of Louie at least, since Josh was a lost cause, but old habits died hard. "Heck out of me," I went with instead, even though he'd heard words much worse than 'hell' and 'Jesus'.

"I'm sorry, *Tia* Diana," Louie whispered in that sugar-sweet voice that immediately had me forgiving him for everything he'd ever done and everything he would ever do.

"Lou." My heart was still beating fast. God. I was too young to have a stroke, wasn't I? I let the covers drop to my lap, still rubbing my chest. "You okay?" I whispered in return, trying to will my heartbeat back to a respectable pace.

He nodded seriously.

He didn't have nightmares often, but when he did, he always found his way to me... regardless of whether I was awake or not. Based on how groggy I felt, there was no chance I'd been asleep longer than a couple of hours. Sleeping in a new house wasn't helping my situation any. This was only our third night here. My body wasn't used to the bed facing a different direction. Everything smelled and sounded different, too. I'd had a hard enough time relaxing even back at our old apartment, so I wasn't surprised when I found myself in bed the last two nights messing around on my phone until I started dropping it on my face from how tired I was.

A small-fingered hand landed on my leg over the sheets. "I can't sleep," the little boy admitted, still whispering like he was trying not to wake me up even more than he already had by scaring the Holy Spirit and a couple drops of pee out of me. The darkness in the room hid Louie's blond hair and those blue eyes that still made my heart ache every so often. "There's alotta noise outside. Can I sleep with you?"

The yawn that came out of me lasted about fifteen seconds, ugly and choppy, my eyes watering in the process. "What kind of noise?"

"I think somebody's fighting by my window." He hunched his shoulders as he patted my leg.

That had me sitting up straight. Lou had an active imagination, but not *that* active. He'd spared us from having imaginary friends, but he hadn't saved me from pretending the toilet was a birdbath and he was a parrot when he was three.

A fight? *Here?*

I'd seen at least fifty houses before coming to this one. Fifty different sale listings that didn't work for one reason or another. They had either been too far from good schools, the neighborhood had looked sketchy, the yard hadn't been big enough, the house needed too much work, or it had been out of my price range.

So when my real estate agent mentioned having *one more* to show me, I hadn't been too optimistic. But she brought me to it anyway; it was a foreclosure that had only been on the market for a few days in a working-class neighborhood. I hadn't let myself get my hopes up. The fact it had three bedrooms, a huge front and backyard, and only needed a minimum amount of cosmetic work had been enough for me. I'd jumped on it and bought it.

Diana Casillas, homeowner. It was about time. I had been more than ready to get out of the two-bedroom apartment the boys and I had been holed up in for the last two years.

After all the dumps I'd been to, this place had been the light at the end of the tunnel. It wasn't perfect, but the potential was there. Despite not being in some fancy new subdivision in the suburbs, the surrounding schools were great. The greatest surprise of all was that it was close to where my job was being relocated, so I wouldn't waste hours of my life driving back and forth.

The thing was, I'd met a few of the new neighbors over the course of the month and a half it took to close on the house, but not all of them. The people who lived closest to Louie's bedroom were an elderly couple, not exactly the kind of people who you would imagine fighting in the middle of the night. The rest were nice families with little kids and everything. A neighborhood with a history of crime was the kind of shit I had been trying to avoid.

Nobody was supposed to be fighting, much less in the middle of the night.

"You can stay with me. Just don't kick me in the stomach again, okay? You almost cracked my rib last time," I reminded him in case he'd forgotten the giant bruise he'd given me that had me gasping for breath every time I bent over. I reached over to turn on the side lamp, nearly knocking it off the nightstand. Swinging my legs off the side of the bed, I tugged on the back of Louie's pajama pants to give him a partial wedgie as I got to my feet.

"It was an accident!" he giggled like he hadn't caused me weeks of pain by using my midsection as a ball, making it apparent he could have a career in soccer if he ever wanted to. We already had two soccer players in our extended family; we didn't need another one. With the light on, that tiny mischievous smile that owned my heart had the same effect on me it always had: it made everything in the world more bearable.

"Sure it was." I winked at him before yawning again and stretching my arms over my head to get some blood pumping throughout my body. "I'll be back in a minute, but try to go to sleep, okay? Grandma is picking you up early."

"Where are you going?"

There was always a hint of worry in his tone any and every time I went somewhere without him, like he expected me not to come back. I hated it. "To check on the noise. I'll be right back," I explained calmly, trying to tell him without words that it would take a weapon of mass destruction to keep me from him. But I didn't make the promise out loud. He needed to believe that on his own without me reminding him every time.

Louie nodded, already climbing under the covers, easing my conscience just a little. He was all gangly legs and arms, and that glowing peach skin that was his inheritance from his mom's Danish ancestry and our Mexican side. There wasn't a tanning bed or self-tanner in the world that could replicate his shade of gold.

"Go to sleep."

Turning off the lamp again, I slipped out of the bedroom, leaving the door cracked behind me. Thankfully, I'd put on shorts before I went to sleep. My hand went out to the walls to try and navigate my way around; I wasn't familiar with the layout of the house yet. The boys weren't scared of the dark, so we didn't bother with nightlights. As long as I could remember, my brother and I had convinced both of them that the bogeyman should be afraid of them, not them of it. I hadn't gotten around to hanging up anything yet, so there was no chance of me knocking pictures off their hangers as I steered down the hallway that separated my room from Louie and Josh's.

When the boys had first come to live with me, I would find myself waking up at least once a night to check on them, to make sure they hadn't magically disappeared like some *Unsolved Mystery*. Now, I only did it on nights like this one when Louie woke me up.

The first thing I spotted on Josh's bed was the long furry body that seemed to take up most of it, our family's 160 pound, worst bodyguard in the world. Mac was passed out, completely oblivious to me coming into the room, and to top it off, he hadn't even reacted to me screaming when I'd found Louie hovering. Higher up on the bed was the top of Josh's brown head of hair, so much like mine and Rodrigo's, peeking out from below the plain blue comforter he'd chosen two weeks ago. It was a miracle I hadn't started blubbering like a baby in the middle of the store. It had killed me a little when I had asked him if he wanted a Ninja Turtles set, and he'd opted for a basic blue one. He wasn't even turning eleven for a few more weeks, and he already thought he was too big for cartoon characters. I could still remember him in onesies like it was yesterday, damn it.

I left Josh's door mostly closed and headed toward Louie's room, the smallest one of the three and the one closest to the front of the house. I'd barely made it to his door when I heard shouting. *There was no way that was coming from the elderly neighbors next door.* The people living on the other side in a bungalow were a couple around my age with a baby.

The neighborhood had seemed like a safe one. Most of the driveways nearby had new-ish cars, but there were some filled with models that had been redesigned years ago. I hadn't been able to help but notice the lawns were all well taken care of, the houses nice and neat, even if they were all built before I'd been born. All signs pointed toward this house being a great place to raise two kids. It reminded me of where I had grown up.

Rodrigo would have approved.

Moving Lou's blinds as stealthily as possible to look out the window, it didn't take me long to find where the noise was coming from. Across the street, two houses to the right were a pair of cars parked in a way that blocked traffic from being able to pass, if there had been anyone driving around in the middle of the night on a weekday. But it was the four men highlighted beneath the street lamp on the sidewalk that had me zoning in on them.

They were fighting, just like Louie had hinted at. It only took me a second to realize that three of them were circling one. I'd seen enough fights on television to know that when three guys circled one, it didn't mean anything good was about to go down.

Was this really happening? I couldn't have gotten like a six-month grace period before things like this went down at a neighbor's house? A stranger was about to get jumped, and I could only assume someone I was now living across the street from was a part of it. Was the man on his own my neighbor? Or was my neighbor one of the guys trying to jump the single one?

It was right then, in the middle of trying to guess what the hell was happening, that the man in the middle of the circle had a punch connect with his jaw. He dropped to a knee, swinging back wildly, missing all of his attackers. The other three took advantage and lunged at the guy on his own.

Oh my God. They were going to kick his ass, and I was standing there watching. *Watching.*

I couldn't go out there.

Could I?

I had Louie and Josh now. Jesus Christ. I didn't need to look around the room to know it was still full of boxes of toys and clothes. How a little boy had so much stuff was beyond me. I'd just bought him an Iron Man comforter for his twin-sized bed.

It wasn't just me I was responsible for, I thought as I witnessed the guy get kicked in the ribs. What if the men had guns? What if—

Through the window, I kept watching Guy On His Own get punched repeatedly by the same person. Over and over again. It was an ass beating if I had ever seen an ass beating. If that wasn't bad enough, another man stepped in and took over. My heart grew about four sizes. *Jesus.* Jesus. He was getting his ass whooped. Guy On His Own fell to his side, kicked over and over again the minute one of his attackers had an opening. They were like hyenas on a wounded gazelle. They were going to kill him.

And I was standing there. Still.

I thought about my brother, feeling that familiar ache pierce my heart and flood it with grief and regret and anger all at once. Hesitating could be the difference between life and death, didn't I know that?

I couldn't live with myself if something happened that I could have prevented. I didn't think about the possibility of them having guns or someone coming after me in retaliation, and I sure as hell didn't take into consideration how my parents, much less the boys, would handle me doing something so reckless. But what kind of person would I be if I just stood inside my house and did nothing to help someone who obviously needed it?

Before I could talk myself out of it, I ran out of the bedroom and toward the front, my feet bare. I didn't want to waste time running back to my room for my phone or shoes, but I clearly remembered Josh leaving his baseball bag by the front door so he wouldn't forget it when he left with his grandparents' tomorrow. If I made it through tonight, I really needed to start calling around to find him a new baseball team, I reminded myself before shoving the plan away for a better time.

I needed to go help because it was the right thing to do and because I needed to be a role model for the boys. And running from obstacles wasn't something they needed to learn from anyone.

The fact was, it was down to the Larsens, my parents, and me to mold them into who they'd become later in life. That was one of the first things I'd had to come to terms with when I became their guardian. *It was up to me.* If I messed up with them... I couldn't let that happen. I wanted them to grow up to be good, honorable people even if it seemed like I had forever until they were something more than the little boys who could barely aim their pee into the toilet and not miss. I didn't want Rodrigo's kids to turn out differently just because he wasn't around to raise them, because I knew exactly whose fault it would be if they grew into little shits: mine.

I didn't need that on my conscience.

Right where he had left it, I grabbed the bat sticking out of Josh's bag, testing the weight of the composite. It wasn't until I eased the front door closed behind me that the urge to run back into the house really hit me. The part of my brain that realized how stupid of an idea doing this was wanted to be back in my room under the covers. It didn't want to have to make this decision—risk my life or not risk my life? But just thinking Rodrigo's name kept me going.

As I ran down the three steps leading from the deck to the walkway, I sent a silent prayer, hoping this wasn't going to backfire on me. My feet had just hit the cement when I noticed the man all by himself was still surrounded, still getting his ass beat. Panic climbed all over my shoulders. *How did no one else hear this?* I wondered before figuring it didn't matter. I had to do what I had to do, and that was help this guy out and get back in my house in one piece.

"The cops are on their way!" I yelled at the top of my lungs, raising the bat up high. "Leave him alone!"

In the greatest surprise of my life, the three men stopped instantly; one of their legs was suspended in the air midkick, and they looked at each other in obvious hesitation, giving me a blurry view of their bland, unremarkable faces. There was nothing special about them; they were tall-ish and had thin builds.

"Back up!" I screamed, my voice cracking, when they kept standing there. I really, really hoped it was my neighbor on the ground and not one of the other guys, or else getting in and out of my house was going to be real awkward for a long time.

Why wasn't anyone out here helping? I wondered one more time, not understanding why no one else had come out. They weren't exactly being quiet.

My heart was beating a mile a minute, and I was already sweating like a pig. I was on my own; terrified even as adrenaline pumped through me, but what the hell was I supposed to do? Stand there with my thumb up my butt?

"Back up!" I yelled again with more balls behind my tone, pissed beyond reason that this kind of shit would even be happening in my neighborhood.

There was a single harsh whisper, and then one of attackers took a step back toward the man on the ground and kicked him hard before pointing. "This isn't over, motherfucker!" he hissed.

As cowardly as it was, I couldn't help but feel more than a little thankful when two of the jerks jumped into a car together and the other got into the second vehicle without a second glance in my direction, tires peeling onto the street.

The man on the ground barely stirred as I stepped closer to him, my legs trying their best to imitate noodles. The guy was on his back, his heels dragging back and forth across the grass as he writhed in pain, silently. His arms, both covered in tattoos to the wrist, were around his head. I was crossing on to the yard when his head tipped up. He didn't take much time rolling onto his side, then finally to his hands and knees, pausing in that position.

I dropped the bat on the lawn. "Whoa, buddy, you all right?" was the only thing I could think of to ask as I went to my knees right next to my more-than-likely neighbor. His attention was still focused on the ground. His breathing was choppy and uneven; a line of saliva and blood trailed from what I could only assume was his mouth to the grass. He coughed and more rose-colored fluids dribbled out.

Distracted and, honestly, pretty damn close to panicking, I noticed the hands holding him up were covered in tattoos too, but it was the splotches covering both sets of his knuckles that were a telltale sign he'd tried to fight back at least. Maybe he didn't know how to fight, but he could get an E for effort.

"Hey, are you all right?" I asked again, slipping my gaze over him, searching for some sign that said he was okay even though chances were he probably wasn't. I'd seen how much they had hurt him. How could he be fine?

His choppy breathing got even rougher before the man bowed his back and spit; his exhale afterward rattled and sounded painful.

I looked him over; the fluorescent street light made his hair look dark blond. The T-shirt he had on was spotted with blood. But it was his bare feet that said everything; he had to be my neighbor. Why else wouldn't he have on shoes? Had he opened the door expecting everything to be okay and then gotten jumped?

"What can I help you with?" My voice was shaky and low as he started trying to get off his hands and solely onto his knees, either not realizing I was there or not caring. I moved closer and was caught off guard when an arm reached up toward me.

I only hesitated for a second before taking his wrist, sliding my shoulder under his arm as the blades of grass rubbed against my bare knees. His weight came down on me as his inner elbow settled around the back of my neck. A hint of some kind of liquor hit my nostrils as I slung my arm around his lower back. Anxiety prickled my belly at his closeness. I didn't know this fool. I had no idea what he was capable of, or what kind of person he was. I mean, who got jumped outside their home? That wasn't some random, being-in-the-wrong-place-at-the-wrong-time crap. It was personal.

It didn't matter. At least a small part of me recognized that it shouldn't matter. Three against one were shitty odds even if they were deserved.

When he tried getting to his feet, I did too, huffing and struggling a lot more than I'd like to admit as he used me for support. "Pal, I need you to tell me if you're okay or not," I told him, swallowing the heartbeat knocking around in my throat as I pictured him keeling over on me from internal bleeding. That would make my night. "Hey, can you hear me? Are you all right?"

"I'm fucking fine," was his wonderful answer as he spat out more saliva.

Uh-huh, that wasn't really believable when he sounded like he'd tried running a marathon he hadn't trained for and bailed halfway through. But what was I going to do? Call him a liar even as he leaned half his weight on me? "Is this your house?"

"Mm-hmm," the man grumbled the response deep in his throat.

Keeping my gaze low, I glanced around the lawn, trying to ignore what was probably close to 200 pounds using me as a crutch. Just like nearly every other house in the neighborhood, the one we were in front of had a deck built three steps up leading to the front door. I raised my free hand and pointed toward it. "I need you to sit down for a second, all right?" My back was about to give out.

Out of my peripheral vision, he seemed to nod or gesture in agreement, but I only caught a glimpse of a jawline covered in a thick beard that belonged on a hipster or a lumberjack. Thankfully, he must have sensed my spine was about to snap in half because he took weight off me as we walked forward ten feet that felt like half a mile. His body was slightly hunched, his breathing rattled. At the steps, I turned to lead him down so he could sit, letting me get a good look at him up close.

At first glance, I realized he was older than me. Maybe ten years, maybe twenty years, some men were hard to guess, and he was one of them. His cheeks had pink-colored patches highlighting spots across them. There was a big split along his eyebrow, and a smaller but just as bloody cut on his bottom lip. I couldn't put my finger on what shade his skin tone was with only the crappy night lighting to illuminate the area we were in, but it was obvious he was a little pale. He was good-looking under normal circumstances, all right. But it was his eyes that had me staying in a crouch just a foot or two away from my new neighbor. Red streaks stretched out along irises whose color I couldn't figure out, a sign that he'd been drinking.

Or did the bloodshot eyes mean something else? Shit.

"Are you all right?" I asked him again. I wasn't a doctor; I didn't know what different symptoms meant.

An ink-covered throat bobbed with what I could only assume was a swallow as he opened and closed his eyes slowly like he was disoriented or something. He was looking at me, but it was almost as if he was looking through me. Could he have brain damage?

"Hey, should I call an ambulance or the cops?"

That had his eyes snapping up to me. His answer was sharp and a little ugly. "No."

I watched him. "You're bleeding." Just as I said it, a line of red trailed along his temple from his eyebrow right in front of me. Jesus.

"No," the stranger repeated, his forehead lining with a frown that had me forgetting he was attractive because stupidity wasn't cute. It just wasn't.

"You are." I'm sure my eyes were going wide in a "are you fucking kidding me" look. He wasn't even bothering to wipe the blood away as it made a path down his cheek.

"I told you. I'm fucking fine."

I had to choke back the urge to snap at him for talking to me like that. The only thing that kept me from opening my big mouth was that I thought about how I'd feel if I'd gotten beat up, and I probably wouldn't be very nice either. But I still sounded grumpier than I had a second before as I gritted out, "I'm trying to help you. They were kicking you. You might have a broken rib… or a concussion…."

The trail of blood made its way toward his ear. How the hell could he tell me he was fine?

"You're bleeding right in front of me. Look. Touch it if you don't believe me," I told him, tapping my index finger against my face in the exact spot I wanted him to do the same, like *hello idiot, listen to me.*

The man shook his head, letting out a slow, painful exhale as he finally reached toward his face and wiped at the blood, making a bigger mess. He glanced at his stained fingers and frowned, his mouth drooping at the sides like he couldn't believe he'd been injured after everything that had just happened. "No cops. No hospital. I'm fine," he insisted, his tone getting ruder by the syllable.

Jesus Christ.

Men. Fucking *men*.

If it were me, I would have already been on an

ambulance wanting to get checked out. But I could already tell from the expression on his face—I could smell a stubborn-ass a mile away; I could recognize my own kind—there was no way I was going to talk him out of his decision.

What a dumbass.

"Are you sure?" I asked again, just so my conscience could be sure I'd done what he had requested even if I thought he was being a fucking idiot.

His blink was slow as he looked at me one more time, a slight grimace pinching one cheek before he could mask the fact he was human and hurting. "I said yeah."

I said yeah.

This asshole was about three seconds away from me finishing off the job the other guys started if he didn't keep that tone to himself. But the blood all over the front of his shirt had me keeping my mouth closed for maybe the fifth time in my entire life. He was hurt. He seemed to have trouble breathing. What if he had a punctured lung? What was I supposed to do?

The answer was: *nothing*. I couldn't do anything unless he wanted it.

He was a grown man. I couldn't force him to do anything he didn't want to.

I should go back to my house. I'd already done enough. I didn't want to deal with this, but… I knew I couldn't go back inside until I was sure pretty sure he wouldn't pass out on the lawn.

"All right, come on then. If you're going to lie and

say you're fine, at least let me help get you inside your house," I pretty much muttered, frustrated that I couldn't just say "okay" and let him go on about his business. I was even more frustrated that he was blowing this off like it was nothing and that there wasn't a chance there was something genuinely wrong with him.

His eyelids hung low over his eyes for a moment before my neighbor nodded, flicking his gaze in my direction. Another rattling breath came out of his chest, all reluctant and stupid.

I held out my hand to help him up, but he ignored it. Instead, it took him a moment to get back to his feet, while my hand waited in midair in case he changed his mind. He didn't. Slowly and on his own, he climbed up the stairs, and I followed behind him, there to break his fall. With his back to me, I realized he wasn't just heavy, he was a pretty big guy overall. Even without him standing straight up, it was easy to tell he was around six feet tall and definitely a lot heavier than me. He grunted under his breath as he took one step after another up to the deck, and I had to tell myself that, if he didn't want me to call the cops, I needed to respect his wishes.

Even if I thought he was being a giant idiot and there was a chance he could die from his injuries.

I couldn't keep my mouth from opening one last time, anxiety riding me hard. "You really should go get checked out."

"I don't need to get checked out," he insisted in what was the rudest tone I'd ever heard.

You tried, Di. You tried.

There was a metal security door blocking a regular wooden one, and my neighbor reached out to open the first and then the second, going inside with me following after. All of the lights were off as he stumbled in, him grunting in the process. I couldn't see a single thing as the drunk and beaten-up man stumbled forward. My bare feet were on carpet, and I prayed he didn't have needles lying around or anything. A few seconds later, there was the sound of a thud and then a double click before a side lamp flickered on.

It was one of my worst nightmares.

His house was *a mess*.

There were piles of clothes that may or may not be clean on the couch and two recliners in the living room. A giant television was mounted to the wall, lines of cables dangling out from the bottom, linking it to two gaming systems I recognized. Cans of soda and beer were all over the side tables; balled-up napkins, receipts, socks, wrappers for fast food, and who knows what the hell else covered the floor.

He was huffing in pain as I kept looking around, catching sight of a baseball in a dusty glass case and an equally dirty trophy on the console table to my left. This whole place reminded me of the first apartment I'd had with Rodrigo. We'd been pigs after we had moved out of our parents' place, but that was because our mom was a clean freak, and for once in our lives we didn't have to pick up after ourselves religiously. Nowadays, with two boys and a job that was over full-time hours, I was pretty lenient with what I could live with.

But this place had me side-eyeing everything, scrunching up my toes.

The guy—*man*—let out a long groan as he slowly lowered himself onto a recliner, one hand gripping the side arm.

"Are you sure you don't want me to call an ambulance?"

He let out another "Uh-huh" as he laid back, his head dropping against the headrest, his colorful throat bobbing with a swallow.

"Sure?"

He didn't even bother replying.

I hesitated as I took in the red stains on his clothing and the swelling spots on his face, and thought about him getting kicked again. "I can take you to the hospital. I'll just need a few minutes." The idea of waking up Josh and Louie was an awful one, but if I had to do it, I would.

"No hospital," he murmured, swallowing hard again. His eyes were shut.

I stared at him for a minute, taking in the sharp lines of his profile. I hated feeling useless, I really did. "Is there anyone I can call for you?"

My neighbor might have shaken his head, but the movement was so restrained it was hard to be sure. "No. I'm fine."

He didn't look fine to me.

"You can leave now," he muttered, those hands of his gripping his thighs so hard the knuckles turned white.

I didn't want to be in his house with him, but I knew I couldn't just skip on out either. The idea of being in a strange man's house at night alone sent about a thousand alarm bells ringing in my head. This was the kind of stupid shit women in movies did that got them dumped into a deep hole in some psycho's basement. But bailing wasn't the right thing to do, and if it made a difference, people didn't usually have basements in the Texas Hill Country. I looked around and kept my question about whether he had a first aid kit or not to myself. "Do you have anything I can use to clean your cuts?"

The man's eyes were closed, and from his lap, a couple of his fingers on his left hand wiggled in a dismissive gesture that had me narrowing my eyes.

"Do you know how many germs people carry around on their hands?" I asked him slowly.

I wasn't a fan of the look he slid my way with only one opened eye.

And he wasn't a fan of my persistence. "I'm not joking. Do you have any idea?"

He stared at me for all of maybe a second before closing his eyes and making another dismissive gesture that insisted he was going to be an idiot about this. "I already said I'm fucking—"

"What the hell is going on?" an unfamiliar voice spoke up out of nowhere, just about scaring the shit out of me.

Standing in the space where the living room transitioned into what was either a hallway or the kitchen was a half-naked man. A half-naked man rubbing at his eyes and frowning.

"Nothing. Go back to sleep." The grumpy idiot on the chair couldn't even talk without groaning.

The sleepy man kept frowning and blinking, still obviously out of it. He reached an arm out toward the wall behind him, flicking the overhead fan light on.

And God help me.

God help me.

The new guy, the not-beat-up dumbass, was only in black boxers. It was obvious even from the ten plus feet between us that he was tall, maybe even taller than Beat-up Dumbass. His hair was cut nearly to the scalp, his face was stubbled but not really bearded, and he was built like those long-limbed male models with brawny chests, six-packs, thighs for days, and a giant brown and black tattoo that seemed to cover everything from his upper arms, across his pectorals to the notch at his throat and continuing to arch up above his trapezius muscles, disappearing somewhere on his back.

He was built like a porn star. The really attractive, muscular porn stars.

Or I guess a male calendar model.

I'd obviously been watching too much guy-on-guy porn lately for that to be the first kind of body I associated him with.

I knew the exact moment his tired eyes noticed I was there because he stood straight up and all of those muscles went tight. "Who are you?" he asked slowly, dryly, his voice rough with sleep.

Dropping my hand from where it was over my heart—I didn't even remember reaching up—I caught the ragged breath in my chest and held up my palms so that they faced toward him in surrender, taking in his features that weren't from the neck down. His face was all angles and sharp lines like a gangster in a Russian mafia movie. Not exactly handsome but there was something about it... I coughed. *Focus.* "I just helped him outside," I explained, standing there like a deer caught in the headlights.

Wasn't that obvious? The beat-up guy was bleeding. Why else would I be standing there?

The half-naked stranger stared at me, unblinking, unmoving before his gaze switched back to the man on the recliner. "What happened?"

Beat-up Dumbass shook his head and lay back against the couch, waving his fingers dismissively. "Nothing. Mind your own fucking business and go back to sleep."

Was I...? Should I...? I should go. I should probably go, I decided. I cleared my throat and luckily neither one of them glanced at me. "All right, well, I'm going to head out now—"

"What happened?" the half-naked man asked again, and it didn't take a genius to know the question was directed at me... because his gaze was locked on mine, all hooded eyelids and a frown that made me uncomfortable.

"I already fucking told you nothing!" Beat-up Dumbass hissed, raising a hand to his eyes and draping it over them.

The not-beat-up guy didn't even glance at the other man. I was pretty sure his nostrils had flared at some point, and I could definitely see his loosely hanging hands were opening and closing into fists. His voice was low and almost hoarse. "Can you please tell me why the hell he's on the chair, looking like he just got his ass beat?"

Because he had? I opened my mouth, closed it, and mentally shrugged. I wanted to get the hell out of there, and it wasn't like I had some allegiance to the beat-up guy. "He got jumped, and I helped him. I didn't want to leave him out there." My eyes bounced back and forth between the chair and the muscles—I mean, the guy in the boxers that only covered about a third of his thighs.

"Jumped?" One of the man's thick eyebrows seemed to creep up a half inch on his broad forehead.

I'd swear his chin jutted out as he picked at my words to repeat. I'd had enough experiences pissing people off in my life—specifically my mom—to know those three traits were a sign of someone who was angry but trying not to be and failing miserably.

I probably made it worse by adding, "On the lawn outside."

The width of his shoulders seemed to double, bringing attention to bulky biceps flexing to life with the hands he was fisting in pretty obvious anger. I couldn't tell how old he was... but it wasn't like that mattered.

"He got jumped on the lawn outside?" the newest stranger asked stiffly, his shoulders rolling back, his stubble-covered chin inching out a little more.

Why did I feel like I was tattling to Dad? "Uh-huh."

The man on the recliner groaned in exasperation.

I would have been worried about being a big mouth except Beat-up Dumbass didn't look like he'd make it five feet on his own.

The half-naked man's biceps became even more bunched as his hand—a large one—went up to grip the top of his buzz-cut dark hair. "Who?" the man asked in that raspy, deep voice of his that had nothing to do with a head cold, like mine did. I had a feeling it wasn't a sleep-induced voice either.

"Who what?" I asked slowly, trying to decide the best way to bail on this conversation as quickly as possible.

"Who did it?"

Should I have asked them for their names and addresses? I shrugged, my discomfort growing by the second. *Get out, Diana,* a little voice inside my head warned me.

"It's none of your fucking business," Beat-up Dumbass muttered as angrily as someone who may or may not have internal injuries was capable of.

But at the same time as he gave his response, I blabbered, "Three guys."

"Outside this house?" Half-naked Man pointed toward the floor with an index finger.

I nodded.

There was a moment of silence before:

"I'm gonna fucking kill you," the man hissed, not completely under his breath, his head swinging over in the direction of the recliner. The hand dangling at his side tightened into a fist that had me eyeing the door and taking a step in reverse.

And it was probably that, that had me blurting out as I took another step back, "All right. I'm going to bounce now. I'd go to the doctor if I was you, buddy. I hope you get better—"

The not-beat-up guy's attention slid back to me as a shaky exhale left his broad chest, his hand went loose once more at his side, and he blinked. "Who are you?"

I didn't like telling strangers where I lived, but it wasn't like I was Batman, saving strangers in the night because I was trying to save the world from crime. I was just an idiot who couldn't ignore someone in need if I had the power to help them. Damn it. Plus, if either one of them—or both of them—lived in this house, they were going to eventually see me around. "I just moved in across the street."

The man with the hard face and tiny boxers seemed distracted as he looked me over, like he was trying to sniff out if I was lying or not. I'm sure the only thing he would be able to tell was the fact that I was really regretting trying to be a good person and getting involved in this awkward-ass situation.

Glancing back and forth between the man standing there and the other one on the recliner, barely holding it together, I figured I could leave. I wasn't leaving the beat-up guy alone, and maybe the other man was pissed off at him, but who the hell knew what the backstory between them was. You didn't say you were going to "fucking kill" someone unless they'd pissed you off enough times in the past. I'd been there. Maybe he was right to be mad. Maybe he wasn't. All I knew was that I had tried my best and it was time to get the fuck out.

"All right, well, bye and good luck," I said. Before either one of them responded, and later on I realized I hadn't learned anyone's name, I was out the door and walking across the street, going home. That had been uncomfortable and not something I'd want to go through again. I had tried. I just hoped it didn't come back to bite me in the ass.

I took my time walking back. The adrenaline pumping through me had disappeared, and I was tired. I picked up Josh's bat off the lawn and crossed the street, wondering what the hell that had all been about but knowing my chances of finding out were slim to none. As I made it to my lawn, I zeroed in on a short, skinny figure standing behind the screen front door in just a T-shirt that was a size too small and underwear, his hands were on his hips.

"Lou? What the fu—dge are you doing?" I snapped, raising my hands at my sides.

The smile that came over his face said he knew exactly what I'd been on the verge of saying, and I wasn't surprised. Of course he knew. My brother had thrown around the word "fuck" like it was the name of his imaginary third kid. Not for the first time, I remembered my parents had never complained to him about how he needed to stop saying certain words in front of the kids. Huh.

"I didn't know where you went, Buttercup," he

explained innocently, pushing the door open as he used his nickname for me.

And just like that, my irritation at him for staying up crumbled into a thousand pieces. I was such a sucker. I opened the screen door fully and bent to pick him up. He was getting bigger every day, and it was only a matter of time before he said he was too old to be carried. I didn't want to think about it too much or anticipate it, because I was sure I'd end up locking myself in the bathroom with a bottle of wine, snotting everywhere.

Bouncing him in my arms, I pecked his temple. "I went to make sure the neighbor was okay. Let's go to sleep, all right?"

He nodded against my mouth, already a mostly limp weight. "Is he okay?"

"He's going to be okay," I answered, fully aware that was a partial lie, but what else could I say? *I hope he doesn't die from internal bleeding, Lou?* No. "Let's go to bed, Goo."

CHAPTER TWO

"DIANA," MY MOM CALLED OUT FROM THE KITCHEN AS MY DAD and I maneuvered my flat screen on to the entertainment system he had just finished building with my assistance. My job had mainly consisted of handing him screws, tools, and his bottle of beer. Before that, he'd installed Mac's giant, human-sized doggy door in the kitchen while I'd sat next to him watching.

I wasn't the handiest person in the world, and the fact I was exhausted after the last five days didn't make me the best assistant for building and installing things. Looking back on it, I should have changed the date for when I closed on my house so that it wouldn't have fallen at almost the same time my job was being relocated. It was a lot more work than I had expected. I was lucky it was summer and the boys were now gone with their other grandparents, the Larsens, for the rest of the week. They'd been picked up the day before, and that, at least, had worked out perfectly since I'd offered to help paint the new salon, which had taken a twelve-hour day with multiple people handling rollers and brushes.

"*Si, Ma?*" I called out in Spanish as my dad wiggled his eyebrows, raising his hand in a C-shape that he tipped toward his mouth, the universal gesture for wanting a beer. I nodded at the only steady man in my life, purposely ignoring all the lines around his mouth and eyes—all the signs of how much he, like my mom, had aged over the last few years. It wasn't something I liked to focus too much on.

"*Ven*. I made some *polvorones* for you to take your neighbors," she answered in Spanish in that tone she'd used since I was a little kid that left no room for argument.

I didn't completely manage to muffle my groan. Why hadn't I expected this shit? "Mom, I don't need to take them anything," I shot back, watching my dad choke back a laugh at what I'm sure was my are-you-kidding-me facial expression.

"*Como que no?*" What do you mean no?

My mom was old fashioned.

That was an understatement. She was really, *really* old fashioned and had been my entire life. When I first moved out of the house, you would have figured I'd gotten pregnant at sixteen in the 1930s in Mexico. More than ten years hadn't dulled her reaction every time she was reminded I didn't live under her roof anymore. Her values and ideals were no damn joke.

She *would* be the only person moving into a new

neighborhood that would want to take her neighbors something instead of vice versa. She didn't seem to understand that most people probably wouldn't want to eat food from people they didn't know because everyone assumed there was going to be Anthrax or crack in the ingredients. But even if I told her my reasoning for not wanting to take her treats around, she probably wouldn't listen anyway. "Its fine, *Mamá*. I don't need to take them anything. I already met the people on both sides of me. I told you, remember? They're really nice."

"You need to be friends with everyone. You never know when you'll need something," my mom kept going, telling me she wasn't going to let this go until I agreed.

I dropped my head back to look at the television, suddenly getting reminded of being a little kid at her mercy all over again, of all the times she made me do something I really didn't want to because it was the 'polite thing.' It drove me nuts back then, and it drove me nuts now, but nothing had changed. I still couldn't tell her no.

Out of the corner of my eye, my dad was taking DVDs out of a box to set in the compartments underneath the entertainment center, purposely not getting into the middle of our discussion. Wuss.

"Come get them. They're better when they're warm," she insisted, as if I didn't know that firsthand.

I blew out a raspberry and swung my gaze up to the ceiling, asking for patience. Lots of it.

"Diana?" Mom called out in that tone I refused to

believe I used on Josh and Lou.

For one brief moment, I felt like stomping my feet.

Resigned to the inevitable, I headed to the kitchen. The cupboards were a faded, stained oak, but they were real wood and still in excellent shape. The countertops were tiled and dingy, the grout a shade of color only found on things that had been around before the Vietnam War, but not much worse than the ones at the apartment the boys and I had been living in. Luckily, my dad had already told me he'd help me fix up the kitchen when I was ready, claiming we could do it ourselves with a little help from my uncle. On top of the kitchen remodel, the floors needed some tender loving care and the appliances the owners had left were from the nineties. I wanted to repair and replace those things before I even looked at the cabinets. The fence had seen some shit go down, too. But everything did what it needed to do for the most part, so I'd get to it all eventually. Someday.

"Diana?" my mom called out again, unaware that I was standing right behind her. At an even four foot ten inches tall and with a personality that was nearly saint-like 75 percent of the time—the other quarter of the time she tapped into her inner Napoleon—she didn't outwardly seem like a force to be reckoned with. Her black hair, shot through with chunks of silver in the last couple of years, was brushed down her back. Her skin tone was darker than mine, almost bronze, her frame stouter, but there was no doubt about it, I might take after my dad more physically, but I knew my pushiness came from her. To give her credit, I also got my loving side from her, too.

"I'm here," I said to Mexican Napoleon, who I'd barely realized had a Rubbermaid tower stacked up behind her. Where she'd gotten the plastic containers from, I had no idea. Half my set didn't have lids anymore.

"Do you want me to go with you?" she asked, glancing at me from over her shoulder.

I took my mom in one more time, shaking my head, remembering when I used to go door-to-door selling cookies for my Girl Scout troop and she'd tag along, half the block behind me; it had been her way of showing me she was there if I needed her, but at the same time letting me know what it was like to stand on my own two feet. I hadn't appreciated that kind of stuff when I was a kid, thinking she was hovering, but now... well, now I understood her all too well. Most of the time at least. In this case, I didn't want to. *"Esta bien.* I'll be right back," I replied more than a little whiney. I didn't want to go.

She narrowed her nearly black eyes at me. "Stop making that face. You want them to like you, *no?"*

And then I wondered where I got my need to be liked from, damn it.

While I got my dad another beer, my mom split the containers into two plastic grocery bags, and I headed toward the front door, yanking on a chunk of my dad's short hair on the way out as he finished tightening something on the entertainment center. He let out a hoarse *"Oye!"* Like he was surprised I'd done it.

Not dragging my feet at all, I went ahead and

dropped by the neighbors on either side of me first. The younger couple wasn't home, but the older one thanked me even though I was positive they had no idea what *polvorones* were. Somehow I managed not to laugh when I first noticed my mom had taped my business card to each of the red-lidded containers along with a Post-it that read in her slanted handwriting **FROM YOUR NEW NEIGHBOR AT 1223**. She'd also thrown one of Louie's old markers into the bag. Out of the corner of my eye, I noticed a red car pulling over in front of the house of the guy who had gotten beat up, but I didn't pay much attention to it while I talked to my neighbors. His business wasn't my business.

Once I was done with them, I crossed the street, heading to the house not directly in front of mine but just to the left. When no one answered the door, I left the cookie-type dessert on the doorstep.

Next was what I thought was the most beautiful house in the neighborhood. I'd been admiring the buttery yellow bungalow from the moment I first drove down the street. I hadn't seen who lived there yet; the old Buick hadn't moved once from the driveway, and if it had, I hadn't noticed. The flowerbeds and yard were so perfect, with so many varieties I couldn't even begin to name them. Everything about the landscaping was well-maintained and thought out, from the stone birdbath to the gnomes hidden within the flower bushes—it was like something out of a magazine. I walked up the concrete steps, looking around, getting ideas for what I'd love to do to the front yard when I had the time and money, so maybe around the time Josh was off to college. There wasn't a doorbell, so I knocked on the slab of wood next to the small glass window built into the center of the door.

"Who is it?" an elderly female voice, higher pitched and nearly squeaky, asked from the other side.

"Diana. I just moved in across the street, ma'am," I called out, taking a step back.

"Dia-who?" the woman asked just before the lock on the door turned and a head of perfect, nearly transparent white hair peeked out from the cracked door.

I smiled at the lined, pale face that appeared. "Diana Casillas. I'm your new neighbor," I offered like that would help.

Two glaucoma-ridden eyes blinked at me before the door swung open wider and a woman smaller than my mom—and thinner too—appeared in a pink house robe. "My new neighbor?" she asked, blinking those milky eyes at me. "With the two boys and the big dog?"

At first glance, her eyes said she couldn't see well, but her knowing I had the two boys and being aware of Big Mac, told me I couldn't let this woman fool me. She knew what was up. I could appreciate that. "Yes, ma'am. I brought you some cookies over."

"Cookies? I love cookies," the elderly woman commented as she slipped glasses over her fragile nose with one hand. The other rose toward me, thin and heavily veined.

"Mexican cookies," I explained, picking one of the containers out of the bag.

And the smile melted right off the woman's face. "Mexican cookies." Her voice had changed, too. "You Mexican?" she asked, her eyes narrowing at me as if she was barely noticing I had some yellow and tan in my skin tone.

Unease tickled my neck, making me hesitate. "Yes?" Why the hell was I answering like it was a question? I was and it wasn't some secret. I couldn't exactly hide it.

Those small eyes got even smaller, and I didn't really like it. "You look a little Mexican, but you sure don't sound Mexican."

I could feel my cheeks start to get hot. That familiar burn of indignity scorched my throat for a brief second. I'd lived in multicultural cities my entire life. I wasn't used to someone saying the word "Mexican" like the greatest food on the planet wasn't from there. "I was born and raised in El Paso." My tonsils tickled, my face getting hotter by the second.

The old lady hummed like she didn't believe me. Nearly hairless eyebrows went up. "No husband?"

What was this? A CIA interrogation? I didn't like the tone of her voice before, now the husband thing... I knew where this was going. I knew what she was going to assume considering she was already aware of Josh and Louie's existence. "No, ma'am," I answered in a surprisingly calm voice, holding on to my pride with both hands.

The thin slivers of her white eyebrows went up half

an inch on her forehead.

That was my cue to get the hell out of there before she could ask something else that was going to make me mad. I smiled at the woman despite being pretty sure she couldn't see it and said, "It was nice meeting you, Miss—"

"Pearl."

"Miss Pearl. Let me know if you need anything," I forced myself to offer, knowing it was the right thing to do. "I work a lot, but I'm usually home Sundays. My phone number is on the container," I said, holding the Rubbermaid right up against her hands, which were clasped in front of her.

She took the container from me, her expression still a little off.

"Well, it was nice meeting you," I said, taking a step back.

Were her eyes still narrowed or was I just imagining it? "Nice meeting you, Miss Cruz. I hope these Mexican cookies are good," she finally replied in a tone that said I shouldn't hold my breath.

I blinked at the "Miss Cruz."

With a sigh punching at my throat to get out, I jogged down the steps and headed toward the next house. Unsurprisingly, no one answered. It was the middle of the day on Tuesday. Most people would be at work. I didn't need to look at the bag to know there was one more container of *polvorones* to deliver. One more set of cookies for the home where I'd helped break up a fight and seen a man in his undies. I'd be damned if I went back home with them, or worse, tried to hide them because I didn't want to have to listen to my mom rail me for not doing what she requested.

I blew out another breath as I climbed down the steps of the second to last house, distractedly noticing that the red car that had pulled over while I'd been talking to my next-door neighbors was still there. Huh. In the day since the beat down, I hadn't seen any cars in the driveway. But a red sedan didn't exactly seem like the kind of car either man that had been in the house would drive.

For a moment, I hesitated. Then all I had to do was think of my mom waiting for me in the house, and I knew I didn't have a choice unless I wanted to hear about it all night, or worse, have her threaten to go meet the neighbors herself because I hadn't. Was I ever not going to be scared of her?

Down and around the sidewalk leading up to the house I had been in once, I jiggled the cookies in my hand. I eyed the Chevy for a second as I walked by it and headed up the neat walkway toward the front door. It was a better-looking cousin to my place… only this one was hiding the horrors within.

At the door, I knocked but there wasn't a single noise from inside. I rang the doorbell, and when still nothing stirred, I set the container of cookies on the deck on top of the doormat, ripped my business card off the lid, leaving only the Post-it, praising Jesus that I'd gotten out of talking to this neighbor—or his friend or roommate or whoever that man had been—at least for a little while longer. It wasn't that I was embarrassed. I wasn't. I hadn't done anything other than save the man's ass, but I didn't want to seem like some stalker showing up to their house just two days afterward.

"Hey!" a feminine voice called out.

Turning around, I frowned at the black-haired woman standing on the side of the sedan furthest away from me.

"Yeah?" I called out, squinting against the sun.

"You know if Dallas lives here?" the woman asked.

"Dallas?" I made a face. What the hell was she talking about? We were in Austin.

"*Dal-las*," the woman said slowly like I was an idiot or something.

I was still making a face at her, thinking she was the idiot. "You mean Austin?"

"No, Dallas. D-a-l-l—"

"I know how to spell Dallas," I told her slowly. "Is that supposed to be a person?" Either that or she really was an idiot.

Pinching her lips that matched the color of her car together, she nodded.

Oh. "I don't know anyone named Dallas," I answered back in a tone nearly as snappy as hers as I walked down the steps. What kind of a name or nickname was Dallas anyway?

"About this height, green eyes, brown hair...." She trailed off when I didn't say anything. That sounded suspiciously like a description of half the men in the world, including both of the men I'd seen at the house. The one who had gotten beaten up had dark blond hair but some people might think it was brown.

More than anything though, how was I supposed to know who she was talking about even if it was one of them? I didn't know their names. Even if it was the beat-up guy, I didn't want to get sucked in to some stranger's life more than I already had. That guy just seemed like a bunch of drama I didn't need or want in my life. The other one... well, I didn't want or need that in my life either, even if he did have an incredible body. "Don't you live around here?" she asked, still using that snarky voice that called to my inner attitude like a siren.

I bit the inside of my cheek as I walked down the path, telling myself I couldn't pick a fight less than two weeks after moving in. I couldn't. *I couldn't.* I was going to live here for a long time, I hoped. I couldn't be starting some kind of beef so soon. But my voice backstabbed me, coming out exactly how I was feeling. "Yeah, I do, but I haven't lived here long, *sorry.*"

I think the woman might have stared at me for a moment from the silence between us, but I really couldn't tell. I heard her sigh. "Look, I'm sorry. I've been calling this asshole all day, and he won't answer. I heard he was living here."

I shrugged, my temper starting to ease at her apology. Technically, even if my neighbor was named Dallas, or Wichita or San Francisco, I didn't know that and therefore didn't know a Dallas, so I wasn't lying. Plus, I could barely keep track of my own schedule, much less someone else's. I tried to think of Beat-up Dumbass's face, but could only get a clear image of all that horrible bruising while he'd been lying on the recliner. "No. I'm sorry. I don't know anyone."

With a long and aggravated sigh, the woman dipped her head just as I got within a foot of her car, close enough to really see her face. She might have been older than me, but she was really pretty. Her face was oval, her makeup perfectly done, and she was wearing skintight clothing on a curvy body, even I could appreciate. Once upon a time, I'd put on makeup and curled my hair just to go to the grocery store. Now, unless I had to work or was going someplace where pictures were going to be taken, it wasn't happening.

"All right, thanks, honey," the strange woman finally said. With that, she ducked back into her car.

Honey? She couldn't be that much older than me.

For one brief second, I wondered if the man who had gotten beat up was this Dallas person, then pictured the other man—the bigger one—clearly in my head, and then I shoved the curiosity aside. I had other things to worry about than the neighbor and his might-be friend. Back inside my house, I found my mom in the living room alongside my dad, hanging up picture frames.

Sure enough, the second I closed the door behind me, my mom's eyes swept over the empty bags I held in my hands. "You gave them all away?"

I gave the plastic in my hands a squeeze so they crinkled. "Yes."

My mom bobbled her head, mocking me. "*Que te dije? No me hagas esa cara.*"

I let my smirk fall off my face a little slower than she would have liked.

We worked alongside each other in peace for the next few hours, hanging frames and some of my best friend's artwork I'd collected over the years. Neither of my parents said anything when we pulled out the framed photographs of Drigo and Mandy. I didn't want the boys to forget their parents. I didn't want to stuff their memories into a box so that I wouldn't feel that pull of sadness every time I remembered what we had all lost. What I did notice was my dad looking at a picture of the entire family at my high school graduation with this intense expression on his face, but he didn't say a word about it.

Neither one of my parents ever wanted to talk about my brother.

Every once in a while, when I was at the really low point where every cell in my body missed Rodrigo and got mad that I would never see my brother again, I'd wish that I could bring him up, that I could talk to them about it. But if there was one thing I'd learned over the course of the last few years, it was that everyone dealt with grief differently. Hell, we all dealt with life differently.

My mom eventually made dinner with the pitiful ingredients I had in the fridge and pantry, we ate, and they took off. They lived almost an hour away in San Antonio, in the same subdivision as one of my aunts and uncles. After twenty-something years in El Paso, they had sold my childhood home and moved to be closer to my dad's family. I had been living in Fort Worth at that time; for eight years that had been my home. Their moving and my ex were the reasons why

I'd left Fort Worth and moved to San Antonio before I got the boys. It had been my decision to move to Austin with Josh and Louie to have another fresh start.

Once I was alone, I finally finished hanging all my clothes from the boxes where I'd packed them.

In my room, I had barely taken my jeans off when the doorbell rang. "One second!" I yelled, tugging my stretchy shorts up my legs before waddling over to the door, inspecting the living room to see what my parents might have left. It was probably my dad's cell; he was always leaving that thing lying around. "*Papá*," I started to say as I undid the lock and opened the door, my attention still on the living room behind me.

"Not your daddy," a low, unfamiliar masculine voice replied.

What?

It definitely wasn't my daddy on the other side of the front door with his hands buried deep in the pockets of stained denim jeans under the porch light.

It was the man. The man I'd seen inside of my neighbor's house; the man with the big biceps and short, dark brown hair. The guy who'd been in his boxers.

This was a surprise. Up close, without the weight of exhaustion from being woken up in the middle of the night and nerves from dealing with a moody asshole who didn't want my help after I'd freely given it, I finally got to take in that the man was in his mid-thirties, maybe close to forty. I blinked once and gave him an awkward smile. "You're right. My dad's half a foot shorter than you are." He probably weighed sixty pounds less too.

I'd figured that day in the house he had to be taller than Beat-up Dumbass, but now I got to confirm that. He was easily six foot two. I'd had a boyfriend once who had been about that height. Fucking jackass. But this man in front of me was built a lot more muscular. *A lot.* There was no doubt about it. If I could get up close and personal with the seams of his black T-shirt, I wouldn't have been surprised if the stitching had been holding on for dear life. He was all super straight spine, broad chest, and veiny biceps and forearms. And that plain face with its high, sloping cheekbones, proud, straight nose, and square jaw was not hot or handsome, but there was something about the structure of his face that I didn't mind looking at.

Nope. I sure didn't mind looking. I could still see that big tattoo across the upper half of his chest if I closed my eyes.

The corner of the man's mouth—*this stranger's mouth*—went flat instantly.

Had he figured out I was checking him out? Movement around his waist had me eyeing the familiar-looking plastic container he was holding in one hand.

Shit. If he'd caught me eyeballing him, it was done; I might as well not be shy about it. Rubbing at my hip, I looked him directly in the eyes and smiled wider. Their color reminded me so much of a forest; somehow brown and gold and green at the same time. Hazel. After Louie's, it was one of the prettiest shades of color I'd ever seen, and I couldn't help but stare at another body part of his, even as I wondered what the hell he was doing here. "Can I help you with something?" I asked, not breaking our eye contact.

"I came by to say thanks," he answered in that voice that was still as deep and raspy as it had been in the middle of the night, somehow perfectly fitting for that angular, henchman-like face of his. A crease formed between his thick, dark eyebrows as his gaze strayed from my eyes to my chest and back, for a moment so quick, I might have imagined it.

One of those big hands I'd seen clenched in aggravation days ago went up to tug at the collar of the plain, black T-shirt he had on. He flicked those greenish brown eyes back in my direction, tugging again at his clothes, showing off a hint of the tattoo at the base of his neck. "I appreciate what you did."

I had to tell myself twice to keep my gaze on his face. "You don't have to thank me for your friend—"

"My brother," the man cut me off.

His brother? The idiot who got beat up was his *brother*? I guess they were both big…. Huh. His brother. That explained the wanting to "fucking kill" him part perfectly, I guessed. I raised a shoulder. "If he wants to say 'thank you,' he can do it himself, but he doesn't have to. Thank you anyway." I kept smiling at him, hoping it wasn't as forced as it had originally been.

"That'll never happen." The man's hazel eyes slid over my face, and I was suddenly extremely aware I hadn't put on makeup that day and had two nice scabs on my forehead from picking at my face the last time I'd gone to the bathroom to pee. "I appreciate it though."

His nostrils slightly flared when I didn't glance away from his eye contact; he stood up taller, his lips pursing. Maybe the staring was too much.

Too bad for him, because checking out his biceps to guess how much he curled would have been even more inappropriate. The man shrugged too roughly to be casual. "He doesn't need to be bringing his shit over here, is all. I'm sorry about that."

I blinked. "It would be nice for that not to happen again."

"You live here with your boys?" the man suddenly asked, those pretty irises still locked on mine. No one ever really stared at me right in the eye for this long before. I wasn't sure how I felt about it. Plus, there was something more important for me to deal with: how the hell was I going to answer his question? Should I lie? His question seemed casual, but there was something a little off about it. I didn't know how he knew about Josh and Lou, but obviously he'd seen us at some point. That was nothing to freak out about. He could have seen us from a distance.

Couldn't he?

I narrowed my eyes at him.

He narrowed his right back.

My mom had always said you could tell a lot about a person by their eyes. A mouth could be formed into a million different shapes, but eyes were the windows to a person's soul and shit. I could remember in the month after my last ex and I had split, how I had sat there and wondered where the hell I'd gone wrong.

The sad reality was, when I thought about the upper half of his face... I accepted that I had been blind at that point in my life. Blind and dumb.

Stupid, really. God. I'd been so fucking stupid back then. I couldn't be that stupid ever again. Maybe he didn't have black holes as a reflection of his soul in his eyes, but I moved the door in closer behind me just an inch, more of a reflex than anything. I'd misjudged others before. I could never forget that, especially when I had other people I needed to watch out for.

I said "yes" before I could think twice. They were my boys. Maybe they hadn't come straight from my body, but they were as mine as they could get. Plus, what did it matter if he thought I was a single mom? I was a single aunt. A single guardian. That was basically the same thing.

His answering nod was slow, a definite dip of his chin that had me glancing at his pink mouth. "This is usually a quiet neighborhood. You don't gotta worry about your kids. What happened won't be happening again." That hard face, with crow's feet at his eyes and the brackets at his mouth, told anyone who looked at this man that he wasn't unused to smiling. But I couldn't picture it. He hadn't looked happy the first time I'd seen him and he didn't look particularly happy to be here in front of me right then either.

Was he nice or not? Here he was taking responsibility for someone else's actions. He couldn't be that bad.

Could he?

I just kind of shrugged. "Well, thank you for...

caring." *Caring? Really, Diana?*

It was impossible to miss one of his large hands forming a fist all over before going loose. "Well, just wanted to thank you," he started, sounding uncomfortable all over again. He gave the container a shake, holding it slightly away from his body. "Here's this before it got lost in my things."

"You're welcome." Jesus Christ. He'd eaten all the *polvorones* already? I'd just dropped them off. I took the container from him, still wondering how he'd downed that much sugar before something about his words tickled my thoughts.

His mess?

"He lives with you?"

The man's eyebrows twitched. "Yeah. I'm your neighbor. He's only staying with me."

This was my neighbor.

All this was my neighbor?

What the hell?

This tall, muscular, tanned-skin man with tattoos to his elbows and a body that made me want to pray he did the lawn with his shirt off was my neighbor. Not the other guy.

I wasn't sure why I was so relieved, but I was. Maybe he wasn't exactly giving me a hug, but he wasn't being a rude prick either like his brother. And he'd brought my mom's plastic container back. Even I didn't do that. People who knew me didn't let me borrow stuff because they never got it back.

There was no way this guy could be so bad if he was here apologizing for something he hadn't done.

Could he?

I looked into his hazel eyes again and decided probably not.

Blowing out a breath of air, my cheeks puffed out like a chipmunk before I gave him the second awkward smile of the day. "I thought—never mind. In that case, I'm your neighbor Diana. Nice to meet you."

He blinked and the hesitation, or caution or whatever it was floating around in his brain, flashed across his eyes briefly before his hand extended toward me, and I saw it.

He had a wedding ring on.

"Dallas," the man introduced himself.

He watched me with that straight face of his, a crease back between his eyebrows, his grip firm. Dallas. *Dallas.*

Oh shit. This was the man the lady earlier had been asking about. He was a real person, so she wasn't an idiot.

He was a married real person, and some lady who didn't know where he lived was asking about him. Hmm. I wondered what she wanted for one second before telling myself it wasn't any of my business.

Once my hand was my own again, I put it on my hip and went for the third weird smile in the last ten minutes. "Well, it was nice meeting you, Dallas. Officially. You're welcome for everything. Let me know if you ever need anything."

He blinked and I suddenly felt like I'd done something wrong. But all he said was, "Sure. See you around."

I didn't look at his butt as I closed the door behind him. He was married, after all. I'd seen enough. There wasn't a whole lot in this world I took seriously, but a relationship, especially a marriage, was one of those things, even if he had women coming over to his house looking for him. Staring at a man's butt was a lot different than checking out the front half of him when he'd been the one to come out half naked.

I wasn't going to be sitting on my deck with a glass of lemonade on days he did the yard after all, damn it.

I flipped the lock just as my cell phone started ringing from where I'd left it in my bedroom. I ran down the hall and picked it up, not surprised when ALICE LARSEN showed up on the screen. "Hello?" I answered, knowing exactly who was really calling.

"*Tia*," Louie's voice came through the line. "I'm going to bed."

Plopping my butt down on the edge of the bed, I couldn't help but smile. "Did you brush your teeth?"

"Yes."

"Are you sure?"

"*Yes.*"

"Positive?"

"*Yes!*"

I snickered. "Did Josh?"

"Yes."

"Where is he?"

"Playing video games in the living room."

"Do you love me?" I asked him like I did every night just to hear him say it.

"*Yes.*"

"How much?"

"*A lot!*" his little boy voice giggled in amusement, reminding me why I still asked.

"Are you having fun?"

"Yes."

"You're ready?" I asked.

"Yes," the five-year-old answered quickly. I could already picture him in my head, lying back against his pillows with his covers up to his neck. He liked sleeping like a mummy, wrapped up completely. "Can you tell me the one about daddy saving the old lady's cat again?" he asked with a tired, nearly dreamy sigh.

God, I really needed to quit saying "old lady" around them. I couldn't count the number of times I had told Josh and Louie the same story, but I always let him choose what he wanted to hear. So, for what was more than likely the twentieth time, I told him about the time Rodrigo climbed up a tree to save our elderly neighbor's cat back when we had lived together along with my best friend. "The tree was so big, Goo, I thought he was going to fall and break his leg...," I started.

CHAPTER THREE

I WAS *THIS FUCKING CLOSE* TO BANGING MY HEAD ON THE steering wheel. Oh my God. It was too early for this. And if I was going to be totally honest with myself, noon would have been too early for this. Six in the evening would have been too early for this.

"I don't have any friends." Josh continued the same rant he'd been going on for the last small eternity about how unfair starting fifth grade at a new school was.

He'd been going at it for twenty minutes exactly. I'd been eyeing the clock.

They were twenty minutes I would never, ever get back.

Twenty minutes that seemed like they were going to span the next six months between this moment and my thirtieth birthday.

Twenty minutes that had me silently begging for patience. Or for the end. For anything to make him *stop*. Oh my God. I was crying invisible tears and sobbing silently.

I'd been dropping Josh and Lou off at school and daycare for a long time, and in that period, waking up before seven hadn't gotten any easier. I doubted it ever would. My soul cried every morning when the alarm went off; then it cried even more when I had to keep after Josh to wake up, get out of bed, and get dressed. So listening to him complain for the hundredth time about the unfairness of starting all over again was too much to handle before lunchtime.

To be fair, a huge part of me could understand that having to make new friends sucked. But it was a better school than the one he'd been at before, and Josh—not counting this moment—was the kind of kid I was proud to be mine, who made friends easily. He got that from our side of the family. I'd give him a week before he had a new best friend, two weeks before someone invited him for a sleepover, and three weeks before he completely forgot he had ever complained in the first place. He adapted well. Both boys did.

But *this*, this was making it seem like I was ruining his life. At least that was what he was pretty much hinting at. Me destroying a ten-year-old's life. I could cross that off my bucket list.

When his grandparents had dropped him off the night before after being gone for a week, and he'd already been in a terrible mood, I should have known what I'd be getting myself into.

"Who am I going to sit with at lunch? *Who is going to let me borrow a pencil if I need one?*" he pleaded out the question like a total drama queen. I wasn't sure where the hell he'd picked that up from.

My real question was: why wouldn't he have a pencil to begin with? I'd bought him a value pack *and* mechanical pencils.

I didn't bother answering or asking about the pencil situation, because at this point, I thought he just wanted to hear himself talk, and anything I said wasn't going to be helpful. Commentary was pointless, and frankly, I didn't trust myself not to make a sarcastic comment that he would take the worst way possible because he was in a mood.

"Who am I going to talk to?" he kept going, undaunted by the silence. *"Who am I going to invite to my birthday?"*

Oh dear God, he was worrying about imaginary birthday parties already. How rude would it be if I turned on the radio loud enough to zone him out?

"Are you listening to me?" Josh asked in that whiney voice he usually spared me from.

I gritted my teeth and kept my face forward so that he wouldn't see me glaring at him through the rearview mirror. "Yes, I'm listening to you."

"No, you're not."

I sighed and gave the steering wheel a squeeze. "Yes, I am. I'm just not going to say anything because I know you're not going to believe me when I tell you that you're going to make friends, that everything is going to be fine, and when your birthday rolls around, you'll have more than enough people to invite, J." I kept my mouth shut about his non-pencil problem for both of our sakes. When he didn't respond, I asked,

"Am I right?"

He grumbled.

Just like my damn brother. "Look, I get it. I've hated starting at a new job where I didn't know anyone, but you're a Casillas. You're cute, you're smart, you're nice, and you're good at anything you want to be good at. You'll be fine. You'll both be fine. You're amazing."

More grumbling.

"Right, Louie?" I glanced into the rearview mirror to see the upcoming kindergartner in his booster seat, grinning and nodding.

"Yeah," he replied, totally cheery.

Seriously, everything about that kid made me smile. Not that Josh didn't, but not in the same way as Lou. "Are you worried about starting school?" I asked the little one. We'd talked about him starting kinder plenty of times in the past, and every single time, he had seemed stoked about it. There was no reason for me to think otherwise. My biggest worry had been that he might bawl his eyes out when I dropped him off, but Louie wasn't really that type of kid. He'd loved daycare.

Ginny had warned me that I'd cry taking him to his first day, but there was no way I could or would break down in front of him. If I cried, he'd cry even if he had no idea why. And I'd be damned if that happened. When I'd taken his picture in front of the house a little while earlier, I may have had one little tear in my eye, but that was all I was willing to give up.

"Nope," he replied in that happy five-year-old

voice that made me want to snuggle him until the end of time.

"See, J? Lou's not worried. You shouldn't be either." In the rearview mirror, Josh's head drooped before falling to the side to rest against the glass window. But it was the huge sigh that came out of such a young body that really got me. "What is it?" I asked.

He shook his head a little.

"Tell me what's really wrong."

"Nothing."

"You know I'm not going to drop it until you tell me. What's up?"

"Nothing," he insisted.

I sighed. "J, you can tell me anything."

With his forehead to the glass, he pressed his mouth to it, steam fogging up the area around his lips. "I was thinking about Dad, okay? He always took me to school the first day."

Fuck. Why hadn't I thought of that? Last year, he'd gotten pretty grumpy about starting the school year then too. Only it hadn't been this bad. Of course, I missed Drigo, too. But I didn't tell Josh, no matter how much I needed to sometimes. "You know he would tell you—"

"There's no crying in baseball," he finished off for me with a sigh.

Rodrigo had been firm and tough, but he'd loved his kids, and there wasn't a single thing he didn't think they could do. But he'd been that way with everyone he loved, including me. A knot formed in my throat and had me trying to clear it as discreetly as possible.

MARIANA ZAPATA

Was I doing the right thing with Josh? Or was I being too tough on him? I didn't know, and the indecision burrowed a notch straight into my heart. It was moments like these that reminded me I had no idea what the hell I was doing, much less what the end result would be when they grew up, and that was terrifying.

"Your new school is going to be great. Trust me, J." When he didn't say anything, I turned to look at him over my shoulder. "You trust me, don't you?"

And just like that, he was back to being a pain in the ass. He rolled his eyes. "Duh."

"Duh my ass—butt. I'm going to drop you off at the pound on the way home."

"Oooh," Louie cooed, forever an instigator.

"Shut up, Lou," Josh snapped.

"No, thank you."

"Oh my God, both of you be quiet," I joked. "Let's play the quiet game."

"Let's not," Josh replied. "Have you found me a new Select team?"

Damn it. I slid a look to the side window, suddenly feeling guilty that I still hadn't even started looking for a new baseball team for him. Once upon a time, I would have lied to him and said that I had but that wasn't the kind of relationship I wanted to have with the boys. So I told him the truth. "No, but I will."

I didn't have to turn around to sense the accusation in his gaze, but he didn't make me feel bad over it. "Okay."

None of us said anything else as I pulled up to the

curb at the school and put the car into park. Both boys sat there, looking at me expectantly, making me feel like a shepherd to my sheep.

A shepherd who didn't always know the right direction to go.

I could only try my best and hope it was good enough. Then again, wasn't that the story to everyone's lives? "Everything is going to be okay. I promise."

"MISS LOPEZ!"

I shut the car door with my hip later that day, with what felt like fifty pounds of grocery bags hanging off my wrists. Louie was already at the front door of our house, the two smallest bags from our shopping trip in each of his hands. While I usually tried to avoid taking them to the grocery store, the trip had been inevitable. The salon wasn't scheduled to open until the next day, and I was partially thankful that I'd been able to pick them up their first day of school. Considering that even Louie hadn't looked like school had been everything he might have hoped it would be, grocery shopping had gone well; I'd only had to threaten the boys twice. Josh paused halfway to his brother with full hands too, a frown growing on his face as he looked around.

"Miss Lopez!" the frail voice called out again, barely heard, from somewhere close but not that close. I didn't think anything of it as I stepped toward them, watching as Josh's gaze narrowed in on something behind me.

"I think she's talking to you," he suggested, his eyes staying locked on whatever it was he was looking at.

Me? Miss Lopez? It was my turn to frown. I glanced over my shoulder to find why he would assume that. The instant I spotted the faded pink housedress at the edge of the porch of the pretty yellow house across the street, I forced myself to suppress a groan.

Was the old woman calling me Miss Lopez?

She waved a frail hand, confirming my worst guess.

She was. She really, really was.

"Who's Miss Lopez?" Louie asked.

I blew a raspberry, torn between being irritated at being called just about the most Latino last name possible and wanting to be a good neighbor, even though I had no clue what she could possibly wanted. "I guess I am, buddy," I said, lifting up the hand that had the least amount of groceries on it and waving at the old woman.

She gestured with that bone-thin hand to come over.

The problem with trying to teach two small humans how to be a good person was that you had to set a good example for them. All. The. Time. They ate everything up. Learned every word and body language that you taught them. I'd learned the hard way over the years just how sponge-like their minds were. When Josh was a baby, he'd picked up on "shit" like a duck to water; he'd used it *all the time* for any reason. He'd knock over a toy: "Shit." He'd trip: "Shit." Rodrigo and I had thought it was hilarious. Everyone else? Not so much.

So, trying to teach them good manners required me to rise above the instincts to want to groan when something frustrated or annoyed me. Instead, I winked at the boys before looking back at our new neighbor and yelling, "One minute!"

She waved her hand in response.

"Come on, guys, lets put up the groceries and go see what the"—I almost said *old lady* and just barely caught the words before they came out—"neighbor needs."

Louie shrugged with that signature bright smile on his face and Josh groaned. "Do I have to?"

I nudged him with my elbow as I walked by him. "Yes."

Out of the corner of my eye, his head lolled back. "I can't wait? I won't open the door for anybody."

He was already starting with not wanting to go places with me. It made my heart hurt. But I told him over my shoulder, even as I unlock the door, "Nope." Once I got him started on staying home alone, there would be no going back. I knew it, and I was going to cling to him being a little boy as long as possible, damn it.

He groaned, loud, and I caught Louie's gaze. I winked at him and he winked back... with both eyes.

"I need my bodyguards, Joshy Poo," I said, pushing the door open and waving my youngest one inside the house.

Said "Joshy Poo" blew out his own raspberry as he passed by me into the house, only slightly stomping his feet. He didn't say anything else as we unpacked the things that needed to go into the refrigerator and left everything else on the counter for later. We crossed the street, with Josh dragging his feet behind him and Louie holding my hand, and found the door to the yellow house closed.

I tipped my head toward it. "Goo, knock."

Louie didn't need to be told twice. He did it and then took two steps over to stand by me. Josh was almost directly behind us. It took a minute, but the door swung slowly open, a poof of white hair appearing in the crack for a moment before it went wide. "You came," the woman said, her milky blue eyes going from the boys to me and back again.

I smiled at her, my hand going to pet the dark blond head at my hip almost distractedly. "What can we help you with, ma'am?"

The woman took a step into the house, letting me get a good look at the pale pink dress she had on with snap buttons going down the middle. Those thin, very white hands seemed to shake at her sides, a tale of her age. Her lined mouth pulled up at the corners just a little. "You cut hair?"

I forgot I had given her my business card. "I do."

"Would ya mind givin' me a little snip? I was supposed to have an appointment, but my grandson has been too busy to take me," she explained, swallowing, bringing attention to the wrinkled, loose skin at her throat. "I'm startin' to look like a hippy."

I usually got pretty annoyed with people when they first found out I was a hair stylist and wanted preferential treatment: a free haircut, some kind of at-home service, a discount—or worse, when they expected me to drop everything to take care of them. You didn't ask a doctor to give you a free check-up. Why would someone think that my time wasn't as valuable as anyone else's?

But…

I didn't need to look at the trembling, heavily veined hands at Miss Pearl's sides or her cloud of thin white hair to know there was no way I could possibly tell this woman I wouldn't do what she was asking of me, much less charge her. Not just because she was my neighbor, but because she was old and her grandkid was supposed to take her to get a haircut and hadn't. I had loved the hell out of my grandparents when I was a kid, especially my grandmother. I had a soft spot for all of my older clients; I charged them less than I did everyone else.

Ginny had long ago stopped asking why I gave them discounts, but I'm sure she understood. Sure, it was unfair to give some people a discount, but the way I looked at it, life wasn't fair sometimes, and if you were going to cry about an elderly person paying less than you, you needed to get a life.

And this elderly, judgmental lady… I gave Louie's shoulder a squeeze. "Okay. I have time right now if you'd like me to do it."

Josh muttered something behind me.

The old woman's smile was so bright that I felt bad for groaning when I had realized she wanted me to cross the street to go talk to her. "I wouldn't be putting you out?"

"No. It's no problem. I have shears at home. Let me go grab them and come back," I said.

~

"Don't cut too much."

"That's too much."

"Could you go a little shorter?"

"My beautician doesn't usually do it like that. Are you sure you know what you're doing?"

I should have known after her first comment that the haircut wasn't going to go as easily as I would have liked. There were two different types of customers in my profession: the kind that let you do whatever the hell you wanted, and the kind that nitpicked every single strand of hair. I used up all of my patience on the boys most of the time, so I loved the customers that genuinely didn't care. I felt like I had a good idea with what worked best for people's faces, and I would never give someone a haircut that needed a lot of maintenance if they didn't have time for it, unless they begged.

But I kept my mouth shut and a smile on my face as I listened to my elderly neighbor and tried to cut her hair the way she wanted.

"Where do you usually get your hair done?" I asked as I worked my way around her, being extra careful around her paper-thin skin with the super-sharp edges of the shears. The last thing I wanted or needed was to accidentally cut her.

"Molly's," she replied.

On the floor a few feet away, Louie was lying on his belly with a notebook he was drawing in while Miss Pearl's ancient cat sniffed his shoes, and Josh had a handheld game system in front of his face. He'd asked me again if he could stay home, and I'd told him the same thing I had originally. I wasn't sure why he was in such a grumpy mood today, but I wasn't going to worry about it too much. He had his days. I couldn't blame him; I did too.

"Do you know where that's at?" Miss Pearl asked after she rattled off side streets that weren't familiar.

I shook my head. "No."

"Oh? You're not from here?"

My chest ached for a moment. An image of Rodrigo filled my head briefly, and I swallowed. "No. I'm from El Paso. I lived in Fort Worth for a few years and San Antonio for a little bit before moving here."

"Divorced?" she blatantly asked.

And that was why I loved old people. They didn't give a single shit about how their questions could make you feel. She had already asked if I had a husband last time; now she went in for clarification. "No."

The "oh" out of her mouth was just about the most disapproving thing I'd ever heard, and it took me a minute to realize how she was going to take it.

But I didn't care about what she was assuming. There was nothing wrong with being a single, unmarried mom. Or in my case, a single, unmarried aunt.

I wasn't imagining the sneer that came over the

elderly woman's face. I also didn't miss the apprehensive expression that Louie shot our way. That kid was the most emotionally intuitive person I'd ever met and always had been. Where Josh understood my moods like he had some kind of emo-location, it was only with me. Lou was something else.

"Well," she hummed. "Me and my George were together for fifty-eight years before he kicked the bucket—"

I coughed.

"My sons knew what they were doin', too. They married good girls. Their kids..." She literally went "harrumph" and rolled her eyes as she thought about her grandkids. "But my girls, neither one of them had a man for longer than a few years atta time. Not that I blame them. My girls are pains in the you-know-what. All I'm tryin' to say is that you're better off not having a man than having a lousy one. You got your own house with your boys, so you can't be doin' too bad."

And just like that, I went back to snipping away. Maybe this lady wasn't so bad after all. "You're right. You are better off being alone than with someone who doesn't make you happy." I'd learned that shit the hard way.

"You got a pretty face. I'm sure you'll find somebody someday that doesn't mind you havin' kids."

And I retracted my statement on how she wasn't so bad for a second or two.

She was really old, and she pretty much got a free pass for most things, but I wasn't used to brutal honesty by someone so new in my life. My parents and best friend were usually honest with me about everything, regardless of whether it would hurt me or not, but they'd had years to reach that level of trust. Sure, I knew some men might run screaming the other way if they met someone with two kids, but it wasn't like I wanted to date some twenty-one-year-old whose greatest commitment was paying for his own Netflix plan. My imaginary future boyfriend might have kids of his own, and that would be okay. I didn't know if I would have the energy or patience to date someone who didn't know how to act around two boys. As long as my imaginary boyfriend wasn't in love with anyone else, I wouldn't care he'd been in a long-term relationship before me. Better that than him having slept around with a thousand women.

Then again, I wasn't planning on dating any time soon. I was doing fine on my own. My hand kept me company just fine, and I'd swapped out my shower sprayer for a handheld one. I was never without company unless I wanted to be, which was the case more often than not lately when I was tired, aka all the time.

I happened to look up and see Josh sitting in the living room staring over at us, his face way too interested. These guys were so nosey. I made sure his gaze met mine, and I gave him a wide-eyed look so that he wouldn't be so obvious about eavesdropping.

"Your babies' daddy, is he in the picture?" the older woman blatantly asked.

I told her the truth. "No."

The "huh" that came out of her mouth was a little too suspicious, and I really didn't feel like bringing up my brother since she already assumed Josh and Lou had ripped through my birth canal. "I'm just about done. Do you want to look at your hair in the mirror?"

One pale hand went up at her side. "There's a little mirror in my bathroom. Will you bring it? It'll take me half the day to get in there and back."

I squeezed my lips together so that I wouldn't smile. "Sure. Where's your bathroom?"

Miss Pearl pointed at the hall connecting to the kitchen. "First door."

I gently touched her shoulder as I walked around and headed down the hall. The walls were painted a pale, pale pink and were lined near the ceiling with a strip of flowered wallpaper. I caught a few pictures frames mounted to the wall, but I didn't want to be nosey since I knew she could see me. I ducked into the doorway, finding a small full bathroom with an elevated toilet seat decked out with handles and a clean looking bathtub with a long metal bar bracketed to the wall. Sure enough, over the toilet with a shelf behind it was a fairly large handheld mirror like the one I had at work.

I was only slightly nervous when I handed her the mirror and let her take in the front of her haircut. She moved her chin from side to side and handed it back to me. "Half an inch too short, but you did better than the grumpy bat who's been cutting my hair. That darn woman tried giving me a mullet," she claimed.

"I think you dodged a bullet with the mullet," I

joked.

She let out a tiny snort. "You're telling me. How much do I owe you?"

Like every time I dealt with someone much older than me, an image of my grandmother flashed through my head for a brief moment. I sighed and smiled, resigned. "You don't owe me anything." Chances were, she was probably on social security. There was no way she was getting very much money, and she was my neighbor. There was also no way her hair grew fast enough for it to be a burden on my schedule. There were only a certain number of people whose hair I cut that got it for free, and one more wouldn't be the difference between arthritis and... not arthritis. "It's a neighborly discount," I let her know.

Her eyes narrowed in a way that was pretty creepy. "Don't insult me. I can give you the twelve dollars I usually pay," she argued.

Her offer only made me want to give her a hug. "Please don't insult me," I said gently, trying to sound playful. "I'm not going to charge you anything."

She let out this exaggerated, long sigh that told me I'd won.

"Point me in the direction of your broom, please."

She did, and five minutes later, I had managed to sweep up the hair and use her handheld vacuum to pick up the fine clippings left behind. Noticing that I was wrapping up the haircut, Josh and Louie were standing in the living room... staring at the old woman. And the old woman was staring back at them. I was 99 percent sure none of them blinked.

"I'm hungry," Louie finally said, keeping that blue-eyed gaze on our neighbor.

Packing my shears back into their case, I picked up my keys and raised my eyebrows at him, but he still had his attention on the woman. "We can start on dinner in a minute." I walked toward them and smiled at our neighbor, who had, at least, stopped staring back. "We should get going before you can start hearing their stomachs grumbling. Let me know if you need anything, okay, Miss Pearl?"

She nodded, her eyes meeting mine before shifting back to Louie for a moment. "I will. Thank you for the 'do."

"You're welcome."

"I have your number on my freezer," she let me know as if I hadn't seen it when I'd first gone into her kitchen. "Y'all ever need something, you let me know."

"That's really nice of you, thank you. Same goes for you." I nudged Josh who had moved to stand next to me. Oh dear God, his mouth was cracked, his eyes narrowed as he took in the woman who was older than his grandparents. "It was nice seeing you." I poked at Josh again.

"Bye, miss," he kind of mumbled, still dazzled and lost in his trance.

I made my eyes go wide at Louie who had at least managed to catch on to us leaving. "Bye, lady," he added, shyly.

Lady. God.

I smiled at Miss Pearl and waved the boys toward the door, trying to ask myself where I'd gone wrong with them. Staring. Calling our neighbor "lady." My mom would be horrified. We filed out, and I made sure to lock the bottom lock on the door before closing it behind me. We made it to the street before Louie did it. "How old is she? A hundred?" he asked, completely curious, without the smallest hint of smart-ass in his tone.

If he hadn't been holding my dominant hand, I would have smacked myself in the forehead. "Louie!"

"Don't be dumb. She's like ninety-five, right, Aunt Di?" Josh butted in.

Oh my God. "I don't know. Probably, but you're not supposed to ask that kind of stuff, guys. Jes— Sheesh."

"Why?" they both asked at the same time.

We made it to the other side of the street before I answered, "Because... it's not very nice to say she's ninety-five or a hundred."

"But why?" That was Louie working alone that time.

I hated when they asked me things I really didn't know how to answer. I didn't want to lie either, which just made it that much more complicated. "Because... I don't know. It's just not. Some people are sensitive about their age."

Louie's little shoulders shrugged up against my leg as he pulled me along the lawn... the lawn that needed to have gotten mowed weeks ago. I had to quit putting it off. "But that's good she's old," he explained his reasoning. "She's lasted longer than all her other friends. She said her Georgie died. She won."

It never ceased to amaze me how much they both really absorbed. And it scared me. And reminded me why I had to watch everything I said around them. "Outliving your friends isn't a competition, you little turds," I said to them as we walked up the steps toward the front door.

"It's not?"

Why did they sound so surprised? "No. It's sad. I mean, it's good she's lived for so long, but just…." It was times like these I wished I had Rodrigo around so I could make him deal with answering these kinds of things. What the hell was I supposed to say to them? "Look, it just isn't nice to say she's a hundred, or that it's good all of her friends aren't around anymore." Before they could make another comment I had no idea how to respond to, I asked, "Whose turn is it to help me with dinner?"

All the silence needed was crickets in the background.

Mac barked from inside the house like he was volunteering.

I ruffled their hair. "Both of you are going to help? It's my lucky day."

It was right then that the loud grumble of a truck warned us of its approach coming down the street. All three of us turned to spot a deep red monster of a Ford pickup making its way closer. I could spy two ladders mounted to a frame around it. In the driver seat was my real, actual neighbor—the hunky one with manners. I raised my palm when he passed by, giving us a view of ladders, equipment, and tools I wasn't familiar with in the bed of the truck. I was pretty sure he lifted a few fingers in our direction as he pulled into the garage.

What I also noticed in that moment was that red car from the day before was parked on the street in front of my neighbor's house again. What I also saw was the driver side door opening as we continued making our way toward the house.

Lou went up on his tiptoes, craning his neck toward the house. "Is that the man who was fighting?"

I didn't lie to him. "No."

"Who?"

I glanced down at Josh's tone. "It happened last week. Lou heard someone fighting, and it was the neighbor's brother," I had to explain.

The ten-year-old turned his head to pin me with this expression that was beyond his years, like he knew what I was trying to hide. Or maybe he could guess what I had done.

I didn't need or want him worrying, so I kicked him in the butt, immediately shoving my neighbor's business aside. "Come on. Let's get started on dinner before we have to put Mac on the grill."

"Gross!" Lou gagged.

I swear I loved messing with him. There was something about being young and innocent and gullible that I loved, and to be fair, I used to do the same thing to Josh before he'd gotten old enough to realize I was usually full of shit. The boys had just gone inside the house when my phone started ringing. It was my best friend, Van.

"Diana" was the first thing out of her mouth. "I'm dying," the too familiar voice on the other end moaned.

I snorted, locking the front door behind me as I held the phone up to my face with my shoulder. "You're pregnant. You're not dying."

"But it feels like I am," the person who rarely ever complained whined. We'd been best friends our entire lives, and I could only count on one hand the number of times I'd heard her grumble about something that wasn't her family. I'd had the title of being the whiner in our epic love affair that had survived more shit than I was willing to remember right then.

I held up a finger when Louie tipped his head toward the kitchen as if asking if I was going to get started on dinner or not. "Well, nobody told you to get pregnant with the Hulk's baby. What did you expect? He's probably going to come out the size of a toddler."

The laugh that burst out of her made me laugh too. This fierce feeling of missing her reminded me it had been months since we'd last seen each other. "Shut up."

"You can't avoid the truth forever." Her husband was huge. I didn't understand why she wouldn't expect her unborn baby to be a giant too.

"Ugh." A long sigh came through the receiver in resignation. "I don't know what I was thinking—"

"You weren't thinking."

She ignored me. "We're never having another one. I can't sleep. I have to pee every two minutes. I'm the size of Mars—"

"The last time I saw you"—which had been two months ago—"you were the size of Mars. The baby is probably the size of Mars now. I'd probably say you're about the size of Uranus."

She ignored me again. "Everything makes me cry and I itch. I itch so bad."

"Do I… want to know where you're itching?"

"Nasty. My stomach. Aiden's been rubbing coconut oil on me every hour he's here."

I tried to imagine her six-foot-five-inch, Hercules-sized husband doing that to Van, but my imagination wasn't that great. "Is he doing okay?" I asked, knowing off our past conversations that while he'd been over the moon with her pregnancy, he'd also turned into mother hen supreme. It made me feel better knowing that she wasn't living in a different state all by herself with no one else for support. Some people in life got lucky and found someone great, the rest of us either took a long time… or not ever.

"He's worried I'm going to fall down the stairs when he isn't around, and he's talking about getting a one-story house so that I can put him out of his misery."

"You know you can come stay with us if you want."

She made a noise.

"I'm just offering, bitch. If you don't want to be alone when he starts traveling more for games, you can stay here as long as you need. Louie doesn't sleep in his room half the time anyway, and we have a one-story house. You could sleep with me if you really wanted to. It'll be like we're fourteen all over again."

She sighed. "I would. I really would, but I couldn't leave Aiden."

And I couldn't leave the boys for longer than a couple of weeks, but she knew that. Well, she also knew I couldn't not work for that long, too.

"Maybe you can get one of those I've-fallen-and-I-can't-get-up—"

Vanessa let out another loud laugh. "You jerk."

"What? You could."

There was a pause. "I don't even know why I bother with you half the time."

"Because you love me?"

"I don't know why."

"*Tia*," Louie hissed, rubbing his belly like he was seriously starving.

"Hey, Lou and Josh are making it seem like they haven't eaten all day. I'm scared they might start nibbling on my hand soon. Let me feed them, and I'll call you back, okay?"

Van didn't miss a beat. "Sure, Di. Give them a hug from me and call me back whenever. I'm on the couch, and I'm not going anywhere except the bathroom."

"Okay. I won't call Parks and Wildlife to let them know there's a beached whale—"

"Goddammit, Diana—"

I laughed. "Love you. I'll call you back. Bye!"

"Vanny has a whale?" Lou asked.

I tugged on his earlobe. "God, you're nosey. No, she's having a baby, remember? And I told her she is a whale right now."

He made a funny face. "That's not nice."

"No, it's not, but she knows I'm playing. Come on then and grab an onion and celery for me."

"Celery?" He scrunched up his face.

I repeated myself, getting a nod from him before he turned to get what I asked of him.

I had just started slipping my phone back into my pocket when it started ringing again. I had no idea that in about two minutes, I would be calling myself an idiot for not looking at the screen before I hit the answer button without looking. My muscles had the placement memorized, so I didn't have to. "Did you fall over already?" I joked.

"Diana?" the female voice came over the phone. The voice sounded familiar. "Don't hang up—"

And just like a slap to the face, I realized why it was familiar. Smiling at Louie, I said in a bright voice, "You have the wrong number." And I hung up even as my heart started going double-time.

She had called me maybe once over the last two years—*once*—and this was the second time she'd called in less than two weeks. I wanted to wonder why she would be calling now of all times, but I knew why. The *why* was probably in the living room setting up his Xbox for a game.

The thing was there were plenty of things in life you couldn't escape, including the stupidest thing someone you loved very much did.

"*Tia*, the trash is full."

Hopefully, my smile didn't look as fake as it felt and Louie wasn't paying enough attention to me to notice it was. The second to last person who needed to know who just called was Louie. "I'll change it real quick then. Wash that for me, would you, Goo?" I asked, already heading toward the trash can as a ball of dread formed in my belly. He wasn't big enough to lift the bag out of the can; we'd learned that the hard way, so I didn't mind being the person in charge of taking it out.

I shoved the phone call aside until later when I was in bed, alone without anyone to see me freaking out.

In no time, I took the bag out and replaced it with a new one, carrying the old one out the kitchen door to dump it in the big trash can outside. I had seriously just taken the first step down toward the trash cans when I heard, "—take your ass and go."

Say what?

I stopped in place, fully aware that my fence was only a four-foot-tall chain-link one that anyone on the street could see through. A female voice hollered, "You're a piece of fucking shit, Dallas!"

Dallas as in my neighbor? Was it the lady in the red car out there talking?

"You're not telling me something you haven't called me a thousand times before," the male voice drawled in a loose laugh that somehow didn't really sound very carefree at all. Jesus. How loud were they talking that I could hear their conversation so clearly?

The curse word that exploded through the air had me raising my eyebrows as I stood there with my bag. Carefully, I made my way down the steps from the kitchen door to the yard and paused by the trash cans, mere feet from the fence that would let me look at my neighbor's house. Setting the bag down, I let my curiosity get the best of me as I tiptoed over the grass to the corner of the fence and tried to take a peek, convincing myself they wouldn't see me in the shadows.

The man apparently named or nicknamed Dallas was standing on the porch, and the woman was on the sidewalk, leaning forward in a confrontational gesture. I tried to squint to see them better, but it didn't help.

"I wouldn't call you that if you didn't act like one," the woman shouted.

The man with the short hair seemed to look up at the sky—or the ceiling of his deck, if you wanted to get technical—and shook his head. His hands went up to palm his forehead. "Just tell me what the hell you came all the way here for, would you?"

"I'm trying to!"

"Get to the fucking point then!" he boomed back like an explosion, whatever control he had disappearing.

Under normal circumstances, I wouldn't think it was okay for a man to yell at a woman like that, but they were standing far apart and the woman was yelling like a damn crazy person, too. Her pitch was all shrieks and squeaks.

"I've been calling you over and over again—"

"Why the fuck would you expect me to answer?" he barked back. "I haven't heard from you or seen you in three years. We agreed to go through our lawyers, remember that?"

To be fair, I had no idea what was going on and who was really at fault, but he had a point. If I hadn't spoken to someone in so long, I more than likely wouldn't answer the phone either.

But lawyers?

Lawyers, yelling at each other, his wedding ring… was this his wife? I'd been in enough relationships to know you didn't yell at another person with so much hatred unless you'd slept with them at some point.

"Why would you see me? I told you before you left I was done," the woman yelled back with so much emotion in her voice, I actually started to feel guilty for eavesdropping.

"Trust me, I knew you were done—not like you ever really started anything to begin with," the man replied.

Yeah. Definitely his wife. Why else would they have lawyers and go so long without talking to each other?

And why would he still be wearing his ring after so long?

"What are you doing?"

I jumped and turned to glance at Louie who was standing on the other side of the screen door, looking at me. "Nothing," I told him, taking the two steps over to open the trash can and put the bag inside like he hadn't just caught me eavesdropping.

He waited until I was on the first step to ask, "You were listening to them, huh?"

"Me?" I made my eyes go wide as I opened the door and stepped inside as he backed up to give me room. "No. I'm not nosey."

Louie scoffed. This five-year-old literally scoffed at me.

I couldn't help but laugh. "You think I'm nosey?"

Louie had already gone through his lying phase as a toddler, and even if he hadn't, he knew I didn't like it, and he didn't like to hurt anyone's feelings. Especially mine. But what he said next left me trying to figure out whether I should high-five him or be scared at how manipulative and sneaky he could be. He walked over to me and leaned against my leg with that beaming smile of his. "Wanna hug?"

CHAPTER FOUR

IT WAS A SIGN OF HOW MUCH MY LIFE HAD CHANGED OVER THE course of the last few years that "going out" now consisted of me changing into skinny jeans and a cute top. Years ago—a damn lifetime ago—back when I was younger and dumber and had very few worries in the world, "going out" consisted of taking an hour or two to put makeup on, do my hair, and get dressed in something that would have had my mom asking herself where she'd gone wrong raising me. I'd even seen her doing the sign of the cross once or twice. "Going out" meant heading to some loud bar or club with overpriced drinks to get hit on by guys who manscaped religiously. It hadn't been every night or weekend, but it had been enough.

Now...

Now, half my adult social experiences revolved around birthday parties and baseball practices. The only time my hair was done was when I had to work and that was only because *that was my work.* I'd mastered doing my makeup in five minutes. Time really was more valuable than money.

Well, now, looking at my boss, Ginny, who was dressed almost identical to me in jeans and a short-sleeved blouse, priorities had obviously changed.

We had agreed days ago that we should go out to celebrate the reopening of the salon. *Saturday,* we had promised each other because the salon was closed every Sunday. *We'll go out on Saturday.* Her kids were with their dad, and Josh and Louie were with my parents this weekend. It had seemed like the perfect time to spend some quality time together.

What we hadn't taken into consideration was how tired we were going to be after working a full day following a week of painting and moving furniture from one location to the next.

I had taken a chair at Shear Dialogue a little more than two years ago. Ginny and I had met through a mutual hair stylist friend, who knew she needed help and knew I was looking for somewhere else to work. We'd hit it off immediately. She had three kids, was a single parent in her early forties with a boyfriend, and had this no-bullshit attitude that sang to my own take-no-shit attitude, and the next thing I knew, I was moving the boys and myself from San Antonio to Austin. The rest was history.

But now that the day was here, we'd faced each other that afternoon and said the same thing, "I'm tired." Which meant we both would rather go home and relax but weren't going to because we were so busy we didn't spend enough time together. Kids and relationships—hers, at least, she was getting married in a few months on top of everything—consumed a lot of energy. It was our unspoken agreement that we'd get a couple of drinks and head home before the nightly news came on.

"Where do you want to go?" I asked her as I reapplied deodorant in the middle of the salon. We'd locked up half an hour ago, cleaned the place, and took turns changing in the bathroom. It didn't escape me that neither one of us bothered trying to fix up our hair after a long day of work. Some days I thought that if I had to touch more hair, I would vomit. I'd settled on more lipstick, and Gin had slapped on a little more blush and ran a brush through her shoulder-length, blood-red hair that I colored for her monthly.

She had her back to me as she… yep, adjusted her boobs, and said, "Are you fine with staying close to here?"

The look I sent her through the reflection of the mirror conveyed how stupid I thought her question was.

"Let's go to the bar down the street then. It isn't the fanciest place, but their drinks are cheap and my uncle owns it."

"Deal," I told Ginny. I was no snob. Close and cheap sounded like a plan.

Her uncle also supposedly owned the new building we had moved into. Located in a high-foot traffic side of town, across the street from a real estate company, popular tattoo parlor, and a deli, she couldn't have gotten a better space for the salon. The dog grooming business two doors down from us had got me seeing money signs; I had tons of clients with dogs. Plus, it worked out even more in my favor because my new house was a short drive away.

And that was how we found ourselves, ten minutes later, standing in front of a bar walking distance from the salon. We'd been able to leave our cars in the same lot we left them for work, next to a big mechanic shop that her uncle also supposedly owned.

To be fair, Ginny had told me the truth. It wasn't a fancy place. What she hadn't warned me of was the fact it was a biker bar, if the row after row of motorcycles parked along the front of the street meant anything.

All right.

If she noticed my apprehension about going inside, Gin didn't make a comment as she waved me toward the door. Fuck it. I only partially ignored the three men standing outside smoking and watching us a little too closely, but when I opened the heavy door to go inside, the simultaneous smell of cigarettes, cigars, and weed brutally assaulted my nose. My sinuses immediately started going crazy, and I had to blink a lot as the smoke made them burn.

The place was exactly what I'd picture a biker bar to look like. I'd been to a lot of bars in my life pre-Josh-and-Louie, and some had been way sketchier than this. From behind, Ginny pointed in the direction of rows of liquor along the wall, and I headed over, taking in the loose crowd of men and women in leather and T-shirts alike. They were all ages, all looks. Despite the heavy smell of smoke that I knew was illegal indoors… well, it didn't seem so bad. Most people were talking to one another.

Snagging two chairs in the middle of the counter, Ginny slipped in to the chair beside me. I leaned forward and looked up and down the bar for the bartender, waving when the older man caught my eye. He simply tipped his chin up for our order.

I'd gone out with Ginny enough over the years to know we started off our evenings with Coronas or Guinness, and this place didn't seem like the type to carry my favorite nectar from the mother country. "Two Guinness, please," I mouthed to him.

I wasn't sure he understood what I said, but he nodded and filled two glasses from one of the taps, sliding both over to us, yelling the amount we owed. Before Ginny could get it, I slid two bills across the bar.

"Woo," Ginny cheered, clinking her glass against mine.

I nodded in agreement, taking the first sip.

I'd barely finished swallowing when two forearms came from behind to cage my boss in, a blond head of hair making an appearance right by her ear. Who the hell was this?

As if wondering the same thing, she started to say, "Who…?" before glancing over her shoulder, her body tight and reeling back. It was her laugh a moment later that told me everything was okay. "You son of a bitch! I was wondering who the hell was coming up to me!" She reached up with the arm furthest away from me to pat the strange man, who was wearing a leather vest over a white T-shirt.

"What a fuckin' mouth," the man's low voice claimed just loud enough for me to hear. He pulled back, his attention casually sliding in my direction. The grin that had been on his face as he spoke to my friend brightened a little more as he took me in.

God help me, he was hot.

The dark blond of his longish hair matched the same color crossing his mouth and cheeks in a rough five o'clock shadow. Mostly though it was his easy smile that electrified his handsome face. He had to be a few years older than me at least. All I could do was sit there and smile at the man who was more than likely a biker based on the fact he had a vest on… and that we were at a biker bar. *A biker bar on a Saturday.* You really never knew where life would take you, did you?

The longer I looked at the blond's face… I realized I recognized those blue eyes of his. That particular shade was pointed in my direction from another face, a face I knew well. That blue was Ginny's blue.

"Trip, this is my friend Diana. She works with me at the salon. She's the one I told you about who has the boy who plays baseball. Di, this is my cousin Trip," Ginny explained as my gaze trailed back over to my friend, shaking off the fuzz that had come over my brain from looking at him.

Trip. Baseball. She had mentioned her cousin who had a son around Josh's age who played competitive baseball a couple of times. I remembered now.

"Nice to meet you," I greeted, one hand curled

around my stout, the other extending out in his direction.

"Hey," the grinning blond said as he took my hand in a shake.

"He works at the garage by the parking lot," Ginny explained.

I nodded, watching as the guy named Trip turned back toward his cousin and elbowed her. "Where's your man at?"

"He's at home," she explained, referring to her fiancé.

He gave her a funny look and shrugged. "The old man is back there if you wanna drop by and say hi," he said to her, his gaze straying back to me for a moment as a small, sly smile crossed his mouth.

She nodded, turning to look over his shoulder briefly, as if searching for whoever "the old man" was. Her uncle?

"Go say hi," I offered when she continued looking around the floor of the half-full bar.

Her nose scrunched for a moment as she hesitated. "You sure?"

I rolled my eyes. "Yeah, as long as you don't leave me here all night."

With that, she grinned. "Okay, it's my uncle. It'd be rude of me to not go say hi. Want to come?"

If there was one thing I understood and was all too well acquainted with, it was the politics that went behind big, close families. In mine, you had to tell *everyone* hi. There was no such thing as a group wave unless you wanted your mom hissing in your ear about how much of an embarrassment you were.

"Nah," I answered and tipped my head toward the back. "Go say hi. I'll be here."

My boss smiled and stood up, patting her cousin on the cheek. "Show me where he is," she stated... which was kind of weird. The bar was a good size but not that big. It wouldn't have taken her longer than a couple of minutes to find her uncle, but whatever. The blond man nodded and led her through the small group directly behind us. She carried her stout with her.

I sat there and took a couple of sips, looking up and down the counter at the people sitting there. Really, they almost looked like normal, everyday people, except for all the leather and Harley T-shirts. I had just pulled my phone out of my pocket to check my e-mail —not that there was anything important in there— when I caught sight of a familiar-looking buzz cut and brown hair at the far edge of the bar. It wasn't until the man turned to face forward that I realized it was my neighbor.

Dallas with the asshole brother. Dallas who may or may not be in a marriage with a woman in a red car. Dallas with a giant tattoo across his body. Dallas who was chuckling as he said something to the person who had been sitting beside him.

What were the fucking chances he would be here?

I hadn't seen a motorcycle at his place in the days since I'd first started paying attention to his house after his brother got beat up. I'd only seen his pickup truck. Was he a biker too?

Taking him in, sitting there with his elbows on the

counter, a smile lingering on his sharp face, his attention focused on the television mounted on the wall... I couldn't really picture him in this kind of place. With the way his hair was cut short and from his posture, all straight back and strong shoulders, I would have thought military, not motorcycle club.

Really?

For one shameful moment, I wondered what the hell I had gotten myself into by moving to my neighborhood and living across from someone like him. Him with his marital problems that took place outside and his brother who got the shit beat out of him for who knows what. Him who hung out at a biker bar of all places.

Just as quickly as that thought filled my head, I accepted how dumb and hypocritical I was being. What mattered was what was on the inside, right?

One of the people in my line of view moved and I noticed he wasn't wearing a vest like so many of the men were. Maybe he wasn't in the motorcycle club, or was he?

It doesn't matter. At least, it shouldn't.

He had brought back my plastic container and thanked me for helping his brother. There was no reason to think he was a bad guy now, was there? He had dirt smudged on his neck like Louie sometimes did, and something about that reassured me.

No one was sitting next to my neighbor at that point, and as I looked around, I debated for a minute whether to pretend not to see him or just go ahead and wave to get it over with the lazy way. Then those deeply engraved manners my mom had practically beat into me overrode anything and everything else, like usual. Plus, I hated when people pretended not to see me, even if I really didn't want to say hi, and he'd been polite when he didn't need to be. I wasn't going to count the first day we'd met; no one was ever in a good mood when they'd gotten rudely woken up, especially with some bullshit like his brother had pulled.

After another minute of telling myself that it would be fine to not say anything, I accepted that I couldn't do that. With a grumble, I finally pushed my chair back and got up, grabbing my stout along the way.

One day I would grow into my own person who didn't care about doing the right thing.

One day when hell froze over.

The closer I got to him sitting at the other end of the bar staring at the television mounted high on the wall, the more relaxed I became. He was watching a baseball game. It was Josh's favorite major league team—the Texas Rebels. I only hesitated a little bit as I came up behind him and then tapped him on the shoulder with my free hand.

He didn't turn around, so I did it again. That second time, he finally turned his head to look over his shoulder, a slight frown creasing the space between his full eyebrows. Pale eyelids lowered over those hazel irises, blinking once, then twice and a third time.

Great. He didn't recognize me.

"Hi." I flashed him a smile that was about 98 percent "why did I do this?" "I'm Diana, your neighbor," I explained, because though we'd met twice, apparently he still didn't remember me. If that didn't make a girl feel good, I didn't know what would.

Dallas blinked once more and slowly gave me a hesitant, wary look as he nodded. "Diana, yeah."

I blinked at the most unenthusiastic greeting I'd ever been welcomed with.

And then to make it worse, his frown made a reappearance at the same time his gaze flicked around the bar. "This is a surprise," he said slowly, his forehead still lined with confusion or discomfort, or both. I didn't know why. My boobs weren't hanging out and in his face, and I was standing a reasonable distance away from him.

"I'm here with my friend," I explained slowly, watching as he turned his head enough to glance around me... to look for my friend? Or see where his friend was to get me out of his face? Who knew? Whatever the reason, it made me narrow my eyes at him. I didn't *want* to be here either, thank you very much. "Well, I wanted to say hi since I saw you here...." I trailed off as his gaze switched back to my direction, that almost familiar crease making its presence known one more time between his thick eyebrows. Had I done something wrong by coming up to him? I didn't think so. But there was something in his gaze that made me feel so unwelcome, I couldn't help but feel awkward. Really awkward.

I could tell where I was wanted and where I wasn't.

"All right, I just wanted to say a friendly 'hello.' I'll

see you later, neighbor." I finished in one breath, regretting making the decision to come over more than I had regretted anything in recent history.

That furrow between my neighbor's eyebrows deepened as his gaze swept over me briefly before moving back to the television as he shifted forward in his seat, dismissing me. The action was so fucking rude, my stomach churned from how insulted I was. "'Kay. See you around," he said.

Thank God I had said I was leaving first.

I didn't know him well enough to decide whether he was being unfriendly because he didn't want to have anything to do with me in public or if today was just not the day for small talk. Then again, once he realized who I was, his expression had just turned guarded. Why, who the hell knew?

Slightly more embarrassed than I had been minutes before—I should have just pretended not to see him, damn it—with my drink in hand, I made the walk along the edge of the bar toward my original seat. I'd barely sat down when I faintly heard Ginny's voice over the loud music. A moment later, the seat next to me was pulled out and so was the one on the other side of her.

"Sorry, sorry," she apologized, scooting the stool forward as the blond man she'd called her cousin did the same at the stool beside her.

I shrugged, shoving the moment with my neighbor to the back of my mind. I wasn't going to let it bother me. There wasn't anything *worth* bothering me about the situation. Good for him not being a giant whore, I guess, if that was why he hadn't been friendly. "It's okay."

And then, of course, the blond named Trip leaned forward and tipped his chin up at me. "You know Dallas?"

"The guy over there or the city?" I asked, gesturing toward the end of the bar with a quick and not-so-inconspicuous head jerk.

He nodded with a grin. "The man, not the city."

"Uh-huh. We're neighbors."

That had Ginny turning her red head to look in the direction we'd both gestured to. I could tell her eyes narrowed.

"No shit?" Trip asked, bringing his mug of beer to his mouth.

"He's two houses down, across the street."

"You're across from Miss Pearl?"

How the hell he knew who Miss Pearl was, I didn't understand. "Yep."

"I remember seeing a for sale sign up in front of that house. How 'bout that."

Someone knew my neighbor well.

Meanwhile, I noticed that Ginny was still trying to look over at the other side of the bar to search whom we'd been originally talking about. I touched her elbow and, with my palm flat to the surface of the bar, pointed right at my neighbor pretty damn discreetly if I did say so myself. "The guy in the white shirt."

Then she turned to look at me over her shoulder, her eyes a little too shrewd. "You live across the street from him?"

"You know him too?"

"I didn't…" She flubbed her words before shaking her head and using her thumb to gesture to the blond beside her. "He's our cousin."

That man was Ginny's cousin? *Really?* She had never, ever mentioned him before. I'd pegged him to be about forty, right around her age. The same age as I figured the cute blond on her other side might be also.

"So, you cut hair too?" Trip asked, ending Ginny's explanation of the man at the end of the bar, damn it. I could always ask her about it later… maybe. After the way he'd just been, I wasn't exactly interested in hearing his life story. Plus, he was married. *Married.* I wouldn't roll down that hill even if he'd been interested. Which he hadn't. It was fine. I wasn't interested either.

"Yes," I answered, focusing on the blond's question, even as Ginny snorted into her beer. "I prefer hair *artiste*, but yeah." Doing hair color was my favorite and what I made more than half my money off, but who needed to be specific?

"You wanna cut mine?" the flirt just went ahead and asked.

I scrunched up my nose and smiled. "No."

The big laugh that bubbled out of him made me grin.

"It's nothing personal, I promise," I explained, smiling at him and Ginny, feeling a little like a jerk for how that had come out.

Ginny's cousin shook his head as he continued cracking up, his handsome face getting that much more good-looking. "Nah. I get it. I'll go cry in the bathroom."

My boss groaned as she put her beer mug up to her face, rolling her eyes. "Don't believe anything that comes out of his mouth."

"I wasn't going to." I winked at her, earning us another laugh from the only man talking to us.

"Fuck, you two are brutal."

We didn't even have to say "thank you." Ginny and I grinned at each other over his compliment that wasn't supposed to be one. I had just sat back into my stool when, out of the corner of my eye, I spotted my neighbor's face. He was looking right at us.

Before I could process that, Trip leaned his forearm onto the counter, catching my attention once more, and asked, "What did you say your name was again?"

CHAPTER FIVE

FUCK.

Ginny pulled the words right out of my mouth. "Why is it so bright out today?"

I squinted against the shaft of sunlight beaming through the glass doors and windows of the shop. Despite suffering through the worst of my hangover yesterday, I still wasn't back at 100 percent after our drinking fest. My head ached and my mouth still tasted faintly like a dead animal.

God, I was getting old. Five years ago, I wouldn't still be feeling like shit almost forty-eight hours after going out.

"I'm never drinking again," I muttered to the redhead who had woken up on my couch the day before.

"Me neither," she moaned, practically hissing as the door to Shear Dialogue swung open and even brighter sunshine poured into the salon at eleven in the morning as Sean, the other stylist, stepped inside with his phone to his ear. He gave us a chin dip in greeting, but we were both too busy acting like we were Dracula's children to care.

God.

Why did I do this to myself? I knew better. Hell, of course I knew better than to drink so much in one night, but after we'd left the biker bar, aptly named Mayhem, in a cab together—because there was no way either one of us had any business behind the wheel of a car—we'd gone on to drink a bottle of wine each.

When I'd woken up the day before on my stomach and felt that first stir of nausea and flu-like symptoms hit my body, I'd promised God that, if he made my nausea and headache go away, I would never drink again. Apparently, I had to accept that he knew I was a damn liar and wasn't going to do a single thing to ease my suffering. My mom had always said you could lie to yourself, but you couldn't fool God.

"Why did you make me drink that entire bottle of wine?" Ginny had the nerve to ask.

Slumping deeper into my work chair, I slanted a look in her direction. I didn't trust my neck to do what I requested. "I didn't *make* you do anything. You were the one who said you wanted your own, remember? '*I don't want white. I want red.*'"

"I don't remember that."

"Of course you don't remember it."

She let out a snicker that made me smile until my head hurt worse.

"I don't know how we're going to make it through

the rest of the day."

"I don't have that many appointments left. You?" Mondays and Wednesdays were my slowest days of the week usually; those were the two afternoons I picked the boys up from school.

She groaned. "I've got two hours until I'm busy. I might go take a nap in the break room." She paused. "I'm thinking about going to buy one of those travel-sized bottles of wine from the gas station and drink it. I think it might make me feel better."

Ginny had a point. I had eyed the last bottle I had in the fridge that morning and talked myself out of a few sips to ease my hangover. My next client was in an hour, and then I had a fifteen-minute break between customers after that until I got off. Actually, having clients when you were hungover was a curse disguised as a blessing. "Go. I can wake you up if you want."

We both let out a moan of suffering at the same time Sean slammed the break room door closed.

Slumping in my seat, I folded my arms over my chest and tried not to taste my saliva. "Your cousin is pretty cute."

"Which one?"

How had I forgotten my neighbor was her cousin? I didn't have the energy to ponder Dallas and his brother, whose name I didn't know, being related to her. It didn't make sense. "Trip."

That had Ginny making a noise that sounded like a pathetic attempt of a scoff. "Don't even go there, Di."

"What's wrong with him?"

"How can I say this? He's a great friend and family

member, but a partner in a relationship…? No. He has two baby mamas."

"*Oh.*" Oh. One baby mama? All right. Two baby mamas? Nope.

"Yeah. He's great. Don't get me wrong. He's a great dad, and other than my dad, there's nobody else I love more in my family, but he's a player, and I doubt he'll change any time soon," she explained in a way that gave me the feeling she'd gone through this spiel in the past. So… Trip was her favorite, not the cousin who sat on the other side of the bar from us and not once came up to her to say hi. Shocking. "His oldest son plays competitive baseball like Josh."

Huh. I slid her a look, intending to just mess with her. "So, you're saying we have things in common?"

"I'm doing you a favor, Di. No. Don't go there with him."

"There goes my dream of us being family." I laughed until my brain told me to quit doing stuff like that.

She let out a snort that lasted all of three seconds before she moaned. "I have other family, you know." After a pause, she asked, "So you live across from Dallas?"

"Uh-huh." I thought about it for a second. "He's really your cousin?" The coincidence was almost too much for me to believe it was true.

"Yeah." There was another pause. "His mom is my dad's sister. Trip's dad's sister."

There was something about the hesitation as Ginny talked about this specific side of her family that gave me the clue there was something about them that she wasn't fond of for some reason or another. In the time we had worked together, she wasn't stingy talking about her family. She'd mentioned Trip enough times, but she had never once brought up Dallas. I wondered why; I just didn't want to ask.

Ginny knew me well enough to recognize when I was curious about something but didn't want to be the first to bring it up.

"We're not close. He didn't grow up around here like me and Trip did, and he's younger than we are by a little." Ginny was forty-three; "younger than" her didn't really explain much. "He retired from the marines... or one of those branches. I don't remember which exactly. From what I heard, he moved back a year ago. I haven't seen him but once."

"Oh," was the only thing that came to mind for me to respond with. *But I'd fucking known it!* He had been in the military, long enough to retire. How old *was* he? Before I could stop my big mouth, I asked, "Is he married?"

She didn't look at me as she answered, "I remember someone saying he's separated from his wife, but that's all I know. I've hardly seen him in the last twenty years. I've definitely never seen her around."

Separated. I knew it. That explained everything. The ring. The woman in the car he'd gotten into a screaming match with. Maybe that explained him being weird. Maybe he didn't want anyone to think we were flirting with each other? One of my clients that I'd had for years had gone through a rough divorce. After she'd told me all the shit she and her husband were fighting over, she had pretty much convinced me that everyone should get a prenup.

"I met his brother." I'd more than "met" his brother, but that wasn't my business to share. "He's kind of a jerk. No offense."

Ginny turned her entire body to look at me. "Jackson is here?"

Why the hell did she say his name like she was saying Candy Man? It was my phone ringing that had me snapping straight up with a jolt, immediately forgetting her question. Too lazy to get up, I reached forward as far as I could to grab my purse. I strained and then strained a little more, snatching the edge of it and pulling it toward me with a huff. Sure enough, my phone was in the pocket I always left it in, and I only had to take a quick glance at the screen before I hit the ignore button at the "restricted call."

I had just set my phone back into my bag without a word when it started ringing once more. With a sigh, I glanced at the screen and groaned, torn between being relieved I'd decided to look again and dreading the caller. "Fuck."

"Who is it?" Ginny asked that time, all nosey.

I let my finger float over the screen for a second, knowing I needed to answer it but not really wanting to. "The boys' school."

The look on her face said enough. She had two sons. Getting a phone call from the school was never a good thing. Ever.

"Shit," I cursed one more time before making

myself tap the screen. "Hello?" I answered, praying for a miracle I knew wasn't going to happen. I already had one hand in my purse, searching for the keys.

"Mrs. Casillas?"

I frowned a little at the title but didn't correct the woman on the other line who knew she was about to ruin my day. "Yes?"

"This is Irene at Taft Elementary. There's been an incident—"

NOTHING BEFORE THE AGE OF TWENTY-SIX COULD HAVE prepared me for raising two boys. Really. There wasn't a single thing.

None of the four boyfriends I'd had over the course of my life had prepped me for how to deal with two small people who would eventually grow into men. Men who would eventually have responsibilities and maybe even families—decades and decades from now. The thought was terrifying. I'd dated boys and I'd dated idiots who were still boys no matter how much facial hair they had. And I was responsible for raising a pair to not become like them. I was about as far away from being an expert as you could get. Looking back on them now, my exes were like pieces of gum you'd find beneath a table at a restaurant.

While Rodrigo and I had always been close, at five years older than me, I had been too young to pay attention to those careful years between five and fifteen, to see how he'd survived them. All I could remember was this bigger-than-life personality who had been popular, athletic, and likable. If there had been growing pains, I couldn't remember. And I definitely couldn't ask my parents about it. I also couldn't call the Larsens for advice; they'd raised two girls, not two boys, and in the span of no time, I'd figured out that for a lot of things, boys were a lot different than girls. Josh and Lou had done some shit that I couldn't begin to wrap my head around, and I had no doubt five-year-old me would have thought the same thing.

What the hell was I supposed to do with Josh and Louie? Was I supposed to discipline them differently? Talk to them differently? Was there a leeway with them that wasn't possible with girls?

I didn't think so. I could remember my parents being a lot more relaxed—and that was saying something because they were strict—with Rodrigo than with me. It used to piss me off. They would use the excuse that he was a boy and I was some sort of innocent flower that had to be protected at all costs as their reasoning behind why I would get grounded for weeks if I got home past curfew while he would get a sigh and an eye roll. There had been plenty of other things that my parents had expected of me that they hadn't of Drigo.

So, as I sat in my Honda with Josh and Louie in the backseat, both strangely silent, I still couldn't decide how to handle the situation. After I had picked up Josh from school, neither one of us had said a word as I drove back to work and proceeded to go back and forth between color jobs for my last two clients of the day until it was time to pick up Louie. And as if sensing the tension in the car, Lou had been suspiciously quiet, too.

The fact was Josh had punched a little boy in the face.

Now I had been pissed off about it for all of ten minutes until I'd shown up at their school to talk to the principal and Josh himself, to find out that *yeah*, he had hit someone in his class. But he had punched him because the little shit had been beating up on a different kid in their class in the bathroom. The fact that they were in fifth grade doing this kind of crap didn't escape me at all. Josh had supposedly intervened, and the little shit had then turned his attention and aggression on my nephew. The slight amount of irritation I'd felt having to go pick him up had disappeared in an instant. But the principal had something up his butt and was talking about how severe the offense was and blah, blah, blah, *the school doesn't condone violence*, blah, blah blah.

The asshole then proceeded to try and suspend Josh for a week, but I argued until I got it down to two days with a promise to have a long talk and consider disciplining him.

That was where my problem came in.

Diana, the aunt, wanted to give Josh a high five for standing up for another kid. I wanted to take him for ice cream and congratulate him on doing the right thing. Maybe even buy him a new game for his Xbox with my tip money.

Diana, the person who was supposed to be a parent figure, knew that if it had been me who got in trouble at school, my parents would have beat my ass and grounded me for the next six months. My mom had slapped me once when I was fourteen for yelling at her and then slamming the door in her face. I could remember it like it was yesterday, her throwing my bedroom door open and *whack*. Getting suspended from school? Forget about it. I'd be six feet in the ground.

So what the hell was I supposed to do? What was the right path to go down?

Sure, my parents had an iron grip on my life back then and I had turned out okay, but there had been problems along the way. I couldn't count the number of times I had thought that my mom and dad didn't understand anything, that they didn't know me. It hadn't been easy feeling like I couldn't tell them things because I knew they wouldn't get it.

I didn't want Josh or Louie to feel that way toward me. Maybe that was the problem between being an aunt and being a parent figure. I was one, but had to be the other.

So where the hell did that leave me?

"Am I in trouble?" Louie randomly asked from his spot in the backseat on his booster chair.

I frowned and glanced at him through the rearview mirror, taking in that small, slim body angled toward the door. "No. Did you do something I don't know about?"

His attention was focused on the outside of the

window. "'Cuz you're not talking, and you got Josh outta school early and not me."

Josh let out an exasperated sigh. "You're not in trouble. Don't be stu—" He caught the "stupid" before it came out. "—dumb. I got in trouble."

"Why?" the five-year-old asked with so much enthusiasm it almost made me laugh.

Those brown eyes, so much like Rodrigo's, flicked over toward the rearview mirror, meeting mine briefly. "Because."

"Because why?"

"Because," he repeated, shrugging a shoulder, "I hit somebody. I'm suspended."

"What's suspended?" Lou asked.

"I can't go to school for a day."

"What!" he shouted. "How can I get suspended?"

Josh and I both groaned at the same time. "It's not a good thing, Lou. If you get suspended to miss school, I'll kill you."

"But... but... how come Josh isn't going to get killed?"

Those blue eyes met mine through the mirror again, curiosity dripping from the corners of those long lashes. "Because I'm not going to get mad at you guys for getting in trouble when you're doing the right thing —"

"But why would you get in trouble for doing the right thing?" Lou blurted out.

What the hell was I supposed to say? I had to pause to think about it. "Because sometimes, Lou, doing the right thing isn't always considered the best thing for everyone. Does that make sense?"

"No."

I sighed. "Okay, like Josh, do you have bullies in your class? Someone who picks on other kids and tells them ugly, mean things?" I asked.

"Umm… there's a boy who tells everyone they're gay. I don't know what that is, but our teacher said it wasn't a bad thing and called his mom."

Jesus. "I'll tell you what gay is later, okay? But it isn't a bad thing. Anyway, so that kid tells other kids things to try and make them sad and mad, right? Well, that's a bully. It's someone who picks on other people to try and hurt their feelings. That isn't nice, right?"

"Right."

"Exactly. You should be nice to other people. Treat them with respect, right?"

"Right."

"Well, bullies don't do that, and sometimes they're mean to people who don't know how to defend themselves. Some people can ignore those mean comments, but other people can't handle it. You get what I'm saying? They might cry or feel bad about themselves, and they shouldn't. There's nothing wrong with someone not liking you, right?"

"Right?"

The question in his voice almost made me snort. I had to let it go. "So, this kid in Josh's class was picking on another kid…. Josh, tell him what happened."

Josh sighed. "He was telling him he was a fa—" He stopped and shot me a look through the rearview mirror. What the fuck? Kids used the "F" word when they were ten? What decade was I living in? When I was his age, getting called "fart face" was about the biggest insult getting thrown around. "He was calling the other kid ugly names like Shrimp because he's short, and making fun of his shoes because they weren't Nikes—"

Oh hell. I hadn't heard that part in the office.

"I told him to stop saying that stuff, but he wouldn't. He started telling me... stuff."

What kind of shit had he been telling Josh? And why did I suddenly have the urge to go kick some ten-year-old's ass?

"He kept pushing and pushing me, and I told him to stop. But he started saying stuff about me and the other boy—"

I wasn't just going to kick the kid's ass, I was going to kick his mom's ass too. And after I was done kicking his mom's ass, I was going to kick his grandma's ass to teach the whole family a lesson.

"He kept flicking me on the ear and my neck, stepped on my shoes, kicked me a bunch of times, so I punched him," he ended simply while I was still thinking about maybe even hunting down an aunt or two of the little shit's.

"*Oh*," was Louie's serious, thoughtful response.

I put off my plan for later, reminding myself I needed to be an adult for now. "So, the principal got mad at Josh for hitting him, even though he hadn't been the one to start anything. I think it's stupid he got in trouble even though the other kid was the one being an asshole—"

That had Lou giggling.

"Don't tell your *abuelita* I said that. I'm not going to get mad at Josh for what he did, even though the principal doesn't think it's right. If you aren't purposely trying to hurt other people—and you can hurt them with your words and your actions—and you're trying to help someone or defend yourself against somebody who is trying to do something wrong to you, I'm not going to get mad. Just tell me. I'll try to understand, but if I don't, we can talk about it and you can tell me what happened. You should never pick a fight with someone for no reason though. Sometimes we all make bad choices, but we can try and learn from them, okay?"

"I don't make bad choices," Lou argued.

The fact that Josh and I both laughed at the same time didn't go unnoticed by the youngest person in the car.

"What?" the five-year-old argued.

"You don't make bad choices." I laughed and reached back with my palm up; Josh smacked it. "I told you not to stick foil in the microwave like a dozen times and you still did it and broke it!"

Josh slapped his palm into mine again. "Ding-dong, remember that time you said you really had to poop and we told you to go use the bathroom—"

"Be quiet!" Lou shouted. I didn't need to look to know his face was turning red.

"—but you didn't, and you pooped in your underwear?" Josh continued, laughing his ass off.

"It was an accident!"

My shoulders were shaking, and it was only because I was driving that I didn't fall apart on the steering wheel while remembering Louie's sharting accident last month. "It was an accident, and you learned to quit prairie dogging it, didn't you? So see? You learned your lesson about making bad choices when it comes to poop."

"Yeah," he muttered, sounding so defeated it only made me laugh more.

"And that's what matters." I snorted just as I pulled the car into the driveway to our house. "You just had to shit your shorts to learn your lesson."

"*Tia!*"

There were tears in my eyes as I got out of the car, holding my stomach from how hard I was laughing. Once the boys were out too and we were walking toward the front door, I pulled on a strand of Louie's hair so he would know we were only messing with him. "It isn't that hot today. You want to play some catch?" That principal could suck a big ding-dong if he thought I was going to punish Josh for what he'd done. In the back of my head, I realized that my parents and the Larsens probably wouldn't agree with my glorifying his choices, but they could make all the faces and comments they wanted. I was proud of my kid.

"Can we play tag too?" Lou asked.

An Alka-Seltzer, Gatorade, a Coke, and a lot of water had dulled the sharpest edge of my hangover the day before, but if I was being completely honest with myself, not playing something my five-year-old wanted all because I'd had too much to drink made me feel awfully guilty. I could throw up in the bushes later if it came down to it, I guessed. "Sure."

"And can I ride my skateboard after?"

"Yeah you can."

"Have you found me a new team?" Josh asked with hopeful hesitation in his voice.

Fuck. I kept forgetting. "Not yet, J, but I will. Cross my heart. I really will find you one." We had already talked about how it would more than likely take a couple of months to find Josh a new Select baseball team to play for, and to give him credit, he hadn't been hounding me about it even though we were coming up to the two-month mark since we had talked about it. But I knew how important baseball was to him. Luckily, in the meantime, Mr. Larsen had been taking him to practice with his catching coach and batting coach.

Five years ago, I had no idea there was even a thing called a catching coach or someone who just worked on batting skills. Literally, he was a coach that worked with Josh to perfect his skills as a catcher and another to correct and improve his batting. I'm not sure what I had thought about baseball before that, but I sure as hell didn't realize how much work went into it, much less how competitive and cutthroat it could be before boys even hit puberty. There was none of that fun, fair, positive crap going on with the kinds of teams Josh played on. They played to win. If it didn't make Josh so happy, I would have been fine with him doing something else with his free time.

A few minutes after getting home, we had all

changed into nonschool and work clothes and had made our way to the backyard with Mac, who was beyond stoked to have us all home. I eyed Louie's outfit for a second and kept my comment to myself. The red Spiderman pajama pants and purple collared shirt my mom had bought him at some point didn't match. At all. But I didn't say a word. He could wear whatever he wanted to wear. I caught Josh side-eyeing him, but he didn't tell him anything either. We both just let that boy live his life in mismatched clothing.

Somehow we started off playing tag in the backyard, even though I was pretty sure we had intended to play catch first. The three of us chased each other around with Mac running after us, trying to play too. Over the chain-link fence, I heard the rumble of cars passing by, but when Louie slapped his hand on my back to "get me," I completely forgot what I was thinking about as I ran after him.

We didn't stop until we were all panting and sweating, and then Josh and Lou picked up their gloves to start playing catch.

The sun was hot, but none of us let it get to us as we took turns tossing the ball at each other; it was a pointless game for Josh's skills, but I liked that he still did little-kid stuff to hang out with Louie.

"Can I bat some?" Josh finally asked after we'd been tossing the ball for a while.

I scrunched up my nose and looked around at the nonstop fence lines in our neighbors' backyards, imagining the worst.

"You don't throw that fast, and I won't hit it as

hard as I can," he said like I wouldn't take it offensively.

"*'You don't throw that fast,'*" I mocked to mess with him. "Yeah, sure. Just be careful. We don't need to be breaking any windows."

He rolled his eyes like what I was asking for wasn't a big deal, and maybe for him it wasn't. He wouldn't be the one paying for a new window or going to apologize if it happened.

"Let's go to the front at least so we don't have to jump any fences to get into people's backyards." I eyed Louie. "I'm talking to you, you little criminal."

"I don't do anything!" He laughed, putting both of his hands to his chest like he couldn't understand why I would pick on him.

I loved it.

"Uh-huh. I know you're always up to nothing good."

He chuffed.

"I'll get the bat," Josh said, already moving toward the house.

It didn't take him long to get his bat, and we moved toward the front yard, leaving Mac in the back barking and whining, but that was what he got since he'd run across the street last time. Soon enough, I was tossing underhand pitches at Josh, watching him hit one after the other, proving that his batting lessons were coming in handy. Sure, I didn't throw the balls with any real power behind them, they were slow, but something was something. He was hitting them, rocketing them into our neighbors' lawns and making Louie run after the balls at our urging... and a promise I'd pay him five bucks.

It was probably about fifteen bats in that I spotted the two male figures across the street in front of Dallas's house, talking. One of them had to be him; I didn't know anyone else with that buzz-cut hair and brawny build that would be standing there of all places. And it was about two seconds later that I realized it was Trip, Ginny's cousin—*other* cousin—next to him. The longer I looked at them, at how one was leaning forward and the other wasn't, the more I realized they might have been arguing. But in the time it took me to glance at the boys and back across the street again, both men were making their way over. It was the blond who had me smiling in their direction, remembering his teasing from two nights ago. The love and friendship he had with my boss had been obvious. I'd liked him more and more the longer we stayed at the bar talking, especially when he had offered to walk us outside to catch our taxi.

And just as suddenly, I thought about the brush-off the man beside him had given me. Right after that memory, I made myself remember how he had come by my house to thank me for helping his brother. I could give him some credit for that.

And he was married and having marriage problems. I could respect that. After every time I'd split up with someone, I'd sworn off the entire male gender —except for those related to me—for a lifetime, which in reality usually only lasted a few months.

Josh didn't notice our visitors until they both

stopped on the sidewalk a few feet away as Trip's hands came up flat in a pacifying gesture. "Not trying to scare y'all," he apologized when the ten-year-old shot him a wary who-the-hell-are-you look, which I was pretty sure he'd picked up from me. I was also pretty sure I noticed him getting a better grip on his bat.

"Hi, Trip," I greeted my newest acquaintance before acknowledging my neighbor. "Hi, Dallas." I eyed both boys. "Josh, Lou, this is Ginny's cousin Trip, and our neighbor Dallas." Should I mention that I knew he was related to my boss? The boys liked Gin. Saying her name would be like a seal of approval, and I wasn't sure if this man deserved the honor or not, but I made a spur of the moment decision. "He's Ginny's cousin, too."

Neither one of the boys reacted until I gave Louie a wide-eyed stare, and he shouted out a "Hi" at our visitors.

Dallas had his gaze settled on Louie the instant he'd opened his mouth. He smiled so easily at him it totally caught me off guard. "How's it going, buddy?"

So it was like that.

"Good," the light of my life answered easily, his eyes shooting to my direction quickly as if searching for a clue for what he should do or say. Just because he'd been kind of cool and distant with me didn't mean I had to lead by a bad example. I winked at Lou.

"Hi, Diana," my neighbor finally greeted me next, all subdued and shit.

"Hey," I returned, glancing back and forth between

Trip, Dallas, and Louie.

What were they doing coming over? I wasn't going to believe it was a coincidence that Trip was over at my neighbor's house two days after we'd met and he'd found out where I lived, but... well, I wasn't going to think about it too much. Ginny had told me what he was like. As cute as he was, that was it. Plus, he hadn't acted *that* interested in me. He had just been doing what a man like him did best: flirt.

"These your boys?" Trip asked.

I would never deny them to anyone, especially not in front of their faces. So I nodded. "The little devil is Louie and that's Josh." Josh was frowning at the strange men while still holding his bat in a weird way and looking them up and down judgmentally. Ginny's family members or not, he wasn't impressed. I wasn't sure where he'd gotten that habit from.

"You've got a great swing," Dallas said to my older boy.

Just like that, with one single compliment, Josh's who-the-hell-is-this look melted into a pleased one. God, he was easy. He also threw me under the bus. "She's pitching slow."

I kind of choked, and Josh threw me a playful grin.

"Nah. There's a good arc to it," my neighbor kept going like nothing had happened. "Your posture, feet, and hand position are good. You play on a team?"

My gaze met Trip's and he flashed me that easy, flirting grin of his. If he remembered Ginny's comment from two nights ago, he knew Josh had played on a team.

What was happening?

"Not anymore," Josh answered, not needing me around from the sound of it.

Dallas's eyes narrowed just slightly as he looked at my nephew. "What are you? Eleven?"

"Ten."

"When's your birthday?"

Josh rattled off the date coming up in less than two months.

Under normal circumstances, the exchange might have been creepy, but in the last two years, I'd sat through so many Select parents talking about ages and sizes, that I knew this was baseball related. It all suddenly came together for me. Ginny had mentioned a handful of times in the past about her *cousin* coaching the baseball team his son was on. A son that was around Josh's age. I also faintly recalled seeing a baseball trophy at Dallas's house when I'd gone in there. For whatever reason Trip had come over, both he and Dallas had scouted Josh from our playing on the front lawn.

Huh.

Wait. Did that mean Dallas was a coach too?

"We have an 11U team this year," Trip explained, answering my question without even meaning to. "Tryouts are next week and we need a couple new players." Those blue eyes that were exactly like my boss's shot back in my direction for a split second before moving back to Josh damn near instantly. "If you're interested and your mom lets you—"

Bless Josh's soul, he didn't correct him.

"—you should come by."

The overly excited "Yeah?" that came out of Josh's mouth made me feel terrible for not making more of an effort to find him a team sooner.

"Yeah," my neighbor replied, already patting around on his back pocket. He pulled out a worn, brown leather wallet and fished through it for a moment before taking out a business card. To give him credit, he handed me one first and then Josh another. "We can't make any promises you'll get on the team, but—"

"I'll get on the team," Josh confirmed evenly, making me smile. What a cocky little turd. I could have cried. He was a Casillas through and through.

Dallas must have gotten a kick out of his confidence too because he smiled that genuine, straight, white-tooth smile he'd used on Lou earlier. "I'll hold you to it then, man. What's your name again?"

"Josh."

Our big, rough-looking neighbor with a shitty brother, who hung out at a motorcycle club's bar, but somehow also coached little kid baseball with a biker, thrust a hand out at Josh. "I'm Dallas, and this is Trip. Nice to meet you."

CHAPTER SIX

─────────

"Joshua!"

"I'm coming!" the voice down the hall yelled in reply.

I tipped my chin into the air, eyeing the clock on the wall with a grimace. "You said that five minutes ago! Let's go or you're going to be late!" And we all knew how much I hated being late. It was one of my biggest pet peeves.

"Thirty seconds!"

Louie's snort had me glancing down at him. He had his backpack on, and I knew without looking that it was filled with either the tablet he and Josh shared or his handheld game console, snacks, and a Capri Sun. I didn't think Louie knew what it was like to not be prepared; he got that from his Larsen side because God knew he hadn't gotten it from his dad. He had his shit together better than I did, as long as I didn't take into consideration the number of things he lost after they left the house.

"He's lying, isn't he?" I asked him.

Sure enough, Lou nodded.

I sighed again, gripping the strap of my bag tighter. I'd stuffed it with three bottles of water and a banana. Where Lou was the prepared one, Josh was not.

"Josh, I swear to God—"

"I'm coming!" he hollered, the sound of what I was sure was his bag hitting the wall confirming his words.

"You got everything?" I asked as soon as he stopped in front of us, his bag thrown over his shoulder, bulky and heavy. I stopped asking him if he needed help a year ago. Big boys wanted to be big boys and carry their own stuff around. So be it.

"Yeah," he replied quickly.

I blinked. "You got your helmet?"

"Yeah."

I blinked again. "So what's that on the coffee table?"

His face turned pink before he lunged for the helmet he'd left there the night before. Last year, I'd made him a laminated checklist he needed to go through before going to practice. If I'd had to drive back home to pick up a glove or socks again, I would have screamed. Looking back on my childhood now, I wasn't sure how my mom hadn't dropped me off at the fire station. I used to forget everything.

"Uh-huh," I muttered before waving him forward to go through the door first, followed by Lou and then Mac.

Josh was huffing and puffing as we drove to the

facility where the 11U Texas Tornado played. In the two weeks since Trip and our neighbor had invited him to try out for his team, he'd been making either my dad, Mr. Larsen, or me go out and play with him nearly daily. I could tell the fire in the furnace of his little heart was stoked and more than ready to go for a sport he'd been playing since he was three years old, running to the wrong base.

We'd both looked up the team one night to make sure they were legit. They were; they'd won a good number of tournaments, too. The last two years, they won State, and they'd done well at Worlds. Sure enough, both Trip and Dallas were shown in several of the pictures posted on their page, tall and obviously tattooed and not looking at all like the kind of men who would coach boys a fourth of their sizes. I'd also learned my boss's cousins' full names: Trip Turner and Dallas Walker.

I'd met a lot of parents who ended up coaching their children's teams because they had been unhappy with who had been teaching their kids in the past, but it was still weird. Trip was a member of a motorcycle club, for God's sakes. I had no idea if Dallas was or not, but I figured that was a negative because I'd yet to see a motorcycle come down the street. Weren't bikers supposed to be doing biker stuff instead of spending entire weekends at tournaments and teaching kids values? And what was biker stuff anyway?

The important lesson I seemed to keep forgetting was that you couldn't always judge a book by its cover.

So, if Josh wanted to try out, I wasn't going to stop

him. All I could do was hope he kicked ass and kept it together. None of us liked to lose. Him especially.

The facility where the team practiced at was about a twenty-minute drive away, located near the edge of town. They shared the space with a softball branch. With only ten minutes to spare before the tryouts were set to start, I rushed Josh and Lou out of the car.

The facility was almost as nice as the one where Josh used to practice. His last team's practice spot was too far from where we lived now, and even if it wasn't, we still wouldn't be going back there. Josh rushed ahead, waving at me as I stopped to fill out the paperwork to register him for the tryout. We'd gone to get a check-up for him at the doctor just a couple of days ago in preparation for this, and I'd brought a copy of his birth certificate. The form wasn't too long, but it still took me a few minutes to get through it. Louie stood by me, already messing with his game console. Out of the corner of my eye, I found Josh standing by a group of boys about his size. He was such a freaking trip thinking he wouldn't make friends, but he always did almost instantly. The kid was magnetic.

I finished, and Louie and I made our way outside to the field the team used, taking seats at the bleachers where there were already about fifty other people sitting around, watching the kids. A few adults were clustered together by the entrance to the field, and soon enough they all started filing out, each one with a clipboard. Dallas was one of them... and when I squinted at the sight of the head of blond hair, I was pretty sure that was Trip right by him. And standing a few feet away from both of them was the rude guy who had gotten jumped. What had Ginny called him? Jack? Jackson? Someone Who Didn't Know How To Say Thank You?

More than twenty boys age ten and eleven lined up along the field and started tossing the ball back and forth as the adults moved around, jotting things down on their clipboards, watching. Then, the batting part of the tryout began with Dallas pitching to the boys. They ran through a few other drills and split the kids up into two teams to play a game that seemed to last forever.

I was pretty smug when Josh whooped some ass at every drill they made him run. He was a great catcher, an excellent batter, and he was fast. He got that from my side of the family obviously.

But...

It was impossible not to listen to the two women sitting in front of me talking about some of the kids who had been previously on the team and other parents. Nothing they said, from gossiping over crazy-ass moms who made their kids practice too much, to couples who had split up, was anything I hadn't heard or experienced with Josh's previous team. That was the one thing I'd come to realize: there was always the same kind of people everywhere you went, regardless of location, skin color, or income.

And then they started up with the coaches. One in particular at least: "the hottie with the body." I tried. I really tried not to pay attention, but I couldn't help myself.

"God, what I wouldn't give for him to pitch me

some balls," one of them muttered a little too loudly, making Louie glance up from his game and give me a funny look. If I had wondered which of the men they'd been talking about, I now knew for sure it was Dallas. He was the only one pitching.

"Mind your own business," I mouthed to him, earning me a disappointed frown.

"I've tried offering him money to coach Derek in private, but he never agrees," the other woman said.

"He says he's too busy."

"With what?" the first lady asked.

"Working. What do I look like? His secretary?"

I snickered and had to throw a hand over my mouth to hide my reaction from them when one of the ladies turned around to see what I was making noises over.

"I know he works a lot. He's been redoing the floors at Luther's place," she paused and let out a sigh that sounded totally charged. "You'd figure he could spend some of that money he's getting from his retirement on some new clothes. Look at those shorts. Are there holes on the pockets? Those are holes in the pockets."

"But then the new ones wouldn't mold to that ass, would they?" the woman cackled.

"Good point," the other one agreed.

What a bunch of horny bitches.

I think I already kind of liked them. They were funny.

I'd barely thought that when a sour-faced woman, maybe a few years older than me, leaned over—she was sitting on the same bench as the other two women talking—and hissed, "Have a little respect, would you?"

One of the two women groaned loudly. "Mind your own business, Christy."

"I would, but I can't hear myself think over you two gossiping," the woman to the side grumbled.

"Yeah, I'm sure," one of the ladies muttered.

The woman named Christy shot the pair a glare before sitting up straight and focusing on the game again. But the two moms started mumbling just loud enough for me to hear something about "a stick up her ass" and "delusional if she thinks he'd give her ass the time of day." After that, I couldn't hear much else.

By the time the tryout had been wrapped up, followed by a long talk that I couldn't listen in on that consisted of Dallas standing in a circle of kneeling boys, I was ready to get home. With Louie holding my hand, we hopped down the bleachers and walked around the front to wait for Josh, who had his bag over his shoulder. The kid was sweaty and flushed, but he was smiling.

"Somebody kicked ass," I whispered to him as he approached us.

Josh grinned, shrugging his shoulder. "I know."

I bumped him with my hip. "That's my boy."

Louie even held up a hand, earning a high five from his big brother.

"Is there anything else you need to do or are you done-done?"

"We're done-done," he answered. "He said they'll

post the list online next Friday." He let out a visible shiver of excitement. "I'll make it."

It had taken me years to build up the kind of self-confidence that Josh had. Hell, even now, I still struggled with it more than I would like to admit. I had never been really good at anything growing up, much less so good that I had a reason not to ever doubt myself. Then there were people like my cousin who was slightly older than me, who, even when we were kids, walked around with this kind of internal swagger and confidence that was hard to ignore. She'd always been an amazing athlete, like Josh. But that awesomeness had skipped Rodrigo and me.

I had an eye and a hand for cutting hair, and it paid the bills. Plus, I really liked what I did. I accepted that I was never going to win a gold medal or be on the cover of a Wheaties box. But I knew Josh could do whatever the hell he wanted to do with his life. He could be anything.

Seeing the joy on his face made me happy, happier than happy. I loved knowing that was my boy on the field who was so good he made other parents jealous. But I knew that, even if he wasn't the best, I would still root for him and think he was the shit anyway. That kind of stuff was important to a kid. I wanted him to know I would always love him anyway.

With a hand to his shoulder, I hugged him to my side and felt him hug me back with a hand on my waist.

"Ready then?"

"Yeah," he replied easily. "Can I call Grandpa on

the way home and tell him how it went?"

Mr. Larsen had called that morning before school, stating he had come down with a bug and wouldn't be able to make it to tryouts. Under normal circumstances, he would have had a front row seat to it. "Yeah, just grab my phone when we're in the car."

We had just gotten on the sidewalk to cross the parking lot when Josh lifted a hand, his head tilted to the right past me and Louie, who was still holding my hand, and waved. "Bye, Mr. Dallas!" he yelled.

Sure enough, standing on the sidewalk surrounded by two kids and four adults, one of whom was wearing a vest just like the ones I had seen at the bar, our neighbor nodded and waved briefly, his eyes flashing to me for a brief second before returning back to the people he was talking to.

Okay. If that didn't make it obvious we weren't going to be besties, I don't know what other clue I would have needed. All right.

NONE OF US WERE SURPRISED WHEN A WEEK LATER, WE checked the roster online and found Josh's name near the top of the list for the baseball team. It had been in alphabetical order; otherwise, I didn't have a doubt his name would have been first. Of course he'd made the team. I had probably been more excited than he was.

It was another new beginning for us.

Going to the first day of baseball practice with a new team was a lot like starting a new school year.

There were e-mails and schedules, and expensive uniforms to be bought and eventually lost. Fun stuff like that. For the boys already on the team, the season never ended. Select baseball players for the most part did it year round; they didn't have seasons. They always had games, only some months were slower than others because of the holidays and weather. So, for an established team to pick up a few new players, it seemed like making a kid start school halfway into the year. The people who were old news were sitting around inspecting the new blood. Measuring, judging, watching.

Parents and kids alike considered every new person competition, which was fair enough. They were. One new kid could take another boy's position. I couldn't blame them for being paranoid.

So on the first day of baseball practice with the Tornado—as Josh's new team was called—I put an extra watchful eye out on the parents and the kids. Josh could handle himself, but he was still my little guy at the end of the day, regardless of whether he was only inches away from being as tall as me. And as my little guy—as my *guy*, my Josh—there wasn't an ass I wouldn't whoop if I had to. For my kids, I would do anything.

When we got to the new facility and Josh left me to go with the rest of the kids on the field behind the building, I took a spot on the bottom row of the bleachers and prepared myself mentally.

Make friends.

Be nice.

When a few parents came up to me to shake my hand and introduce themselves, it relaxed me. The parents were all ages. Some older—maybe they were grandparents—and there were a few who looked younger than me, too, but most of them seemed like they were over my nearly thirty. I spotted the two moms that I'd been eavesdropping on at the tryout but didn't get a chance to officially meet them.

Somehow, by the end of the practice, I'd ended up with two dads sitting on the same bench I was on. It was only my big canvas bag between us that I felt kept them from scooting closer. The one sitting the closest to me had mentioned no less than four times how he was divorced. The guy sitting beside him, who had blatantly ogled my boobs every single time he talked to me, wore a wedding band. My best guess was that his wife had missed practice and he hadn't wanted to get busted sitting on my other side. Schmuck. I knew the difference between flirting with someone I wanted to flirt with and accidentally flirting, and I made sure to keep the conversation easygoing and about the kids.

But when Josh made his way toward me after practice, his eyes narrowed on the dads who were still sitting where I'd left them on the bleacher. He gave me this look that said he wasn't amused by the two strangers sitting so close. He usually didn't like men talking to me, and in this case, nothing had changed.

"What do they want?" he asked immediately.

"Oh, hey, J. I'm glad practice went well. I'm doing fine, thank you," I replied in a mocking voice.

Josh didn't even blink as he jumped into our

imaginary conversation. "That's good."

I stuck my tongue out at him and waved him to the side. "Ready to go?" I changed the subject. There wasn't a point in explaining anything about the dads.

"Ready," he answered, shooting the two men a wary look before walking next to me down the pathway that led from the team's practice field to the parking lot. The complex had four other fields and one of them was being used for a girls' softball team practice. "Are we gonna pick up Lou now?"

Setting my hand on his shoulder, we kept walking. "Yeah. I'll make dinner when we get home." Earlier in the day, Louie had called from the school's phone saying he wasn't feeling well. With a day full of appointments, I had checked with my mom to see if she could go pick him up and she had. She'd said he hadn't been running a fever but that he'd been complaining of a headache and sore throat. She'd offered to keep Louie overnight, but he'd said he would rather come home. He didn't like sleeping away from Josh if he didn't have to, and I didn't have the heart to force him to sleep somewhere else.

"What are you making?"

"Tacos."

"Gross."

I stopped walking. "*What did you just say?*"

He grinned. "I'm playing."

"I thought I was about to have to drop you off on the side of the road and make you find your own way home, kiddo."

That made my serious Josh laugh. "You—uh-oh."

He stopped in place and immediately dropped his bag on the ground, his hands going to the rim of it to spread the material wide.

I knew that movement. "What did you forget?"

Josh rummaged through it for a couple of seconds longer. "My glove."

He knew the same thing I did. I had just bought him that glove a couple of months ago. I'd made him swear on his life he wouldn't lose it; it was that expensive.

"I'll be right back!" he shouted, already taking a step away as he gestured toward the bag that was beginning to topple over. "Watch it for me!"

I was going to kill him if he lost it. Slowly. Twice.

Feeling my eyelid start to twitch, I snagged his bag before it fell over and hefted it over my shoulder. What did I do? I just stood there, looking around at the people on the team who hadn't left yet. In one of the bigger groups of parents and kids, I could see Trip's blond head. I hadn't gotten a chance to tell him hi, but I figured it was all right since it was the first day of practice and everyone probably wanted to talk to him. It wasn't like I had anything to ask yet or be annoying for.

As I continued glancing around, waiting for Josh, I spotted Dallas, his brother, the bitchy mom named Christy, and her son walking almost side by side toward the parking lot, which was where I was standing. It seemed like the woman was the one talking while Dallas just nodded along, and the other two seemed off in their own world. For a brief moment, I thought about tying my shoelace that didn't need a retie or pretending I was on a phone call. Then I realized how cowardly that made me feel. All because Dallas hadn't been Mr. Friendly at the bar? I had to face it. I was going to be around these people for a while. I wasn't scared of them, and I wasn't going to be shy and shit.

If he didn't like me for whatever reason in the world he might have made up for not being my fan, then too damn bad. My grandma had told me once you couldn't make someone love you or even like you, but you could sure as hell make someone put up with you.

So, the second they were close enough to me, deep in a conversation that didn't require a whole bunch of mouth movement, I let out a breath, reminded myself that two of these people were Ginny's family, one was a child and the other... well, I wasn't worried about her, and I said, "Hi, guys."

The greeting I got in return didn't amuse me.

One glare from the mom for a reason I couldn't even begin to figure out.

One weak smile from the little boy on Josh's team.

And two grumbles. Literally. One that sounded like "Mmm," and the other didn't really sound like anything at all.

Had Mac mysteriously broken out of the house, taken a shit on Dallas and Jackson's front step, and lit it on fire without me knowing? Had I done something wrong or rude to the mom? I didn't know. I really didn't know, but suddenly I felt a little betrayed. A part of growing up was accepting that you could be nice to others but shouldn't expect that kindness to be returned. Being nice shouldn't require a payment.

But as the group of four walked by, honest to God making me grateful that no one had seen that encounter, it aggravated me. More than a little.

A lot.

If I had done something, I could understand and accept responsibility for my actions. At least I wanted to believe that. But I hadn't. I really hadn't done anything to either one of them.

And most importantly, Josh had been picked to be on the team. So....

"Don't worry, I found it," came Josh's voice from my left, tearing my thoughts away from the men who lived across the street from us.

I slanted one of the few people in this world who wouldn't dishonor me a look. "Worried? You should have been the one worried you weren't going to make it to turn eleven if you hadn't found it."

ABOUT AN HOUR AND A HALF LATER, THE THREE OF US WERE driving down our street when Josh piped up, "The old lady is waving."

"What old lady?" I asked before I could stop myself from calling her that. Damn it.

"The really old one. With the cotton hair."

There were two things wrong with his sentence, but I only focused on one: I couldn't tell him to stop calling her old when I'd just done it, but hopefully I would remember next time. "Is she still waving?"

Pulling the car into the driveway and parking it, he unbuckled his seat belt and turned to look over the backseat of the SUV. "Yeah. Maybe she wants something."

There was no way in hell her hair needed cutting so soon, and *it was almost ten o'clock at night*. What the hell was she doing awake? The boys shouldn't even be up at this point either, but that was just part of the beast called Select Baseball. The three of us all got out of the car, tired and ready to go to sleep after we'd eaten at my parents' house, and a huge part of me hoped that, as I got out of the car, Miss Pearl didn't actually need anything. I'd barely slammed the door shut when I heard, just barely, a near whisper this far away, "Miss Lopez!"

We were back to Miss Lopez.

I just managed to hold in my sigh as I turned to face her house. I waved.

"She's waving at you," Louie's helpful ass explained.

Damn.

"I'm sleepy," he added immediately afterward.

I didn't need to look at Josh to know he had to be exhausted too. They were both usually in bed by nine on nights that didn't fall on baseball days. "Okay. You two can go inside while I go see what she wants, but lock the door behind you, and if someone tries to break in"—this was highly unlikely, but stranger shit had happened—"Lou, call the cops and blow that train horn under your bed I know your Aunt Missy bought you for your birthday while Josh tries to break a skull in with his bat. Got it?"

They both seemed to deflate with relief that I wasn't forcing them to go over to Miss Pearl's.

"I'll only be fifteen minutes tops, okay? Lock the door! Don't turn on the stove!" I said, watching them nod as I started off across the street. I turned around once I was on the other side to make sure the door looked securely closed and not left half open. By the time I made it up to Miss Pearl's driveway, she was at her doorway, wearing a snow-white robe over a dark purple nightgown with her cat in her arms. "Hi, Miss Pearl," I greeted the older woman.

"Miss Garcia," she said, smiling at me a little. "I'm sorry for botherin' ya in the middle of the night—"

I chose to ignore the "Miss Garcia" and smiled at her calling ten the middle of the night.

"—but the pilot light on my water heater went out. If I get on the floor, I might not be able to get up, and my boy isn't answerin'. Would ya mind helpin' me out?"

Pilot light? On a water heater? I could faintly remember my dad working on ours as a kid.

"Sure," I said, not knowing what other option I had. I could look it up on my phone, I hoped. "Where is it?"

Maybe that was the wrong question to ask because she gave me a funny look. "In the garage."

I smiled at her and immediately reached for my phone in my back pocket. As she walked me through her house and into the garage, I quickly looked up how to turn a pilot light on a water heater and managed to glance at the basics behind it. So when we stopped, I asked, "Do you have a lighter or a match?"

That must have been the right thing because she nodded and walked over to a work table pressed up against one of the walls, pulling a box of matches out of one of the drawers. I shot her a tight smile when she handed them over, hoping like hell she wouldn't be one of those people who stood there watching and judging.

She was.

I pulled my phone out of my pocket again and, in front of her, looked up the model of her water heater on the Internet and read the instructions twice to be on the safe side. When I set my phone down, I made sure to meet her gaze; I smiled and then did exactly what I was supposed to. It took a couple of tries, but it worked. *Thank you, Google.*

"All done," I let Miss Pearl know as I got to my feet and dusted off my knees before handing over her matches.

The older woman raised one of those spiderweb thin eyebrows as she accepted the matches. "Thank you," was her surprisingly easy answer without any comments about what I'd done.

"You're welcome. I should get going back home. The boys are waiting for me. Do you need anything else?"

She shook her head. "That's all. Now I can get my bath in."

Beaming at her, I walked toward her front door and waited until she caught up. "It was nice seeing you,

Miss Pearl. Let me know if there's anything else you need later on."

"Oh, I will," she agreed without any hesitation. "Thank you."

"No problem. Have a good night," I said to her, already three steps down her deck.

I had made it to the intersection of her walkway with the sidewalk when she yelled, "Tell your older boy good luck with his baseball practice!"

"I will," I told her, not thinking anything of her comment. She'd probably seen him lugging his equipment around. It wasn't some big secret.

Two minutes later, I was inside the house after banging on the front door for a solid minute and then having Josh ask, "What's the password?"

To which I responded, "If you don't open the door, I'm going to kick your butt."

Which got me: "Somebody's in a bad mood."

I had barely closed the door when I got bum-rushed from behind. Two arms went around my thighs and what felt like a face smashed into the small of my back. "I know what you can tell me tonight."

"You feel good enough for a story?"

He nodded. He looked like he wasn't feeling well, but he wasn't dying yet. My heart ached just a little as I turned around in Louie's arms to look down at him. "What are you in the mood for, Goo?"

Those blue eyes blinked up at me. "How did Daddy know he wanted to be a policeman?"

CHAPTER SEVEN

——————

"I SOLD ALL YOUR STUFF WHILE YOU WERE WITH YOUR grandparents," I told Josh on Sunday after his grandparents had dropped them off following their weekend together. Both boys looked tanner than they had before leaving for the weekend.

I didn't know what I would do without their involvement in our lives. That saying "It takes a village to raise a kid" was no joke. Louie and Josh had five people who cared for them full time, and sometimes it still didn't seem like enough. I seriously had no idea how single parents with no close family to help made it work.

Not even Louie fell for my joke; they both just ignored me before heading into their rooms to drop off their bags with Mac trailing behind them, ignoring me too.

Grumpy much?

"We have to do the lawn. Don't take forever," I

yelled after them.

It was Josh who let out a drawn-out grumble, pausing at his doorway. "Do we have to?"

"Yes."

"We can't do it tomorrow?"

"No. I get off work too late and the mosquitoes will be bad."

"I have homework," the little ass lied.

"You're full of crap," I stated. He always got his homework done on Friday; I'd bet my life on it. I had my brother to thank for getting him on that path early on in school. He hadn't let him go out and play until he got his stuff done.

There was another drawn-out sigh and the sound of a door—a closet door probably—slamming shut. Good grief, I hoped he was going to get over this crap soon. Wasn't it only girls who went through the horrible hormonal phase? Even then, wasn't that when they were in their teens?

Luckily, neither one of them gave me any more verbal grief as we all trudged out the back door to fish the lawn mower out of the shed in the back. Mac was terrified of the noise it made, so he was left inside the house. There were three huge spider webs on the door, and I only screamed once as something scuttled across the floor as I pulled out the mower and the two rakes I'd taken from my dad's house on my last visit.

I handed the boys each a rake. "You rake the leaves. I'll pull out weeds."

Josh frowned fiercely but took the garden tool from me. Louie... well, Louie wasn't really going to get much done, but I didn't want to raise a lazy butt. He could do his best. With gardening gloves on—I double-checked for roaches living in the fingers—we spent the next hour doing the first half of the yard, only taking a break for water and Gatorade and to put sunblock on the boys when I noticed the back of Lou's neck getting pink. How could I have forgotten about putting sunblock on him?

Once the weeds had been yanked out and bagged, and half of the leaves were lumped into multiple small piles throughout the yard, the boys stood off to the side, wiping sweat off their faces and looking so done I almost laughed.

"Is that it?" Josh asked.

I slid him a look. "No. We still have to pick this all up and mow the lawn."

He dropped his head back and let out a groan that had me blinking, unimpressed.

"J, you're basically a grown man—" I started to tell him.

"I'm ten."

"In some countries in the world, you could be married right now. You're pretty much the man of the house. You're almost as big as I am. I'm going to let you mow the lawn—"

"I'm a little boy," he argued.

"You're not that little. What do you want to do? The front or the back?"

Despite everything, Josh knew what and how much he could get away with, and he had to be aware that he wasn't going to get himself out of the mow job. It was happening no matter what he said. So I wasn't surprised when he sighed. "The back, I guess."

"You want to go first or second?"

"First," he grumbled.

"I can do the other part," Lou interjected.

"Goo, the handle is taller than you are. You'll end up running your brother and me over, hitting a car, mowing down a cat or two, and catching something on fire. No thanks. Maybe when you're sixteen."

He took it as a compliment, his expression practically beaming. "Okay." Like he was really proud of the mayhem I thought he was capable of.

"Let me show you how to turn it on, J," I said and went on to instruct him how to use the machine even though I knew for a fact he'd done it with my dad a few times.

By the time Josh was done, I'd shoved and tripped Louie into three different piles of leaves, and then we had to clean them up afterward. The backyard wasn't perfect, but I wasn't going to bust Josh's balls over it, and I settled for sticking my pinky in his ear. "Good job, hambone. Now you have to bag the leaves in the front with Goo."

The expression on his face made it seem like I was trying to poison him or something. His shoulders slumped and he lumbered toward the front yard with Mac barking from inside the house; I'd closed the dog door on him so he wouldn't sneak out while we'd been busy. I finally let him out, shutting the gate in his face to leave him in the backyard. Josh was still bumbling around when we got to the front, and I didn't think twice about putting my index finger to my lips while his back was turned and telling Lou not to say anything.

He didn't.

In what would probably be one of the last times I was capable of, I picked Josh up in a cradle hold while he screamed, "No! No! You better not!"

I laughed, noting subconsciously how heavy he was.

He shook his head as he thrashed in my arms. "No!"

Obviously, I ignored him even though he was inches from my face. "Louie, he's saying yes, right?"

"Uh-huh," the little traitor agreed, his hands over his mouth as he giggled.

Eyeing the biggest pile of leaves, I walked over to it, struggling more than just a little with Josh's weight as he yelled, "Don't do it! Don't do it!"

"Do it? You want me to drop you in the leaves?"

And as he kept yelling for me to have a heart, I dropped him like a sack of potatoes. He'd live. My dad had done it to me enough times as a kid in piles smaller than this one. A couple of bruises weren't going to kill him.

And sure enough, he acted like he'd gotten shot.

I wasn't sure how it happened, but somehow I ended up on the ground, too. Before I knew it, Louie went flying squirrel on us and dove on top of his older brother. At some point, I noticed my shoes had been thrown across the yard. It wasn't until they were both draped on top of me, trapping me on the ground and pressing an elbow down on my crotch while a forearm squished my boob, that I started smacking the palm of my hand down on the grass. "I give up. Jesus—"

"*Abuelita* said you're not supposed to be saying that," Lou corrected me from his spot the furthest away from my face.

"I know what *Abuelita* says," I groaned as the elbow over my pubic bone pressed down on it again, making me cringe and try to buck Josh off. "But you know what else *Abuelita* says? Don't be a snitch."

"She doesn't say that," Josh argued, crushing my mams.

"Yeah, she does. Ask her next time." They wouldn't ask, and I'd bet my mom didn't know what a snitch was anyway. I hoped.

Mac was howling in the background from the yard, fully aware he was missing out on playtime and losing his mind.

Josh hopped up to his feet, giving my poor chi-chis a break, and then held out a hand to help me up— which filled me with a stupid amount of pride. It wasn't until I was standing that I looked around the yard and saw the mess we made. Fuck. "Shi—oot."

"Ugh," was his response.

"Let me grab the rakes so I can help you get this all together." I sighed again, tiptoeing over to pick up my shoes and put them back on.

"I got it," Louie said, already running toward the gate that led to the backyard.

I wasn't thinking, otherwise I would have remembered that Mac was going to barrel right through him once the door was opened. Just as I yelled, "Wait, Lou," the big, shaggy, white beast did just what I had expected. He knocked Lou to the side as he sprinted across the front yard, zig-zagging in excitement like he'd been imprisoned for the last decade.

And like the paranoid, worrywart I was, I immediately envisioned him running onto the street and getting hit by an imaginary car.

"Try to grab him," I instructed the two youngest Casillas in our family, as I shoved my feet into my shoes.

Yeah, it didn't work. Mac was too fast and too strong and too nuts.

When he darted across the street, I yelled his name like a crazy person. I felt my heart drop to my feet until he made it to the other side.

"Wait for me here while I go get him, okay?" I called out to the boys. They nodded, my eyes immediately going to Louie who was wringing his little hands. "I'll be right back."

Not bothering to close the gate in case I could get Mac back by simply calling his name—a girl could dream—I looked up and down the street, trying to spot the biggest Casillas in the house. He was such a good dog... until he got loose. He always had been. I could remember like it was yesterday, Rodrigo bringing him by my apartment, so excited. "You're dead," I had told him even as I'd picked up the Irish Wolfhound puppy and cradled him to me, one of the few and rare times before he'd gotten too big. Now...

Well, now he was my oversized monster.

"Mac!" I hollered.

Nothing.

"Mac!" I yelled again, holding my hand up to shade my eyes as I glanced down the other side of the street.

Sasquatch's cousin was a lot of things, but he wasn't an idiot. He usually didn't go anywhere further than ten feet away from the boys or me, but every once in a while, especially since we were in a brand-new neighborhood with brand-new smells... he liked to go exploring.

"Mac! I'm not playing with you! Come on!" I yelled again, just as something moved in my peripheral vision.

Sure enough, to my right, the very tip of a white tail peeked out from behind the top of a trash can that had been pulled onto the curb. Relieved out of my mind, I jogged across the street heading to the house squished between Miss Pearl's and Dallas's. It was nearly identical in size and style to the homes on either side of it, blocked off by a chain-link fence similar to the one in my backyard. From the highest point of the roof, an American flag hung loosely thanks to the absence of wind.

"Mac," I groaned loudly enough for him to hear me as I approached the wagging tail on the other side of the trash can. "Mackavelli, come on, man," I called him again.

His tail just waved in the air more aggressively.

Of course he would ignore me.

He'd been spoiled rotten since he was a puppy, and

I hadn't treated him any worse. Hell, he slept in my bed on the nights he didn't hog Josh's. I knew for a fact Mandy had never let him on the couch back when he'd lived with them, but I hadn't upheld that in two years.

"Mac Daddy, *now*, come on," I called out just as I walked around the trash cans to find the tall, long-limbed, grayish-white Wolfhound with his nose to the ground, his butt in the air, and that nearly three-foot long whip-like tail still wagging.

He raised his head and seemed to give me that face that said he was completely innocent of whatever I was assuming he'd been doing. "Come on," I muttered, slipping my fingers underneath his leather collar, his wiry long hair brushing against the backs of my fingers.

I'd barely begun to tug him back in the direction of the house when a voice called out, "I hope he's not taking a shit."

I turned around quickly, caught off guard by how much I hadn't been paying attention to not notice someone approaching. Sure enough, at the edge of the driveway between this house and Dallas's was the same man who I'd helped weeks ago. The one who had gotten jumped. The brother. Jack, Jackson, Jackass, whatever his name was; it hadn't been included on the team's website.

The yellow discoloring over half his face confirmed it was him even if his features weren't too familiar to me. He was just as tall as I remembered, and finally seeing him without blood covering his face, I could see he was better looking than the man who was my real neighbor, his brother.

I shook my head, a little uncertainly. Did he have an attitude or was I imagining it? "No. He's smelling the trash can." Why did I feel like I'd gotten caught doing something bad?

The man frowned, his gaze darting to Mac, who at the sound of a stranger's voice had straightened his head and cocked his ears back, his lean body turned in the stranger's direction. All his attention was focused on the person who was on the verge of standing too close to me. Or maybe he didn't like the sound of his voice. Knowing Mac, it could be either or.

"I hope you're watching him. Nobody needs to be stepping into dog shit," the man grumbled.

I'd put my neck on the line for this asshole? His brother had been the one to come thank me—not that I had needed or wanted a thank you for helping him out —but it would have been nice. "If he poops, I'll pick it up. But he hasn't," I said to him calmly, trying to figure out what might have crawled up his butt.

"I don't see a bag in your hand," he tried to argue.

Did he think he was the neighborhood watch?

"He just ran across the street, why would I have a bag on me?"

"Jackson, cut it out," a deeper, rougher voice chimed in before either one of us had a chance to say something else.

There was only one person that voice could have belonged to: Dallas.

The man's face went red and his entire body went stiff at getting called out by his supposed brother. He turned his body as the other man, Dallas, made his way down the pathway from his door, arms loose at his sides as he came toward us. But it wasn't the ancient jeans he had on or the one-size-too-large dirty T-shirt he had on that caught my attention. It was his facial expression. There was a scowl on Dallas's face that said he couldn't believe what the hell he'd been hearing and he was disappointed by it. I would know, I'd been the cause of that look on my mom's face enough times in my life.

Dallas kept coming, his gaze frozen in place, on his brother to be specific, who wasn't moving. Neither one of them said a word until he stopped right next to the man talking to me, his forehead furrowed as he said in a low voice that wasn't low enough for me to not hear, "We talked about this shit." He spat each word out, anger lining each syllable.

I'd be a liar if I said I didn't wonder what kind of shit they'd talked about. Being a jerk? Unfriendly? Both?

"I already told you to quit being an asshole to the neighbors."

That explained it.

Somehow I must have disappeared to both of them because the man I could only assume was named Jackson turned to face Josh's head coach. His neck was red, and I'd bet five bucks it wasn't the sun to blame. "You're not my fucking dad, asshole, and I'm not a fucking kid. You don't get to tell me what to do—"

This was awkward.

And I wasn't going anywhere.

I glanced from one man to the other, noticing their similarities, which were quite a bit actually. They both had the same long, straight nose, heavy brow bone and strong jawline. Both were handsome in a way, depending on how you looked at them, but Jackson was prettier even though he looked older, more like a cover model, where the only thing cover model about Dallas was his resting bitch face that was too aggressive to be on the cover of anything other than a survival guide magazine. That was it as far as similarities went though. Where one of them had long hair, the other had it shaved down. One had a beard; the other had thick stubble. Blond and brown. Green eyes and hazel ones. A jerk and not as much of a jerk. That last one was still out for judgment. Dallas's saving grace was that he'd been nice to Louie and Josh.

"I get to tell you what you fucking do since you're living at my house," the man named Dallas kept going as if I wasn't there. "My house, my rules. We went over it already. Don't make it seem like I'm springing this on you."

Maybe hanging around wasn't a good idea after all.

I eyed the distance between my house and where I was. Then I squeezed Mac's collar tighter. When Rodrigo and I argued, we had always done it away from other people... and a day later, we were usually on good terms again.

"Fuck off," the Jackson guy spat, shaking his head, his rage clearly obvious to anyone within a quarter of a mile. "I've had about enough of your shit. I don't need this."

Dallas laughed that same bitter, wretched laugh I'd heard out of him the day he'd been arguing with the woman outside of the house. I couldn't tell if it was out of rotten humor or if he was genuinely bothered and trying to cover it up, but… it hurt me. "All I'm asking is for you to be nice to the fucking neighbors and quit doing dumb shit, Jack. There's nothing for you to have 'enough of.'"

"Fuck off. That's the story of your life and you know it. Everyone ends up getting tired of your shit eventually," the Jackson guy continued so angrily it finally triggered Mac's growl.

If I hadn't overheard the conversation Dallas had with the woman in the sedan who may or may not have been his wife, I would have no idea what he was talking about. But I did hear it. And the comment had me feeling defensive of this poor man who might be a gigantic asshole to the people who should have been the most important in his life, for all I knew. But still, harsh, much?

Jackson raised a middle finger as he walked by his brother and pressed the front of it against Dallas's forehead as he walked by. What the hell was wrong with this man? And my neighbor, the real one, didn't move an inch as his brother did that. He kept those hazel eyes locked on the other man even as he disappeared up the driveway for a moment before the loud roar of a motorcycle filled the air. Before I knew it, a beefy Harley was getting rolled down the driveway —where the hell was that thing parked? In the backyard?—the person behind the handles wearing the same clothing Jackson had on a second ago. Then he was gone.

That was interesting.

Unsure what I was supposed to do, I just stood there. Awkward. Maybe he wouldn't notice I'd listened to everything said between them. A girl could dream.

And that was exactly what didn't happen because the man named Dallas turned his attention to me.

Of all the things I could have said or asked, I went with, "Are you the older brother or the younger one?" before I could stop myself.

I didn't realize how offended someone could get over that question until after it came out of my mouth. If someone had asked if Rodrigo was the younger one, I would have slapped them.

He let out a noise in his throat as he glanced in the direction his brother had disappeared to and shook his head.

That said more than enough.

Luckily, after a moment or three, my neighbor settled for blinking down at me with that remote expression on his face. What did he think I was trying to do? Get information to steal his identity? "Older," he finally answered.

"Ahh." That explained everything. I would like to think it was because I didn't know him that I said, "I'm sure my older brother wanted to kill me a few times in his life." I could probably count at least fifty different occasions when he would have wanted to shake me at some point. God, I missed him. "That's family for you."

Something about that must have been the wrong thing to say because the dark-haired man shrugged like he was shaking off something he didn't like, his gaze darting to Mac quickly. "Make sure to be careful with him running off. We don't get a lot of traffic, but shit happens," the rough-voiced man warned me, forcing the smile off my face.

I didn't know why his concern irritated me from one second to the next, but it did. "Yeah. I will." Did he think I was stupid and didn't know that?

"*Buttercup!*" Louie yelled from across the street where he was standing on the front lawn, waving me over violently.

I waved back at him before turning to my neighbor one last time, trying to tell myself I didn't need to get annoyed with his suggestion about keeping better track of Mac. He probably hadn't meant anything condescending by it. "I should get going. Thanks for —" I pointed in the direction that his brother had gone in. "I don't know what I did to make him mad, but see you."

He took my leaving instantly, that sharp, serious face making a dismissive sound but I didn't miss the way his gaze slid back in the direction of his house. "You didn't do anything." His attention shifted to the five-year-old waiting impatiently on the lawn and stayed there for a moment. "Later."

I smiled at him. "See ya." Tugging on Mac's collar, we took a few steps toward the street before I used my grown-up voice on the stubborn-ass and whispered into his floppy ear, "The things I do for you."

With his head turned over his shoulder, he gave me that silly dog grin of his that erased every frustration I felt toward him. He followed me across the street without a single problem, where the boys were waiting and watching.

"What are you doing standing around? That's not what I pay you for," I called out to them.

Louie gaped before asking his brother, "She pays us?"

~

"Son of a *bitch*."

From her spot inside the break room, I heard, "Did you cut yourself?"

I shook my head, not bothering to see if Ginny had peeked out at my words or not. My eyes were laser-focused on the e-mail I'd just gotten. "No. I just got the schedule for Josh's baseball team. They want to bump practices up to three times a week. *Three times a week.* Like four hours during the school week isn't enough on top of him already going to batting and catcher practice. When am I supposed to have an afternoon to poop in peace?"

"Diana!" Ginny laughed, her voice getting louder, telling me she either had stuck her head out or she'd walked out.

"Who agreed to this?" I asked myself more than her. Practice three times a week and tournaments twice a month *minimum*. Jesus Christ. At this rate, I was going to need to buy a sleeping bag and just camp out at the facility every day.

"One of my cousins," she sacrificed them both. "It's that bad?"

"Yes!"

Out of the corner of my eye, I saw her approach me with a bowl of whatever she'd brought for lunch. "Why don't you call Trip or one of the other coaches and complain? You can't be the only one thinking about buying real estate by the field if it's that bad."

She had a point. I also didn't fail to catch that she didn't suggest Dallas, who was the head coach, to be the one I called.

When the team mom had e-mailed all of us after posting the roster, we'd been given all the coaching staff's phone numbers and all the fellow parents' numbers. I'd called Josh's last coach just about every week for one reason or another. I'd had that crazy, moody asshole on speed dial I talked to him so often.

So calling Trip or Dallas wouldn't be some crazy unheard of thing.

Would it?

"You have a tournament one week in Beaumont and the next week in Channelview? That's a pickle," Ginny said from over my shoulder.

Blinking at the list on my phone, I reeled back as I took in the information she had just told me about. Those were both three-hour plus drives! What in the hell? I could only take off one weekend a month, and every other month I managed to get two off. The Larsens wouldn't hesitate to take Josh somewhere that far away, but it seemed unfair to have to ask them to do that.

Without even thinking about it, I exited out of that e-mail and opened the one with the phone numbers, almost angrily punching Send on the screen when Trip's phone number transferred to the correct screen. "This isn't going to work," I said to Ginny as the phone rang. "They're out of their minds. I'm calling Trip right now."

I did and he didn't answer. Damn it. Facing the list of four phone numbers for each staff member—including that rude one, Jackson, who only ever talked to the boys—I eyed Dallas's digits for a moment, wondering whether he should be my next option or not. I hesitated. Then I reminded myself of how I was going to be stuck dealing with him for a while; it didn't need to be weird for whatever reason it could or would be. I hadn't done anything to make him feel strange around me.

So I copied the number and pasted it into the keypad. "Your cousin didn't answer so I'm calling Dallas."

There was a short hesitation before she said, "Might as well."

"Yeah. This is stupid." Why was she hesitating so much, I wondered as the line rang. "Hey, is there something wrong with—"

"Hello?" a raspy, masculine voice answered on the other end.

I paused for a second, my words to Ginny hanging off my tongue before I snapped to attention. "Hi. Dallas?"

"This is me," he replied evenly, almost professionally.

"Hi. This is Diana Casillas. Josh's—" What the hell was I going to call myself? "Your neighbor."

There was a brief pause while I'm sure he tried to remember who I was. His neighbor. The one who had saved his brother's ass. The same one who had a nephew that was—in my opinion—the best player on his team, not that I was biased or anything like that. "Oh." There was an awkward pause. "Hi."

That sounded real friendly and honest. Not. "I was calling about the e-mail I just got regarding the schedule," I tried to prep him.

The deep sigh that escaped him made me feel like I wasn't the first person to reach out to him today about the same exact thing. "Okay," was his answer that pretty much confirmed that suspicion.

So I just went right for it like I would have with Josh's old coach. "Look, I don't know what you guys were smoking when you put the schedule together, but this is way too busy." I was doing it. Fuck it. I was a terrible bullshitter. "Three practices a week? He already has coaching two other days. All that with weekend tournaments multiple times a month isn't going to work either. They're kids. They need some time to do... kid stuff."

There was a pause on his end, a controlled exhale. "I get what you're saying—"

This wasn't going to end well. I needed to go ahead and accept that.

"—but this is just preparation for when they're

older, playing more competitive ball." He ended in that deep tone that sounded like he'd lost his voice once and never regained it.

"I think we have three or maybe four more years for that. I think they'll be fine playing tournaments once or twice a month, and practicing two times a week. There's no way I'm the only person that this isn't working for."

"Three other sets of the parents approved the schedule before we sent it out," Dallas said in a voice that reminded me how Ginny had mentioned him being in the military. He was *telling* me this information.

Unfortunately for him, I had a problem with people telling me what I could and couldn't do.

"Well, those three parents must only have one kid, no lives, and that one kid must hate them because they don't do anything that isn't baseball related," I grumbled back, surprised at what he was telling me. What the hell was wrong with these people?

There was a shout in the background that sounded surprisingly like "Boss!" Then a muffled shout back that I was pretty sure came from Dallas before he returned in a cool, quick voice. "I gotta go, but I'll think about what you said and somebody will get back to you about the schedule."

That was it? "Somebody" was going to get back to me? Not him? "Please think about it—"

"I gotta go, sorry. Bye," he cut me off a split second before the line went dead.

With a groan that came straight from my gut, I

pressed my finger against the screen and ground down on my molars. "Damn it."

~

WHEN THREE DAYS WENT BY AND I HADN'T GOTTEN A NEW E-mail about the schedule being changed for the better, I started to get a little frustrated. When another day went by, including a practice, with half of the parents complaining to one another about their outrage regarding practices and tournaments, and *still* none of the staff commented about anything being done... I got more frustrated. But it wasn't until four more days passed, including another practice, with nothing changing and no one saying anything, that I realized the truth.

Nothing was going to happen.

And that just wasn't going to work.

I'd already talked to my parents and the Larsens about Josh's insane schedule and they had all assured me we could make it work between all of us, but that wasn't the point. What about the parents who didn't have four extra people to help them out? What about the parents with more kids, who all had other sports and activities? What about my Louie who liked going skateboarding and riding his bike from time to time?

I understood how highly competitive sports worked. I had family members who had grown up to be professional athletes, but a ten-year-old completely sacrificing all of their free time? That didn't seem like the best idea to me. They needed a couple more years to be kids, didn't they?

So between clients, I picked up the phone and redialed the numbers I had saved in my contacts a week ago. And when it went to voice mail, I left a message. Four hours later, when I still hadn't gotten a response, I called Trip again and left him a voice mail. In my desperation, I called again and left another message on Dallas's phone. I may or may not have been making faces the entire time it took me to get home from work at seven that evening, making up all kinds of random excuses why I hadn't gotten a call back from the team's head coach *when I lived across the street from him* and worked with the assistant coach's cousin, who worked down the block. The only thing that had kept me from walking to the mechanic shop where I'd overheard Trip worked was that would be creepy and crossing the line. A work place was a work place.

"This is bullshit," I finally whispered to myself as I sat in my car before opening the door and heading up the path to my house. Unfortunately for Dallas, I dropped my keys on the ground and it took forever to wipe the fob off on my pants, otherwise I might have missed him getting home. The fact was I didn't miss anything. As an old, Ford pickup rumbled its way down the street and turned into his driveway, I stood there. In the cab, I spotted that familiar buzz-cut dark head of hair behind the wheel of his big, old F-350.

I stood there, watching and debating whether to leave Dallas alone or not.

I went with not leaving him alone.

Before his truck had even disappeared into the garage set back along his driveway, I was already crossing the street and making my way over, hands tucked into the back pockets of my black jeans.

"Hi," I called out to him as I approached. He already had one leg hanging out of the driver side, the door flung open wide.

"Hey" was his response as he got out, his eyes going a little wide into what I knew couldn't be exasperation, right? Dressed in a long-sleeved, button-up, navy blue work shirt and khaki cargo shorts with more holes in them than pockets, Dallas was dusty as hell. I still hadn't figured out what he did for a living, not that it mattered or that it was even my business.

I smiled at him, trying to be as sweet and nonthreatening as possible. My *abuela*, God rest her soul, had always told me you get a lot more out of life being nice than being a *cabrona*. God, I had loved that woman. "I wanted to see if you had changed your mind about the schedule," I said, still smiling, trying to be all nice and innocent.

Almost as if sensing my bullshit, Dallas narrowed those hazel eyes at me. "It's been brought up, but nothing has been decided," was his political bullshit answer.

I was a lot of things, but a quitter wasn't one of them. "Okay. In that case, I hope you guys see reason and change it because it's crazy."

Maybe I shouldn't have gone with the "C" word. Maybe.

When those light-colored irises went even smaller, I

decided that yeah, I probably shouldn't have. "I'll make sure you know if anything changes." His tone clearly said, "get out of my face," so I knew he was full of it.

"Please," I peeped, getting desperate. "Everyone was complaining about it. Even Josh said he was tired just looking at it, and he doesn't really have an off switch."

Dallas eyed me one last time before starting to make his way around me. "I got you," he threw over his shoulder, not bothering to spare me another glance. "We'll see what we can do."

"Thanks!" I hollered after him, squeezing my fists at my sides at the brush-off he'd just given me. Son of a bitch.

The man whose brother owed me the teeth in his mouth lifted a hand as he walked into the house right before the security door slammed closed behind him. I was getting sick and tired of him brushing me off. If he wasn't going to listen to me, then damn it, I knew other people would. Because like my grandma would also say, *if being nice doesn't work, que todos se vayan a la fregada.*

BY THE TIME THE WEEKEND CAME AROUND, I HAD SPOKEN TO nearly half the parents on the team and gotten a definite feel that I wasn't in any way, shape, or form the only one who wasn't okay with the revised schedule from hell. We wanted it changed and no one in power was willing to do it. Governments had fallen thanks to pissed off citizens. Why couldn't Tornado parents or guardians do the same thing on a smaller scale?

Over the course of those days, the parents I talked to reached out to others they knew and soon the entire team had been contacted. There was a handful that genuinely didn't care about the schedule or understand why we were upset by it. Suck-ups.

But there was no way a big group of us could all be ignored. I figured, if nothing was done, those of us who disagreed could plan to not show up on the new date that had been added during the week. I wasn't just doing this for me; I was doing it for Josh and Louie. When the hell would I manage to do things with Louie if we were always busy with Josh? He was at such a delicate age for memories and shaping the outcome of the kind of person he would become. I didn't want him to ever feel like he was less important than his brother. I knew what that felt like, and I'd never want either of the boys to experience that.

Someone decided that at the end of practice, we were all going to talk to the coaching staff. And that was what happened. A swarm of parents descended on the head and assistant coaches of the Tornado. It looked like a mob with the three men and one woman in the middle. Some people were shouting to get heard; there was some finger pointing, but mostly there was a ton of "Yeah!" when someone overheard a good point another person made. Somehow I'd gotten wrangled into the middle of the circle, right at the center of the action. My head had started hurting earlier in the day, and the near shouting didn't help it at all.

I was only partially surprised as Dallas, while in the middle of saying, "Stop yelling. I can't think when you're in my face," looked right at me. He'd been glancing from face to face from the moment he'd been surrounded, but as soon as his gaze landed on me, it stayed there.

What the hell had I done now? He'd brought this on himself, hadn't he?

"It was brought to our attention," he said, staring right at me, "how unhappy you are with the schedule. I get it. I'll get together with the rest of the staff and see what changes we can make." He repeated the same words he'd told me days ago.

I looked from side to side as discreetly as possible, but when my eyes went forward again, Dallas still hadn't looked away. Why? I hadn't been the only one to complain.

"Some of us don't mind the schedule the way it is," one lone, ballsy parent piped in. It was the woman who had complained during the tryouts when the two women sitting in front of me had been talking about Dallas's body.

"Some of us have a life, Christy," one of the parents, whose name I couldn't remember, shot back. "Our kids need lives too."

"It isn't that bad," Christy kept arguing, her gaze landing on me and narrowing. What the hell was happening? Why were multiple people looking at me like I'd caused this? Hadn't I tried to prevent it? "We never had problems like this before. Some *people* need to realize they aren't always going to get their way."

The fact that she was looking right at me didn't help the situation at all. The schedule *hadn't* been like that before. One of the parents I talked to told me that.

Plus, I wasn't an idiot. Josh hadn't left his old team on good terms. His coach had moved him to second base to give his own son the catcher position and we'd complained. Soon afterward, the team had picked up another player and Josh had gotten screwed over again. Coincidence? I think not. It had been his idea to leave, and I had supported him 100 percent... even though I'd called his ex-coach a prick when we finally walked out of there for the last time. Had rumors gotten around here already about that? I knew how tight this community was. There might be two degrees of separation between everyone.

Either way, I knew this parent was talking about me. *Us.* I'd have to be an idiot to not recognize that. And I didn't like it.

From what I'd learned, only three new boys had joined the Tornado at the same time Josh had, and I didn't know where the hell the parents of those kids were. If they were even here. Regardless, with parents of kids in competitive teams, you had to assert your dominance before your voice was lost forever. And I sure as hell wasn't going to put Josh into that position of having the parent that was just okay with everything. If anyone ever picked on him, they were going to learn the hard way my family didn't get messed with.

Those were the excuses I was going to go with to justify what happened next.

"Why are you looking right at me as you say that?" I asked the woman calmly. Was today "Pick on Diana Day" and I hadn't gotten the memo?

The woman sneered, and I swore a couple of people standing right by her took a step away. "I didn't say your name, did I?"

I didn't have an anger problem. I never had because I didn't bottle up my emotions, except for that one stupid period at the age of twenty-six when I wasted months of my life on the second worst thing that ever happened to me: my ex. If I had a problem with someone, I dealt with it, and if I happened to stay mad afterward, it was no one else's fault but mine.

But I was going to beat the shit out of this woman the second there weren't any witnesses around, I decided instantly. "You didn't have to say my name. You were staring right at me. Am I the one having a hissy fit about wanting things to go 'my way'?"

The woman had the urge to shrug.

I made sure not to break eye contact with her as I stayed pretty damn calm. "I'm not having a hissy fit. The schedule is ridiculous, and I'm not the only one who thinks so, so don't put this on me, lady." Looking back on it, maybe I shouldn't have used the "L" word. Someone had called me that once and it had the same effect on me as the "B" word did.

"But you started it," she argued.

"I didn't *start* sh—anything. My kid needs a day off during the week. This has nothing to do with me. My kid is ten. He isn't in the majors yet. You want him getting Little League elbow or stress fractures in a couple of years? I don't want Josh to have to get surgery before he's even out of high school because I wanted him to win a fu—damn tournament he isn't going to remember when he's sixteen," I snapped at her, irritated.

"I do care about my son," she tried to argue.

"I didn't say you didn't."

It was shameful how much I enjoyed her cheeks going red. "But you implied it!"

I shrugged right back at her the same way she had at me, and it sent her into a rage. Bitch. "Well, you have an awesome way of showing it when I just told you about how he could injure himself by overdoing it, and you're still arguing with me over something that's had plenty of studies done on."

"I do care about my son, *Teen Mom—*"

God help me. I took a step toward her. I didn't know what the hell I was thinking about doing to her, but it was something, damn it.

The expression on my face must have said just that because the woman shut her mouth and took a step backward, her hands immediately coming up to her face.

"Okay! Okay!" An arm was waved up and down. "That's enough. Christy, go home. You're out of here for the next two practices for that," Dallas ordered. When the woman started opening her mouth, he blinked, that alone working better than any "zip it" gesture. "You started it and you know it."

I almost stuck my tongue out at her when her gaze swung over to me.

"Diana, make sure somebody else brings Josh to the next practice."

What? Was he fucking *kidding* me? I hadn't even done anything but defend myself!

Just as I opened my mouth to argue that fact, Trip jumped in. "Everybody else, we'll talk over the next couple of days and come to some agreement on changing the schedule. We'll e-mail you," he concluded with a whole hell of a lot of finality to his voice. Where was the guy who had hung out with me at the bar?

I was pissed. As the mob finally split up, I stood there, stunned and about five seconds away from pepper spraying half the parents.

I turned to try and find Trip, who had done little more than smile at me from twenty feet away lately, but he was surrounded by parents deep in conversation already. Dallas... I had no clue where the hell he had disappeared to. And Jackson was standing off to the side with his arms over his chest, looking so unimpressed with life, I wasn't sure why he bothered still breathing.

I couldn't believe it.

"*Tia?*"

The sound of Josh's voice almost immediately ripped me away from the edge of diving back into Diana From Years Ago who would have told everyone to lick a dick. First, I had to mentally picture myself smacking everyone in the back of the head, and then I cut off the rage that had started taking over. It was maybe only ten seconds after my nephew called me that I managed to turn around with a nearly serene smile and find him looking up at me with a suspicious expression on his face.

"What happened?" he immediately asked.

My head hurt, but I knew that wasn't what he was picking up on. If there was someone in the world who was my spirit animal, it was this kid. I wasn't sure how I ever forgot it. And since Louie wasn't here, I told the one who had already heard everything and more in his life the truth. "I'm about five seconds away from going to kick Jonathan's mom's ass, and then kicking her mom's ass afterward to teach them both a lesson."

The kid burst out laughing, reminding me of how young he was beneath it all. "Why?"

"She's out of her mind. We were having a parent meeting and she started talking nonsense. I might go kick Jonathan's ass too for being the reason she's here."

Josh laughed again, shaking his head. "You're crazy."

"A little," I agreed, winking at him, suddenly feeling whatever was left over of my rage disappear. How could you stay mad when you had so many great things in your life? "You ready to go home?"

He nodded, his grin a mile wide. "Yeah."

"All right, come on." I waved him toward the walkway, pausing until he was by my side. "According to your coach, I can't come to practice with you next time because of that psycho, so tell your grandpa tomorrow that he'll have to bring you. I'll call him, but you tell him too, okay?"

That had Josh stopping and frowning. "Why can't you come?"

"Because, I told you, she was saying crazy stuff about how it's my fault that we're trying to get the schedule changed, and I might have said something about how she didn't care about her kid and that's why she thinks the schedule is fine," I explained to him honestly, not wanting him to consider me a liar. I felt like, if I didn't lie to him, I hoped he would learn not to lie to me either. No one was perfect, and I didn't want him to believe he needed to be. He just had to be the best kind of person he could be and stand up for himself. Being "right" was so subjective.

"And because of that you can't come?"

I nodded, giving him an "I know, right?" face.

The downturn of Josh's mouth deepened and he shook his head. "That's not fair."

"I don't think it is either, but I guess I did egg her on, too, J. I didn't have to say anything back to her. I could have just let her think whatever she wanted to." That simple truth had me resigned. I *could* have let it go. I really could have. "Too late now. It's okay. It's just one practice, and hopefully they will change the schedule so it'll be worth it."

"That's stupid."

I shot him a look.

"That's dumb," he amended.

I shrugged, reaching up to rub at my temple with my index and middle finger. "She's just mad her kid is in the right field."

CHAPTER EIGHT

MY GOOD MOOD LASTED UNTIL THE NEXT MORNING. WHEN your first thought after waking up includes the word "bullshit" in it, it shouldn't be a surprise when you're grumpy the rest of the day. But the fact was even though I was well aware that I had thrown verbal lighter fluid into my talk with the baseball mom at practice yesterday, what resulted from it was still a whole load of horseshit. The more I thought about it, the angrier it made me. What was I supposed to do? Stand there and get blamed for something that wasn't my fault? I was dreading having to call Mr. Larsen and tell him that I wasn't going to be able to take Josh to practice, and then have to explain why. It made me feel like a kid who had gotten caught cheating on her test.

Josh was too sleepy to notice that I was grumpy, and Louie, well, who the hell knew what was going through that kid's head. The last time I asked him what he was thinking about, he'd said "buttholes." Since then, I kept that question to myself. But Ginny, who happened to open the salon with me that morning, immediately picked up on my mood.

"What's wrong?" she'd asked, already smirking.

"How can you tell something's wrong?" I asked, shoving the last piece of smores flavored Pop-Tart into my mouth.

"Because you eat Pop-Tarts when you're mad or aggravated." Her smirk grew. "And I know you. I can sense it."

She was right. Pop-Tarts were my comfort food in time of need. The boys already knew that when they caught me eating a package, something was wrong. I slid her a look as I unpacked my lunch and put it into the refrigerator, chewing and swallowing the last bit of my makeshift breakfast. To balance it out, I'd scarfed down a banana first. "You get into one little argument with another parent at baseball and you get suspended from a practice."

I didn't have to look at my boss to know she'd hunched over when she started laughing. I could hear her, and I knew her. And it was the sound of her laugh that made me smile so hard my face hurt from trying not to do the same. It did sound ridiculous.

"Trip did that?" she asked, wiping at her eyes.

"No, your other cousin did. Trip just stood by and let it happen." We weren't friends, I'd accepted that while I sulked on the way to work that morning, but I still couldn't help but feel betrayed.

That had her cracking up all over again. "What happened?"

So I told her in detail, and when she nodded at me in response, I knew I hadn't done some crazy, unheard of thing. Plus, Ginny really had been nineteen when she'd had her first child. Of course she was going to get at least a little offended. Luckily for both of us, she didn't offer to call Trip and put in a good word for me. I would never ask her to do that and she knew I could handle my own battles… unless I specifically asked for help. When she patted me on the back and shared half an orange with me, I told myself again it wasn't a big deal, that I shouldn't get so bent out of shape.

I had acted wrongly, but I still wouldn't change what I'd said. I could be a grown-up and accept responsibility for my actions. Somehow my mood spiked after I accepted that reality, and the next few hours went better.

Until I went to the deli for two soft drinks during a small break between customers right around lunch.

It wasn't a surprise that the line to order and pay was long. They kept the sodas behind the counter. With two people ahead of me, the door chimed open, but I didn't turn around. I was too busy looking down at my phone, browsing through flight times to visit my best friend.

"How's it going?" a male voice asked behind me.

I didn't realize they were talking to me, so I kept looking at my screen.

There was a short laugh. "Diana, you gonna ignore me?"

Wondering who the hell would be talking to me, I glanced over my shoulder and immediately went from being confused to not amused. It was Trip, my not-friend. "Hi. I didn't know you were talking to me."

That signature bright smile of his went up a notch, indifferent to my tone and mood. "Who else would I be talkin' to?" he asked, still grinning.

I shrugged, that slight taste of resentment on my tongue. "I don't know."

Unaffected, he asked, "Gettin' some lunch?"

"No, just two drinks." I paused, fighting the urge between being rude and polite. The champion winning as it always did. "You?"

"Lunch." If he knew he wasn't exactly my favorite person in that moment, he didn't let it get to him. "How's your day goin'?"

"Good." I kept my mouth flat. "You?"

"No complaints." That pretty pink mouth of his twitched and he raised his eyebrows, his impressive smile growing by the second. "You mad at me too?"

My mood felt like a balloon that had been pricked by a needle. I sighed and took a step closer as the line behind me shifted. "Maybe."

He straight up smirked. "Aww, honey, don't be like that. We gotta be fair. The boys can't see y'all goin' at it and think there's no consequences if they get into fights."

I started to open my mouth about how we hadn't gotten into a fight, but closed it just as quickly. The thing with being an adult sometimes, was that it sucked. I hated admitting I was wrong to other people, even though last night while I'd been talking to Josh I had admitted having a part in what happened. But

Trip was right.

"If it matters any, I would've been rootin' for you and not Christy."

How could I stay mad after that, especially with that beaming grin he had aimed in my direction? "At least you would have. I don't know what I did to your head coach. He makes me feel like I have cooties. Every time I talk to him, it's like I'm a burden on his soul. If he didn't want Josh or me on the team, he could have said something before, or just not put him on the team to begin with."

"What?" Trip chuckled, his forehead scrunched up in confusion as he did it. I was starting to see this man laughed more than he did anything else. It was so cute. "Dallas?"

"Yeah." I wasn't about to tell him about the first day we met. It wasn't any of his business what had happened to Dallas's brother, family or not. I didn't know what Dallas could or would have told others about that night. Maybe he had told them everything. Maybe he had told them nothing. But it wasn't my news to share with other people. I would hate for him to spread my business around.

The blond's forehead became lined even more, and he shook his head just slightly in disbelief. "He was the one who pointed out your boy in the first place." He paused and shook his head again. "He's being like that?"

I nodded.

"Nah. That doesn't make any sense. I've known him my whole life and I've never seen him get mad at anybody. He's pretty fuckin' chill."

Were we talking about the same person? I had seen him get mad at two people in the handful of times I'd been around him.

He seemed to think about it for a moment before making a noise deep in the back of his throat. One of his eyes went a little squinty. "You hit on him?"

The snort that burst out of me was so insulted, there was no way he could have taken it a different way. No fucking way. "*No.*" I didn't even have to think about it. I hadn't. Not even a little. Maybe I'd checked him out a tiny bit, I wasn't a saint, but I hadn't told him to come out of his room in only his boxers. But I'd cut myself off from looking at him below the neck the instant I learned he was married.

Trip looked more than a little amused. "I'm just askin'. He gets a little sensitive about that shit." Because he was married or separated or whatever the hell he was? "He hasn't said nothin' to me about you."

Not knowing what to think or say, I rubbed my hands across the front of my pants nervously. "I just don't want things to be awkward if we have to see each other all the time. I swear I didn't do anything to make him dislike me. He was pretty nice at first—" At that moment, I realized I was complaining to a grown man about his cousin. I needed to stop. There were plenty of pointless things you could do in your life and whining to a man about another man seemed like it would be at the top of the list. "I just don't know what I did, and I don't want things to be awkward."

"I'd ask him. I don't always get what climbs up his

ass and what doesn't," Trip explained casually, so openly it caught me off guard since we didn't really know each other well. "You're easy on the eyes, honey. I know I wouldn't mind you flirtin' with me."

"I didn't flirt with him," I practically ground out, replaying every conversation I'd had with the man. Nothing. I couldn't see any flirting in there.

Trip raised his shoulders in this casual gesture, still grinning; that could have meant "I believe you" or "I don't know what to tell you."

Great. I scoffed, taking into consideration his words for later, and then focusing again on the man in front of me, grinning. "Stop smiling at me like that," I said, watching him.

That only made his smile wider. "Like what?"

He knew exactly what he was doing. I wasn't a fool. He definitely wasn't one either. "Like *that*. I'm a lost cause. Don't waste all that—" I waved my hand in a circle. "—on me."

His laugh reminded me so much of Ginny, in that moment, it seemed like I'd known Trip half my life. "I don't know what the hell you're talkin' about."

"You're a damn liar." I snorted at him, smiling seriously.

The more he laughed, the more the edges of us not knowing each other chiseled away and made me feel like we were friends already. "Gin already told me to pretend you were married and had warts all over your face." His hands went up to pat the stained white T-shirt he had on. Something told me she wasn't the first person in his life to make that distinction clear to him.

"She said her scissors would slip or some shit like that if I tried anything."

Oh, Ginny. I wasn't sure how I got so lucky to not just have one great friend, but to have two just seemed like a blessing not many people got in their lives. "You don't mess with a girl and her shears." I raised my hand and made snipping motions with my index and middle finger, eyebrows raised.

"I know how to behave."

I eyed him. "I don't believe you."

The smirk on his handsome face, all five o'clock shadow and yellow-gray hair, confirmed just how full of shit he was. At least he wasn't going to bother continuing. And now that the ground rules between us had been set into place, it made me feel even more at ease with him.

"How's Josh likin' the team?" he asked, as if sensing that our lines had been drawn.

I told him the truth. "Good. He's ready to start competing." I had already started mentally preparing myself for sitting through game after game, hour after hour, for the next chunk of my life. Competitive baseball was probably one of the hardest things I'd had to adapt to when I first got Josh.

"How long has he been playing?"

"Since... tee-ball when he was three." That was almost eight years ago. I'd been almost twenty-two when he'd started. If that didn't have the ability to make me feel like life had flown by, I didn't know what could.

"Your boy's got that look in his eye. I kinda feel like

a dumbass now that I never paid much attention to Gin when she'd bring up her coworker's boy that played."

I shrugged. At least he knew he should feel dumb. "She said your son is on the team too. Which one is he?" I'd been trying to figure out which of the boys on the team was his son, but I hadn't put it together yet. Both coaches were always surrounded by at least two boys, and maybe I hadn't paid enough attention, but I hadn't caught him singling one out more than the others.

"Dean. Yellow hair. Hyper. Never stops talking."

There was a dark blond boy on the team who had been a giant goofball even during tryouts. At practice the day before, he'd been singing theme songs each time a different boy went up to bat during practice. "And you have another one, don't you?"

Trip made a sound in his throat. "He's two. I don't get to see him much," he admitted so easily I wasn't sure how to take it. His tone hadn't changed, but... well, I didn't know him well enough to be sure if there was something else hidden under there, but there easily could have been. Trip didn't know I knew he had kids with different people, and I wasn't positive how much he would like Ginny telling me things like that, even if it hadn't been with bad intentions or a lack of affection on her part. She was just watching out for me.

The line behind me moved until I was next.

"You only got your two boys?" he asked.

"Yeah," I answered. "They're actually my—"

His phone started ringing, and he winked at me as

he reached into his pocket. "Gimme a sec," he said, bringing it up to his face and answering.

I turned around to give him some privacy, promising myself I'd tell him about the boys some other time.

~

"Who is it that we don't like?"

I almost snorted out the water I'd been in the middle of drinking.

"Cat got your tongue, Di?" the older man chuckled, slapping me on the back as I coughed for breath after his question.

Louie, who was sitting on the other side of his grandpa on the same bleachers as us leaned over, his face all worried and soft. "*Tia*, you okay?"

I coughed and then coughed some more, the hand I'd slapped over my mouth to keep from spitting on the people in front of us, coming off more than a little wet from what I hadn't been able to catch. I looked at Mr. Larsen out of the corner of my eye, trying so hard not to laugh, and nodded at Lou. "I think a bug flew into my mouth, Goo. I'm all right."

He winced. "I hate it when they do that. They don't taste like chicken."

What the hell?

Before I could ask him why he would assume bugs tasted like chicken, Mr. Larsen shot me a horrified expression that we shared for a moment. He raised his shoulders and I raised them right back. I was going to blame his side of the family for that. Then I whispered to the older man, "She isn't here. They aren't letting her come to two practices. It was only me that got suspended from one."

He had "oohed" and "ahhed," a total sport after I'd had to admit to him why I couldn't take Josh to practice. Without missing a beat, he asked afterward, "What time does he need to be there?" My love for the Larsens didn't know an end or a beginning. I had a big family, but sometimes you met people who fit so perfectly into your life, you couldn't imagine them ever not being a part of it. And these two people went above and beyond. Their ability to love knew no bounds.

The next hour flew by with us running commentary on Josh's practice and how much he was improving since he'd started getting help from additional coaches a year ago. I'd gotten off work and headed straight to the facility, despite knowing the Larsens were going to keep the boys tonight and take them to school the next morning. When Trip and Dallas called the boys into a circle to dismiss them, we all got up and headed toward the gap in the fence by the field to wait.

Josh kind of grinned when he spotted us afterward but didn't run screaming or anything. I liked to tell myself he was excited to see us, but he was just growing up. The days of him screaming "*Diana!*" at the top of his lungs every time he saw me were over. He let us pat him on the back before immediately saying, "I'm hungry."

I had already waved at Trip earlier when he'd tipped his chin up at me through the other side of the fence, our conversation still fresh in my mind. It had bothered me a little when he had made the comment about Dallas feeling off around women who flirted with him. Was it just because he was technically still married or whatever the hell the situation was? That didn't offend me at all—honestly, it was probably the exact opposite now that I knew the truth—we were going to see each other pretty often. I didn't like drama and awkwardness, and definitely didn't want to face it a minimum of twice a week for who knows how long all because he'd gotten the wrong impression of me.

So I found him a little attractive—he had a great body, anyone with eyes could see that—but I found a lot of men attractive, and I hadn't flirted with him to begin with.

It wasn't like I had a way of knowing he would be inside of his house when I helped his brother. After that, I had left cookies with most of the neighbors who lived close to me, not just him. But the second time we'd met, he had come over. I hadn't gone to him.

Everything after that... I could see why he *might* think I'd been flirting. Maybe if he was an idiot. Coming up to him at a bar, calling him and walking up to his house, even though it had all been baseball-related and only baseball-related.... I could cut him a little bit of slack. Just a little.

But I still wanted to kick this white elephant out of the neighborhood.

So as I hung around the parking lot as the Larsens and the boys took off in their minivan, I kept an eye out on the adults still hanging around the perimeter of the facility, trying to find the specific person I was looking for so that I didn't have to show up unexpectedly at his house and make him more uncomfortable. I had just decided that he might have left without me noticing when I spotted him standing by the bed of a black truck with Trip right next to him.

"Diana," Trip called out to me over his cousin's shoulder when he noticed me walking toward them.

"Long time no see." I slid my gaze over to Dallas, pasting a funky, tight smile on my face. "Hi, Dallas."

Before my neighbor said a greeting in return, Trip threw his hands in the air. "I'm gonna get goin'. Dean's waitin' in the truck. Dallas Texas, I'll see you tomorrow. Honey, I hope I'll see you tomorrow." Trip winked as he walked away. He was something else, and that something else had my not-so-smile turning into a real one.

It was just as awkward as I figured it would be as Trip got into his truck, making us back away from the bed as he pulled out of the lot. I spotted a head in the back cab. There weren't a lot of parents left hanging around, but there were enough, and I couldn't help but feel the weight of their stares on us. I wasn't a fan of being gawked at, but it was inevitable, wasn't it?

Just as Dallas opened his mouth to say whatever was on his mind, I beat him to it. "Hey, I just want to clear the air between us. If I've done something to make you feel uncomfortable"—*coming up to you at a bar* or *being really aggressive about getting the schedule changed* were both options I accepted freely—"I'm sorry. I didn't mean anything by it. Sometimes I try to be helpful, but maybe I should mind my own business instead, but really, I don't mean anything by it that isn't professional or friendly."

The stare he gave me wasn't discouraging at all. Not.

"Just so you know, yes, I think you're a good-looking guy, but you're not my type. I swear I'm not trying to get in your pants or anything. I can see your wedding ring, and I don't do that kind of thing."

He still hadn't said a word, and just to make sure he understood, I kept going. "You and Trip scouted Josh out. It wasn't like I was trying to get him on the team to seduce you or something." I'd gone with "seduced." All right. I'd never used that word out loud, but there was a first for everything. There was another awkward, brief pause before my big mouth kept rambling. "I'd like us to be friends since we live across the street from each other, but if that's not something you're willing to do, it's okay. I'm not going to cry about it."

There was a huge chance that last part was unnecessary, but I didn't know what else to say. What were you supposed to do when someone didn't want to be your friend or at least be friendly, and you'd tried your best? I thought I'd been a pretty good person. A pretty good neighbor. I hadn't done anything to make him feel uncomfortable. At least, I genuinely didn't think I had.

I rubbed my hand against my upper thigh and let out a deep breath at the weight that seemed to have lifted off my shoulders. I met his gaze head-on, wanting to make sure he could see there weren't hearts and stars in my eyes. My mom had always told me I was about as subtle as an elephant. "So? Should I fuck off or not?"

My neighbor's eyelids swung low over the brown-green-gold color of his irises. "Anyone ever told you you have a staring problem?"

I made sure not to close my eyes for a second, even though the urge was strong. "Has anyone ever told you that you have an active imagination?"

Neither one of us blinked. I wasn't going to lose this shit. He was obviously trying not to lose either. I could respect that.

The small smile that crawled over his mouth was not the first, second, third, or fourth thing I would have expected coming from him. I would swear on my life for years to come that his eyes sparkled—but it was probably just the streetlight giving them that impression. Then he blinked.

Thank God, I blinked too.

Dallas   I-Wasn't-Sure-If-That-Was-His-Real-Name-Or-Not made a noise straight from his nostrils. His eyelids went back to their normal position as his arching eyebrows took center stage. "I don't get 'uncomfortable,'" he started. His mouth stayed in that same partial-smiling position it had been in a moment ago. It was a sad cousin to the smile he'd given the boys and his friend at the bar, but I'd take it. I didn't need more. "You haven't made me 'uncomfortable.'"

Uh-huh. Sure. That was why he was complaining about eye contact and trying to win our staring competition.

And using his fingers as quotation marks. Sure.

What had to be his tongue poked at the inside of his cheek as he watched me carefully. "You were coming on to me—"

I exploded. "What?" The chances that my face was scrunched up was high. Very high. "When?" From the sound of the words coming out of my mouth, I hadn't realized that *me* assuming he'd thought I'd been flirting with him was completely different from *him* admitting he thought I had. I hadn't.

"You brought cookies over—"

"That my *mom* made for the eight houses closest to me. Go ask the neighbors." Hadn't I told him this already? He was good-looking, but he wasn't *that* good-looking. I had better things to do with my precious time than bake him cookies. The fuck was he thinking? Was he one of these idiots in the world who thought every female was interested in him? Sure, he had an amazing body, but all you needed to do was go on social media and search for a fitness model to find one just as nice.

Trying to tell myself that I didn't need to get all riled up for no reason, I let out a breath through my nose and tried to let out the most controlled exhale I was capable of. Basically, I still sounded like a dragon. "No offense, pal. I'm nice and I have manners, and I pretty much saved your brother's life. I was not trying to get in your pants after only seeing you one time." Maybe that was harsher than it needed to be, but I was insulted.

Those gold-green-brown eyes narrowed as he

seemed to process what I was saying. Even the mostly-grin on his lips melted off.

Feeling more indignant than I probably had any right to be, I figured I should go ahead and bring up anything else he might try and use as examples before they pissed me off. I held up one finger. "I went to the bar, Mayhem, with my friend and boss, Ginny, who is Trip's cousin, who is your cousin, too. I work down the street from there. Please ask anyone who knows Ginny."

I raised another finger. "The only reason why I told you hi was because you were the only person there that I knew, and I didn't want to be rude."

A third finger rose. "*And* before I called you about the team's schedule, I called Trip first each time. The only reason I didn't go over to his house to complain was because I don't know where he lives."

In my head, I added "fucker" to the end of that. In reality, I did not. Sometimes I even amazed myself.

The silence between us was thick. And he finally said, with his gaze sharp and his mouth back to a firm line, "I'm married."

I lost it. "Good for you. Did I say you weren't?" Jesus Christ. I'd already mentioned I knew he was married and didn't want to have anything to do with that. "I have married guy friends, and by some miracle, I've managed to keep my hands to myself every single time I've spent time with them, if you can believe that."

We stared at each other for so long, eye to eye, one smart-ass expression to another that it didn't immediately hit me that both of our facial features eased gradually. He had been wrong and I... hadn't. Dumbass.

It was almost as if he could read my mind because he raised his eyebrow.

I raised mine right back, repeating the word in my head. *Dumbass.*

His eyebrow stayed where it was and so did mine.

Once you bowed down to someone, you were their bitch. And if there was one thing I'd learned about myself over the course of the last few years and last few dozen mistakes, that wasn't exactly a title that sat well with me, and it wasn't one I would willingly take ever again. Especially not from this man who didn't put food on my table and clothes on my back. I was usually a lot nicer than this, but this was basically how I treated people after they'd known me for a while. It was his fault he brought this out of me so soon.

I repeated the word to myself, hoping he could read my thoughts: *dumbass.*

Dallas's mouth twitched, highlighting the fact his bottom lip was fuller than the top one; the lines across his forehead eased, and eventually he extended his hand in my direction, those hazel eyes still on mine. He thought I had a staring problem? He had one too. "We're good," he announced to the world, steadily.

Like I wanted to be friends with him by that point.

Trip, I liked. Dallas on the other hand, I didn't know what the hell to think. Maybe I could have reasoned that the woman in the red car had pushed him over the edge, but I wasn't going to go there. His brother seemed like he might be a jackass. Jackass

Jackson. But…

I was going to be an adult and accept that we all made mistakes. Didn't I know that by now?

Fuck it. He wasn't spitting into his hand and I wasn't spitting into mine to form some kind of undying friendship, like I'd done with Vanessa so many years ago. We might as well make the best out of this situation. Life was a lot easier spent next to a pine tree than a cactus. Plus, this was for Josh. For him, there wasn't anything I couldn't or wouldn't do.

And Dallas and I were going to be stuck with each other for a long time. Literally.

I snuck my hand into his. The callused, much larger body part that consisted of a palm and fingers swallowed mine whole. At least he had the grip of a man. "All right. We're good." We shook, and before he'd let go of me, I asked with my face straight, "So has the schedule been changed?"

CHAPTER NINE

JOSH'S WORDS HAD ME FREEZE-FRAMING IN PLACE. I HAD TO glance over my shoulder with a long, marinara-covered spoon in hand so I could read his lips and make sure I hadn't imagined his words. "What did you say?"

The almost eleven-year-old with his head in the fridge peeked out, a gallon of orange juice clutched in his hand. He faced me as he said the words I'd been hoping to have misheard: "Can my friends spend the night?"

My initial thought was *no, please, Jesus Christ, no.*

I didn't even have to try and pull the memories of the last time his "friends" had slept over. Friends? More like demons from the ninth circle of hell.

My soul had been scarred; it hadn't forgotten for one single second about the broken bunk beds, cracked dishes, clogged toilet, or, God help me, the yelling and the running through our apartment. I'd thought boy sleepovers would be like the sleepovers Van and I had damn near every weekend: we'd hang out in my room, look through magazines, watch movies, paint our nails, talk about boys, and eat all my mom's snacks. Boy sleepovers were fucking hell, at least at Josh's age. I took for granted how well behaved Josh and Louie were on their own. I really did. For all the shit they lost, things they forgot, toilet seats they peed on, food products they shoved into the cushions of the car, and the dirty socks they left *everywhere,* they were pretty damn great.

It wasn't until I was around other people's kids that I remembered why—before Josh and Louie—I hadn't planned on having kids for a long, long time. If ever.

And somehow I'd gotten away with not having more than Josh and Louie at the same time for almost a year. It had taken me a year to recuperate from the beasts Josh had invited to stay over. Hell, I still hadn't gotten over everything. I'd gotten lucky he hadn't brought it up before.

Unfortunately, my time had run out.

How could I tell him he couldn't have friends over so close to his birthday? He had already told me he didn't want to have a party, but in the words of my mom, *how could he not have a party?* I'd always thought get-togethers were more for the adults than for the kids, but now I knew for sure that was the truth. Josh really could have been perfectly happy getting twenty bucks and going to the movies or the batting cage.

"Please?" the boy asked with so much hope in his voice it crushed my soul.

Please don't do this to me, I thought, but what really came out of my mouth was more like "Sureeee…. But no more than three, okay?"

Was it too much to hope that he would say he really only wanted one friend over?

It was.

Because his response went: "Three's good."

God help me. I was paying for everything I'd ever put my parents through with interest.

"SEE YOU TOMORROW MORNING!" I CALLED OUT TO THE MOM getting into her car, waving a hand with a little too much enthusiasm.

I'd bet she was excited. She'd just admitted her only child was spending the night at my house. Of course she was going to be ready to get the hell on with her Friday night. She hadn't even bothered coming inside the house to make sure I didn't have cages or a torture chamber. The boy on the Tornado team had been kicked to the curb: my curb.

Two out of three boys were over, and I could already hear them stomping around inside my house.

Oh my God. What had I done? Why had I agreed to this?

I wasn't built for sleepovers.

If I could have hunched over and cried silently, rocking back and forth, I would have. Something was going to get broken before the end of the night, and I had no way of knowing what it would be. My sanity maybe. God, help me. I'd already eaten two packets of Pop-Tarts from how stressed I was and I had another foil-wrapped package tucked into my back pocket in case of an emergency.

When the sound of a truck engine idling had me opening my eyes again, I let out a deep breath and watched as the passenger door to a black Dodge pickup truck opened and out hopped a blond boy with a backpack in his hand. I'd forgotten Josh had mentioned that he was one of the kids spending the night. I smiled as he bounded up the pathway, not even turning around to pay attention to Trip who had parked the truck and was making his way around the front grill.

"Hi, Miss Diana." The little blond smiled in a way that would have been shy on any other boy except him. On him it looked like… I don't know what it looked liked. Trouble, more than likely. He'd come right up to me at the last practice and introduced himself. If I thought Josh had confidence, he had nothing on this kid. It reminded me of someone I knew: his dad.

"Hey, Dean. How are you?"

"Good." He was still smiling.

So was I. He was cute. "Josh and the other boys are inside. Want me to show you where?" I asked him, glancing up to see Trip coming behind him, a knowing smirk on his playful, handsome face. From the looks of it, he had the ability to smell his own kind too, except his was trouble.

"I can figure it out." Dean blinked those blue eyes just like Ginny's. "Thank you for letting me spend the night."

"You're welcome," I said, stepping aside to let him in the house.

Trip watched his son as the boy went in without a second glance behind him, calling out, "Bye, Dean!" in a sarcastic tone. To which he got a shouted reply of "Bye!"

Just "bye." Not "bye, Dad," no nothing. Even that hurt me.

Trip and I both shook our heads. I grimaced and he just looked resigned. "It's the beginning of the end, isn't it?" I asked the blond man still coming up the pathway.

Dressed in jeans, his usual motorcycle boots, and signature white T-shirt minus his motorcycle club vest, he looked freshly showered and too good-looking with his dark yellow scruff covering the lower half of his face. "It's been the beginning of the end since he started talkin'. I'm gonna be payin' for all the stupid-ass shit I did with that boy."

I laughed because I could tell, *like father like son.* And hadn't I just thought the same thing about Josh?

He winked as he stopped in front of me on the deck, his face playful, eyes bright.

"Hi, Trip," I greeted him, grinning wide.

"Hey, honey."

Feeling a little shy, I held out an arm and he leaned into me, throwing his own arm over my shoulder to give me a hug. The big smile on his face as he pulled back reminded me of how much I liked him. Part of it was because he reminded me so much of Ginny, but I really did feel like I knew him and was comfortable around him.

"Thanks for inviting Dean over," he said, resting his hands on his hips.

The laugh I let out was all balled up nerves and dread and panic, and that must have been noticeable on my face because the older man burst out laughing.

"You just figured out you're in for a world of shit tonight, huh?" Trip cackled out the statement.

Oh my God, I really cracked up that time, everything bubbling up inside of me. "I am, aren't I?" I wheezed. "I'm scared to go in there. I really am."

That only made him laugh harder.

"I'm just going to lock them in the room together and see what happens," I joked, not knowing how else to cope but to make a joke so I wouldn't cry. "Jace's mom pretty much just kicked him out of the car and waved at me from the driver seat, and Kline's mom came up to the door with him and burned rubber getting the hell out of here," I told him.

"Jace *and* Kline are here?"

Oh God. "I messed up, didn't I?"

"You got Benadryl?"

"Yeah…."

"I know me and Kline's mom wouldn't even be a little mad if you slipped 'em some Benny later." He could barely get the words out. "I'm just sayin'."

What had I done? I should have asked for report cards and shit to approve the boys before they'd come over. Incident reports from other parents. Interviews. Something.

I groaned. Then I groaned a little more. I wasn't going to cry this early in the evening. I wouldn't.

Just messing around, I asked, "You got plans tonight? I have a few steaks in the fridge I was going to make for dinner tomorrow. I could be convinced to grill tonight..." I trailed off, half laughing as I said it.

One blue eye peered back at me, the corner of a grin caught high. "I was plannin' on headin' over to Mayhem since you're keepin' Dean tonight." He pursed his lips together. "I could run to the store and get some beer and come back."

Well shit. I hadn't exactly expected him to take me seriously, but now that he wasn't disagreeing... I eyed him a little, hoping he hadn't gotten the wrong message from my invitation.

"As long as you promise you're not gonna hit on me or anythin'." He pretty much gurgled out in a laugh.

Goddammit. I couldn't believe it. Dallas had told him. I threw my hands up as I leveled a glare at the blond. "Just friends, Jesus Christ. The little one is here, too. There will be supervision."

"I'm fuckin' with you, honey," he chuckled. "Need anything from the store?"

I had already stocked up that morning since it had been my day off. "I'm good, thank you."

Trip winked. "All right. I'll be back then."

I was beyond relieved to have someone else in the house with me while *they* were all over, even if that person was Trip. I gulped and turned to head back into my house as my new dinner buddy made his way toward his truck. Inside, the living room was empty, but I could hear a racket coming from Josh's room. With Louie nowhere in sight, I peeked into his room and found him sprawled width-wise across his bed with his tablet in hand going at whatever game he was playing.

My guts went as far as to look into Josh's room to find four boys in there. Josh had already asked me if we could move the Xbox into his room for the night, and I'd agreed. His other aunt had given him a small television for his last birthday, so if they broke anything, at least it would be his TV and not our forty-five inch. Before I got caught, I snuck back out and headed toward the kitchen.

I got as far as wrapping some potatoes in foil and seasoning the four steaks I'd bought the day before, with the intention of inviting my parents to dinner, when the doorbell rang. Through the peephole I found the back of Trip's head on the other side, the phone he held to his face just barely visible.

"I told you where I'm at. Across the street. Diana has Dean." Trip turned around in midconversation as the door creaked while I opened it. He held up the six-pack he'd run out to buy. "I just bought a six. Hold on." He pulled the phone away from his face and asked, "You mind if Dallas comes over and has a beer?"

Huh. I shrugged and shook my head. We had made amends. Sort of. "Nope." At least I had enough food. I'd planned on ordering Josh and his friends pizza later.

"Diana said to come over. She's scared of Jace and Kline," he told his cousin.

"Shut up," I hissed at his exaggeration, earning me another wink.

"'Kay, later," Trip finally said before getting off the phone. "He's coming over."

The words had barely come out of his mouth as the boys started yelling all together loud enough to be heard down the hall, "Kill him! Kill him! KILL HIM!"

And that was exactly how I found myself in a house with seven males on a Friday night.

"I TOLD GINNY TO COME OVER," I TOLD THE TWO MEN LEANING against my kitchen counter, each cradling a bottle of the beer.

"She coming straight from the salon?"

I shook my head, flipping the steaks over with a fork. "No. She's meeting up with Wheels for dinner and after that she said she'd come by."

It was impossible to miss the slight sneer that came over the blond's face, even though my attention wasn't centered anywhere near him. I was too busy trying to coat the steaks in the oil evenly.

"You don't like Wheels?" I asked him, referring to Ginny's fiancé.

It was Dallas who let out a snicker in response that had me swinging my gaze over in his direction. He hadn't said much since he'd showed up a few minutes ago, freshly showered and with a bottle of Jack in one hand and a cardboard container with four glass bottled Cokes in the other, which had me eyeing him, wondering if I'd been selling this man short all along. Oblivious to me checking out his excellent taste in sodas, all he'd said was, "Hi, Diana" and I'd said, "Hi, Dallas. Come in. Trip's in the kitchen." That was that.

We had just agreed to be friends—or at least friendly—so this should be no big deal. I didn't want to make it weird, and I was glad he didn't either. We could figure this out. Luckily, Trip talked enough to make up for any awkwardness there might be lingering between us.

So for Ginny's fiancé to be the first thing he decided to comment on after Trip and I had argued about how to properly cook a steak, I was caught off guard. Then for him to shrug and be all casual about it, threw me off even more. "He's all right…." Trip trailed off.

"You can't tell me he's all right and not tell me what you don't like about him," I said.

The two exchanged a look I wasn't familiar with.

"Really? You're not going to tell me?" I thought about it and straightened my spine, one sentence away from getting really angry. "Is it bad? Did he do something to Ginny?"

Trip hooted. "Not if he wants to keep livin'."

Oh. "Then what is it?"

"Have you met him?"

"Yeah, a few times. He always seemed like a pretty good guy."

Trip and Dallas shared another glance.

"What is it?" I asked again. "He's always nice to

me."

It was only Trip who snorted that time. "Why wouldn't he be nice to you?"

"Because no one *has* to be nice to anyone else. I've met plenty of assholes."

Dallas snickered at the same time Trip snorted.

I went back to Ginny's fiancé. "Is that all that's wrong with him? You guys just don't like him?"

The blond bobbed his head as if thinking about the question. "If Ginny was your family and you knew the stuff he's done and the people he's... messed around with, you wouldn't be all about him being with her either," he finally managed to explain. "But that's who she wants to be with, and she knows all of his shit, so we can't say nothin' anymore."

I could smell bullshit from a mile away, and that was exactly what I had a whiff of as he spoke his reasoning. Ginny loved Wheels. I'd seen them together enough. I'd overheard their phone conversations. And Wheels had always been really sweet to Gin. He brought her flowers, brought her lunch from time to time, texted and called her regularly. For whatever he might have done before her, he was nice to her now, and Gin was a grown woman. If she knew his business, then she could deal with it. If I was in her shoes, not so much, but I wasn't.

"I'm sure she appreciates the thought behind you wanting the best for her, but she knows what she's doing," I told them.

"I'm not saying she doesn't."

"Yeah, but you're saying you don't like him

because of what he's done in the past, right?" I peeked at Trip over my shoulder to try and soften what I was going to say next. "Imagine if you found someone you wanted to be with and her family didn't like you for the things you'd done ten years ago. That isn't fair. I'm not the same person I was when I was twenty or even… twenty-six. Some people don't change, but other people do. They grow up."

"It's different," Trip started to argue.

"How is it different? Are you going to tell me that you guys have only slept with women who you've been in long-term relationships with?" Neither one of them said anything, even though I looked at both of them with a smirk on my face, knowing how they were going to answer. Of course they hadn't. "No. Exactly. We've all done stupid things we regret. And if Gin knows all this and still wants to be with him, then let her do what she wants. Just saying."

"You're saying you'd marry somebody who's messed around with half the women you'd have to see at get-togethers?" Trip asked with a goofy grin on his face.

"Me?" I scoffed. "No way in hell. But if she can handle it, let her go for it."

That had Trip busting out with a big laugh. "That's some kind of hypocrite shit!"

"No it's not!" I laughed. "I'm possessive, and I get jealous. I know that. I accept it. I own up to it. I would be picturing this imaginary person I love having s-e-x," I whispered the word just in case, "with whoever he's been in a relationship with, and I'd want to stab each one of those girls. But not everyone is like that. That's part of the reason why I don't have a boyfriend. I know I'm crazy. I already feel sorry for whatever poor bastard ends up with me some day, but he'll know what he's getting into. I don't hide it."

Trip shook his head, grinning wide. "You said it. You're fuckin' nuts."

What was I going to do? Deny it?

"Diana, I hate to tell you, I don't know anybody like that."

I frowned. "That's okay. I'm sure there's some nice, divorced Catholic boy out there somewhere in the world, who waited to lose it until he got married and now he's waiting again for the right girl."

"Doubt it."

I gave Trip a face before checking on the steaks again. "Quit killing my dreams."

"I'm just keepin' it real for you, honey."

"Okay, maybe if he's really nice to me and good to me, and I'm the love of his life, and he writes me sweet notes on a regular basis telling me that I'm the light of his life and he can't live without me, I'll give him ten women tops. *Tops.*" I let out a breath. "I'm getting mad just thinking about it."

Both of them groaned before Trip began cracking up. "Ten women and you're already getting mad at the poor bastard."

"Life is too short to not get what you want," I argued with him, smiling so wide my face hurt even though I was facing the skillet. With my back to them, it took me a moment to remember that Dallas was still in the kitchen with us. He hadn't said a word during our back and forth, so I glanced at him over my shoulder. He was leaning against the kitchen counter, looking tired.

We could do this. We could be friendly.

"What do you think?" I asked him.

He kind of closed one hazel eye as he asked, "How old are you?"

"Twenty-nine."

His face went a little funny, a little smirk-ish before he squinted one eye. "You're young, but not *that* young."

I choked out a laugh that I swore had a tiny smile curling Dallas's mouth.

He finally ended with, "Unless you're hoping to find some kid still in high school, I think you're shit out of luck."

I hoped he understood that the look I shot him wasn't a nice one, but I was going to let the age thing go. "What? Eleven women then?"

Trip closed his eyes, shaking his head just slightly. "I don't know why Ginny didn't bring you into my life before, honey."

"Because she didn't want you crushing my dreams and making me plan to spend the rest of my life alone?"

"I think you might just be able to make a family man outta me if you tried," Trip joked.

I raised my eyebrows at Dallas, reminding myself that this wasn't going to be weird between us, damn it, and shook my head quickly, pursing my lips together.

"No thanks."

The blond man sagged as he laughed, but it was Dallas I was looking at, and I didn't miss his quick smile.

That was something.

"Buttercup!" Louie's voice shouted from another room.

I didn't move as my five-year-old stomped into the living room, his face pink and a mix of pouty and hurt. In blue swim trunks and an orange German national team soccer jersey my uncle had given him for his birthday a few months ago, he already looked like a mess without even taking in the watery blue eyes of his that went from Dallas to Trip and finally to me.

"What is it, Goo?" I asked.

Louie stalked toward me, his chest puffing. "They won't let me play with them."

I crouched down to get eye level with Lou, who was hesitating closer to the stove. "Video games?"

He nodded, closing the distance between us quickly, his forehead going straight to my collarbone. I hugged him. "He never lets me play when he's with his friends," he whispered.

I sighed and held him for a minute. "He likes playing with you. It's just his birthday coming up, and he wants to hang out with his buddies, Goo. He still loves you."

"But I wanna play with them," he whined.

"I'll go tell them to let him play," Trip offered.

Louie just shook his head against my cheek, embarrassed.

"They'll let you play," Trip kept going. "Promise."

"I don't wanna," the little boy whispered, changing his mind all of a sudden. His arms slipped around my neck. His body went soft in resignation.

"I got an Xbox at my house. I can bring it over and we can play." Dallas's suggestion had Lou and me both glancing over at the man still leaning against the counter.

"You do?"

"Sure do, buddy."

I remembered seeing a couple of game consoles at his house and his massive TV, but I couldn't really picture Dallas—this muscled mountain of a man who had been so serious every other time we'd spoken—sitting on his messy couch playing video games, at all.

Lou took a step away from me. "What games do you have?"

"Louie," I hissed at him.

Dallas smiled, his entire face bright and welcoming. I narrowed my eyes, taking in the way he went from good-looking to more like stunning by using the muscles around his mouth. What kind of trickery was this? "A lot of them," he told him. "What do you like to play?"

The little boy said the name of a game I wasn't too familiar with, but Dallas nodded anyway. "I got it."

That seemed to perk Louie up because he looked at me for approval, and I smiled at him.

"I'll be back in a few minutes," the older man explained.

"Can I come with you?" Louie blurted out.

"Louie, come on, you can't invite yourself places," I told him softly. Plus, he didn't even know this guy. What the hell was he doing?

Dallas glanced at me with a shrug, a partial smile on his face courtesy of the five-year-old in the room. "I don't mind. We'll only be a minute."

Did I trust this practical stranger with Louie at his house?

"Please, please, please, please, please." That was Louie.

Our neighbor met my gaze evenly and lowered his chin. "I'll leave the front door open."

"One minute, *Tia,*" he begged.

I hesitated for a moment. This man spent hours with boys. Lou looked so hopeful... Damn it. I met my neighbor's gaze. "If you don't mind holding his hand."

"Nope." He was back to smiling down at Lou, resembling a different person with that expression on his face. Had he really been so serious and distant because he thought I was coming on to him? *Really?*

"Okay. Then go with Mr. Dallas and don't steal anything."

Louie's face went red. "I don't steal!"

I couldn't help but grin at the other man, grateful at his kindness and still slightly unsure about him taking Louie somewhere. But I reminded myself I let this man spend a whole lot of time with Josh and so did plenty of other people. "He's got little butterfingers. Watch him."

"I'll make him empty his pockets before we leave my house," he said dryly, as he extended one of those big hands toward the little boy. "You can help me cross the street."

I watched Lou and Dallas walk out of the house hand in hand and it sent this terrible bittersweet grief straight through me. All I could think about was my brother and how I would never get to see him do that with Louie. How Louie would never get to experience that with his dad who had loved him very, very much. This knot formed in my throat and didn't seem to want to go anywhere despite how many times I swallowed in the time I kept facing the direction they had gone, even though they were out of the house.

Before I knew it, I had reached up to wipe at my eye with the back of my hand.

How was it possible that I lived in a world where my brother didn't exist anymore?

"You all right?" Trip asked, reminding me he was in the room.

I nodded at him, distracted and sad at the same time. "Yeah, I just..." I forced myself to clear my throat. "I just remembered his dad, is all. Does he have kids?" I forced myself to ask, not able to explain what had gotten me so upset in more detail. I wouldn't be surprised if he'd somehow found out that the boys weren't my biological kids or not, but I didn't want to bring it up right then.

"Dallas?"

"Uh-huh."

Trip shook his head, his mouth going firm for the first time since I'd met him. "No." He took a swig of his beer and stayed quiet for a moment. "Why, you interested?"

"No." God, why did everyone seem to think I was trying to—

"I'm fuckin' with you."

I got mad all over again, remembering Dallas admitting he thought I was flirting with him all because of some *polvorones* and a few phone calls. My panties needed to get out of the wad they were in and remember he'd realized how stupid he'd been. Because he'd been real stupid to think that.

"Don't take it personal, honey. His ex, or soon-to-be ex, whatever the fuck she is now, did a real number on him. It doesn't have nothin' to do with you," he explained.

I was being sarcastic when I asked, "What? She was a single parent too?"

"Uh, yeah, she was," was the remark that suddenly had me feeling like a giant schmuck. Shit. I guess I couldn't blame him for being hesitant with me. "Don't worry about it though. He knows he 'isn't your type.'" He chuckled at that last bit, and I frowned. "You actually got a type?"

"Yeah, from the sound of it, I do now," I said, facing the cast iron skillet popping on the stove once more. "High school virgins."

Trip and I laughed so hard it filled the time until Dallas and Louie came back with two plastic grocery bags filled with a console, two controllers, and multiple games. I hadn't bothered ordering Josh and his friends pizza yet. The last time I had checked, the cupboard's two bags of chips, one container of cookies, and six sodas had already gone missing. I could force food on them later. Trip disappeared into the living room as I finished cooking the first two steaks.

While I kept an eye on the meat and checked the potatoes in the oven, I thought about Dallas and his single-mom-ex for all of a second before starting a mental list of what I needed to get done before Josh's official birthday party. I was in the middle of flipping the steaks again when I heard the distinct sound of glass shattering from the living room.

"I'm sorry!" That was Louie.

The response was so low I couldn't hear it. I flipped the flame off the stove, ready to go and make sure everything was okay. I'd barely turned around when Trip appeared in the kitchen. "Louie's all right, but you got a vacuum or something? There was a glass cup on the coffee table…"

And it got knocked over.

Reaching under the sink, I pulled out the little handheld vacuum my parents had bought me years ago and started toward Trip, but Dallas appeared behind him, his attention focused downward. It wasn't until he shouldered past the blond man that I saw his hands. They were cupped together and in them were shards of glass along with a decent amount of blood pooling in those wide palms.

"I got it," Trip said, taking the vacuum from me as I watched Dallas make his way toward the trash can.

"Jesus Christ. Let me see your hand." I went after him.

"I'm all right. It's only a cut," he answered with his

back to me.

"There's blood all over you. You're not all right." I stopped right behind him, too close when he turned around to face me, one hand still holding the other.

"I'm fine," the stubborn-ass insisted. "I tried to save it, but it shattered in my hand."

Maybe he was fine and maybe he'd had a lot worse in his life, but I couldn't help myself.

"Let me see it. I promise I won't stick my hand down your pants," I told him, only half joking.

The look he gave me almost made me feel like I was getting called to the principal's office, but I didn't take my words back or refocus my gaze. That was what he got for thinking something so stupid about me. He must have understood, because he didn't say a word.

Without asking for his permission, I wrapped my fingers around his wrist and pulled him toward the sink.

He let me.

When I shoved his hand under the tap, him standing slightly behind my side at an angle, he still didn't move or say a word as the cold water hit his wound. I hovered my face over the cut that sliced around the front of his thumb. "Let me make sure there's no glass in there," I offered. "It might hurt."

"I'm fi—" He groaned and grunted as I pressed on the sides of the wound and pinched them together.

I bet he was fine.

"I'm sorry," I whispered as I did it again, watching blood pool and stream out, swirling in the empty, metal sink, the water diluting the red.

Dallas let out a low groan deep in his throat again.

"I'm so sorry, but I need to do it again."

"No, it's—" That third time I did it, he cleared his throat, and I couldn't help but cluck my tongue to keep from grinning as I stopped what I was doing and let the cut sit under the faucet for a second before adding a drop of hand soap and dabbing it around the wound, rinsing it off as gently as I could. He cleared his throat once more, and that time I couldn't help but glance up at him. His face was maybe three inches away; his arm pulled so far away from his body it was like I was forcing him to hug me around one side. Up close, I could see the lines at his eyes clearly and his sun-weathered face perfectly. How old was he exactly?

"Are you laughing at me?" he asked in a low voice as I reached to turn off the water and grab a paper towel afterward.

I didn't even try to bullshit him. "I told you it was going to hurt," I explained as I dabbed at the skin around his poor thumb, trying to dry it. "You have thick calluses." I glanced up at him one more time. His gaze was on his hand, thankfully. "Are you a mechanic like Trip?" I doubted it since I'd seen the ladder and other tools on the back of his truck before.

Those hazel eyes flicked in my direction, so close I could see the golden ring around the pupil. I turned back to his hand. His voice was gruff. "No. I do home renovation jobs. Painting and flooring mostly."

That explained the paint-stained clothes I'd seen him in. "That's nice. On your own?"

"Mostly," he groaned low as I touched the top of

his cut.

"You don't ever accidentally hurt yourself on the job?"

"No. I know what I'm doing." Someone sounded insulted.

Dropping my gaze to look back at his hand, I let out a snort. "Not around sharp objects by the look of it. Hold on for a second so I can put a Band-Aid on you."

"I don't need a Band-Aid," he tried to argue in that husky voice of his as I let go of him. The sound of the handheld vacuum turning on in the living room had us both glancing in that direction.

"You need one," I insisted, even as I reached into one of the kitchen drawers and pulled out one of the many small first aid kits I had hidden around the house in case of emergencies. "You're still bleeding. At least leave it on for today, please? I feel really bad. I knew I should have moved that glass earlier and I didn't."

His sigh was long, and he was giving me a flat look with that not-so-plain face when I glanced at him. Someone was not amused by my request. "Sure" was the word that came out of his mouth reluctantly, but his face said a different word completely.

Not wanting to waste any time before he changed his mind, I went up to him. He was so tall the bottom of his butt was pressed to the counter. I set the kit aside and pulled out a jar of honey from one of the cabinets. If Dallas thought it was strange that I was bringing it out and opening it, he didn't say a word.

His fingertips *were* really rough and callused as I

flipped my palm up to hold his hand in place. His fingers stretched out past the tops of my own. His hand was so much wider and almost as tan as mine; you could barely see my hand beneath his. Giving him a quick, reassuring smile that wasn't exactly returned, I scooped out a drop of honey and set it on his cut with the tip of the butter knife I'd used, still holding him steady.

"Louie's allergic to first aid cream. He gets a rash and blisters from it, so I don't bother buying it anymore," I explained. With a skill I'd picked up after taking care of so many of the boys' cuts, I unpeeled the paper off the bandage with one hand and carefully wrapped it around his thumb, the pad of my thumb brushing against the side of his injured one, my other fingers dancing across his hard skin.

His question came out of the blue. "What happened to your finger?"

I blinked and glanced at my own hands. It took me a second to find the finger he was talking about, and I flexed it. There was a ragged line about a half-inch long on the index finger of my left hand from where I'd cut myself with my shears during a haircut two days ago. "I cut it at work." And it had bled like a bitch.

"What did you put on it?" he asked, obviously taking in the goopy line along the seam of the wound.

"Super glue. It works like a charm, but yours isn't deep enough to need it," I explained, my attention downward. "I'm really sorry about your cut."

"It was an accident," he replied, sounding really close to me.

That had me lifting my head, grimacing. "Still, I'm sorry."

Those hazel eyes were even and steady on my boring brown ones. He was probably six inches away from me, tops. He drew his hand away from mine and took a step back. "You don't have anything to be sorry about."

The smile I gave him was so tight it made my cheeks ache. "All right. If you insist." I tilted my head toward the stove. Sometimes friendships were built on baby steps, weren't they? He could have said he didn't want to come over when Trip invited him, and he could have pretended he didn't have an Xbox for Louie to play on. He was trying, and I damn well was, too. I could do this. "How do you want your steak cooked? Burnt, perfect, or pink?"

His mouth twisted to the corner as he blinked. "Burnt."

"Burnt it is," I said, turning to face the stove.

There was a moment of silence before he asked, "We good?"

Of course, I turned to look at him over my shoulder. "Yeah, we are." I blinked right back at him. "If I do anything to make you uncomfortable, just let me know. I don't really have a verbal filter." I thought about it for a second and added, "And I'm a little touchy-feely, but I don't mean anything by it, so just tell me. It's not a big deal. I won't cry. I'll tell you if I have a problem with something."

Dallas made a sound that might have been a snort. "I'm getting that."

I smiled awkwardly and maybe a bit tightly at him then turned back to face the stove when his question came.

"Since we're good, can I ask why you have Pop-Tarts in your back pocket?"

CHAPTER TEN

"Josh, I swear to God—"

"I'm coming!"

I did the sign of the cross with one hand, eyeing the face of my cell phone with a grumble. We were running fifteen minutes late, and while I didn't have to be at work until eight forty-five, I still hated Josh and Lou getting to school after it started. Rushing drove me bonkers, even though I seemed to be running behind half the time anyway. More like three-fourths of the time if I was going to be totally honest with myself. And if I was going to be even more honest with myself, this whole not-getting-places-on-time business didn't start until the boys became mine.

"*Joshua!*" I yelled just as Louie lifted his red school Polo shirt up from his spot next to me, showing the empty space where a belt needed to be. "Goo, you forgot your belt."

He looked down like he didn't believe me and

immediately took off down the hall back toward his room with his shoulders stooped. That should have told me what kind of day it was going to be. Louie didn't usually walk anywhere like he was headed for his execution.

"Joshua Ernesto Casillas," I hollered again, two seconds away from losing it. I'd woken him up at the same time I always did. He'd even stood up and started putting his pants on right in front of me before I left the room, but by the time fifteen minutes had passed and he still hadn't come out of there, I had gone to check on him, only to find him asleep again, sitting on the mattress with his pants at his knees in only his tighty-whities.

"I said I'm coming!"

"You also told me last week you were going to stop 'resting your eyes' after I woke you up, but from the looks of it, that hasn't happened either," I snapped, gripping the very edges of my patience.

There was a pause before, "I'm sorry!" What a faker.

He should be sorry, but I knew I needed to accept his apology before he stopped giving them. I was worried, if I guilt-tripped him too much, at some point it would stop being effective. "I forgive you but come on, man! Chop, chop!"

Two seconds later, the older brother followed the younger one down the hall, clutching two backpacks, two jackets, and a baseball bag between them. The Larsens were taking him to batting practice tonight. I waved them on, locking the door behind them as we basically all ran toward the car… until Josh stopped and threw his hands up. "I forgot my helmet!"

Oh my God.

"What happened to checking off your list?" I asked him.

"I was trying to hurry!" was his excuse.

The look I gave him went pretty much ignored as I tossed the keys in his direction, lunging like I was going to give him a wedgie as he ran back to the house. Turning back to face Louie so I could tell him he might as well get into the car while we waited, I stopped and took in the little boy standing a few feet away. Did he look pale or was I imagining it? And were there bags under his eyes or was I imagining that too?

"You okay, Lou?" I asked him, frowning.

He wasn't looking at me when I questioned him, but his blue eyes swung to me and he nodded the most unconvincing nod I'd ever seen.

"Are you sure? Did you sleep bad?" The longer I took him in, the worse he looked.

"Yeah," he answered, scrunching up that adorable nose for a moment. "My head hurts."

I'd heard that excuse before from Josh. "A little or a lot?"

He shrugged.

Well, it couldn't be that bad if he wasn't complaining. "Can you try to go to school?"

He nodded.

In my gut, I knew that was a weird way for him to respond. Josh was the body language one of the two; Lou usually said whatever was on his mind. But I still

MARIANA ZAPATA

dropped to a knee and gave him a hug, touching his cool forehead and cooler cheeks. His coloring was off, but he wasn't warm. His arms wrapped around my neck and he gave me a squeeze.

By the time Josh came back, Lou was already buckled into the booster seat that he hated and I had just slammed his door shut. Josh tossed the keys over and I asked just to be sure, "Did you check that the front door really closed?"

He shot me a look as he opened the other passenger door. "Yes."

"Okay, attitude." He made it seem like he hadn't left it unlocked before. Jesus.

"*Tia*, your purse," Louie mentioned in a soft voice the minute I opened the driver side door to get in.

My—

Damn it. I'd left it inside.

Ignoring the smug look I would bet an ovary Josh was throwing my way, I ran back to the house, in and out of it in less than two minutes. As I jogged toward the car, I spotted that big Ford pickup backing out of the driveway. I waved, not sure if Dallas had even seen me or not.

At their school fifteen minutes later, I had to get out of the car and go with them to the principal's office to get tardy passes, earning a snarky comment from the secretary who had to write the notes about how important it was for "children to get to school on time." Like she never occasionally ran late. Ugh.

My day didn't get any better once I got to work.

Sean had shown up to work over an hour late,

complaining about how he wasn't feeling well and wasn't sure he'd be able to stay all day, and put me on edge. When my cell started vibrating at nearly noon, I was in the middle of a wash and couldn't answer. It wasn't until an hour later, in-between appointments, when my phone started vibrating again that I was able to answer. My mom's name flashed across the screen. Eyeing my coworker and his customer out of the corner of my eye, I headed outside.

"*Bueno*?"

"Diana, I've tried calling you three times," my mom hissed, catching me totally off guard.

"I'm at work, *Mamá*. I can't pick up the phone if I have a customer," I replied, frowning and wondering what was up with her. She knew all of this. I wouldn't call her while she was working and get all bent out of shape if she didn't answer.

"*Si, pues* maybe you can get a job where you can," she said in Spanish, her tone exasperated and pretty damn brutal.

"I don't think jobs like that exist," I replied, wondering what I'd done to deserve another bad attitude so soon.

She obviously didn't see the truth in my words because the attitude she called me with went nowhere. "Maybe if you would have gone to college like we wanted you to—"

Oh, fuck my life. It had been at least a month since the last time she'd given me this talk. It didn't matter that I did okay at a job I enjoyed and was pretty damn good at. It also didn't matter that I had only *once* asked to borrow money from my parents soon after I'd moved out; *I hadn't gotten a degree. What had I been thinking?* She brought up me not going to college at least three times a year, if I was lucky. If I wasn't lucky, it came up once a month or more.

"I'm at work. Do you need something?" I cut her off, not even remotely caring that I was being just as rude as she was. There was something about not wanting to have this conversation right by the salon that had me looking both ways and crossing the street, wanting to get away so that Sean and his customer couldn't see, much less hear whatever shit was about to come out of my mom's mouth and mine. It felt too personal already.

"If you would've answered, you would know Louie *se enfermó.* You didn't answer so they called here. I went to pick him up already, and I took him to the *clínica* at the pharmacy. He said he hasn't been feeling good for days—"

My heart sank. I knew he hadn't looked well that morning, but I'd asked him. I started pacing up and down the sidewalk outside.

"He has strep. Do you know if Joshua is feeling okay?"

Rubbing my forehead, I told her the truth. "He hasn't told me he was sick. I think he's fine."

"*Ay,* Diana. You don't ask if they're feeling okay?"

I almost told her that it wasn't like she'd asked me daily if I was feeling fine or not, but I kept my mouth shut. "No, *Mamá.* They only tell me if they aren't."

"Well, Josh might be sick too. Maybe you should

ask from now on, *no*? You have to remember you don't only take care of yourself now. You have to take care of them too. Pay more attention."

It wasn't very often my mom flayed my parenting skills, but when she went beyond a little comment here and there, she went in for the kill. This was one of those moments. My guilt for not insisting that Louie tell me he was feeling crappy was bad enough, but my mom's words just severed all the veins and arteries that connected my heart to the rest of my body. I should have asked more questions when I'd noticed his pallor. She was right. It was my fault, and I felt awful instantly.

In a cool, smaller voice, I said, "Okay. I get it. Thank you for picking up Louie. Let me know how much I owe you for the doctor's visit, and I'll pay you back—"

"You don't have to pay me anything."

Well, I sure as hell didn't want to owe her a cent after the reaming she'd just given me. "No, I'll pay you for it and the medicine. I'll call Josh's school right now and check on him. Thank you for picking up, Lou."

"You don't have to thank me," my mom said as if she could sense the distance I was throwing between us. This had always been our relationship: she went in like a battering ram and didn't worry about what she damaged until afterward. I didn't want to think too much about how similar we might be from time to time.

"Well, I want to. If he isn't feeling well, I'll call the Larsens and see if they can pick up Josh so you don't have to. You've done enough. Thank you."

"Diana—"

"I need to get back to work. If it's an emergency call my work. I gave the school the number for the salon, but I guess they didn't write it down. I'll make sure to take your number off the contact list—"

"*No seas asi.*" Don't be like that, she said.

How else could I be when she tore all the love, time, and effort I put into Josh and Louie to shreds in seconds? How? I didn't do everything for them, but I did a lot, and no one could say I didn't put them first. But that was exactly what my mom had implied and it hurt a hell of a lot more than it should have. I didn't think she ever would have told my brother what she had just said to me if he hadn't been able to get off work to pick them up.

"I get off work at seven. I'll pick Lou up then...." For one brief, hurtful moment, I thought about not telling my mom I loved her. Every single time we got off the phone, I made sure to. That went with all of my loved ones. But as quickly as the thought came into my head, I knew I couldn't do it, no matter how angry I was. So I rushed it. "Love you, bye."

I hung up on her and didn't even feel bad about it.

I had done a lot of stupid, selfish things in my life, but I didn't want Louie or Josh to ever be affected by those kinds of decisions. Not ever. But my mom had stomped on me and made me feel like the biggest douchebag on the planet, even if I had asked Louie if he was okay.

I was trying my best, I thought. Most of the time I did pretty well.

Pon más atención.

Oh man, it felt like she'd sucker punched me. I *did* pay attention to them. How could she make it seem like I didn't?

All this weight settled nicely on my chest, and I let my heart swim around in my mom's words. I had just let out a deep, shaky breath when I heard, "Diana!"

Literally standing three feet away from me, in the opposite direction I'd been facing, were Trip and Dallas right outside of the tattoo parlor next door to the deli I had, at some point, stopped pacing in front of. Great. Had they overheard? "Hi," I greeted Trip a little weakly, knowing he was the one who had called my name.

He didn't even try to pretend he hadn't listened in. "You okay, honey?"

Being judged and found lacking by the people who were supposed to love you never left anyone feeling all right, and I didn't see a point in pretending otherwise when chances were he had heard enough to know I wasn't. I wasn't trying to impress him, or much less Dallas, by not being upset at something so personal. "You ever disappoint your parents?" I asked the blond with a forced smirk, trying to make light of something I wanted to believe happened to every child no matter what the age—something I didn't want to ever have Lou or Josh feel.

Trip's chuckle was so rich and honest, I knew I had done the right thing by not going the strong route. "Only every day."

I couldn't help but smile a little, even if he was

lying.

He winked at me before asking, "Getting lunch?" with that flirty grin that didn't do anything for me right then.

"I just needed to get out of the salon for a minute to deal with this," I said, giving my phone a shake as I kept my gaze on Trip and not the brown-haired man beside him who had eaten dinner at our place two nights ago. "Getting a tattoo on your lunch break?" I tried to joke.

It was my neighbor who responded, forcing me to glance in his direction. "No. I'm getting some work done," he explained just like that.

"Oh." I nodded and looked away from him, not sure how long it was okay for me to make eye contact before I crossed the fine line of our friendship or whatever it was. "Umm, my little one is sick right now, and I'm not sure if Josh caught it or not."

"What's wrong with Louie?" Dallas asked almost instantly about the little boy who had sat beside him—and a couple of times partially on top of him—for hours, playing some shooting game.

My shrug was more helpless than I would have liked for it to be. "Strep throat."

Both men winced and I nodded.

"I need to give Josh a call and check up on him, he's supposed to have batting practice tonight but I don't know if he's sick or not." God, I hoped not. "I'll see you later."

"Okay, see ya, honey," Trip said.

I smiled at him and just as I did that, Dallas added,

"Hope Lou feels better."

I smiled at him too and watched as both men turned and headed down the street toward the parking lot or mechanic shop, wherever they were going.

Not bothering to cross the street again, I dialed Josh's school from where I was on the sidewalk, asking first and then demanding that they put him on the phone so I could make sure he was feeling fine. I waited outside the deli until his voice came over the line.

"Hi?"

"J, it's Di. You okay?"

"Uhh, yeah, why?" He quickly added, "Are you okay? Is everything okay?"

Here went another ton of guilt. I was such an idiot. "Everything is fine. Don't worry. I'm sorry. Louie got sick and your *abuelita* had to go pick him up. I just wanted to check with you and make sure you're feeling okay."

The long exhale out of him made my heart hurt. "I thought...," he whispered, his relief evident. "I'm not sick, but you can come pick me up if you want."

This kid. I couldn't help but laugh. "Get back to class. Your grandpa is picking you up today," I said, even though I was sure he hadn't forgotten. Our schedules hadn't changed much over the last two years.

"'Kay, bye."

"Bye, I love you."

"Love you too," he whispered right before the line went dead. At least someone loved me.

Wiping at my eyes with the back of my hand, I didn't realize until right then that I'd gotten teary-eyed at some point. Jesus. I wasn't sure why I let my mom's words bother me so much; it wasn't the first time she'd said a variation of me not doing a good enough job with the boys. It wouldn't be the last either.

~

"What you're trying to tell me is that you've reached blue whale status?"

Vanessa's laugh on the other end of the phone made me smile as I steered the car down the street toward my house. "Shut up."

"You're the one carrying a full-sized kid. I'm only speaking the truth, and you can't handle the truth."

"The doctor said he's in the highest percentile in size—"

"No shit."

"But he's not *that* big—"

"Compared to what exactly? A baby elephant?" Some days, all a girl needed was to talk to her best friend to make a day that hadn't been great better. I had done enough thinking and replaying everything that happened with my mom. I didn't want to deal with it any more than I already had, so I'd been relieved when my phone rang and Vanessa's name had flashed across the screen.

She groaned. "I haven't gained that much weight," she argued. "I'm all belly."

"Until the belly eats the rest of you," I joked,

earning a big laugh out of her that made me smile. "I promise I'm going to try and schedule my trip to visit you. Everything has just been hectic lately. I barely have time to use the bathroom, and even then, someone is banging on the door asking for something."

"I know, Di. It's fine. I wanted to tell you I mailed Josh's birthday present yesterday. Are you ready for his party?"

I almost groaned. The party. Ugh. "Almost," I answered vaguely.

"That sounds convincing. Fine, I won't ask. How's it going with his baseball team?"

Spotting my house coming up, I turned the wheel to pull into the driveway. "He really likes it so far." It was me who had been having issues with it. "I already got suspended from practice for getting into an argument with a mom on the team."

"Diana! What did she do? Say something about Josh?"

In normal circumstances, she knew me too well. "She called me *Teen Mom*."

There was a pause. Vanessa was a product of a parent who had become one as a teenager. "What a bitch."

"Uh-huh. It's fine. He likes it, I'm not worried about it, and the coaches are…" I let out a low whistle. "Not my type, but they're nice to look at."

She laughed. "Have your parents brought up him doing soccer again?"

I almost grumbled. That a sore spot in my family. No matter how many times I explained to my parents that, just because I had two cousins who played professionally, didn't mean every person with the last name Casillas was going to be good at it. "Nope."

"And Louie?"

"Still no. He mentioned wanting to try karate, but he's happy skateboarding for now."

"I'm sure it'll—shit. I need to go pee, but I need both hands to get off the couch—"

I just about shouted out a laugh, imagining her trying to get off the couch and failing.

"Shut up. I'll call you later, okay?"

"Okay." I snickered again. "Love you."

"Love you too," she replied.

"Bye," we both said at the same time.

Tossing the phone into my open purse, I was cracking up all alone. Imagining Vanessa trying to hoist herself off the sofa again only made me laugh harder, easing my memories of the day further and further away. Out of the car, I opened the rear passenger door and reached in, slipping my hands through several grocery bags. My mom had sent me a text before I had gotten off, saying she would bring Louie home later, and with the Larsens taking Josh to batting practice and keeping him overnight, I had decided to hit the store on my way home. I'd stocked up on sick-kid necessities.

"Diana?"

I froze. Each wrist had four plastic grocery bags hanging off it. My cell phone was in my purse.

My heart started beating so fast there was no way I

would want to know what my blood pressure could possibly be in that moment. I'd heard that voice before. It only took a second "Diana" for the tone to register with the part of my brain that didn't want to recognize it.

It was Anita.

She had found my house.

She was here.

I wasn't above admitting there wasn't a reason for me to lose it, but I was going to do it anyway. I was more freaked out than angry, and that pissed me off. A knot filled the very center of my chest and my throat closed up. That part of me that didn't want to deal with this—that never wanted to deal with this—said I should just get in the car, close the door, and get the hell out of there as fast as possible.

But I thought of Josh, and I knew I couldn't do that.

Anita knew where we lived. *She knew where we fucking lived.* Arguably the biggest mistake of my brother's life had somehow found our address.

My hands went numb right before they started trembling. I squeezed them into fists. I closed my eyes too, hoping this was a bad dream but knowing it wasn't.

Slowly, I let out a long breath and ducked out of the car too hesitant when that was the last reaction I would want to have if I ever looked back on this moment. Like a bad dream, she was there.

Josh's mom.

Josh's *birth* mom.

I hadn't seen her since Rodrigo's funeral, where

she'd pitched a fucking fit in the parking lot when she saw Mandy, my brother's wife—Louie's mom and Josh's stepmom, who had always been more than that, until she wasn't.

"Hi," she said in a calm tone like the last time I'd seen her, she hadn't called me a stupid bitch while she'd been drunk as a skunk. I could forgive her for that. We had all been in a bad place at that point. What I couldn't forgive her for was trying to fight Mandy while she'd been grieving, and yanking on Josh's arm when he hadn't wanted to go with her. Why would he? Before the funeral, which I had no idea how she'd even heard about, she hadn't seen him in three years. I could count on one hand how many times she had been with the boy she'd given birth to and given up parental rights to at nineteen.

I had nothing to be freaked out about. Absolutely nothing. But that was a lot easier said than done.

"How have you been?" she asked almost casually.

"Fine and I hope you have too, but you need to go," I managed to tell her calmly, carefully, despite the fact that my hands and forearms had started tingling with discomfort and I was feeling about eighty other different emotions I wasn't ready to classify.

"I just want to talk," Anita tried to explain, one of her hands going to cup the elbow of the opposite arm. She looked thinner than the last time I'd seen her. The whites in her eyes were more yellow, and I couldn't help but wonder what was wrong with her.

I'd told her very plainly when I'd shoved her toward her car after pulling her away from Mandy and

Josh, "*If you ever want to see Josh again, you need to clean your life up.*" And from the yellow that was supposed to be white and the flat color of her hair, she hadn't done that.

I *knew* Anita. At least I knew the person she used to be. She'd been this teenager who had fallen in love with my brother after meeting him at a club back in Fort Worth. She had been nice enough, partied a lot, laughed really loudly. I guess you could say we were a lot alike. Anita had only been seeing my brother for about two months when she told him she was pregnant with his kid. She was only a year older than me, but as I took her in, I saw this person who seemed to have aged physically faster than I had. What had started off with her "not being ready to raise a baby" had turned into this person in front of me who got mixed in with one bad decision after another.

She was Josh's biological mom, but in all the ways that mattered, he was mine, and I would only share what he was willing to give. He had been mine before Mandy, and he was still mine even after Mandy. I was the one who helped bottle feed him after he'd been released from the hospital. I'd been the one who took turns with my brother waking up in the middle of the night when he cried. I had cleaned his dirty baby butt, bought him clothes, blended his food when he'd gotten off formula. I was the one who cried when my brother met Mandy and announced to my best friend and me that he was moving out and getting a place with her. I was the person who had missed the shit out of Josh when I didn't live with him for those years their family had been together.

Not Anita.

"Go. Now. There's still the restraining order against you. You can't be here," I said, using that no-nonsense voice I'd practiced on the boys countless times.

Pink bloomed across her cheeks, and it reminded me of the expression on her face the first time she'd tried to see Josh when he was a year and a half. He'd started crying, sobbing actually, and she'd been so embarrassed, I had felt terrible for her. Then again, no one had made her disappear. No one had made her say and do the things that led to my brother filing a restraining order against her for Josh's sake.

"Diana, please. It's been so long—"

"If you want to see Josh, it's not going to be like this. You can't just show up here. You need to go. Now."

Yeah, the rose color deepened and her eyes darted away. "Diana—"

"Anita, *now*," I insisted, knowing damn well there was still an hour left until Josh got home from batting practice.

She groaned, her hands going up to the sides of her head as she swallowed hard. "Would you listen to me for a minute? That's all I need."

"*No.* I want you to go. Right now. I'll give you my e-mail address. Contact me that way. I don't want to talk to you, and I don't want to see you, but we can message each other." You'd figure she'd gotten a clue the last two times she'd called and I'd either hung up on her or ignored it. I wanted to have whatever she said in writing just in case.

Her mouth—that mouth that had called my beloved nephew a mistake once upon a time—opened, but it wasn't her voice that came out.

"Pretty sure she's telling you to fuck off."

Something tickled at the back of my throat. Relief? I turned to look over my shoulder to spot Dallas stepping onto the sidewalk toward my house. And despite the fact that I wanted to yell at her and tell her all the ways she'd hurt my Josh, I couldn't help but take in the scene called my neighbor.

And it wasn't because he was dirty and sweaty and his shirt was clinging to him like a wet T-shirt.

Mostly.

Because, Jesus Christ, it was like my brain forgot who was standing next to me for all of the fifteen or thirty seconds that I watched this damn near stranger walk over. Unless Anita was blind, she was taking in the same thing I was. I knew what she saw. That "fuck off" face. The powerful upper body. Old, worn-in jeans with stains all over them, and scuffed, paint-stained, black work boots. The shirt he had on must have shrunk at some point because the sleeves barely covered his shoulders, highlighting the dark ink that covered his biceps, but I made myself look at his face before I got caught.

"You gonna get going or do I need to walk you to your car?" Dallas asked as he stopped right beside me, his shoulder inches away from my head, completely surprising me. I wasn't going to deny a gift when it was given to me, even though it was from someone I didn't know how I could repay.

"I just want to talk," the woman, who had given my brother so much hell, said.

"Pretty sure she doesn't wanna talk to you. Am I right?"

I was still looking at Dallas when I said in a distracted voice, "Yes."

My neighbor shrugged, his attention laser-focused on the woman a few feet away. "You heard her. Get gone."

"I just need a damn minute, Diana—"

Somehow, the use of my name managed to get me to lift my eyes to meet hers. "Don't make me call the cops. Please. I told you, get your life together, Anita. Don't show up to my house unexpected. This isn't the way to do this."

My neighbor had turned his head to look at me for the first time, slow, slow, slowly when I first said the c-o-p-s word. I turned my body so that, out of the corner of my eye, I could see him blink. A muscle in that sharp cheekbone of his twitched. His nostrils flared just enough to be noticeable.

"The cops?" the man who lived across the street asked in a calm, cool voice. And Dallas—I could have hugged him right then, kissed him even—lifted one of those big, callused hands of his and pointed it along with his head to the side. "Leave." One word and only one word was necessary. "Now." One more word cemented that harsh command.

As if sensing her impending demise at the fact I was about to tell someone bigger than both of us that she was breaking the law, Anita made a short, sharp noise in her throat. "Forget it. I'm leaving."

I didn't watch her hightail it and neither did Dallas; he was too busy staring a hole straight into my eyes. A part of me regretted starting this staring thing with him, but it was too late now. If he wanted to do it, we could do it.

It was the sound of a car starting nearby that snapped us both out of the world we had built up around us. Dallas turned to look at something over my shoulder, his expression darkening for the first time, lines forming horizontally across his forehead as he glared at what I could only assume was Anita's car taking off. It was a black Chevy. I wouldn't forget it.

Just like that, those murky eyes flicked down to mine, and my neighbor's expression changed from a disturbed one to a worried one that pinched his facial features together. "You all right?"

All I could do was nod, too quickly, but there wasn't a doubt in my head that my anxiety was written all over me. Anita had no legal claim to Josh. I knew that. She wouldn't be able to just *take* him. I could share. I really could. But only if there was some way for me to know she wouldn't hurt him like she had countless times before. And only if he wanted.

I made myself let out a breath, then another one, and finally nodded. I knew I was good. And if maybe I wasn't completely all right, I would be eventually. "I'm fine."

"Okay." A small frown framed my neighbor's mouth. "Lemme take that," he said, even as his hands went to mine.

I shook my head. "It's fine. I got it."

The downturned corners of his mouth went flat. Dallas blinked, those eyes of his sliding from one of mine to the other as if he was trying to measure something. Maybe he was. My stubbornness. "I'll take it," he finally said slowly, carefully grabbing ahold of the grocery bag handles, wrapping them around his own wrists as his gaze stayed on me.

I couldn't even find it in me to keep protesting, to tell him I could take the bags on my own and let him know he'd done enough, that I didn't need his help. He didn't need to come into my house and feel all weird or make up some other thing in his head about me stalking him. But I didn't have the fight. I just followed after him, stiff, stiff, stiff. I unlocked the door and watched as he went in while I grabbed the rest of the bags from the car and followed after him.

I was fine. She was never coming to my house again, and if she did, it would be years from now. This was how it always worked with her. She'd show up and years would pass before we ever saw her again.

Dallas was in the kitchen taking things out of the bags when I found him. My heart thudded a little and my stomach was still unsettled. "You really don't have to do that. I can do it."

"Okay," was his simple reply, even as he kept going.

I sighed. "Really. You don't have to. I don't want you feeling weird being in here. I swear, I'm not trying to do anything."

Those big, callused hands paused in their motion. The breath he let out was so deep I could hear it. "I know you're not."

I was so distracted by Josh's mom, I couldn't even think of a comeback or focus on the strained silence between us. Shame filled me from my belly button to my chin, but I knew I had to say something to him about what had just happened. "Thank you for that out there." Yeah, it sounded just as awkward as I was afraid it would.

He finally glanced up at me through long, spiky eyelashes I'd never noticed before. "She'd been parked outside your house for a while," he explained casually. "I thought something wasn't right."

His comment only made me feel slightly guilty for eavesdropping on the conversation he'd had with the woman in the red car, his maybe-separated, maybe-almost-divorced wife. I had no business knowing about her, much less thinking about her when I had something genuinely more important to focus on. Fucking Anita.

She couldn't take Josh. She couldn't. There was no way, I reminded the lump that had formed in my stomach.

Maybe I should call his school tomorrow or talk to his teacher about the situation so they could be more vigilant with who he went home with.

"Is there something I should know?" he asked quietly, more gently than any other sentence I'd yet to hear come out of his mouth.

Was there? Palming my forehead, I closed my eyes

and willed my heart to beat slower.

Something metallic clanked against the kitchen countertop. I could picture him taking cans of soup out and setting them there, keeping those big hands busy. "I can help, if you tell me what you need."

He was offering to help me after he hadn't been able to get away from me fast enough. Who would have known? Who would have fucking known?

Tears seemed to fill my closed eyes, but I wiped them away as I dragged my hand down my face. At what point had I turned into such a crybaby? When I opened my eyes again, my attention went to the cabinet in front of my face. The words out of my mouth were the truth. Lies and I weren't friends. "That was Josh's biological mom," I told him steadily.

He didn't say anything.

Turning around to face him, I found him with his hand on one of the cans I must have heard him taking out of a plastic bag. I met his eyes for a moment as I took one of the bags next to him and started pulling things out of it. "He's not supposed to see her any more. She tried taking him out of daycare when he was three, and we had to put a restraining order against her. She hasn't done anything like that since then, but she only comes around every few years." I shrugged and balled up the plastic bag when I was done with it. I squeezed it in my fist and swallowed as I looked up at him over my shoulder, shrugging again. What else was there to say?

"Okay," he said, damn near softly. Those hazel eyes locked on mine. There was only a tiny crease between his eyebrows then. "Okay," he repeated on an exhale that seemed nearly painful. "I'll keep an eye out."

My mouth formed the shape of a smile that wasn't really one. What a mess. "Well, thank you for that. I can't—" God, this entire situation made me awkward. A part of me still couldn't wrap my head around her showing up after so long. Why would she do that? When she'd shown up in the past, it had always been to troll on Rodrigo. I genuinely didn't think that she had some deep love for Josh. Then again, what did I know? I would probably do the same thing if I were in her shoes. We all made mistakes we regretted. "I really appreciate it."

"You don't need to thank me. I wasn't gonna leave you to handle her alone." His hand went up to touch the back of his neck in a gesture that didn't seem as casual as it should have. He probably didn't like getting involved in things that didn't include him. I couldn't blame him. But the thing he said next explained it. "I owe you."

"You don't owe me anything," I said to him slowly, meeting his gaze.

That wary face didn't move a single muscle. "You've been nothing but nice to my family. I owe you," he repeated himself.

Figuring he was talking about Dean and Trip, I focused on his other words. What the hell was I going to do with this man? Be ungrateful about what he'd done even if it had mainly just been moral support? I knew I should take what I could get for whatever reason.

We worked in silence for a few minutes. He'd take things out of the bags and set them on the counter while I put them where they needed to go. A few times I caught him looking around the kitchen, I'm sure taking in the crappy cupboards and the paint that needed to be redone... and the floors that had seen better decades, but he didn't comment on them. I didn't let myself get all bent out of shape over him being in my house, this near stranger.

"If you wanna call the cops, have them come over, I can be your witness she was here," my neighbor offered in that easy voice that reminded me this was the type of man who didn't want to talk to women who flirted with him because he was married and who also coached little boy baseball.

I'd been thinking about it while putting up groceries. The truth was, I didn't want to involve the police, mostly because I didn't want this getting back to my parents and stressing them out, and I also didn't want the boys getting involved in it either. Josh had made me promise him something I would never take lightly that night after the funeral. *You don't ever have to see her again if you don't want to, J. I won't let her take you. I promise.*

"I'm not," I told him. "I really don't think she'll come back."

The noise that churned in his throat didn't say whether he approved of my decision or not.

For a moment, I thought about telling him about Rodrigo, but I didn't. Seeing Anita had given me enough to deal with. Talking about my brother was a mountain I didn't want to tackle yet with this man who was slowly becoming friendly with me.

When we were done a few minutes later, Josh's coach gave me a serious, solemn look. "I'm gonna get going, but I'll be home the rest of the day. Holler if you need anything, but I'll keep a look out and make sure you don't get any more visitors."

"You really don't have to do that," I tried to insist.

Dallas let his head lull to the side a moment, watching me with those eyes. That pink mouth opened just enough so I could see the tip of his tongue tap the corner of his lips. "You're friends with my family. We're neighbors." His eyelids hung low in a way that was almost a glare. "Give me a call if you need anything."

The look I gave him must have said *"You sure you're not going to freak out about me calling?"* because I would swear he scowled.

"Holler," he repeated in that bossy tone.

I nodded at him, not completely convinced calling him was something I wouldn't get unfriended for. "Thanks again."

Dallas shrugged one rounded, muscular shoulder. "Make sure your doors are locked, all right?"

The nod I gave him was slow. That prideful part of me wanted to say I could take care of myself. Because I could. I had. I took care of two boys and me. But I kept my trap shut. I knew when to accept help and when not. It wasn't like I had anyone else.

"Hey!" I called out to him all of a sudden. "Josh is having a birthday party next weekend. If you have nothing better to do, feel free to drop by. We'll have food, and I'm inviting some of the other neighbors, too." I didn't need him thinking I was trying to reel him in.

Dallas hesitated for a moment, already walking away. His back was to me. "All right." He didn't move for a moment. "Keep an eye out next time you get home."

Indignation flared in my chest at being treated like a stupid kid. What was with this man and his bossiness?

Those golden-brown eyes glanced over his shoulder. That familiar line formed between his eyebrows. "Don't get pissed off," he said, turning forward again before tossing out, "I only want to help. See you later."

CHAPTER ELEVEN

"LOUIE CHEWY," I SAID HIS NAME CALMLY.

He didn't look up at me. He knew what I was about to ask. I had eyes. So did he, and he was using his to look at the not-so-interesting sky.

I scratched the tip of my nose. "Where is your shoe, boo?"

Even after I asked him about the missing sneaker, which I knew for a fact he'd had on when we'd left the house—because why would he leave the house with only one sneaker on?—he still didn't look down at his sock-covered foot. The same sock-covered foot that suddenly had curled toes inside of the blue and black material as if he was trying to hide. Jesus Christ.

He tilted his head to the side and shrugged those small shoulders. "I don't know," he whispered.

Not again. With his attention focused on something other than me, I didn't feel bad about pinching the bridge of my nose. He knew I only did that when it was deserved, and this would count as one of those times. If someone had told me four years ago that little boys randomly lost their shoes for no reason at all, I would have laughed and told them "that sucks." If Josh had ever misplaced a sneaker at a young age without being in my presence, Rodrigo hadn't told me about it. Who the hell loses a shoe and isn't blackout drunk? How the hell does someone lose a shoe to begin with? I wouldn't walk around bragging about it either.

But now, two years into this guardian slash parenting gig, I understood how possible it was. Three-times-in-a-year possible. How my little biscuit of love, who was usually more prepared than me, had something go missing was beyond my brain's capacity to comprehend. The fact was he did. Like him sneaking into my room and scaring me half to death, I should have been used to it. At least, I shouldn't have been surprised he managed to do it.

As we stood near the bleachers at the field where Josh practiced, I glanced around, hoping to magically see a shoe that my gut expected was gone forever.

Fuck.

Crouching down, I set my bag on the ground next to us and placed a hand on his shoulder. "I told you to tell me when this stuff happens, Lou." He still hadn't made eye contact.

"I know." I could barely hear him.

"Then why didn't you?"

"Because."

"Because what?"

"I lost my shoe last week." He had? "Grandma

bought me the same ones, and she made me promise not to lose 'em again."

Motherfucker. And here I went feeling bad when I kept stuff from the Larsens.

Pressing the tips of my fingers to his jaw, I gently made him look at me. His features were so remorseful I was tempted to tell him it was okay and not to worry about it, but all I had to do was imagine him growing up into a liar and know that was the worst thing I could do. "I'm not going to get really mad at you if you tell me the truth, and I don't like it when you lie to me. You can lie to me by not telling me anything too, Louie. You really have to be more careful with your stuff."

"I know."

"I know you know. But now I'm not going to buy you another pair that you like until I know you can take care of them—"

He gasped. "But—"

"Nope."

"But—"

"Nuh-uh."

"But—"

"I'm not, Lou. I warned you already. Now show me where the last place you saw it was. Maybe we can find it."

He sighed but kept his argument to himself, finally.

On the other side of the fence, the players were huddled around their coaches as practice came to an end. Keeping an eye on them, I turned around to let Louie jump on my back and stood up. "Where to?"

He pointed straight forward to the area where he'd

been playing for the last hour with other brothers and sisters of the team's lineup. There were still plenty of kids running around, and as I watched them, I wouldn't hold it past one of them to have grabbed his sneaker and taken off with it. Kids were little shits sometimes.

With only the flashlight app that came on my phone, I moved the beam around the ground, CSI style, trying to find a trace of a shoelace or something.

"You lost your shoe again, dummy?"

I didn't bother turning around to talk to Josh. "Don't call your brother that... even if he did lose it."

"I said I was sorry," Louie muttered.

I smirked as I kicked a broken branch over to make sure it hadn't mysteriously found its way beneath it. It hadn't. "Lies. You never said you were sorry."

He made a humming noise on my back. His breath was warm on the little hairs on my neck. "I did in my head."

Despite everything, that made me laugh.

"I'll go look over there." Josh sighed, already moving away from us, his attention focused on the ground.

"What are you doing?" a voice asked from somewhere nearby a moment later.

Straightening, I glanced over my shoulder to find my neighbor there, his expression a confused one. I couldn't blame him. I could only imagine what I looked like stumbling around in the dark with a five-year-old on my back.

"Hi." This was the first time we'd seen each other

since the day Anita had dropped by unexpectedly. Way unexpectedly. "We're looking for a shoe about this size." I used the fingers of one hand to give him an approximate length.

Dallas hummed and immediately glanced at the ground. I'd noticed during practice he'd trimmed his facial hair. The worn, red ball cap that he usually wore during baseball practice was pulled low on his forehead. "My mom used to say my shoes would just pick up and walk out of the house on their own."

I eyed Louie over my shoulder and he turned his face away. Uh-huh.

"Where did you leave it, bud?" our neighbor asked as he walked around us to search the ground further ahead.

"I don't know," the boy on my back answered in a muffled tone I recognized as him being embarrassed.

I tried to keep my snicker as quiet as possible, but it was still loud enough for Dallas to hear it and turn around. The way his eyebrows were shaped said he was amused. I couldn't say I didn't like that about him. After he'd brought his Xbox over, I'd watched how patient he was with Louie. Maybe he was still acting a *little* weird with me, but he hadn't been the same way with either of the boys that night. When Josh and the boys had come out of the bedroom, demanding to be fed, they had all been excited to see Dallas there. Kids were awesome at sniffing out assholes, and I guess this man couldn't be so bad if none of them complained. God knows Josh wouldn't keep his opinion to himself on someone.

It also helped that the thing Trip told me about Dallas's ex helped me not take his coolness personally.

"We'll find it. Don't worry," he assured the monkey on my back.

Obviously, he'd never lost a child's shoe before, because it wasn't that often they were found. A lot of times they disappeared never to be seen again like socks in the dryer. But I didn't want to ruin his optimism. A few kids streaked by us, oblivious to our treasure hunt. We probably searched for another five minutes before a boy ran right in front of Dallas. Quick as lightning, he struck his hand out and grabbed the kid on Josh's team by the back of his workout jersey, hauling him to a stop.

"Dean, you seen a shoe?" Dallas asked Trip's son, the hand on the back of his shirt moving up to touch the back of the kid's neck in an affectionate pat.

The dark blond, a little taller than Josh, frowned. "No." He seemed to think about it a second. "What kinda shoe?"

Our neighbor gestured toward Louie and me. "Little boy shoe. A tennis shoe."

"Oh." The kid swiveled his attention to us, his smiling creeping up in a way that didn't seem like it belonged on a boy about ten or eleven. "Hi, Ms. Diana."

"Hi, Dean." I smiled at him.

The grin on his face really was something else. "I'll find it," the boy said right before taking off in the direction he'd come, back toward a small group of kids younger than him.

Not really expecting much, I figured I'd wait a few more minutes before we headed home. I was resigned to the inevitable: having to buy another pair of shoes, this time from Walmart. Plus, it was getting late, and I'd left chili cooking in the Crock-Pot that morning. It was more than likely only a minute later before Dean rushed back toward us, his hand extended. In it was a red and black tennis shoe that I now accepted was brand spanking new. Mrs. Larsen really had tried to pull a fast one on me. Huh.

"What do you say, Lou?" I asked as I took the sneaker from him.

"Thank you," he mumbled a little lower than he usually would have.

"Thanks, Dean," I emphasized. "We really appreciate it."

The boy did that smile again that my gut said was all trouble. "Anything for you, Ms. Diana."

This kid was something else.

"Thank you?" I said, shooting a glance at Dallas, who had this ridiculous expression on his face like he didn't know what to think either.

"See ya, Josh," the boy called out to my nephew before bumping fists with Dallas and running off again. "Bye, Uncle Dal."

Louie slid off my back, plopping down on the dirt, oblivious to the fact he was wearing his khaki school pants and the ground was damp from an earlier rain shower. He started putting his shoe on, slapping the Velcro straps over to the other side.

"Thank you for asking him to look," I told our

neighbor, keeping an eye on Lou at the same time to make sure something else didn't magically disappear.

"Yeah, thank you, Mr. Dallas."

"Dallas, and you're welcome. I told you we'd find it."

Lou climbed to his feet, rolling onto his knees as if getting his butt dirty hadn't been enough. "We're gonna have chili tonight. You wanna come?" he asked so suddenly, it caught me completely off guard.

I froze, snapping my gaze up to Dallas, smiling tightly.

He is married, I reminded myself. Married. The last thing I wanted to do was give him the impression we were trying to wrangle him in to our lives more than he needed to be.

Those hazel eyes bounced back and forth between Louie and me. "Chili?"

"It's real good."

Louie didn't know a damn stranger. He was so honest and innocent in his answer it made me wish everyone was so upfront. It also made me want to protect his feelings that much more. "I'm sure Mr. Dallas—" I started to say before getting cut off by our neighbor.

"Just Dallas," he cut in.

"—has plans already, Lou. We can invite him another day, not at the last minute."

The boy blinked up at the man with those blue eyes that could conquer worlds if he ever put his mind to it. "You got things to do?"

Our neighbor opened his mouth, hesitation *right*

there, an apology, an excuse, something, on his tongue, but he closed it just as quickly. He seemed to take in Louie completely, and I knew what he was seeing: the cutest boy in the world. "It's real good?" he asked Louie, a soft, gradual smile crossing his mouth.

The enthusiastic nod of my boy could win over the biggest Grinch. It was both a blessing and a curse. He used it on me on a regular basis.

Our neighbor was done.

"If your mom doesn't mind...." He trailed off, giving me an almost apologetic look.

To anyone else, the frown that came over Louie's face at the "M" word wouldn't have meant anything other than a kid not liking the chance he might not get his way. But to me, I knew what that frown was for, and Louie's answer didn't make me feel better. He ignored the "M" word and went with, "Buttercup doesn't care, do you?"

～

"CAN I HELP WITH ANYTHING?"

Glancing over my shoulder, I shook my head at the tall man standing in my kitchen for the third time in a week. "It's only a couple of dishes. I'm almost done."

Dallas scanned the kitchen, eyeing it the same way he had the first time he'd come in, probably looking at all the imperfections I would get to fixing eventually. "Thanks for dinner."

Rinsing off the last dish and setting it into the rack, I dried my hands on the towel I had hanging off the stove. "You're welcome." I turned to face him as the sounds of the boys in the living room told us they were arguing. What was new?

"It was real good," he said, and if I wasn't completely imagining it, there was a playful hint to his tone.

I couldn't help but smile at him. Dinner had only been a little awkward at the beginning, thankfully. We never really used the dining room table unless my parents or the Larsens were over, and this time hadn't been an exception. The four of us had sat around the coffee table with bowls and pieces of bread, Josh and Dallas talking about professional baseball nearly the entire time. Meanwhile, Louie and I had taken turns opening our mouths at each other when they were full of chili.

"Thank you for coming. Lou doesn't really…" How did I say this? "He doesn't really spend a lot of time with men who aren't in their sixties since his dad died, and you've always been really nice to him. He likes you. Thanks for that, by the way. That's really nice of you."

Some nerve in that hard face seemed to jump in disbelief or discomfort, I couldn't be sure. I didn't realize I'd mentioned Rodrigo's death until after I was done. Dallas reached up to scrub at the trimmed hairs along his jaw, shaking his head. "Don't thank me. He's a good kid. They're both good kids." His hand moved along to palm the back of his neck. "My dad died when I was young. I'm sure I would've been the same way when I was his age. I get it."

His dad had died? I didn't know that. Then again, how would I? I wondered how old he'd been, but kept the question to myself, focusing on the good part of what he'd said, and part of me hoped he wouldn't ask about my brother, so I switched the subject.

"I'm sure that mindset helps when you're coaching little boys. I can tell they all really like you." I could. When Dallas talked to them, their attention was zeroed in on him. He was patient with them even when they didn't listen to his instructions and kept doing the wrong thing over and over again. I don't think I would have been able to keep it together so well.

That amazing hazel-eyed gaze slid over to me, and he raised a brawny shoulder casually. "That's why I do it. I like the idea of being there for somebody who maybe doesn't have anyone else around, teaching them what I didn't have someone around to teach me." He stated it like what he'd been through as a kid without a father was a fact. Like not having a dad was just something as uncomplicated as him not having a dog growing up. He didn't say it like it was some huge, secret burden. It just was what it was, and I thought that was why his words hit me so hard. He actually liked what he did for a good reason.

I swallowed and somehow kept myself from smiling at him, knowing that would probably just make the situation awkward. "I'm not saying this to flirt with you..." The sides of his mouth flexed the slightest bit at the same time I made that comment, but I kept going. I was just messing with him, I told myself, trying to keep this as light as I could. "But that's really nice of you. You never know when even a little bit of kindness might change someone's life."

Dallas's smile slowly melted into a serious expression and a stiff nod. "I know."

He knew. After rubbing my hands on my pants, I reached over for the towel I had next to the sink and started to refold it. "So, how'd you end up with the Tornado?"

"Trip wanted to start his own team because he had a falling out with Dean's old coach, and got me drunk enough to agree to take one on with him as an assistant. He didn't know shit about baseball, but he's learned. I had to read a couple of books about the rules. I hadn't played in years," he explained.

"Did you play ball when you were younger or what?"

"Little league and high school. I watched it more than I played it. I didn't go to some fancy school for it or anything."

There was something in his tone then that didn't sit right with me. "I didn't go to some fancy school for anything either." I needed to stop looking him in the eyes unless it was necessary. "I hated college. I did a semester of basics and decided it wasn't for me."

"You cut hair?"

"And color it... and style it," I added in a joking voice before stopping myself. God forbid he think I was flirting. "I mostly do color now."

Dallas leaned a hip against the kitchen counter, crossing both arms over his chest. I'd already noticed all the dirty smudges along his forearms and biceps from practice. He'd taken off his cap before he'd come over. "Trip said you won't cut his hair."

And I thought I had a big mouth. "Nope."

Those dark brown eyebrows knitted together like he couldn't believe I would say no to his cousin. "Why?"

"I'm doing just fine with mostly only women, some kids, and the few men who have stuck with me for a while now. I'm not worried about it. The last time I took a new male client, he tried to stick his face between my boo—chest." I shrugged. "No more for me."

He frowned. "People do that?"

"Yeah. One of my coworkers is a guy and he's always getting his butt pinched," I explained to him before making a face. "But he doesn't mind half the time as long as he gets a good tip."

The shocked look on his face made me laugh.

"Mr. Dallas, do you wanna play Xbox with me?" came Louie's singsong voice from the living room.

What the hell? It was after ten. The only reason I hadn't sent them to bed yet was because I'd been washing dishes.

"Isn't it his bedtime?" Dallas asked in a lowered voice.

I nodded at him. "Louie! Play Xbox my ass—butt. Come tell Mr. Dallas goodnight so you can get to bed," I called out, rolling my eyes at this sneaky kid.

I heard an "aww man" from the living room.

It took a couple of seconds for Louie to trudge into the kitchen, heading straight toward the neighbor. He still hadn't even bothered putting his pajamas on yet. His school pants were even dirtier than I'd imagined. His face seemed flush, but I ignored it. "Goodnight, Mr. Dallas." He sounded grumpy. Too bad.

"Night, Louie," Dallas answered back, that big, gruff hand lowering so he could get a high five from a hand so much smaller than his.

Louie gave him a little smile as he slapped his hand down as hard as he could. "You can come by tomorrow if you want. Right, Buttercup?"

Uhh...

"I got something I gotta do tomorrow, but maybe after that. We'll see, buddy, yeah?" the man reasoned, saving me the trouble of having to find a way to tell Lou our neighbor had other things to do.

If Dallas didn't know it, he found out then: my Louie was the most innocent soul in the universe. He didn't ask for much. He didn't need much. And Dallas's vague words were enough. "Okay. Goodnight." He turned around and started to head out of the kitchen again, leaving me standing there before he finally whipped around. "See you in my room?" he asked, finally remembering I was in the same room. Traitor.

"Yeah, Goo. I'll see you in a minute."

"'Kay. Night!" he seemed to holler at us both.

I turned to face Dallas with another apology and assurance ready, but he beat me to it.

He lowered his chin to say, "Don't. I know neither one of you is doing anything, or coming on to me." He met my gaze evenly, seriously.

I couldn't help it. "You're sure?"

"I'm sure."

I wasn't completely convinced. "I promise. Cross my heart. I'm keeping my hands to myself, and the boys and I are fine the way we are. I'm not looking for a sugar daddy. I just don't want you to hate me since we have to see each other all the time. Promise."

The man didn't miss a beat, even the corner of his lip curled up as he murmured in that husky voice, "I know." His mouth almost instantly went flat. "And I don't hate you. I thought you wanted to be friends."

CHAPTER TWELVE

My head was pounding a couple of days later.

I wanted to throw up. I didn't get migraines often, but when they did come a knockin', hell had to be paid. I woke up that morning with a throbbing sensation behind one eye and it had only gotten steadily worse as I drove the boys to school. I should have known what was happening. When a call from a restricted number popped up on my screen just as I pulled into the lot at work, the pain went to another level.

Fucking Anita again. I knew it was her.

Thinking about her usually left me with a headache, but with her recent visit and phone call today… it was so much worse. I was nauseous and my brain wanted to burst out of my skull.

By some miracle, I made it through my work day without throwing up or crawling under my station, thanks to over-the-counter migraine medication we kept in the break room for emergencies and so much coffee, my hand shook while I did a couple of trims. It was a miracle I hadn't cut myself. My phone had rung twice more, once with Trip's name flashing across the screen and the second with Dallas's name. I hadn't felt like dealing with their baseball business and didn't bother answering, letting both calls go to voice mail. It was my turn to pick up the boys from school afterward. I didn't need to look in the mirror to know that the discomfort from my migraine was written all over my face.

They were both sweet and watched me carefully as I drove back. I'm sure they caught on to me not feeling my best, but they didn't comment. To put the topping on the cake of how sensitive they were, when we got home, Josh offered to make them a snack so I didn't have to.

All I could manage to do was thank him and ruffle his hair.

Both of them, along with Mac, headed into the backyard to play who knows what at the same time the next dose of medication I'd taken started kicking in just enough so that the light coming through the windows didn't make me feel like I was on the verge of dying.

So when a knock came from my front door, I was a little confused. My parents rarely came over without calling first, and the Larsens never came unannounced. No one else of my friends would come over without double-checking. Hardly anyone had the new address.

Looking through the peephole, I was more than a little surprised to see a familiar face on the other side instead of a Girl Scout or a Jehovah's Witness.

"Hey," I said hesitantly and more than a little weakly once I'd opened the door.

When I'd peeked through the peephole, Dallas had had just about the most pleasant expression on his face I had ever witnessed coming from him, but the second his gaze landed on me, that expression went straight into a frown. "What's wrong with you?"

Was it that bad that someone who was just shy of being a complete stranger could tell there was something wrong with me? "I don't feel well."

His frown deepened, his gaze raking all over me again in a way that made me feel like he was making sure I didn't have some contagious disease. "You look like hell." Was I supposed to look like a beauty queen when my eyeball felt like it was about to abandon ship from my skull? "Migraine?"

I started to nod before remembering that would only make it worse. "Uh-huh. I don't get them that often, but when I do...." Why was I telling him this? And why was he here? "Do you need something?" I asked a little more harshly than I intended for it to come out.

He ignored my question and tone. "When did you last take something?"

I shrugged; at least I think I shrugged. "A few hours ago."

"Did you make dinner already?"

"No." Honestly, I'd been thinking about making Josh call something in. I didn't even want to bother with preheating the oven to stick a frozen lasagna in there.

Dallas glanced over his shoulder, hesitating when he faced forward again. His jaw jutted out for a moment. He let out a long breath through his nose, and then nodded, more to himself than to me, that was for sure. He rolled those massive shoulders of his and met my gaze, straight on. "I'll close the door. Go lay down. I'll take care of dinner," he stated in that no-nonsense bossy way of his, like he wasn't someone I'd met and hung out with a handful of times.

Who was this man and why was he doing this? The tiny head shake I did was more than enough to send bile creeping up the back of my throat. I couldn't try and hide my cheeks puffing out as I kept the acid down. "You don't have to do that."

"I want to," he said, still not breaking eye contact.

Was he using my own tactic against me?

I swallowed. "I'm sorry. Thank you for the offer, but we'll be fine. Is there something you needed or can we just e-mail later?" Plus, since when had he ever come over to talk Tornado in person? Never. What else would he be coming over for?

To give him credit, he didn't do much more than tip his face toward the sky and blow out a breath before shifting his attention back down to me, his facial features smooth and not amused. "Are you always this stubborn?"

I would have narrowed my eyes if it didn't make my pain worse. So I told him the truth, mirroring his expression. "Yes. Is your real name really Dallas?"

That thick, dark eyebrow of his rose a half inch.

"Yes."

"Why did your parents name you that?" I asked even as my head gave another nauseating throb.

That eyebrow of his rose a quarter of an inch more than it already had. "My dad lost a bet on a football game, and it was either naming me Dallas or Cowboy." He didn't miss a beat and went ahead with going back to the original subject. "Let me help you."

I would have gone with Dallas, too. I let the name thing go and waved my hand weakly. "You've done enough. I'm not trying to take advantage of you or cross some line. We'll be all right," I whispered, closing one eye when the pounding became even more concentrated.

Dallas was staring me down, but I didn't care. His voice was so low I had to strain to hear it. "I get that you're not trying to come on to me, now or ever, all right? Can we never bring that up again? I'm here. You're not feeling well. Let me help."

I closed both my eyes and frowned, wanting this conversation over with.

He sighed. "I know what it's like for a single mom to get a migraine every once in a while. If you want to call mine and make sure I'm not shitting you, you can."

I didn't have the energy or the willpower to contemplate his words. I opened my eyes. Who the hell used their mom as a reference anyway?

The way he was looking at me was like he was blowing out a breath of exasperation in his head. "Take a picture of my driver's license and send it to somebody if it makes you feel better," he suggested calmly.

I didn't think he was some kind of crazy pervert. Not at all. Mostly, I was worried about making things weird between us. He claimed to have accepted that I wasn't trying to put the moves on him, which was good because it was the truth. He was nice to look at, his body even more so, but so were plenty of men.

"I can call in a few pizzas and sit with your boys for a while." He raised those thick, brown eyebrows when I didn't immediately scream my gratitude.

"It's—" I started to say before Dallas cut me off.

"Look, I came over to tell you face-to-face that we're scaling back the tournaments we're doing and the practices. I tried calling you, but you didn't answer or call back."

Tournaments. Fuck. I didn't even care about baseball or even continuing to live right then. All I heard was "pizzas" and "sit with the boys." A wave of nausea and pain suddenly hit me right behind the eyeballs.

"Fine." I felt so crappy I backed up, eyed him again, then went inside like an obedient puppy and headed straight into the living room. Dallas followed after me. I headed over to the couch, fully aware that this semi-strange man was in my house, about to figure out dinner for the boys.

Was this a mistake?

I watched from the couch as my neighbor disappeared out the back door of the kitchen and faintly heard the deepest reaches of his voice in the air, even though I couldn't actually process what exactly he was saying.

When he didn't come back in after twenty minutes, I sat up and peeked through the opened door from the kitchen into the backyard. Josh and Louie were about fifteen feet away from him, forming a triangle. Mac was lying on the grass, watching the three of them lazily. When a baseball flew from Dallas's side to Josh's, I couldn't help but smile before plopping back down on the couch, letting out a silent prayer that this migraine would go away soon.

The clock on the wall kept me informed as twenty more minutes passed, and then ten more on top of that.

The sound of the door being opened warned me that someone was coming in before Josh and Louie's arguing confirmed it was them. Dallas followed after the two, the door creaking shut right before a knock sounded at the front door.

"I got it," my neighbor said, touching one hand to the top of Louie's head as he passed him up and headed in the direction of the knock, crossing in front of the turned off television.

"He got pizza," Josh offered up before plopping down on the recliner perpendicular to the big couch I was on. "Meat supreme."

I didn't even have the energy to stick my tongue out at him. Hell, all I wanted was to disappear into my room, but I wasn't about to leave Josh and Lou alone with a man I didn't know that well. My parents were definitely never finding out about this. "I don't know what's wrong with you not liking pineapple."

"On a *pizza*?"

He and his brother said it at the same time just like

they did every other time we argued about pizza toppings—which was every time. "*Gross*."

"Your faces are gross." Maybe I wasn't feeling bad enough not to argue with them.

"No, just Josh's," Louie chimed in, making me snort. He was too young to have the kind of comebacks he did, but from time to time, he surprised me with them and I loved it.

Sure enough, Josh elbowed Lou and the younger one elbowed him right back. Dallas closed the door and appeared with three boxes, stacked from the biggest at the bottom to the smallest at the top. He set them on the coffee table and gestured toward the boys.

"Little man, can you get some plates and napkins?"

Lou nodded and got up, heading toward the kitchen. By the time he came back with a stack of paper plates and a roll of paper towels, Dallas had spread the pizza boxes out, opening one box after the other, showing that he had ordered an extra-extra-large pizza... and that one of the boys had tattled and told him how much I loved Hawaiian pizzas because the medium sized box had one inside. The last box was filled with chicken wings.

Passing out the plates, our neighbor didn't even ask as he went straight for the pineapple and ham pizza, using his fingers to pull up two small slices and setting them on the plate Louie handed him, then passing it over. "Ladies first."

"Thank you," I said in a weak voice I hated.

"Lou, what do you wanna eat?" he asked my littlest.

He pointed at the meat pizza and then jabbed a finger at the hot wings. "One." I held up a finger at him, squinting with one eye, and he added, "Please."

Dallas's eyebrow went up at the please, but he scooped up a slice and set it on the plate. His hand hovered over the container of hot wings before he asked, "These are spicy. Can you handle it?"

I could only blame myself for the shit that came out of Louie's mouth next. I really could. Because I said the same thing in front of him a dozen times in the past. "I'm Mexican. *Yeah.*"

Those hazel eyes swung in my direction, wide and completely fucking amused. "All right, buddy. If you say so." And just like that, he picked up the leg of what was probably the smallest wing in the box and set it on the plate with the slice.

"Josh, you?" he asked.

Three minutes later, the four of us were sitting around the table, stuffing our faces. I swore the cheese had some kind of magical healing ingredient that made my head stop hurting at least while I was eating. Josh chowed down three slices total and two more wings before throwing himself back on the floor and groaning. Lou wasn't a big eater, but he picked at enough of his food. I wasn't sure how much Dallas ate, but it seemed like a lot; I had no idea where all that food went. There wasn't a hint of bloating or a pooch anywhere.

Some people had all the luck.

"Your head hurting any less?" he asked from his spot on the floor in front of the television, alongside the coffee table. He'd thrown a hand back to hold his weight up, his facial expression lazy and pleased like only pizza was capable of giving someone.

With my clean, pizza grease-free hand, I flipped the palm up and down. "Better than before eating." I smiled at him. "Thank you. Let me know how much I owe you."

"Don't worry about it," was the no-nonsense answer that came out of his mouth.

I knew when my battles were pointless and when I had a chance, and in this case, there was no use in wasting my energy. Plus, I just didn't feel like arguing. I could pay him back later. "Thank you again then."

Before I had a chance to remind the boys what manners were, they piped up, one after the other, filling me with a stupid amount of pride. "Thank you, Mr. Dallas."

The older man gave them a look too. "I told you, you can call me Dallas."

"Mr. Dallas is nice," Louie commented hours later as he climbed into bed.

"He is, isn't he?" I asked, plopping down on the corner of the mattress. My headache had eased enough to at least be able to do this one thing for my boy.

"Yeah." He pulled his sheets up to his neck as he settled in. "Josh hit the ball over the fence and he didn't even get mad. He told him not to say he was sorry because he didn't do nothing wrong."

"'Anything' wrong, Lou. But that was pretty nice of him to say that." As I got older, I realized more and more the things I found attractive. Like patience and kindness. When I was younger—and a hell of a lot dumber—I'd always gravitated toward hot guys with nice cars. Now, there were things like credit scores to worry about, employment histories, and personality traits that couldn't be picked up over dinner and drinks.

"He said our fence was messed up and we needed to fix it."

I winced and nodded, adding the fence to the dozen other things that I needed to repair around the house at some point. "I know."

"You gonna tell *Abuelito*?"

I winked at him. "I don't want to, but maybe you, me, and Josh can fix it. What do you think?"

Those baby-soft features fell instantly. "Maybe *Abuelito* can help."

"Why? You don't think we can do it?" To be honest, I wasn't positive we could either, but what example would I be setting if I constantly asked my dad to do things?

From the words that came out of Louie's mouth next, I had already set a bad example. He looked me right in the eye and said, very seriously, "Remember my bed?"

I shut my mouth and changed the subject. "All right, what do you want to hear tonight?" I asked, using my hands to tuck the sheets in, starting at around his feet, close to my hip.

He made a thoughtful "hmm" sound. "A new one." Thank God he let the bed thing go.

"You want to hear a new one?" I asked, still tucking him in, glancing back and forth between what I was doing and his face above the covers.

"Yes." I drew out the look I gave him until he added. "Please. I'm sorry, I forget."

"It's okay." I drew my finger up the sole of his foot through the sheet, knowing it was going to make him flail and mess up the cocoon I'd been working on. "A new story, then. Hmm." Despite having a lifetime of memories of Rodrigo, some days it was hard to remember things about him that Lou hadn't heard a million times before.

When I had first found out my brother died, the minutes that ticked by after my dad broke the news seemed to have lasted a million years. The memory of sitting on my bed afterward, my soul a dimension away, was one I could never forget. We had all fallen apart. Every single one of us. I hadn't slept in bed with my parents since I'd been a little kid, but I could remember physically forcing myself to go back to my room after I'd stood at their closed door for who knows how long, wanting comfort that they weren't ready to provide.

It wasn't until I saw the boys a day or so later, when I realized that Mandy was in no place to do anything for them, that I had made myself shed and bury as much of my grief as I could—at least in front of them. Just thinking about her and all the signs she'd given us about how she was dealing, made guilt flood every nook inside of my soul. But it was done. We had all been to blame, and I didn't want Josh or Lou to ever forget her.

"You want to hear a funny one or... maybe one with your mom?"

I almost missed Lou's wince—it happened every time I brought up his mom, but it only made me do it more.

"A funny one," he said, not surprisingly.

I raised my eyebrows and smiled, letting it go. "One time, your dad and I were driving back to El Paso to visit *Abuelita* and *Abuelito*, right? Josh hadn't been born yet. We had stopped to eat somewhere and the food was really crappy, Lou. I mean, both of us had stomachaches about halfway through eating, but we made ourselves finish it. Anyway, we left the restaurant and kept driving because we didn't want to spend the night somewhere... and your dad starts telling me how he's going to poop himself. He kept saying how much his stomach was hurting, how bad it was, and how he thought he was going to have a baby."

Lou's little-boy laugh egged me on.

"Once he started threatening me that he was going to poop in the car, I finally pulled the car into the first gas station I could find and he ran inside." I could picture the memory so clearly in my head, I started laughing. "He had his hands behind his butt like he was trying to hold it in." By that point, there were tears in both of our eyes, and it was really hard to get the rest of the story out. "My stomach was still hurting but not *that* much. It had to be thirty minutes later, your dad comes back out of the gas station, sweating. He's soaked in it, Lou. No lie. He was covered in sweat. He gets into the car and I'm looking at him, and realize he didn't have any socks on. So I asked him, *what happened to your socks?* And he says 'There wasn't any toilet paper in the restroom.'"

Lou was laughing so hard he'd rolled onto his side, clutching his stomach.

"You like that one, huh?" I was smiling huge at him busting a gut.

He just kept huffing out, "Oh my gosh" over and over again, a true testament of my mom's influence on him.

"His birthday was a month later, and I got him a roll of toilet paper and a bunch of socks."

"Grandpa showed me a movie of Christmas, and you gave Daddy socks and he threw them at you," he said between these great big chuffs.

I nodded. "He made me promise never to say anything about it again, so I didn't. I just kept giving him socks."

"You're good, *Tia*."

"I know, huh?"

He nodded, his face flushed pink and happy. Even happy, he said, "I miss him."

"Me too, Lou. Very, very much," I said softly, feeling a bitter ball in my throat as I smiled. Tears stung the back of my eyes, but by some miracle I kept them in. I wanted this to be a happy thing between us. I could cry later.

The little boy blinked sleepily up at the ceiling with a dreamy sigh. "I wanna be a policeman like him when I'm old like you."

His comment made my heart ache so bad I couldn't even focus on how he'd referred to me as being old. "You can be whatever you want to be," I told him. "Your dad wouldn't care as long as you always did a good job."

"Because he loved me?"

He was going to be the death of me, this little kid. "Because he loved you," I promised. I gulped and hoped and prayed that he couldn't see the struggle written all over my face. Tucking the covers in around him faster than ever, I leaned over my favorite five-year-old on the planet and kissed his forehead, earning a kiss on my cheek in return. "I love you, poo-poo face. Sleep good."

"I love you too, poo-poo face," he said as I made my way toward his door, thinking about his words and grinning even as a tiny piece of my heart broke off.

"*Tia*, you can buy me socks if you want," Louie added just as I made it to his door.

Maybe if I'd been expecting it, his offer wouldn't have felt like a battering ram to my sternum followed by a nuclear bomb being detonated where my heart used to exist.

My legs went weak. Grief and something close to misery boxed in my throat, and with a strength I didn't think I had in me, I turned to look at him without letting the tears burst like Niagara Falls out of my eyes and nodded. Goose bumps broke out over my arms. "I think your dad would like that. Goodnight, Lulu."

"Night, dudu," he called out as I mostly closed the door behind me, biting my lip and swallowing, swallowing, swallowing hard.

I pressed my back against the wall next to his door.

Oh my God.

Oh my God.

My nose started burning. My eyes began watering, and I gasped for air, for strength, for anything that could get me through the pain slicing through everything that made me, me.

How did it never get easier to know that life was unfair?

How did it never hurt any less to know I would never see someone I loved again? Why did it have to be my brother? He hadn't been perfect, but he'd been mine. He'd loved me even when I got on his nerves.

Why?

I hadn't moved a single inch when I heard Josh peep up, "Aunt Di."

Fuck.

"You're ready for bed?" My voice sounded cracked and splintered even in my own ears as I made my way to his room.

"Yeah," he replied, the sounds of the bed creaking, confirming his statement.

Wiping at my eyes with the back of my hand and then pulling up my shirt to dab at them, I did the same to my nose and took a deep, calming breath, which probably didn't do anything because I was three seconds away from bawling. But I couldn't put off seeing Josh before he fell asleep. It was one of the last few things he still let me get away with every so often.

When I had myself about 10 percent under control, I forced a smile and stuck my head through the doorway. Sure enough, on the mattress was Josh and right alongside him was my third boy, Mac, with his head on his paws, one eye on me at the door. His tail swished right by Josh's face.

"What story did you tell Lou?" he asked immediately, like he knew it had killed me inside. He probably did know.

"I told him the story about your dad and socks."

A small smile crossed his lips. "I know that one."

"You do?" I asked as I went around the edge of his bed to sit on the opposite side of where Mac was. I reached across to put one hand on the dog and another on Josh. If he already knew I was upset, there was no point in me hiding it.

"Yeah. He told me about it."

I raised an eyebrow, slightly surprised.

Josh lazily raised a shoulder, those brown eyes gazing right into my own. "I had to use one of his socks one day when we went to the park," he explained, his ears turning pink.

Those all too familiar tears stung the back of my eyes. He'd told Josh about it at least. Given him another memory I didn't have to. "I've had to flip my underwear inside out a couple of times. No big deal. It happens."

He gave me a horrified look that immediately had me frowning. "Gross!"

"What? I didn't say it was gross you had to wipe your butt with a dirty sock!"

"That's different!" he claimed, gagging.

"How is that different?" I asked, reminded of how many times I'd had this back and forth sort-of arguing with Rodrigo.

He was still choking and gagging. "Because! You're a girl!"

That had me rolling my eyes. "Oh God. Shut up. It's normal. It doesn't make it gross because I'm a girl and you're not. I'd rather be a girl than a boy." I poked him. "Girls rule, boys drool."

He shook and shivered, still supposedly traumatized, and I only rolled my eyes more.

"Go to bed."

"I am," he played around.

I grinned at him and he grinned right back. "I love you, J."

"Love you too."

I kissed his cheek and got a half-assed one in return. On the way out, I gave Mac a kiss and got a lick to my cheek that made me feel just a little better. Just a little. But not enough.

Sometimes I felt like a traitor for how much I loved them. Like I shouldn't, because they weren't supposed to be mine to begin with. Like I shouldn't think they made my life better when the only reason they were mine, lighting my life up, was because of something awful.

My heart hurt. It ached. Throbbed. It was heavier than it'd been in a long time. Tears and some kind of shitty bodily fluids filled my nose and eyes and throat, and for a brief second, I thought about going into my closet to cry. That was the usual place I went to bawl my eyes out, ever since I'd been a kid. But the fact was, this house was old and my closet was too small. Just being inside with this weight made me claustrophobic. The kitchen, living room, dining room, and laundry wouldn't work either.

Before I knew it, I found myself outside, closing the front door behind me as I sucked in huge gulps of breath that battled my lingering headache for attention. Silent tears—the worst ones—poured out of my eyes as my throat seemed to swell to twice its size. I plopped down on the first step, the palm of my hand going toward my forehead instantly, and I curled into myself as if trying to keep this pain from flaring to power. My nose burned and it was hard to breathe, but the tears kept right on coming.

Life was unfair and it always had been. It was nothing personal. *I knew that.* I'd seen that mentioned in the pamphlets I'd read on grief after Drigo died. But knowing all that didn't help for shit.

Grief never got any easier. I never missed my brother any less. Part of me accepted that nothing would ever fill the void his death had left in my life or the boys or my parents or even the Larsens.

Snot poured out of my nostrils like it was on tap, and I didn't make a single sound or bother cleaning myself up.

He'd had two kids, a wife, a house, and a job he'd enjoyed. He'd only been thirty-two when he'd died.

Thirty-two. In less than three years, I'd be thirty-two. I still felt like I had my entire life ahead of me. He had to have thought the same thing.

But he hadn't had years left. One minute he was there, and the next he wasn't. Just like that.

God, I missed his stupid jokes and his bossiness and stubbornness so much. I missed how much he gave me shit and never let me live anything down. He'd been more than my brother. More than my friend. More than the person who taught me to drive and helped me pay for cosmetology school. He'd taught me so much about everything. And the things he taught me the best came after he'd died.

Only he could manage that.

I would gladly go back to being a selfish, self-centered idiot with awful taste in men if I could only have him back.

I missed him. So. Fucking. Much.

"You all right?" a voice carried itself over, damn near scaring the shit out of me.

Without wiping my face or nose, I looked up, confused and totally caught off guard that someone had walked up without me noticing. My chest was puffing in soundless whimpers and my throat constricted. Yet I shook my head at Dallas who was standing at the bottom of the steps leading up to my deck and told him the truth. "Not really."

"Yeah, I can see that." His tone was so soft that it seemed to reach deeper than his concern and presence did. "I didn't know somebody could cry and not make a noise." The frown on his serious face deepened as his eyes scanned over me. That notch between his eyebrows was back again.

My sniffle in response was watery and a total mess, and without realizing I was doing it, I had my bottom lip sucked into my mouth like that would help stop me from crying even more. It wasn't really helping when tears kept streaming down my eyes and cheeks, falling off my jaw no matter how much my brain told my tear ducts to quit it.

"Your head still hurt?" he asked in that eggshell-like voice.

I shrugged, wiping at the wet places on my skin. It did hurt, but it didn't hurt worse than my heart right then.

"Something happen with the boys?"

I shook my head again, still too afraid to use words because I was sure I'd cry my eyes out in front of this man, and I didn't really want that to happen.

He glanced over his shoulder again, that big hand of his going to the back of his neck before he faced me again with a sigh. "If there's something you wanna talk about..." He scrubbed at the side of his cheek, awkward or resigned or both or neither; I couldn't blame him—I didn't want to feel this way. Not now, not ever, and especially not with witnesses who had thought so badly of me in the beginning. "I can keep my mouth shut," he finally got out, making me look up at him. A small smile crossed that hard face of his, so unexpected I didn't know how to handle it.

Tell him? This near complete stranger? I was supposed to say words and sentences to him that I couldn't even share with my parents? How could I even begin to describe the worst thing that had ever happened to me? How did you explain that your brother died, and that the next thing you knew, your life was going up into flames, and you didn't know how to put out the fire because the smoke from it was so thick you couldn't see two feet in front of you?

I wasn't some closed-off person who didn't know how to share her feelings, but this was different. Way different than having someone overhear me arguing with my mom. I could come back from her words. I was scared I'd never be able to come back from the Rodrigo-sized gap my brother had left me with.

"I'm not... I'm not...." I couldn't get the words out. They were jumbled and messy, and I couldn't unscramble them in one breath. I wheezed. "I—I hate this. I'm not trying to get a pity party or attention or anything—"

My neighbor dropped his head back, the long line of his lightly bearded throat bobbed. "I told you earlier, I know," he was still talking low. "I thought we agreed to put it behind us?"

I sniffled.

Dallas sighed again as he dropped his chin, meeting my gaze with those hazel-green eyes. "You gotta stop crying," my neighbor said in a gentle voice that broke the camel's back.

I wanted to tell him "okay," but I couldn't even manage to get that one single word out from how much I was hiccupping, unable to catch my breath.

"I'm no snitch."

He wasn't a snitch. My chest was puffing with those deadly, restrained, silent tears, and even though a gigantic part of me wanted to tell him I was fine, or at least that I would be fine, and explain it was no big deal, my big mouth went for it as my crying went straight to weeping—gasping breaths, shaking shoulders, a headache that went straight to pounding. *"He wants me to give him socks."*

There was a pause and a "What?" in that rumbled voice that got mostly buried beneath my tears and gasps.

It probably didn't even come out of my mouth correctly, but I answered, "Louie told me I could give him socks from now on." I didn't want to believe I was wailing, but it was probably pretty damn close to it.

Through the tears blurring my eyes, Dallas's lips parted and his face went pale. "You can't... you can't afford to buy him socks?"

I put a hand over my heart like that would help the ache pounding away. "No. I can." I wiped at my face as I hiccupped and noticed him closing his mouth. "I used to give my brother socks, and now Louie wants me to give him socks since I can't... I can't... give them to my brother anymore."

There was a pause and then, "This isn't about the socks?"

He didn't even know. How could he know? It wasn't about the fucking socks. At least not totally. It was about everything. About life and death, and white and black and gray. It was about having to be tough when you weren't used to it. About having to grow when you'd thought you were done growing. In the back of my head, I knew what I'd said didn't make any damn sense. But how could I explain? How could I begin to tell him that I had lost a part of myself with my brother's death, and I was trying so hard to keep what I had left together with duct tape and paper clips?

"I miss...." My throat hurt, and I swore my entire chest ached. I couldn't get the words out. Or maybe I just didn't want to. I rarely talked about Rodrigo to anyone except Van, but Van was different. She was my sister from another mister. With a cracked tone that could embarrass me later on, I blurted out what I could never say to my mom and dad, to this man who lived across the street from me. "My brother died, and I miss him so much." My voice cracked; it felt like my soul did the same all over again. I rubbed my palm over my mouth, like it would erase the pain those words gave me. "I miss him so, so much."

"I'm sorry. I had no idea," came Dallas's soft reply.

"It's hard... hard for me to talk about." I shrugged and rubbed my lips again, feeling this crushing weight of heartache and mourning.

How could this hurt so much after so long still?

For some reason, I kept on unloading in front of my neighbor. "I have to tell Louie stories because he doesn't remember him well anymore. I'm pretty sure Josh doesn't either. And they're stuck with me. *Me*. He left them to *me*." I rushed out before another half-gallon of tears streamed out of my eyes uncontrollably. I hadn't believed it after Mandy, and I still couldn't.

They had chosen me, of all the people in the world. "What was he thinking? *I don't know what I'm doing. What if I fuck up more than I already have?*"

I didn't take into consideration that he didn't even know I had a brother, much less know anything about him. He wouldn't understand why I missed him so much. How could he?

"Jesus Christ," he muttered steadily. His gaze was zeroed in on me like he didn't know what to do or say. His forehead was lined, his eyes pinched, his mouth slightly parted. He was stuck, and I mean, what was there to say or do? I was unloading on him and crying, and I didn't even know his middle name.

"I'm sorry." I wiped at my face futilely again. "It's been a long day and you've already been so much nicer than you needed to. I'm so sorry. This is Louie's and his damn sock's fault."

He seemed to study me, some emotion I couldn't completely comprehend tightening the area around his eyes and the skin along his jaw. "The boys... both of them... are your brother's?"

I nodded, sniffling, not even slightly regretting getting all of that out.

His expression only changed for a brief moment, too quick for me to really process it, and then he frowned. He opened his mouth wider and closed it. His hand went up to the back of his neck and he cupped it. Lines appeared at his forehead. He shrugged his shoulders and shook his head, blinking before the words burst out of his mouth. "What the hell are you apologizing for? You're upset and you miss your brother."

I was too shocked to even nod.

In the blink of an eye, he was looking at me like I was crazy. "You're still a kid raising two other kids, and you care enough to worry about what kind of people you're raising them to be. None of that sounds unreasonable to me."

I tipped my face back and fanned at my eyes, trying my freaking hardest to get the crying under control. I gurgled some kind of noise that said I heard him.

Minutes passed with the only sound between us being me making noises. I didn't want to look at my neighbor, so I didn't. Eventually, after however long it could have been, he sat on the second step, so close the side of his arm bumped into my lower leg. "How long has it been?"

"Two years," I croaked, still waving my hand back and forth. Crying usually made me feel better, but in this case, I wasn't so sure if that was the case. "The longest two years of my life."

The breath of air he let out through his mouth had me eyeing him. He had his chin tipped up. A car drove by. "I was Josh's age, I guess, when my dad died, and I still miss him every day. You can get over a lot of shit in two years, but I don't think anybody would argue that's long enough to make losing your brother any more bearable," he informed me in that cool voice that was almost sweet. "Anybody that tells you otherwise has never lost anything or anybody that mattered."

I'd never heard truer words spoken.

"It isn't long enough. Not even close to being long

enough," I agreed. "Are you ever just... okay with it? Is that what's supposed to happen? Does it get easier?" I asked him, not expecting an answer and not getting one either. "I forget sometimes that I can't call him and tell him something funny my mom said, or ask him to come and fix something stupid I did that I don't want my dad finding out about." How many times had I faced that reality? I hiccupped, missing him so much more by the second.

My throat started hurting, and I wasn't sure whether the liquid coming down over my lip was snot or tears. Frankly, I didn't care. "I'm never going to get to see him again or mess with him again. He's never going to shove my face into my birthday cake again or give me birthday licks. He was an asshole, but he was *my* asshole brother. And I want him *back*." The tears started flooding out of me all over again, my chest knotting itself up.

"Assholes or not, they're still your family."

I couldn't stop crying. "*I know.* I had him for twenty-seven years and the boys didn't even get a dime of that with him. It's not fair. I don't want them to grow up with daddy issues, when I know my brother would have killed me so he'd have more time with them. And you know what? I would have been okay with that. If something happened to me, it would have been different." I wiped at my face again. "This is so fucking unfair for Josh and Lou and my parents. It's bullshit. It's just fucking bullshit."

He turned to look at me over his shoulder, the yellow lights of the deck lighting up the side of his strong jaw and straight, long nose. "I'm not saying it isn't bullshit. It is. I don't know why somebody lives and somebody else dies, but it happens and nothing you do can change that. You can't feel guilty for being here and him not. That isn't the way it works."

I let out this moan at his words, shaking my head.

"Diana," he said in that sensitive tone that seemed so foreign on his scratchy vocal chords. "I've seen you with them enough. You don't... it doesn't look like they're not yours. It's clear as day to me that those boys love you like you're more than their aunt. A blind man could see that. They wouldn't love you if you weren't doing shit right. That's gotta mean something, bullshit or not. You got this job to do and nothing is going to take it away from you. At least you're killing it. I don't know your brother, but if he's somewhere looking down right now, at least he knows he made the right choice leaving them to you. You can't hide what you have with them."

There was something in his words and tone that eased just a little of the pain cracking my heart open. *Just a little.* I sniffled and thought about that undying loyalty the three of us shared with each other. Maybe the situation that brought us together sucked, but I loved them more than I'd ever loved anything doubled and tripled. "They really do love me. But they always have."

His shrug made it seem like he'd just solved some great mystery. "I don't got any kids, but I got a lot of friends who do, and if it makes you feel better, I don't think any of them have a fucking clue what they're doing half the time anyway. My mom sure as hell didn't."

I wasn't sure I really believed that, but I didn't feel like arguing.

"Your brother left them to you in his will?"

I nodded and slowly leaned forward to wrap my arms around my shins, my chin going to my knees. I'd accepted that trying to keep my face dry was pointless. "Yeah. It was in his and his wife's will. If anything ever happened to the both of them, I'd be their guardian, not my parents or the other set of grandparents. Me. Those idiots. I never even had a dog before them." Thinking back on the months after Rodrigo passed weren't something I liked reminiscing on, especially not when I thought about Mandy, too. What had started off with me taking the boys for a little while because she'd been out of her mind had become the last permanent thing the boys had.

He nodded, still watching me with those curious eyes that weren't filled with hesitation for once. *What happened to their mom?* I could sense him asking me with his silence.

I answered him back with my own silence. There are some things you couldn't say with words.

He stared at me for a minute before something inside of him said *I get it.* "I think that says it all right there," he finally chimed in. "If you're telling me he loved his kids enough to give you the ax if he could have, he wouldn't have left them to you if he didn't think you could handle it."

No, it was Mandy who should have had them, not

me. But it did end up being me, and like he'd said, there was nothing I could do to change what was already done. "Well yeah. No one's going to love them like I do. I'm the best of the worst." I could say that. It was the truth. I'd pulled myself out of the hole I'd been in for them when other people hadn't been able to, and it had only been because of that love for those two boys who had stolen my heart before they'd even been born, that I'd managed.

His jaw moved and he asked, "They have more family, don't they? I thought I'd seen their grandparents too."

"They have another aunt, who's great, but..." I thought of their aunt and shook my head. "I probably would have taken her to court if she'd gotten them. Knowing the boys, they would have run away to come live with me. I'm their favorite." Saying the words out loud, this truth that I knew to the root of who I was, it made me feel better. Because it wasn't a lie. It was something I believed and had always believed, even if I forgot about it sometimes. Who the hell else would do a better job than me? Their other aunt? In her fucking dreams. The Larsens were the best, but couldn't handle them all the time. They were in their early seventies; they'd had their girls late in life. And my parents... they were everything good parents should be, even with their strict shit, but they'd never been the same after Rodrigo's death. That was something I'd never admitted to anyone, not even my best friend, and chances were I never would.

My neighbor made a small sound that could have

meant a dozen different things. What I noticed was that this hard, rough man seemed to lose the tightness that lived at his shoulders. He met my gaze and I didn't move it.

I smiled at him, probably the ugliest smile in the history of smiles, and he returned it faintly.

"Thank you for saying those things and making me feel better," I sniffled.

He shrugged like what he'd done was no big deal.

"I appreciate it."

"All I did was sit here." Dallas raised those shoulders again. Easy. "We all go through shit for our family that we wouldn't do for anybody else."

"That's for damn sure," I mumbled, catching on to the hook he'd thrown out and holding on because I'm nosey like that and knew little to nothing about this man who was a male figure in Josh's life. "You let your brother live with you. I'm sure you know." His brother seemed like an asshole.

Dallas shook his head and turned his attention on something across the street, the muscles in his shoulders and along his neck bunching. "My brother's been a stupid piece of shit for so long he doesn't remember how not to be one. The only reason I haven't kicked him out is because I'm the only one he's got left. Our mom's had it with him. Nana's had it with him. If I give up on him too...." He cleared his throat and glanced at me over his shoulder. His eyes were so full of some kind of imaginary weight, only I, who had the same burden, could see it. I felt like I understood. "I won't. It doesn't matter."

Goose bumps rose along my arms. Family was family, and maybe this man had been an idiot before, but we understood that heavy burden. "I haven't seen him in a while, here or at practice."

"Me neither."

I glanced at him. "You think he's okay?"

"Yeah. He's pissed off at me, nothing unusual."

And I thought my brother had been an asshole. I hesitated and wiped at my face again with the back of my hand. "Can I ask you something?"

"I don't know," was his immediate response, making me sit up a little straighter.

"You don't know what?"

"I don't know what the hell he got into a fight over that day you helped him. He wouldn't tell me. A couple of the guys in the club—"

Was he talking about the motorcycle club Trip was in?

"—said they heard he was fooling around with a married woman, but he wouldn't tell me what it was about, just that it was over and that that shit wouldn't happen again," he explained, back to that cool voice I'd heard come out of him before tonight.

"Oh." Well. That wasn't where I thought that explanation was going. Over this conversation about his brother and my brother, I laid my cheek on my knee and told him, "I'm sorry about your dad, by the way. I see how much Josh and Louie hurt from it, and it's nothing any kid should ever have to go through. I can barely get through it."

"He'd been sick for a while," he said almost

clinically, calmly, like he'd had years to deal with it and could somehow say those words without losing his shit. "My dad's best friend and some uncles were there for me a lot after his death. It made a huge difference in my life. I got through it because of them and my mom. As long as you're there for them, they'll be fine. Believe me."

We both just sat there in silence for a while, caught up in the night, in the absence of bugs and the close semblance of quiet that was possible in a neighborhood in a major city. Slowly my grief for my brother went back to that low-level hum that never completely left but became manageable.

"Thanks for putting Josh on the team," I finally got out for the first time.

Dallas sat forward, that lean, muscular upper body curling over his knees as his gaze cut to my direction. "I didn't put him on the team. He earned it," he explained.

I eyed my neighbor as I wiped the last traces of tears from my face and sniffed. "He was the best one who tried out."

Dallas look at me for a moment, his hand going up to the back of his neck as he did it, and with a twist of his mouth, he smiled for the second time, closed-mouth and everything. He didn't agree or disagree. Wuss.

"It's the truth."

His smile curved and grew, and I would swear on my life, his cheeks went a little pink. It made me grin even as my eyes felt bloated from crying so much. I hated pity parties; I didn't know how to deal with them.

"You know it. I know it. It's fine. You're trying not to play favorites. I get it." This deep chuckle, so perfect for his voice, finally sprung out of him, and it made me sniffle one last time. Before I could stop myself, I said what I'd wanted to say to him for a while now. "You know it's bullshit you suspended me from going to a practice."

The chuckle grew into a laugh. "You're still hung up on that?"

Somewhere in my conscience, I noted again that he had a really good laugh. Deep from his chest. Honest. He was still a prick for what he'd done before our truce, despite how nice he'd been to me today, but I could see myself forgiving him for it a lot faster than I would have without.

"You instigated it, and I can't play favorites. You said it." He chuckled for a moment before lowering his voice. "I haven't seen that car from the *other day* again, by the way."

The other...? Oh. Anita. Shit. "Me neither. I don't think she'll show up again. She's probably the reason why I got a migraine today to begin with. Thanks for keeping an eye out though."

"Sure." With that, he stood, brushing the back of his shorts with his palms. I made myself keep my eyes on his face. "You're gonna be fine."

"I'm gonna be fine," I confirmed and then used his words on him. "Thanks for… everything." I wondered if he'd remember that term we'd used when we met for the second time.

He must have because a smile grew out of his laugh. "Yeah, you got it." His hands went to his pockets suddenly. "I came over to see if I'd left my wallet. Mind if I take a look?"

CHAPTER THIRTEEN

"I DON'T THINK YOU BOUGHT ENOUGH BEER," MY DAD commented in Spanish.

I shot him a look over my shoulder as I poured another two bags of ice over the bottles. "*Pa*, it's Josh's birthday. Nobody needs to be getting drunk. Come on. I bought like half the sodas, waters, and juice boxes that the grocery store carried. Everyone can get Capri Sun wasted if they want."

He shot me back an expression that I had no doubt resembled mine all too well. "*Uy*. You could have bought some more, or told me and I would have."

Only in my family did adults come to a children's party expecting beer.

My dad had already paid for all the meat being grilled. He should have known better than to say something like that. Plus, I'd spent a horrifying chunk of my checking account balance on everything else for the party, and that was considering I'd gotten a discount from a client who owned party rental stuff for the moonwalk, tables and chairs. Luckily, I'd already owned the Slip-N-Slide.

I kept telling myself the only person whose happiness mattered today was Josh's. And Louie's. Everyone else could go eat a big pile of monkey shit if there wasn't enough beer to drink, damn it. What did they think I was made of? Money?

Dear God, I was turning into my mom.

"It'll be fine," I mumbled to him, slapping him on the back as I headed back into the house to grab the midnight blue tablecloth I'd been reusing for the boys' birthdays the last couple of years. Inside, my mom was hustling around the kitchen, preparing trays of vegetables and other easy finger foods I'd picked up the night before. She shot me that tight, distressed smile she always had on her face when people were going to come over.

When Drigo and I were kids and the holidays would come around, we'd hide. My mom, who was normally a very clean, very meticulous and tough-loving human being with a pretty good temper—as long as you didn't say something she didn't like or do something that embarrassed her—turned into a walking human nightmare. Not being around when she needed help wasn't very nice, but the crap that came out of her mouth when she was trying to be perfect was a lot more "not nice." A few times, Rodrigo had texted me *RUN* if he'd gotten wrangled into one of her moods.

And in this case, even though this was my house

and it was only a bunch of kids, family members, and the nearest neighbors coming... I wasn't expecting any differently. She'd complained about my lack of baseboard cleaning as soon as she had shown up, and then proceeded to walk around the house with a wet towel cleaning them, before going in my bathroom and the one the boys shared and making sure they didn't have pee and poo stains all over the walls or something.

So I wasn't ashamed of saying I had smiled at her and got the hell out of the house and her way as quickly as I could, busying myself with other things outside.

The box of decorations was right where I'd left it earlier in the living room, and I could hear the boys fighting from Josh's room, more than likely playing video games until everyone showed up.

"Guys, will you help me decorate as soon as you get a break, please?" I called out to them, pausing in the living room with my hands holding the box to listen to their response of "Five minutes!"

I knew better. "Five minutes" was open to interpretation.

"I'm serious! Right when you're done! The faster you help me, the faster you can get back to playing."

They might have groaned, but they might have not. I wasn't positive. All I heard was "Okay!" yelled back distractedly.

A girl could dream.

My mom's back was to me in the kitchen, and I speed walked as fast as possible through it and back out the door so she wouldn't catch me. She didn't. Thankfully.

Surprisingly, only a few minutes later, the boys came outside. Louie immediately asked with a frown, "What's wrong with *Abuelita*?"

To which I responded, "She's a little cuckoo during parties, Goo." The expression he shot over his shoulder as he glared at the door that led inside the kitchen made me crack up. He looked deceived and surprised. The kid had no idea my mom was crazy beneath the surface.

Between the three of us, we set up the rest of the decorations, the moonwalk looming over the yard, calling all three of our names, but somehow we focused and finished organizing everything about fifteen minutes before the time on the invitations stated the party was set to start.

"Diana, did you invite your neighbors?" my dad asked from his spot at the grill.

"Yes," I confirmed with him for the second time. My thinking was, if I invited them, they hopefully wouldn't complain when my visitors parked in front of their houses. Just two days ago, Louie and Josh had walked around, leaving invitations on doorsteps as I waited on the deck with Mac. I'd made them address the envelopes and almost died when I saw how Louie had spelled Dallas's name.

"Hello!" a female voice shouted from over the other side of the fence.

All of us—my dad, Josh, Louie, and me—all turned to look in the direction we'd heard the speaker.

And sure enough, four different people peeked over the chest-high fence. Three of them were smiling; the fourth one not so much, but they were all well-known and loved faces. At the front, the taller of the two women in the group, was the face I'd just seen on television a month or two ago. Pretty, a hair older than me, and at one point, someone I resented a lot because she was so awesome and magnificent, and I was... not.

But that had only been when we'd been little kids. My cousin was nothing short of amazing, especially because she didn't think or act like she was too cool for school. Nobody likes a stuck-up, snobby bitch, and she was nowhere even close to that. I was probably more of a stuck-up, snobby bitch than she was.

"Sal!" I yelled, waving. "Come in!"

She beamed at me, swinging her arm over the top of the fence to undo the latch and push the door open. She filed in first, followed by her mom who was my aunt, and her dad who was my dad's brother, and all the way at the end was her husband. I didn't think I would ever get used to calling that man her husband. Out of the handful of times I'd met the retired soccer player, I'd probably only been able to look him in the eye twice.

Sal smiled as she walked over, her arms extended forward like she hadn't seen me in years. Which was true, it had been almost two years since I'd last seen her in person. Living in Europe most of the year didn't leave her with a whole bunch of time to come back home. "I'm sorry for crashing the party without RSVPing—"

"Shut up," I mumbled, taking her in a hug. "I didn't even know you were in town."

"We flew in yesterday. I wanted to surprise my parents," she explained, squeezing me. Pulling back, she grinned and I grinned back at her. Despite being two inches taller than me, we'd each inherited our dads' eyes and leaner frames. Where hers was a work of lean, muscular art, mine was more a masterpiece of Pop-Tarts and good genes. Average: the story of my life. Slightly lighter skinned, which she got from her mom, and way more freckle-faced, the family resemblance was still there between my cousin and I. Our parents used to say that, when we were really young, we would tell everyone we were sisters. "Rey!" she called out over her shoulder.

Out of the corner of my eye, I could see my uncle and aunt talking to my dad, giving him hugs, and Reiner—I had a hard time not calling him by the name half the world knew him by—standing off to the side by them. At the call of his name, he said something to my dad and came over to us, all long and lean and too good-looking.

By some miracle, I managed to keep my face even. He was my favorite cousin's promised one after all. The love of her life, for real. I wouldn't hold it past her to cut someone if they put the moves on him. She might be well-off now, but she hadn't always been. You could take the girl out of the hood, but you could never take the hood out of the girl.

"Rey, you remember my cousin Diana," she stated rather than said.

"Hi," I kind of giggled for a second before catching myself and extending my hand out toward him. I couldn't be too greedy and ask for a hug; the only person I'd ever seen him hug other than Sal had been her immediate family and my mom. She'd talked about that hug for three months afterward.

"Hello," he stated evenly, shaking my hand firmly.

Switching my gaze back to my cousin so I wouldn't get caught ogling the hottest forty-two-year-old in the world too long, I grinned back at her as if a man worth over three hundred million dollars hadn't just been touching me. "Are you hungry? We have water."

"I'll take some water and some food," Sal said as Reiner reached up to place a hand on her shoulder. "Di, where's your mom? I need to tell her hi before—"

"Salomé! *Mija!*" my mom cried out from the back door at the top step.

Mija. Her daughter. God help me.

I just barely held back an eye roll. She didn't even call me that. Since Sal had gotten married, everyone in the family acted like she was a celebrity instead of the kid who had fallen out of the tree and broken her arm at our house in El Paso. My mom was probably the worst about it; it really got on my nerves. And maybe just *maybe* made me a tiny bit jealous that she was more affectionate and proud of my cousin than me.

It wasn't Sal's fault.

"Brace yourself," I whispered to her.

She elbowed me with a snort.

The next two hours went by in the blink of an eye as a few friends of Josh's from school and their parents showed up, mixed in with the family we had in San Antonio, and the young couple from next door and their kid. There must have been at least fifty people in the backyard and the birthday party was still going in full swing. We still hadn't cut cake, socked the shit out of a piñata, or opened presents.

"You need help with anything?" my cousin asked, coming up behind me with two used royal blue party plates in her hands.

I was squatting by one of the coolers, trying to rearrange more drinks inside. "That's okay. I'm done."

She watched me as I stood up, her pretty face beaming. "There're so many people here."

"I know. I'm pretty sure I don't know ten of them," I huffed, zoning in on the group of adults I really was pretty positive that I'd never met in my life. "Anybody bothering you guys?"

"No." She shook her head. "When he has his hat on, no one pays attention."

That was the thing with Sal: she didn't say *no one knows who I am*. She didn't care. My mom had shown me pictures that Sal's dad had posted online of her face on a billboard in Germany, for God's sake.

"Good, because if they are, tell them to fuck off, or tell me and I'll tell them to fuck off."

Sal laughed and tapped her elbow against mine a little too hard, but I kept my wince to myself. "The boys look great."

For probably the third time in the last couple of hours, that all too familiar knot formed in my throat. The first time had been when I'd overheard Louie in the moonwalk shouting, "This is the best party ever!" The second time had been when one of Josh's friend's moms came into the backyard and referred to me as his mom. Neither one of us had objected to the title, but I'd felt every inch of it. How could I not? I shouldn't be the one throwing the party. It should have been Rodrigo.

"Josh has grown a foot since I last saw him," she commented, her gaze on the moonwalk like she could see him through the net walls. "And Louie's still the cutest thing I've ever seen."

"I know. He really is, and he's the sweetest kid in the world."

"Josh isn't?"

I kind of gave her a side look. "When he wants to be, but he's just like Rodrigo, a smart-ass."

Her chuckle had me glancing at her, frowning.

"What?"

"Don't act like you don't know you're the smart-ass in the family."

"I am not," I scoffed.

"Sure you're not," she laughed.

"Diana?" a male voice asked from behind, pausing our conversation.

I was too distracted to piece together why the rough, male voice sounded so familiar, but I was about to turn my head over my shoulder when it clicked. He'd come.

"Hey," I said to the voice I recognized as Dallas's from the rough texture it had, fully turning around to find him a few feet away with Miss Pearl on his arm. Well. I had no idea they even knew each other, but that was pretty damn cute he'd brought her. "Miss Pearl, I'm so happy you're here."

The older woman smiled. "Thank you for inviting me, last minute and all, Miss Cruz."

And she went there. Okay. I barely held back a laugh at her brutal honesty. "Diana, please. You're welcome. Come on in and let's get you a seat and something to eat and drink," I said, walking around to take her other hand. "I'll find you later," I said to my cousin who simply nodded, head bobbing a hello at the two newcomers. Miss Pearl seemed to eye her for a second too long but followed after me.

I made eye contact with two of my other cousins who happened to be sitting at the table closest to us and mouthed, "Move it" while cocking my head to the side. Luckily, they were polite enough to move, taking their trash with them.

"You didn't tell me with enough time about the party," Miss Pearl started. There we went again. "I couldn't buy your boy a present," she apologized as we settled her into a chair at an empty table.

"Don't worry. He has so many presents already. What can I get you both to drink?"

She requested a Diet Coke and Dallas a beer after I told him what we had.

I was surprised he was here. With a beer and a red cup filled with soda in hand, I made my way back to the table, dodging a horde of kids walking through the yard with their cell phones in hand, not paying attention to where they were going.

"Here you go," I said to both, passing Dallas his

can, skipping his gaze in the process, and handing Miss Pearl her cup of diet. "Are you hungry?" I asked her. "We have *fajitas*, chicken, Mexican rice, beans, nachos…"

"I can't handle spicy. It messes with my digestion. Is any of that fine?"

"Yes, ma'am. None of it is spicy."

"I'll take some chicken and Mexican rice, whatever that is."

My lips quirked. "Okay. I'll bring you back a plate. Dallas? Anything?" I made myself ask before my mom caught me not asking and demanded to know where the hell my manners had gone.

But my neighbor turned toward the older woman instead of responding to me. "I'm gonna grab my own plate. You'll be fine, Nana?"

Wait a second, wait a second.

Nana?

She lifted those thin, gnarled fingers as I stood there and tried figuring out what the hell was going on. *Nana?* "Boy, I was born fine," the woman answered, oblivious to the questions bouncing around in my head.

Dallas raised his eyebrows but grinned that grin I'd only seen him give Louie. "If you say so."

"I say so," she confirmed, raising her entire hand to wave him off. "Go."

Fucking *Nana?* Dallas was related to Miss Pearl? Since when?

"I can get whatever you want," I started to say before he stood up, my gaze bouncing back and forth between the man and woman who lived across the street from me.

"I know you can, but I got two hands. I can help."

Nana? Focus, Diana, focus. I gestured toward the grill where one of my uncles was currently manning it, but really, I glanced at Miss Pearl one more time. I didn't see the relation. I really didn't.

We made it three feet away from the table when he asked, "Why don't you tell her your last name isn't Cruz?"

I eyed him as I snickered. "I don't know. I've told her my last name before, but she keeps calling me Miss Cruz or Miss Lopez. I just let her run with it."

He sighed and shook his head, sliding those hazel eyes toward the table. "She doesn't forget anything. Don't let her fool you. I'll talk to her about it."

Was it my imagination or were things already less awkward and more comfortable between us? I didn't think I was imagining it. Then again, nothing could bring people together quite like seeing a person bawling their eyes out and sharing stories about people who had been loved and lost.

He'd already more than proved to me multiple times he was a good man. A really good man.

"It's not a big deal. It's fine. I know what my last name is." I glanced at him just as we stopped in front of the grill. "I'm glad you came. Louie will be happy to see you."

Freshly showered and wearing clothing that wasn't wrinkled or stained for once, it brightened up everything about him. He shoved his hands into the front pockets of his jeans, and I could see the hint of a smile on his pale pink mouth. Dallas squinted a little as he asked, "Did he write my name on the invitation?"

I couldn't hold it. I burst out laughing. *"Yes."*

I could see the corners of his mouth twitch up a little more. "It said Dal-ass on it. That's how he wrote it. D-a-l-a-s-s. Dalass."

Just thinking about Louie's bad handwriting spelling out his name again made my eyes tear up. I'd let myself lose it once he and Josh had made it across the street. He wasn't picking up on the spelling thing very well, but he was trying. Who was I to knock down his best effort? Especially when it amused me to no end. "I'm so sorry. I didn't have the heart to tell him it was wrong." I gasped. "So wrong."

"Sure," he said, his mouth quirking up that much more until it was 75 percent of a grin. "It made me laugh. Don't worry about it."

I grinned at him and gestured toward the food. "You okay with Mexican food?"

"I don't know anyone who isn't okay with Mexican food."

That distracted me. I raised both my eyebrows at him, impressed. *"Tío. ¿Me das una pierna de pollo, porfa?"* I asked my uncle who had taken over the grill, before turning back to the biggest man at the party standing right next to me. "What do you want to eat?"

"Fajitas," he said in his unforgiving, inflexible English that I barely managed not to smile at.

"Y un pedazo grande de fajita, por favor," I translated, even though my uncle spoke and understood English

pretty well. He wasn't much of a talker and handed over one plate after another with the meat I'd requested.

"You all right?" Dallas asked as I led him over to the table with the sides.

"Yeah." I glanced at the hand he had loose at his side. "I never asked, how's your boo-boo?"

I'd swear on my life he laughed a little, even flexing his hand, too. "Fine. No gangrene, no nothing."

That made me snort and look up at his face. His facial hair had grown in again lately, and I couldn't say it didn't look nice. "You're welcome."

Dallas's smile was this grudging thing that only made mine grow. The more he fought being friendly with me, the more aggressive it made me. The more I wanted it. I'd never been good with people telling me I couldn't have something.

"I invited Trip, but he said he already had plans, so you're on your own today." I'd also invited Ginny, but besides her having to work, I noticed that she and Dallas weren't close for whatever reason. He probably wouldn't care that his older cousin wasn't going to show up, why bother mentioning it?

Trip's name had barely come out of my mouth when the expression on his face fell just a little, *just a little*, but he nodded. "He left for Houston."

He'd explained that to me. I gestured to the trays of food set up on the table. "Grab whatever you want from here. Like I told Miss Pearl, none of it's spicy, except the salsa and hot sauce over there on the end."

Dallas's eyes lingered on me for a moment before

he reached over to scoop rice, beans, and even the small bowl of squash my mom had insisted on putting out, onto his plate. Coming up next to him, I did the same for Miss Pearl's plate, unsure of what she'd want. His elbow brushed mine as he said, "I got Josh a gift card."

Peeking at him quickly, I lowered my gaze back at the food below me. "Thanks. You didn't have to, but I know he'll love it. He thinks he's getting too old for toys." I passed him over a wad of napkins, his light-colored eyes meeting mine dead on. "I'm sure he'll be happy to see you, too. Not just Lou."

"Sure. I don't have anything to do till later. I'll give Josh his thing when I see him," he said, continuing on as I led him back to the table where we'd left Miss Pearl, only to find my mom and Sal sitting alongside her.

"Diana, you never told me who your cousin was." Miss Pearl gaped as I set the plate in front of her.

"Sal?" I asked, taking the seat on the other side of my mom and leaning forward to be able to hear the woman. I'd spoken to Miss Pearl a handful of times, if that, since I had moved in, so I wasn't surprised there was something she didn't know about me.

"Yes." The old woman had those milky blue eyes on said cousin. "She just won the Altus Cup," she practically whispered. "Dallas, *she won the Altus Cup.* Can you believe that?"

I learned something right then: I still stereotyped other people even though I knew better, because the last person I would have expected to know anything about soccer would have been Miss Pearl. And to keep digging the dagger of shame in, the older woman kept going.

"She scored five goals!" she said to no one in particular.

I didn't even remember she'd scored that many goals in the tournament.

My cousin, who was sitting next to Miss Pearl, caught my gaze and grinned, obviously as surprised as I was by her unexpected fan. Here I'd been trying to save her from the people around our age and the one person who knew who she was was somewhere in the ninety range.

"Sal is the star in the family." I shouldn't have been surprised those words came out of my mom's mouth as she sat up a little straighter in her chair, reaching out to touch Miss Pearl's forearm. "We're all so proud of her."

I winked at my cousin, letting my mom's words go in one ear and out the other. "Yeah, Sal, we all yell for you every time we watch a game."

"Diana never liked playing sports. She didn't like getting dirty, but Salomé always knew she wanted to play. Didn't you, *mija*?"

"Diana plays outside with the boys all the time. She doesn't mind getting dirty."

I stopped breathing for a moment and stared at the man who had just spoken up. Dallas was standing behind his grandmother, looking as calm as ever with his arms crossed over his chest.

If Sal shot me a look, I wasn't sure because I was

too busy staring at my neighbor, but she quickly answered, "I did, *Tia* Rosario." Before my mom could make another barb, she leaned toward the older woman, catching her eye. "Thank you for watching. We need more fans."

"Oh, I love soccer. Especially women's soccer. The men? They're good for nothing. Now the foreign players…"

I swallowed and let my mom's words run down my back. I wasn't going to let her bother me. But somehow Dallas happened to meet my eyes and we both just stared at each other. I smiled at him tightly, and I was surprised to see him smile back just as tightly.

～

I WANTED TO CRY.

Looking out on the mess in the lawn, I felt a sob that consisted mostly of me being extra tired, fighting its way up through my insides. Somehow, someway, I managed to keep it down.

The backyard was a fucking mess. God help me. But I wasn't going to cry over it, no matter how badly I might want to, and that was *really, really* badly.

The party had moved into the house when the mosquitoes had come out hours ago, and I hadn't bothered turning on the outside lights after the moonwalk had been picked up. I hadn't wanted to see the damage and not be able to do anything about it, and I was suddenly regretting sending everyone home without forcing them to stay and help clean.

Now seeing it… it honestly looked like Woodstock after everyone had trashed the place. The yard had shit all over it, one of the trash bags had been torn open by possibly Mac, the grass was trampled… even the tree… there was something hanging from it, and I had a feeling it wasn't a streamer.

It was awful.

"Diana?" Dallas's dark head of hair was sticking out of the back door of the kitchen.

It startled me, and I forced a tense smile on my face that was 95 percent fake. "Hey. I thought you left." Hours ago, I remembered seeing him take off with Miss Pearl and holding up a hand when he caught me looking from across the yard where I'd been busy talking to the neighbors next door.

"I did," he confirmed, closing the door behind him as he paused on the stoop and swept his gaze over the yard. His eyes went wide and his "Oh shit" seemed to come straight out of my own mouth.

"Uh-huh" was all I could answer without bursting into tears.

It was a mess.

It was a fucking mess.

I thought I might have choked a little as I took it in one more time.

"You okay?" he asked.

I couldn't even look at him. The yard had me in a trance. "Sure."

"You're not okay," was the statement that came out of his mouth, dry and serious and so, so, so true.

I opened my mouth and swallowed the thick saliva

that pooled in my throat. "It's terrible." I gasped. "It's the worst thing I've ever seen."

He started to shake his head before stopping the motion and nodding instead. "Yeah."

Well, at least he wasn't bullshitting me.

I wouldn't cry over grass. I wouldn't. I just couldn't. At least not in front of anyone.

A hand briefly touched my shoulder, nearly enough to get me to turn away from the aftermath of a nuclear bomb my beloved backyard had turned into. "Hey. It'll still be there tomorrow. Don't worry about it tonight."

The little bit of neat freak in me sobbed that I couldn't leave it until the next day. I didn't want to wake up knowing what lay outside the door. But as I stared at it, I was fully aware that it would take hours to clean up. Hours and hours and a few more hours. All the swallowing in the world didn't do enough to help my suddenly swollen throat get any smaller.

"Diana?" Dallas kind of laughed. "Are you about to cry?"

"No." I didn't even believe myself.

Obviously, he didn't either because one of those rare, belly laughs of his escaped him. "I don't have anything to do tomorrow. You, me, and the boys can knock it out."

I couldn't look away from the destruction, no matter how hard I tried. "It's okay," I mumbled, swallowing an imaginary golf ball again. "I got it."

There was a pause. A sigh. "I know you got it, but I'll help." There was another pause. "I'm offering."

He'd used that soft, smooth tone that seemed so...

inappropriate on his raspy voice, and it made me glance at him, sniffling. Since when had I become this person who was the annoying kind of stubborn and didn't accept help? I hated people like that. "I wouldn't want to take advantage of you," I admitted.

It was too dark to tell whether he was staring me down or not. "You're not taking advantage. I'm offering. I've been up since five, and I'm about to keel over. All I'm asking is that you don't make me stay up all night and half tomorrow morning cleaning up. We'll do it first thing."

I must have taken too long to answer because he crossed his arms over his chest and tipped his chin down. I didn't look at his big biceps. "I won't bail," he seemed to promise, making me move my gaze away.

A small, tiny part of me didn't want to take his promise seriously.

That must have been apparent because Dallas kept going. "You look exhausted too, and Louie is already passed out on the couch. If he hears you doing stuff out here, he'll eventually wake up and wanna come help." I think he might have coughed. "I know you're not planning on molesting me, okay?"

I was so upset I couldn't even laugh. But in that moment, the exhaustion overwhelmed my inner OCD, and I nodded.

"You need help with anything else that isn't...." He lifted a hand and vaguely pointed to the disaster zone I suddenly didn't want to look at any longer.

"No. Not really. I have some food to put up, but that's about it. Thanks." Closing both eyes, I reached up to pinch the tip of my nose and thought for a second, opening one eyelid in his direction. "Did you forget something?"

Tipping his head toward the door, he answered, "No. I just got home from meeting up with some old friends in town and was in my garage about to go inside when I saw everybody had left. I wanted to check and make sure you were all good. Josh let me in." He slid his gaze toward the yard again and winced.

For the sake of my mental health, I told myself I'd imagined it.

I also made sure not to make a big deal about him wanting to come over and make sure I was good. Nope. I wasn't going to think about that for one single second more. How many times had he told me he owed me by that point?

"You have a shit ton of dirty dishes. You scrub and I'll rinse," he offered unexpectedly.

What the hell was happening? Had he backed into my car, felt guilty, and was now trying to make it up to me? "You don't have to do that—"

"I haven't eaten food that good in a long time, and I have two days' worth of dinner in the fridge your mom made me take home. I can rinse some dishes, and if you got any beer left, I'll take one afterward. Deal?"

Maybe he had hit my car. Or broken something. I didn't get why he was being so nice. Two days of food didn't seem like enough of a reason to go out of his way, especially when just about everyone had taken off with leftovers. But…

I sighed and made sure to meet his eyes. "You really don't have to be this nice to us."

Dallas's head tilted to the side just a little, and I could tell he let out his own breath in what might have been resignation. "I know it's tough being a single parent, Diana. I don't mind helping," he said. He shrugged those broad, muscular shoulders. "You three remind me of my family when I was a kid," he explained, smiling almost sadly. "It's no huge burden helping you out and getting fed at the same time."

It was the single parent thing I had working for me. All right. I'd be an idiot not to take the help he was so willing to offer.

"Deal," he said. The one word should have sounded like a question, but it didn't. Not really. It was more like he was telling me we had a deal.

Which we did. "Deal. But knowing my family, chances are, there's only a couple of beers left, but they're all yours. I won't drink them when I have the boys."

Dallas nodded and followed me inside, locking the door behind us. I started organizing the dishes as he asked, "Mind if I get one from the fridge?"

"Nope, make yourself at home," I called out over my shoulder, still arguing with myself about having him help me or not.

Soon enough, I had the plates and glasses organized on the side of the sink and partly inside of it, and Dallas came to take the spot right beside me. Like he'd suggested, I scrubbed and handed them over, letting him rinse and set them in the drying rack.

Maybe in a few months, I could invest in a dishwasher, I thought. But all it took was a look at the floors to know that was a dumb dream. I would rather get new flooring put in than get a washer. I was just tired.

"Most of the people here today were your family?" he asked after a few minutes of silence.

"Yeah. Almost all of the adults. Half the kids are related to us somehow and the other half were friends of Josh's from his new school and his last."

"He looked like he had a good time," he noted, probably remembering the image of Josh doing the Slip-N-Slide over and over again.

"He better have. I almost had to beg him to have a party to begin with. I hope Louie's okay with us going to Chuck E. Cheese's for his because I'd rather not ever do this again."

"Oh yeah?"

"Yeah. You know, it was our first birthday here at this house…." I trailed off and shrugged as I handed him a plate. "The last two years we lived in an apartment and couldn't do much there. We had to celebrate at my mom and dad's house. When I was a kid, my parents always threw me a birthday party at home. I felt like I owed him since we have our own place now that isn't tiny."

The deep grumble in his chest said he understood.

"Next time, I'll just save up more money to hire a cleaning crew afterward, or make my family stay and clean before I let them leave. I'll keep their keys hostage or something. Even my mom and dad bailed."

He laughed, and the sound seemed to travel right

along the sensitive skin at my neck. It had a beautiful, deep ring to it. When he finally spoke again, it was to say the last four words I would have expected. "I liked your parents. I could tell your mom didn't like my tattoos much, but she was still nice."

"My mom, yeah, she is really nice." And because I couldn't help myself, thinking about the incident at the table with Sal, I muttered, "As long as you aren't me."

There was a brief moment of awkward silence, and I thought I had gone too far talking about my mom, but then Dallas said, "I kinda noticed she gives you a hard time."

I hummed. "Thanks for defending me, by the way." Did I sound as bitter as I felt? "What she doesn't remember or tell everyone is how when I was younger, she would get mad when I'd go outside and get dirty. She'd say that's what boys did, but girls weren't supposed to do that kind of stuff. There was a brief phase when she didn't let me wear pants, if you can believe that, but it didn't last long." Just thinking about that made a nerve somewhere on my face throb.

I sighed. "She just... thinks I do everything wrong. She always has, and for a long time, I did do a bunch of stupid stuff. I'm not my cousin or my brother, and I never will be. I think it's her weird way of pushing me, but sometimes all she does is make me feel like I can't do anything right and I never will." I coughed, embarrassed I'd even said that out loud. "That was deeper than I wanted it to go. Sorry. It's fine. We've always had a weird relationship. We still love each other." When we didn't want to kill one another.

God. Had I really told him all that? Why?

"You think she likes your cousin and your brother more?"

I scoffed. "I know she does. My brother was awesome. She always said he was her treasure. Her miracle. It's fine. I was the accident baby that almost killed her." Now that I thought about it, maybe she did have a good reason for me not being her favorite. Huh.

"But your cousin? The one that was here today? You think she likes her more?"

"Yes." Of course she did.

"Why?"

Why? Was he serious? Had he been zoned out the entire time we sat at the table with Miss Pearl talking about Sal's achievements? "Do you know who she is?"

"Your cousin."

"No, ding-dong—"

The laugh that cut out of him was loud and abrupt, and it made me laugh. Standing there so close together, his body heat against the side of mine, for some reason, only made me laugh more.

"I'm sorry. I spend way too much time with the boys. No. I mean, yes, she's my cousin. But she's like the best female soccer player in the world, and I'm not just saying that because she's family. They have huge posters of her plastered all over Germany. When you watch anything with women's soccer, they're going to have her on there in some way. She's the kind of person, when you have a daughter, you tell her *be like Sal*. Shit, I tell Josh all the time to be like her. She's one of the best people I've ever met. I get why my mom loves her. It makes sense."

His elbowed bumped my upper arm by accident. "She's married to that famous soccer guy, isn't she?"

"Yes." I shot him a look. "He was here almost all day with her."

He stopped what he was doing and turned that big upper body to face me. I wasn't going to admire how impressive it was. Nope. "You're fucking with me," he scoffed.

"No. Did you see the guy with the hat sitting with her parents and some of my family? The tall one? The only other white—Caucasian—man that wasn't chasing after little kids?"

He nodded.

"That was him."

"What's his name again?" he asked.

Blasphemy. I wasn't even a big soccer fan but still. "I'm going to tell you the same thing I tell Josh: when you ask a really stupid question, you're not getting an answer."

That had my neighbor bursting out with another laugh that made me think I didn't know him at all. Not even a little bit. God, he really did have a great laugh.

For a married man.

A married man, I repeated to myself.

The look he gave me over his shoulder as he handed me a plate, still chuckling, made my stomach warm. "You shouldn't sell yourself short. There're some people who you'll never make happy no matter what you do," he said to me so evenly, I glanced up at him. It sounded like he'd learned that from experience.

"Buttercup, I'm hungry," came Louie's sleepy voice from somewhere close behind us.

He was standing right where the vinyl flooring of the kitchen met the carpeted flooring of the living room. "Give me a second to finish these dishes, but what do you want? Cereal or leftovers?"

"Chicken nuggets."

I crossed my eyes and faced forward again. "Cereal or leftovers, Goo. We don't have chicken nuggets."

"Okay. Cereal." Silence. Then he added, "Please."

"Give me a few minutes, all right?"

Louie agreed and disappeared.

Dallas's elbow hit me again as he rinsed off the second to last dish. "Why does he call you Buttercup?"

I laughed, remembering exactly why. "My brother used to call me that, but when Louie was still really little, my best friend used to babysit the boys, and they'd watch cartoons together. There's this one we used to watch when we were probably thirteen called *The Powerpuff Girls*, and she'd take those DVDs over for them to watch. It's these three little girls with superpowers, right? One of them is named Blossom, she was the nice, levelheaded one, and he said that was my best friend, Vanessa. And there's another one named Buttercup. She has dark hair, and she's the most aggressive of the bunch. She's the loudmouth, tough one, and for some reason or another, Louie just insisted that was me. He's been calling me Buttercup ever since."

"But why did your brother call you that?"

I shot him a look out of the corner of my eye. "I

used to watch *The Princess Bride* all the time and used to say I was going to marry someone just like Westley someday."

He made a choking sound.

"Shut up," I muttered before I could help myself.

Dallas made another sound that was something between a cough and a laugh. "How old were you?"

"How old was I what?"

"When you watched it all the time?"

I smiled at the dishes. "Twenty-nine?"

He laughed as he set the last plate on the drying rack at his side, his body turning in my direction as he raised his eyebrows, giving me this little smirk. "You remind me more of Princess Peach."

I looked down at my shorts and tank top, and caught the ends of my multicolored brown hair courtesy of careful instruction to Ginny. "Because of my beautiful pink gown and blonde hair?"

Dallas's mouth went flat. "She's surrounded by men, but she's still herself, and she's got her shit together on Mario Kart."

I couldn't help but smile, taking in the sloping bone structure of his face and the way his mouth was shaped at a slant and said, "I always did think I should have been born a princess, Mr. Clean."

The choke that came out of him made me laugh.

"Mr. Clean?" he eventually got out, all choppy and broken.

Peeking at him, I shrugged and tipped my chin toward his head.

"I have hair."

I squinted at him and hummed, trying so hard not to laugh. "Uh-huh."

"I shave it every two weeks," he tried explaining.

"Okay," I coughed out, my cheeks hurting from the effort not to laugh at how bent out of shape he was getting.

"It all grows in evenly—*are you laughing at me?*"

CHAPTER FOURTEEN

"Lou, you wanna go with me and see if Miss Pearl and Mr. Dallas want to come eat dinner with us?" I asked.

His hands paused on the remote in his hands as he seemed to mull over my proposal. "Mr. Dallas?"

"Yes." Josh was over at his friend Kline's house, so it was just the two of us. "Since he helped us with the backyard earlier," I explained.

While I'd been in the middle of a shower, I came up with the idea of inviting him over for dinner as a thank-you for helping us clean up the yard hours ago. It was the least I could do. I knew he had leftovers, but that way they would last longer. He'd shown up at ten o'clock on the dot and stuck around for the next two hours, going above and beyond the neighborly and friendly call of duty.

Problem was, I didn't want to make him feel weird. So I figured, why not invite his nana too? The nana I still didn't understand he had.

With more grace than I figured the average five-year-old was capable of, Louie nodded. "Okay."

"Okay, come on." I gestured toward the door, and Mac, who was lying on the couch besides my kid, sat up, expectantly thinking he was going to get another walk. "I'm making your favorite at least, buster."

"Chicken nuggets?" he gushed.

I blinked at him. "Spaghetti and meatballs."

His shoulders slumped forward. "Oh. Yeah. I like that too."

I sighed. "Let's go."

He followed me, pausing his game as he got to his feet. He'd dressed himself this morning and had on a bright green T-shirt with a pizza on it and red and black striped pajama pants. I thought about telling him to change, but who cared? It was only dinner.

Louie and I crossed the street, holding each other's hands. I reached down and pinched him on the butt as we walked up the path to Dallas's house, and halfway up the steps to the porch, the little turd smacked me on the butt. We were bickering as I knocked on the door and stood back, waiting. I wasn't even sure if he was home or not. I was sticking my tongue out at Louie as the lock was turned.

I faced the door as it opened, expecting it to be a certain brown-haired, hazel-eyed man that I owed big time....

But it wasn't him on the other side of the screen door.

It was a woman. A pretty, natural auburn-haired woman, and she was smiling. "Hi," she said.

It took me maybe two seconds, but I managed to get out, "Hey. Is—"

The door opened wider and the woman stepped back as another face I recognized came forward with his eyebrows furrowed and the sides of a thinner mouth turned down into a frown. "Yeah?" was the ugly, unfinished greeting I got from the man I hadn't seen in a while. Jackass Jackson.

"Hi. Is Dallas here?" I asked slowly, with as much patience as I could drag together—which wasn't much, especially when this small part of my brain wondered if the woman was here with Jackson or... not.

She couldn't be. Could she? Dallas wouldn't do that, would he?

"What do you want?" Mr. Not-Mr.-Rogers asked.

I blinked and ground down on my teeth. "To talk to him."

"Hold on," Jackson droned, scowling as he closed the door in my face.

"Why is he so mean?" Lou asked almost immediately.

I shrugged at him and whispered, "Someone didn't take a chill pill today."

Moments later, the door opened wide. Dallas stood there, an uncomfortable expression on his face that didn't sit well with me. "Hey." His eyes landed on Lou and his smile got a little easier. "Hey, Lou."

"Hi."

"Hey. I didn't know you had company again, sorry," I explained quickly.

"Don't apologize," he said crisply. "He just got

here."

Did that mean the woman had already been there?
It's none of my business. None.

"Well, we just came by to see if you wanted to come by for dinner as a thank-you for helping us clean up this morning," I explained.

I tried not to let the way he barely scrunched up his nose hurt my feelings, but it did, just a little.

"I was going to invite Miss Pearl, too. We're making spaghetti and meatballs."

Lou whispered, "We?"

"But if your brother and your friend are over, obviously, stay with them," I said to the older man.

Dallas's head tipped to the side and his hand went up to pull at the collar of his T-shirt for a second, the tips of his fingers brushing against the bottom of the eagle head that I was pretty sure started right at the sensitive notch at his throat. "Uh…." He trailed off.

She was here with him. This lying, cheating, douchebag who had given me a hard time when he was…. *It's none of my business. None.*

"Don't worry about it," I rushed out. "You can get leftovers another day if you want. I figured you wouldn't take my money if I offered it." My voice sounded a little tight and weird but not too horrible. "Unless you do."

Dropping his hand to his pockets, Dallas took a step forward, closing the door behind him. His foot propped the screen door open as he locked his gaze on me. He wasn't wearing any shoes, and I noticed how big his feet were. "It's not that. I'd like dinner, and I'm sure Nana Pearl would too, it's just... Jackson and his girl of the week just got here. I haven't seen him in a couple of weeks."

Why it felt like a weight had been lifted off my chest, I had no idea. But I could feel the difference. What were the chances he wouldn't see it?

"I get it," I croaked out before clearing my throat. *Get it together.* Was he trying to get me to invite Jackson and his friend over too? I couldn't tell. That didn't seem like Dallas behavior, but... I was such an idiot. Why would I think he'd actually have a woman over?

Because I was an idiot. That was why. Shit.

Like with most decisions in my life, I thought of my mom and what she would tell me to do and sighed. "Come over. It should be ready in an hour. You can bring him and his friend if you want. I mean, I'm not Italian and my spaghetti isn't amazing, but this little squirrel thinks it's all right."

"It's *good*," my mini partner in crime chimed in.

Dallas's mouth twitched as he glanced at the boy. "You think so, bud?"

Lou nodded, totally exaggerating. "Almost as good as chicken nuggets," he confirmed.

"Better than chili?"

There was no hesitation. "No."

I slanted him a look.

Raising his gaze back to me, my neighbor let out a sigh. "You sure about inviting them? He's...." That hand went back to his collar to tug, exposing more of that brown ink over surprisingly tan skin. He swallowed a lot harder than I would expect he needed to do. "There's a lot of sh—tuff you don't know."

I raised my hand, understanding his hesitation and knowing it was completely because Louie was with me. Whatever he wanted to say, he didn't want to say in front of him. So I did what any adult would do—I put my hands over Louie's ears. "He's not going to kill us or anything, right?" I asked.

Dallas blew out a breath as the corners of his mouth bunched into a frown. "I'd never let that happen," he stated so evenly, so matter-of-fact, this ripple of who-the-hell-knows-what shot up the nerves of my spine.

He's just a nice guy. He's married. He has a soft spot for single moms.

You are no one special, Diana, I reminded myself. *You are no one special.*

I cleared my throat and gave him a smile that was really fucking tight, my hands dropping from their spot on Louie's ears. "Okay. Then, it's fine. All three of you can come. We're going to drop by Miss Pearl's after this to invite her."

"Sure?" Both of his eyebrows went up.

"Sure."

~

"You smell like garlic."

"You smell like fart."

Louie choked like he couldn't believe what I'd said before bursting out laughing, his hands busy holding several forks. "You're mean!"

That had me grinning from across the table. "Okay,

you smell like a cute fart. Like a little baby fart."

"Babies smell."

"When have you smelled a baby?"

"With Grandma and Grandpa."

In the middle of setting the table, I stopped. "Are you lying to me?"

"No!"

I really doubted he'd smelled a baby—and really, babies smelled great most of the time, at least until you had to clean their diapers. I'd done my fair share of diaper duty, especially with Josh, but I was positive I'd done it with either a smile on my face or a grimace just because it smelled so awful. Formula poop was the worst.

"Speaking of your grandma and grandpa, don't forget you're staying with them for a week when I go visit Vanny, okay?" This was probably the third time I'd brought my trip up since buying my round-trip ticket to San Diego. I wanted him mentally prepared so he wouldn't assume I was never coming back.

"Can I go with you?" he asked.

"Not this time."

"Why?"

"Because you have school?" I grinned, eyeing him.

He pouted, his upper body deflating.

"We can all try to go visit her another time."

A knock on the door had me raising my eyebrows at Lou and had Mac barking. I grabbed him by the collar and led him toward the back door, so he could hang out in the yard while Miss Pearl was over here. He was great with strangers, but I didn't trust his crazy tail around a ninety-something-year-old. "Make sure it's the neighbors and then let them in, please. Leave the forks so I can set them really quick." I could already picture him running through the house with those tines aimed at his face.

"Okay," he answered, dropping the silverware damn near instantly and running toward the front of the house.

A moment later, the sounds of familiar voices came from the doorway in the living room, and I peeked around to see Dallas, Miss Pearl, and the man whose ass I'd saved, in the living room. The woman was nowhere in sight. Louie was standing right by Miss Pearl, shaking her hand. It almost made me cry.

Setting the rest of the silverware as quickly as I could, I headed toward them, suddenly a little nervous. What if they hated my cooking?

"Hi, Miss Pearl," I greeted the older woman first, taking her cool hands as she extended them in my direction.

"Thank you for inviting us over, Diana."

I nodded and pulled back, my gaze going immediately to Dallas. The first thing that caught my eye was that he was wearing a button-down plaid shirt. It was the most clothes I'd seen on him. The brown and black pattern made his eyes pop. Hell, they might have made my heart pop if that was a possibility. But it wasn't. It absolutely wasn't.

"Hi again," I said to him.

It was right then that I noticed how tight the skin around his eyes was despite the muscles of his cheeks shaping his mouth into a smile. "Thanks for having us...." He trailed off and glanced at the man standing next to him, forcing me to do the same.

Without the screen door between us and now that I'd spent more time with Dallas, the brothers' resemblance was kind of amazing.

Except... despite knowing Dallas was the older one, he didn't look like he was. Not at all. Jackson had more gray in his hair, his forehead more lined... but it was his eyes that aged him the most. There was something fundamentally different about the man who stood an inch shorter than my neighbor. There was just something radiating from him that seemed off. The way his presence made me feel reminded me of when Josh wanted something and I told him he couldn't have it and he pouted over it.

"Jack, you've met Diana."

Oh, we'd definitely met.

To give him credit, he extended his hand toward me even though he looked like he wanted to do everything other than that. I took his hand in mine and shook it, ignoring the way Jackson damn near rolled his eyes. I trusted Dallas, enough at least to let this man into my house.

"Nice to see you again," I lied, taking my hand back.

"You too," the man kind of grumbled, lying too, his eyes going to his hand briefly before he tucked it into his pocket.

At least we both felt the same way about each other.

I glanced at Dallas's face as he stared hard at his

brother. Huh. "Ready to eat?"

Silently, we headed over to the dining room, nestled in between the living room and kitchen. I wasn't going to deny it. It was awkward. From Miss Pearl taking a seat as she scowled at something on the table—maybe I should have put names in front of the plates, I didn't know—to the expression the two brothers shared, the weirdness was there. It was definitely alive and well.

"Need help?" Dallas asked as he stood behind Miss Pearl's seat after pushing her chair in.

"I've got it. There're only two more things I need to grab," I explained, watching as Lou slipped out of his chair and darted into the kitchen ahead of me. "I have help already. Thanks."

I'd barely taken a step into the kitchen when Louie said, "I can help, *Tia*." Grabbing the bread I'd left warming in the oven, I slipped the sticks onto a plate and handed them over to him with a wink before nabbing the meatballs from the oven too.

The head of the table had been left empty and somehow Louie ended up sitting next to Miss Pearl while Dallas took the seat closest to mine with his brother on his right. I had to fight the urge to rub my hands over my pants. Fuck it. "We don't usually pray, but if you want to…"

Miss Pearl guffawed. "Us neither. Amen."

And with that, I started scooping pasta onto her plate first, following it up with sauce and meatballs. Dallas asked Louie for his plate and added pasta, and then taking the ladle from me, he put meatballs with a little marinara drizzled. "Is that good, Louie?" he asked my boy first, and then, "How many breadsticks do you want?"

"Parmesan?" I asked my neighbor, still watching the other two out of my peripheral vision.

"Load me up, if you will," the older woman confirmed.

I was in the middle of sprinkling cheese when Dallas slipped my plate out from in front of me and started adding food onto it. "You want more?" he asked me just as I set the plate in front of his grandmother.

"Yes, please," I said before telling him when to stop. No one, besides my mom, had ever served me food before. No one.

His wife was an idiot. His wife was a giant, fucking idiot with a little crazy sprinkled in.

Dallas finished serving me, then himself, and finally handed the serving utensils over to his brother. None of us talked much as we ate, but Dallas met my gaze more than a few times while we did, and we shared a smirk or two.

"I like my meatballs with more thyme and my sauce with more garlic, but I would come over for dinner again if you invited me," Miss Pearl noted in that brutally honest way of hers as she was finishing up the food on her plate.

All I could do was hold back and smile and nod, biting the inside of my cheek the entire time. "Thanks."

"I'm full," Lou moaned from his spot.

I eyed his plate. "Two more bites, please."

He sighed, blinked at his plate a couple of times, and nodded, shoveling the smallest forkful I'd ever seen into his mouth. Smart-ass.

"Any dessert?" Miss Pearl piped up.

Dessert? Shit. "I have vanilla ice cream."

She was dabbing at the corners of her mouth when she answered, "That sounds lovely."

"Okay."

"Dallas, Jackson, would you like some?"

"I'd love some," Dallas replied quickly, not so subtly eyeing his brother.

Jackson...

"No." Silence. "Thank you."

I nodded and headed into the kitchen. What the hell was wrong with that guy? Was he just embarrassed about what happened months ago? Someone needed to grow up.

I was in the middle of pulling the package of cones out of a cabinet when I heard, "Need help?" In what I now thought of as his usual spot, Dallas had a hip against the counter closest to the dining room, looking even bigger than ever before in his dark shirt.

"Sure. The ice cream is in the freezer, if you can grab it."

Dallas dipped his head before going for the container as I found the scooper in a drawer. He handed it over while I pulled out a cone. I only managed to put one scoop into the first cone before I broke down. "Is your brother still mad about the *thing* outside your place or does he hate everyone?" I whispered.

There was no hesitation in his response, but he did lower his voice. "He hates everyone."

I couldn't help but snicker as I snuck him a quick glance. "I guess that makes me feel better."

His chuckle was so low I could barely hear it, but it made me grin as I dug the metal spoon into the container. Dallas took the cone from me and handed me a new one. "He was a kid when our dad died. He handled it really bad," he explained quietly, his voice a gentle rumble. "I left for the navy and he didn't take that well either. Things went downhill from there."

Something about that didn't sound right. "Downhill how?"

His little hum didn't sit well with me. "He's been in jail."

My hand only paused for a second halfway inside the container. "For what?"

"Mostly drugs."

Mostly drugs. What the hell did that mean? How many times had that fucker been in jail?

"He hasn't messed around with that in a while," Dallas quickly explained as he must have noticed me not moving. "You don't have anything to worry about."

Was this the reason Ginny had been all "Jackson is there" in a gaspy voice? Why wouldn't she bring it up again? Why hadn't Trip said something?

Had he even been at the house when Trip had come by?

"You said people can change," Dallas whispered, taking a step closer to me, forcing me to tuck my elbow into my side as I looked up at his face.

I had, hadn't I?

"He isn't doing illegal shit anymore. All he does is have a bad attitude, but I'm trying to help him get his life together. I know you don't have any reason to trust me, but I promise, you have nothing to worry about with him and the team, much less with him staying at my house."

He was right, I didn't have a reason to trust him, but for some reason, a soon as I thought that, I accepted that I did. Every single thing that had ever come out of his mouth, and every action I'd ever seen him commit, had been one based on loyalty or what was right.

And that acknowledgment was a little terrifying. I trusted Dallas. When the hell had that happened?

To make matters worse, I told him. "Okay. I trust you."

No sooner had the words come out of my mouth than I realized why they felt so strange. Trust felt a whole lot like love. You were giving someone a part of you, if you really thought about it. Which I wasn't.

But when Dallas's brown-green eyes met mine, slightly widened, I'd swear he stood a little taller. And he nodded, saying only one word, "Okay."

CHAPTER FIFTEEN

I LOOKED AT MY SHORTS, AND THEN I LOOKED AT THE WEATHER app on my phone.

According to the screen, it was ninety-four degrees out today. In October. Fucking global warming.

I looked at my shorts again, held them in my hands, taking in the ragged hem for a minute and said, "Fuck it." I'd worn things a lot shorter when I was eighteen. This pair had been with me for the last five years, and I still wore them on a regular basis. The thing was, I usually tried to avoid anything higher than my knees at Josh's games or practices because, while the boys didn't blink twice at me running around the house with only a big T-shirt on or sleep shorts, some boys weren't used to that.

God knew my mom had never worn shorts while I was growing up. She made faces any time I put on anything that wasn't a respectable skirt or loose pants. I could still remember what her face had resembled when skinny jeans and leggings had gotten popular. You would have figured I'd been naked.

It was going to be hot as hell today, and I wasn't going to be showing anybody anything they hadn't seen a hundred times before simply going to the mall. And Josh and Lou had never told me anything about the clothes I wore—except for this one red dress I'd put on to go out with some friends from my going-out days that pretty much made me look like a prostitute. "No" was the one and only thing Josh had told me that night a year and a half ago before pointing in the direction of my room. "No, no, no," he'd repeated again, shaking his head. "No, Aunt Di."

Adjusting the straps of my bra so that they were hidden under my brand new Tornado T-shirt with CASILLAS screen-printed on the back, I slipped on my flip-flops just as Josh yelled, "Are you ready?" from down the hall.

Luckily, I'd already packed the cooler for our day at the park, collected a couple of magazines to look through for new hairstyling ideas, and charged up my tablet so I could catch a couple of episodes of *The Office* when there was nothing else to do but sit around. I had this competitive baseball thing all figured out.

I rushed out of my room, finding Josh in the living room already standing by the door. He was pumped and ready for his first game in months. "You got everything?" I asked as I grabbed the handle of the blue cooler with one hand and the strap of my oversized tote with the other; it was also filled with sunblock, an extra battery pack for my cell, nuts, a hand towel, bug spray, and two ponchos in their small plastic containers.

"Yeah," he answered in that same easy, confident tone he always used... even when he was lying out of his teeth.

I blinked down at him. "Did you grab an extra pair of socks?"

Josh tipped his head back and groaned. "No." Dropping his bag, he ran toward his room. In no time, he was back out, stuffing the extra socks he was always forgetting into his bag. The kid had sweaty feet and needed an extra pair, especially on a day like today.

"Okay, let's go," I said, motioning him forward.

I locked the front door as he threw his things into the back. Glancing in the direction of Dallas's house, I noticed his truck was gone. The fields where the tournament was happening that weekend were almost an hour away, and Josh and I listened to music on my playlist the entire ride, singing along softly half the time. Josh and I were both still half asleep. Our resident ray of sunshine was spending the weekend with my parents at a family member's house in Houston instead of frying under the sun with us.

At the park, we climbed out of the car, yawning. Josh grabbed his bag and then helped me lower the cooler out of the back, tiredly smiling at me when our eyes met. I held my hand out, palm up, right in front of him, and he smacked it.

"I love you, J," I said.

He blinked sleepily. "Love you too."

And in that way that Josh and I had—my oldest

nephew, my first real love—we hugged each other, side to side, by the car. While Louie might be the sun, Josh was the moon and the stars. He was my gravity, my tide, my ride or die. He was more like my little brother than my nephew, and in some ways, we had grown up together. I had loved him from the moment I laid eyes on him. Loved him from the moment I knew he was a spark of life, and I was going to love him every day of my life.

He pulled back after a tight squeeze of my middle. "Okay, let's go."

We went.

By the time we found the group of Tornado members clustered around one of the picnic tables at the center of the three baseball fields, I was already sweating. "Morning," I greeted all the parents and kids who turned to look at us as we walked over to them. I didn't miss the long look two moms shot at me as their gaze went from my mostly bare legs to my face and back. Haters. I also didn't miss the inappropriately long look one of the dads, who I knew was separated from his wife, shot me either. I just chose to ignore them. I wasn't doing anything wrong.

Taking a seat on one of the nearest picnic tables, I waited for the coaching staff to arrive. Dallas was the first one to get there. He had two duffel bags hanging over each shoulder, an orange water cooler balanced in his hands, and his sunglasses and baseball cap on. He was wearing a red Polo shirt that had the team's emblem and what I figured was his name embroidered on it. And just like usual, he had his holey cargo shorts and tennis shoes on. I noticed him glance in my direction and tip his chin up, but he didn't greet me as he headed straight to the main congregation of parents and kids, and eventually broke off to walk the boys over to an empty patch of grass to start warming up. There was still well over an hour left until the tournament started, and I knew there was no rush to move toward whatever field would be used first until later.

I sat there for the next hour flipping through a magazine and browsing random stuff on my phone. When I noticed a few of the other moms getting up and start making their way over to one of the fields, I grabbed my things and followed after them. Parking the cooler on the floor beside the second row, I hopped up and took a seat to wait. Josh was on home, catching the balls the pitcher was throwing at him to warm up, but it wasn't going so well. The pitcher was throwing the ball too high every single time. After about the tenth time, Josh had to get up and run after it. Trip, who had showed up minutes ago, waved the pitcher over to talk with him, giving Josh a break.

Standing up, I snagged a bottle of water from my cooler and walked over to the fence separating and protecting the audience from the game and players. "Josh!" I hissed over at him, the fingers of my free hand clinging to one of the links. Out of the corner of my eyes, I caught the big, male figure that belonged to Dallas standing by third base talking to one of the moms that had been giving me a bitch face earlier. It was the Christy woman I was pretty sure, if I had my hair color correct.

Josh turned around immediately, ripping his facemask off, and walked toward me, his palms facing upward as I tossed the bottle up high to go over the fence. "Thanks," he answered, right after catching it.

"Did you put sunblock on?" I asked.

He nodded, the bottle glued to his mouth as he guzzled a third of it down.

I couldn't help myself. "On your face too?"

"*Yes,*" he replied, one eye narrowed.

"Just checking, attitude," I muttered, noticing the mom who had been talking to Dallas turn around and head over in our direction. It only took a moment for my brain to process who the parent was.

It was definitely Christy, the person who had gotten me suspended weeks ago.

From the way her face was tilted down, even with a pair of aviator glasses on, her attention was focused on the lower half of my body. Something in my brain recognized that this wasn't going to go well, but something else in my brain said that I needed to behave. I could be an adult. I was not about to get suspended again, damn it.

So I smiled at her and said, "Hi," even though I was grinding down on my back teeth, expecting the worst. Where I'd last seen him, Dallas was standing by third base, his head facing our direction. I could tell his forehead was wrinkled, but he didn't make a gesture to move. What was this about?

I'd only seen him at practice once in the week since he, Jackson, and Miss Pearl had come over for spaghetti. We had waved at each other since then and that was it. I could have stayed after practice to talk to him, but by that time rolled around, I still had two boys to feed and put in bed. I didn't have time to wait around for the other parents to give me a chance to talk. I didn't take it personally that he wasn't shouting from the rooftops that we were friends and spent time outside of practice together. There was also that big thing that always seemed to hang around my thoughts while we were at practice: the last thing I wanted was any kind of drama from the other parents thinking something dumb about us.

"Josh, go finish warming up," I told him when Christy didn't return my greeting as she came to a stop at an angle to me on the other side of the fencing. Josh frowned as his gaze bounced back and forth between the other mom and myself. "Everything is fine."

Josh hesitated for one more second before nodding and putting his facemask back on, taking the bottle of water with him.

Before I could even open my mouth to ask what was going on, her words came at me, sharp and straight like an arrow. "You need to go change."

I blinked. "What?"

"Your shorts, Diana. They're inappropriate," the mom, who hadn't spoken to me once since our incident, said.

I went from one to ten instantly, courtesy of her words and choice of tone that was 100 percent bitchy and nothing else. I didn't like her to begin with, so my patience was already in the negatives by the time she'd opened her mouth. But I tried my best to be mature. "I'm a grown woman, and they're not that short or inappropriate," I told her coolly, my hands instantly going to my sides. My fingertips were on the hem of my shorts with my hands straight down; it wasn't like I was palming a bunch of bare thigh.

"I wasn't asking what you thought about them," she said, her reflective sunglasses flicking down to my thighs once more. "I don't want Jonathan being exposed to *that*."

Be mature. Be an adult. Be an example to Josh, Diana, I tried telling myself. I'd say I only halfway failed. "What is *that*? Thighs? Half of a woman's thighs that he's seen every time you've taken him somewhere?" That sounded a lot more smart-ass than I'd intended it to.

She could obviously tell because I could sense the tension coming off her body. "I don't know what kind of places you take Josh, but I don't take my Jonny any places like that. There's children here. This isn't a brothel."

A brothel. Had this bitch really just said *brothel?* As in I worked at one or hung around one? *Really?*

I glanced over my shoulder because she was talking so fucking loud. Couldn't she use her inside voice and just *talk* to me? I wasn't surprised to see about eight sets of parents staring at us. Listening. So I asked her one more time to make sure I wasn't imagining anything, "Excuse me?"

"Go buy some pants," she said so fucking loud, I'm sure the opposing team heard her. In a whisper, with her eyes straight on me, she said, "Look, honey, I know you're Josh's *aunt,* but if you're looking for a husband, this isn't the place. Some of us are *real moms.* Look around. We're not dressed like hookers, are we? Maybe you could learn something about real parenting from us."

Someone cackled loudly enough for me to hear.

My entire body went hot, red hot.

I didn't give very many people the power to hurt my feelings, but Christy's comment went directly to my heart. *Real mom.* It was the real mom that pierced straight through me, robbing the breath from my lungs and the anger from my head.

Realistically, I knew my ass wasn't anywhere close to hanging out. I knew that. It didn't matter that there had been a handful of moms on Josh's old team that made the girl on *Dukes of Hazard* look like a pilgrim. In that moment right then, I *was* the only one with *some* bare leg exposed *and it wasn't even that fucking much.*

I cleared my throat, fighting back the pressure squeezing at my lungs and the heat covering every inch of my skin. What example did I want to set for Josh? That he always needed to come out on top? Some things were worth winning and other things were not. With every inch of self-control in my body, I tried holding on to the very edges of my maturity, because if someone was an asshole to you, you didn't always have to be an asshole back.

"Christy," I said her name calmly, "if you want to talk to me about my clothes"—*fuck off and go to hell,* I said to her in my brain but in reality I went with

—"don't raise your voice at me. I'm not a child. While we're at it, you don't know anything about me or Josh, so don't make it seem like you do."

Of all the replies she could have gone with, she chose, "I know enough about you."

While I'd been friendly with the parents on Josh's old team, none of them had ever been close enough to me to know what happened to turn us three into a family. All they knew was that I was raising Josh and Louie, and that had come up because there were Spanish-speaking parents on the team who overheard him calling me *tia* all the time. When they'd ask, I told them the truth. I was their aunt. I didn't care what they thought; they could all assume whatever they wanted.

"You don't know anything," I practically whispered to her, balanced somewhere between being upset and really pissed. "I don't want to embarrass you or make you feel like an idiot, so please stop while you're ahead with the comments. Talk to me like an adult, because I bet your son is looking over here right now, and we want to teach the boys how to be good people, not big mouths with opinions and a lack of information."

It was her turn for her face to go red and she pretty much squawked at me, "You're going to embarrass me? You embarrassed yourself and Josh coming to a tournament dressed like that. Have a little respect for yourself, or respect for whoever was reckless enough to let you watch their kids."

To a certain extent, I knew what she was saying wasn't the truth, but her words were a brutal reality that managed to pick at those frayed little ends inside of me. Sticks and stones might break your bones but words could also hurt you. A lot. A lot more than they should have because I knew she didn't know *anything*.

But even being aware of all of that, this knot formed in my throat, and before I could stop it, my eyes got misty.

I looked at the fencing to the side away from her as two tears jumped out of the corners of my eyes and streamed down one cheek before I wiped them away with the back of my hand almost angrily. I think I lasted there in front of her all of five seconds before two more tears crashed down my cheeks, falling from my jaw to my chest. It wasn't until I felt my lip start to quiver that I swallowed and turned away from her, embarrassed—humiliated—and feeling so small I could have crawled into a hole and stayed there forever. Worst, I couldn't even argue with her points.

Instead of doing all the things I should have done in retaliation, I turned around and started walking away.

"Diana!" I heard Dallas yell.

One second later, I heard, "*Aunt Di!*" But I couldn't stop.

I speed walked away from the bleachers, my face angled toward the ground. One tear after another slid down my cheeks, falling into my mouth and then down my chin to my chest. My vision went blurry as I stared at the sidewalk before catching a glimpse of the small building where the restrooms were located, and I pretty much darted into it just as three times as many more tears came out of me.

I couldn't breathe. I couldn't even find it in me to make a noise as my back hit the cement wall in the bathroom. My hands went to my knees as I hunched over, my heart cringing and flexing. Aching.

Who was I kidding? I was a fuckup. I was going to ruin the boys. What the hell was I doing raising them? Why hadn't I just let the Larsens take them? I didn't know what I was doing. I couldn't even manage not to embarrass them. I thought that I'd stopped making so many stupid decisions, but I was wrong.

God.

I cried more and more and more, silent tears that didn't clog my throat because it was already full of shame and guilt and anger at myself.

Even as a little kid, I either got mad or I cried if I was embarrassed before I got angry.

"Aunt Di?" Josh's voice was hesitant and whispered, but so familiar it cut right through my thoughts.

I wiped at my face with the back of my hand, keeping my gaze on the cement floor. "I'm okay, Josh," I called out in a weak, hoarse voice that said I wasn't.

He didn't reply, but the sound of cleats clacking on the floor warned me he was coming before I saw him peek around the edge of the wall. His small face was soft and worried, his mouth and eyes downturned. "*Tia*." The word came out of him in a hiss, a claim.

"I'm okay. You should go back to the field. I'll—" I stopped talking when this sob crept up on me out of nowhere. The hand I slapped over my mouth didn't help any.

"You're crying." Josh took another step further into the building. Then another.

Dragging my palm up toward my eyes, I wiped at them. *Get it together*. I had to get it together. "I'm okay, J. I promise. I'll be okay."

"But you're crying," he repeated the words, his eyes flicking across the stalls like he was worried he'd get caught doing something bad but obviously not worried enough because he kept creeping toward me. His hands met at his chest. "Don't cry."

Oh my God. Him telling me not to cry only made me cry even more. Before I could stop myself, as he got closer and closer, I blurted out, "Do I embarrass you?"

"What?" He stopped in place two feet away. He genuinely looked like I'd hit him.

"You can tell me the truth," I said in broken syllables, sounding like a complete liar. "I don't want you to wish I wasn't around if it's because of something I wear or something I do—"

"No! That's stupid." Those eyes just like mine went over my face and he shook his head, looking so much like a young Rodrigo it only made me feel that much worse.

"I don't—" I was hiccupping. "I know I'm not your real mom or even Mandy," the words kept getting broken up the more I cried. "But I'm trying. I'm trying so hard, J. I'm sorry if I mess up sometimes, but—"

His body smacked into mine so hard, my spine hit the wall again. Josh hugged me like his life depended on it. He hugged me like he hadn't since his dad died. The side of his cheek went right along my chest as he held me tight. "You're better than my real mom, better than Mandy—"

"Jesus, Josh. Don't say stuff like that."

"Why? You always tell me not to lie," he said into my chest as he hugged me. "I don't like you crying. Don't do it anymore."

Oh my God. I did the complete opposite and bawled a little more, right into my eleven-year-old.

"Ms. Christy is a witch," he said into my shirt.

A mature adult would have told Josh not to call a person a witch and deny that Christy was being one. Except I'd call her behavior that of a bitch, not a witch.

But I didn't feel very much like a mature adult then. I'd used up all my adulting points of the day. So all I did was hug Josh closer. "She is," I agreed with a sniffle.

"I'll quit," he stated. "I can join another team," my nephew offered, cracking my heart in half.

"Joshy—" I started to say before I got cut off.

"Can I talk to your aunt, Josh?" a rough, voice filled the bathroom, making me look up to see Dallas standing three feet away. When the hell had he walked in without us noticing?

The boy in my arms tensed before he turned around, his stance wide and protective. "No."

God help me, the tears started up all over again. I loved this kid. I loved him with every single cell in my body. There was a lot of things about love that you could only learn after you'd faced the real kind. The best kind wasn't this soft, sweet thing of hearts and picnics. It wasn't flowery and divine.

Real love was gritty. The real kind of love never quit. Someone who loved you would do what's best for you; they'd stand up for you and sacrifice. Someone who loved you would face any inconvenience willingly.

You didn't know what love was until someone was willing to give up what they loved the most for you.

But it was also never letting them make that choice, either.

Dallas sighed, his hands going into his pockets. His thick-framed sunglasses had been shoved up onto the brim of his hat, but I didn't look at his face. I didn't want to. "Please, Josh."

"Why? So you can make her cry too?" my defender asked.

"No. I'm not going to make her cry. I swear. You know me better than that," he explained. "Please. I don't want you to quit. I'd like for you to play the first game at least, for your friends out there, and if you still want to quit afterward, you can. I wouldn't blame you. We're a team, and you don't treat people on your team like that."

Josh didn't say a word.

I just stared at the sink behind Dallas. I had maxed out the amount of times I wanted to cry in front of this man.

"Diana, can I talk to you?" came the nearly gentle question that only made me angry.

Had he told her to talk to me about my shorts so he wouldn't have to?

It only took me a second to decide he wasn't that

kind of person. I don't know why I'd been thinking the worst of him so much lately. He didn't deserve it.

Still insisting on looking at the sink, I let out a breath that made me sound like I had lung cancer. "I don't want to talk to anyone right now," I pretty much whispered.

"Josh? Please?" was Dallas's reply.

"Don't make her cry again," my eleven-going-on-twenty-year-old nephew demanded. "She never cries."

That was a lie, but I appreciated why he'd gone with it.

Maybe my feelings were hurt and a part of me felt like it had been split open, but I didn't want Josh to think I couldn't handle my own battles, even as I bled my feelings all over the place. Slipping my hands over his shoulders, I tightened my grip on him. "Thank you, J, but I'll be okay. Go finish warming up. We aren't quitters."

And my poor, beloved nephew who knew me too well, turned to look at me over his shoulder. Those brown eyes were guarded and worried. "I'll go if you want me to."

Fuck. I touched his shoulder. "It's okay. Play your game. I can handle this. You don't have to quit. I've got this."

He didn't budge.

"Go, Josh. It'll be fine. I'll be—" Where? I didn't want to go back by the bleachers just yet. I wished I could be the bigger person and not let a bunch of words hurt me. "Here. I'll be on the bleachers watching."

He nodded.

Stooping down, I gave him another hug because I couldn't help it, and he hugged me back. I kissed the top of his head quickly and released him, watching as he shot Dallas a look that I knew would eventually become trouble when he got older, and then disappeared through the winding hallway of the door-less bathroom... leaving me alone with his coach. It was a place I didn't want to be.

I'd learned years ago that I didn't have to do things I didn't want. It was a gift of being an adult, getting to choose what you wanted and didn't want in life. You just had to see how many choices you had, and if you didn't have any, then you made some.

And without thinking twice about it, the second Josh was around the corner, I made my decision. I was going to sit and watch the fucking game even if it killed me. In the words of my *abuela, que todos se vayan a la chingada.* Everyone could go to hell.

Except as I walked past the second to last man I wanted to talk to in the near future, fingers reached out and snatched at my wrist. "Diana," my name came out comforting and smooth like warm milk.

I stopped, my gaze going down to the fingers wrapped around my bones. "I just want to watch the game. I don't want to talk to anyone right now."

"I know." At least he wasn't arguing with me. "But I wanna tell you I'm sorry. I know she's been gunning for you, and I didn't put a stop to it."

I swallowed, my throat muscles bobbing hard, making me feel like I was trying to pass an egg, but really it was just my pride.

"She doesn't have any idea what she's talking about," he said softly, with so much kindness and compassion, it unzipped me from the throat down.

Tears filled my eyes and I tried to blink them away, but they just stayed there, making my vision hazy and distorted. "I've never even done anything to her. So we argued. I argue with everyone. I know I'm a pain in the ass sometimes, but I would never go out of my way to be mean to someone who had never really done anything to me."

"I know you wouldn't, and you're not a pain in the ass. We get along just fine, don't we?" he assured me, making me sniffle.

"Yeah." Was I still tearing up? "She doesn't know me. She tried to tell me I wasn't a good parent figure to Josh, that I—I'm not a real one. I am—"

"I know you are," came his low reply, all mellow and tender. "They know you are." I could see him getting closer to me out of the corner of my eye. "They couldn't have anyone better raising them. It doesn't matter what she says. You're great. You know you are."

I sniffled, angry and hurt. "Yeah, well, no one else seems to think I am except you... and them... and the Larsens." My voice cracked. My own mom didn't seem to believe that half the time. But I couldn't say that out loud.

Instead, I started weeping again, silently.

I swore I could feel pressure at the back of my head like maybe he was cupping it. I didn't move. I would swear on my life he made this "shh, shh, shh" sound, like he was trying to soothe me. "This is my fault." When I didn't say anything, he leaned in even closer to me. "Don't cry. I'm sorry."

There was an earnestness in his tone—hell, in his entire body—that seemed to reach into me more than his actual words. I'd been apologized to hundreds of times in my life, but there was something about Dallas doing it that didn't seem false or contrived. Maybe I was being dumb, but I didn't think I was imagining hearing or sensing something that didn't actually exist.

I looked up at him, hating him seeing me with what I was sure were puffy, red eyes with disaster written in the pupils. Dallas's expression was a mournful one. There was a softness to his features that didn't normally exist. And when he blew out a breath that hit the cheek closest to him, I could confirm his guilt.

"I try not to play favorites, and it came back to kick me in the ass. I'm sorry. I should have told her to go sit down when she started going off instead of telling her I didn't have time to deal with her," he said, so close to my face. "You're my friend. I'm sorry for letting you down. I seem to do that a lot."

"You didn't let me down," I muttered to him, feeling embarrassed all over again. "Look, I'm going to go sit in the car until the game starts. I want to be alone for a minute to get my shit together."

He sighed, the fingers around my wrist retreating for a brief moment before they slid up my bare forearm, the calluses grazing my upper arm and shoulder over the sleeves of my T-shirt as they made the trek upward, and then he was palming my shoulders with both of those rough-worked hands. He breathed, rough and choppy. The tips of his tennis shoes inched closer to me, his hands squeezing my shoulders as he said in a whisper, "I'm gonna hug you as long as you promise not to grab my ass, okay?"

I almost laughed, but it sounded more like a broken croak.

I came from a hugging family. I was descended from a long line of huggers before me. We hugged for good things and we hugged for bad things. We hugged when there was a reason and we definitely hugged for no other reason than because we could. We hugged when we were mad at each other and when we weren't. And I'd always loved it; it became a part of me. A hug was an easy way of showing someone you cared about them, of offering comfort, of saying, "I'm so happy to see you" without words.

So when Dallas wrapped his arms around the middle of my back, he swallowed me in something that had always been freely given in my life. And he said words that hadn't always been so easily shared, "I'm sorry, Di."

I smiled into his chest sadly, letting the nickname go in and out of my ears. "It's not your fault, Professor."

His body tightened along mine. "Professor?" he asked, slowly, quietly.

He knew. "Professor X. You know, Professor Xavier."

My neighbor—my friend—made the same choking

sound he'd made back at my house when I'd called him Mr. Clean.

"Dallas?" a voice called from outside the bathroom.

Said man didn't loosen his hold on me even as his upper body started shaking a little. "Yeah?"

"Game's about to start," someone who wasn't Trip told him.

"All right. I'll be out in a sec," the man hugging me answered, his palm making a flat trek up my back to land between my shoulder blades before he slowly pulled back just enough to look down at me. "I need to go." There was a pause. "And I'm not bald. I'm just used to having short hair."

I didn't say anything; I just sniffled.

Dallas reached up and touched my forehead with one of his thumbs briefly before snatching the cap off his head and settling it over my hair. The tips of his fingers brushed high over my cheekbones for tears that had disappeared by that point. "Go watch your boy."

When I didn't say anything, he tipped his head to the side and lowered his face until it was inches from mine, his expression so tight I swore he looked furious. "Where's that person who gave me a stare down and asked me if I wanted to be friends with her or if she should fuck off, hmm?"

The corners of my mouth tilted up just a little, and it made his lips do the same.

He blinked and told me in that bossy, military voice, "Don't leave."

I swallowed and couldn't help but duck my head for a moment.

"Don't leave," he repeated. One of those hands I'd admired a time or two came up and gently brushed my neck before dropping away. "I'll talk to Josh after the game, but if you guys wanna quit, I can't stop you. I'll talk to Christy. We don't treat each other like that here." His thumb moved up to touch right beneath my chin. "I don't want you to go anywhere if that means anything, Peach."

This smooth motherfucker was killing me. How? How was he single? How could his wife be such a dumbass? What could he have done to ruin a marriage? I couldn't see it. I couldn't.

The thought came to me as forcefully as the one the last time we'd seen each other had, scary and unwelcome: I liked him. I liked him a lot, and I had no business feeling that way. None.

That was why I trusted him. Because some part of me really liked this man. Shit.

So I told him something I would probably live to regret. Something that I wasn't supposed to say now or ever. But if I'd learned anything over the last few years, it was that you didn't always have the right time for anything even if, in a perfect world, you were supposed to. "Look, I don't know what happened with your wife—where she is, why you guys aren't together… it's not my business—but all I know is that she's an idiot," I told him.

He blinked those brown-gold-green marble eyes.

But I wasn't done. "You deserve the best, Dallas. I hope you find someone who appreciates you someday, if that's what you want. I'm so lucky to have you as my friend. Anyone who has you as more than that is a lucky bitch." I smiled at him, feeling a rush of heat on my face. "I'm not trying to stick my hand down your pants either, all right?"

His Adam's apple bobbed, but he didn't say a word. Instead, he took a step back, eyeing me with that jutted jaw of his. "Don't leave, okay?"

I'd barely nodded by the time he had disappeared.

The sound of cheering from outside a moment later brought me back to reality. Josh was out there. My pride wasn't worth missing out on Josh playing, that was for sure. Reaching up to touch the brim of the cap that had just been placed on my head, I shoved it down a little further on my head and told myself it didn't matter what these people I barely knew thought about me.

But I still walked with my head down to the bleachers, and I'm sure my face was pink as I did it. Luckily, the spot by where I'd left the cooler was still open and I took it, my hands going to my knees. The boys' team was starting on the field and Josh was right behind home base, in position.

I felt overly self-conscious throughout the game, and I cheered a little more quietly than I normally did when someone on the team did well, and I was definitely a lot more restrained than usual when Josh nailed a ball that hit the back fence. He was more subdued too because he didn't run as fast as he usually did. All in all, the game went well and the Tornado won their pool game—a game that didn't matter in terms of progressing in the tournament. At the end of it, the team huddled together away from the parents while Dallas talked to the boys about whatever it was they talked about, and soon afterward, most of the players went back to the dugout to collect their things and move out of the way so that the next two teams could come on to the field.

At no point did I look around for Christy.

But Dallas and Josh stayed off to the side, talking. From the looks on both of their faces—so, so serious— it was some deep shit. Some deep shit that involved me.

I could tell from Josh's initial body language that he was angry, but I could also tell from Dallas's that the man had the patience of a saint. As the minutes went by with me standing there staring, Josh relaxed a little; his hands dropped from his sides and he seemed more easy, less cagey. At one point, the older man put his hand over his heart and nodded at whatever he was telling his player. And what could have been ten minutes or twenty minutes later, the man held his fist out and Josh bumped it.

I guess that meant we weren't going anywhere, and that was okay. Who was I to make someone change their dream just because I wasn't exactly happy? I couldn't and wouldn't be that person. This was about Josh, not me.

And at that point, I wasn't ruling out tripping Christy if the opportunity ever presented itself.

So as they walked toward me from where they'd been far out in the field, I let out a deep breath and purposely ignored the looks I could feel burning through my skin. My nephew came to me first grabbing the water bottle I'd taken out of the cooler while he'd made his way over. And he smiled this tight, one-sided grin.

"Everything okay?" I asked.

He nodded. "You okay?"

The fact this eleven-year-old was asking me that made my heart feel funny. "Yeah."

Josh twisted his mouth. "Can I keep playing here if I promise never to be friends with Jonathan?"

I steeled myself and smiled. "Whatever you want, J. You can be friends with him if you want. His mom just can't drop him off at our house, is all. Water might end up in her gas tank and she'll never leave."

"*You can do that?*"

Shit. I waved him off, realizing maybe I shouldn't teach him things like that. Yet. Maybe if a girl ever broke his heart, I'd help him do that before I ripped all of her hair out. "I don't know. I'm just making stuff up. But really, you can be friends with Jonathan if you want. I don't care."

"I don't really like him anyway," he whispered.

I was not going to smirk, and I managed not to. "It's up to you, but I'd be okay with it."

"You sure?" he asked.

"I'm positive. I want you to be happy." I could come, mind my own business, not talk to anyone, and go home. For him, I could.

He gave me that narrow side-eye I knew damn well he'd inherited from me. "I want you to be happy too."

That had me sighing. "Your happiness makes me

happy. I'll figure it out. Plus, I'm leaving in two weeks, remember? I don't have to see any of their ugly faces for a while." I reached up to pull at a strand of hair sticking out from under his cap. "I want you to kick some ass so you can go into the major leagues and then take care of me for the rest of my life. You're not putting me in an old folks' home, you know."

Josh groaned and rolled his eyes. "You always say that."

"Because it's the truth. Now go play or whatever it is you do with your friends."

He puffed his cheeks out and nodded, taking a step back before stopping and shooting me another of those looks that was too old for such a young kid. "You'll tell me if you're not happy?"

"You of all people can tell when I'm not happy, J."

"Yeah," he answered easily as if there was no other answer he could have possibly given.

I puckered my mouth just a little and earned one of his dimpled smiles. "I'll be fine. Go get a snack or something and hang out with your friends."

Pulling out a five from my pocket, I held it out and he grabbed it with a "thank you" before he went off to meet up with the other kids on the team who were in line at the concession stand buying God knows what. With the cooler handle in one hand and my big bag over my shoulder, I rolled over to the middle section of the three neighboring fields, taking an empty picnic table that was about ten feet away from the nearest parents on the team. I'd already looked at the schedule the night before. The next game wasn't for another hour.

My phone ringing had me reaching into my pocket, and when the number flashing across the screen was an unknown California number, I hesitated for a second. California? I didn't know anyone except Vanessa—

Oh shit.

I didn't think I'd ever answered another call faster.

"Hello?"

"Diana," the incredibly deep male voice on the other line replied.

I hadn't heard it that many times in person, but I could put two and two together and guess who was calling me. "Aiden?" I wanted to make sure it was my best friend's husband.

He skipped over my question but still confirmed it was him almost immediately. "Vanessa is going into labor. I'll buy you the first ticket out."

He didn't ask if I could come, and he didn't say she wanted me there. It was both those things that touched me the most.

Without thinking twice, I rattled off my e-mail address to him and said, "Get it. I'll be there as soon as I can." There were plenty of people in the world that I wouldn't take a handout from; Vanessa's husband was not one of those people. He could afford to buy the plane if he wanted.

My best friend was having her baby.

I needed to find Josh and call the Larsens.

CHAPTER SIXTEEN

"DIANA, YOU CAN COME INTO THE ROOM NOW."

Almost nine hours had passed from the moment that I'd gotten the phone call about my best friend going into labor. Nine damn hours I spent reading about all the horrible things that could happen to a woman when she was giving birth. I'd wanted to throw up seeing phrases like "stitching layer by layer," "closing a uterus," and "closing a belly." If that wasn't bad enough, there were paragraphs dedicated to clots and a dozen other horrific things that could happen during a pregnancy that had me clamping my legs shut in agony at the airport.

My best friend was giving birth, and I was the one sweating bullets.

Everything after I got off the flight from San Antonio to San Diego went by at the speed of light. I caught a cab to the hospital and found Vanessa's husband pacing outside her room; this massive imposing figure who I called The Hulk had been wringing his hands. The stress of waiting around, only to be told she was going to have an emergency C-section was one of the longest hours of my life.

They had let her husband into the room for the procedure, but I'd had to wait. Not that I thought I could handle seeing her sliced up like a Thanksgiving turkey, but I would have done it for her. And only her.

Aiden had come out what felt like a year later, his face bright and eyes glassy, and said, "She's fine and so is the baby. You can see her once they move her to a recovery room."

It was getting to see her that seemed like another eternity. So when Aiden came by to get me, I started shaking again. It had been years since I'd been anywhere near as scared and upset as I'd been then, waiting to make sure this person who I'd loved almost my entire life was going to be okay. I hadn't even let myself think that she wouldn't.

It wasn't even a little surprising that she was in a private room further away from the general population. If a hospital could be a five-star hotel, this one would have been it. My little Vanny, who had eaten dinner at my house almost every night while we were growing up, had come so far in life. Fancy bitch.

I thought I was okay as Aiden led me into the hospital room. It wasn't like we hadn't known for months she was pregnant. Obviously, it was going to happen. I had told myself I was going to keep it together for her; I wasn't the one who'd had an emergency C-section.

But when the first thing I saw was a baby on a cart beside the bed, something in me was triggered. I sucked in a breath. Then the instant I found her on the bed, pale and looking more than a little high, all weak but somehow still smiling, I sucked in another breath.

And I blinked at her.

She blinked back at me.

I was woman enough to admit I was the one who started blubbering first.

"You have a baby!" I pretty much wailed, throwing my hands up to my face to palm my cheeks.

"I have a baby," she agreed almost softly, tears streaming down her cheeks as she extended a hand toward me.

We both went into this crying that sounded a whole bunch like "buhuhuhu" as I walked over to her, torn between looking at my best friend and the little piece of her sleeping a foot away.

I had loved this bitch my entire life, and she was a mom. What I felt wasn't unlike the emotions I had gone through the first time I saw my brother's boys. It was the exact same, except this time, the reality that this was a new life seemed so much more precious than before.

"I can't believe it," I cried, squeezing in between the bed and the baby, aiming for her. One of her hands went around my back and the other to the back of my head as she led me forward. Pressing my cheek against hers, I tried to give her the best version of a hug I was capable of, not wanting to get anywhere near her stomach after the horror she'd just been through.

Her sniffles went right into my ear as she cried. "I'm so happy you're here."

"I'm so happy I'm here, too," I boo-hooed into her neck. "Someone had to come and make sure you survived that." I gestured with one hand toward the cart, not sure she even saw me since we were hugging each other.

Vanessa's laugh was right into my ear. "*That* is your nephew Sammy."

I choked, pulling back just enough so that I could barely see her through my tears. "My nephew?" She was trying to kill me.

Her eyes were clouded, from drugs or emotions, I was sure. She nodded, gulping. "Well, who the hell else is going to be his crazy-ass aunt who takes him to see R-rated movies before his time?"

The noise that bubbled around in my throat reminded me of the sounds Louie and Josh had made when they were babies. Unlike me, Vanessa had three older sisters. Three bitch-cunt-twat sisters, but they were blood nonetheless. I'd sworn a long time ago that some day before I died, I was going to cut each one of those pieces of crap for what they had done to my best friend when she was a kid. But in that moment, I was reminded of what I had always known—we were sisters, Van and I. Blood or not. Different races and all. She'd been the serious, quiet one who kept us out of trouble, and I had been the reckless, loud one who tried to talk her into getting into trouble. We were each other's yin and yang.

"We'll start with PG-13 when he's eight," I croaked

out, leaning over her again to hug her and kiss her cheek repeatedly as we both cried and snotted on each other according to the moisture on places I couldn't reach. "I can't believe you really did it. You have a baby."

"I can't believe it either."

I pulled back enough so we could look each other in the eyes again. "We've been through some shit, haven't we?" I asked her, smiling.

Her laugh filled the space between us. "We've been through all kinds of shit, D," she agreed, her voice choppy.

I was sure we both thought the same thing: it was only the beginning.

Together we had been through crushes, boyfriends, heartbreak, fights, family problems, twenty miles, thousands of miles, school, a marriage, death... everything. She must have been thinking of those exact same things because Van, who was so much more reserved than me on a regular basis, kissed my cheek again. She squeezed my hand.

I squeezed hers right back. "There's no one else I would rather have gone through all that shit with than you, you baby whale. I love you."

"I love you too," Van said.

We were all wrapped up in each other when something nudged my shoulder, and when I glanced up, my face feeling puffy and wet for the second time that day, I found Aiden standing right by me with that not-so-little baby in his arms.

"Here," this massive, mountain of a man

whispered.

Using my shoulders, I wiped at my cheeks as much as I could, and cried more as he set the baby—Sammy —in my arms. It had been a long five years since I'd held Louie for the first time. And as I took in that little alien face, my heart swelled and swelled and swelled. "I love him," I told his parents, meaning each syllable. "You chubby, little chunky monkey, I love you already." Leaning in a little closer to take in those wrinkled, pink features, I couldn't help but glance up at Van and puff out my cheeks. I tilted my arms so she could see him again. "You made this. Can I have him?"

"I know." She sniffled. "And no."

"You too, Aiden," I added absently, letting my request go and glancing back at the face inches from mine. Then I glanced back at Van. "This was in your vagina—"

"Diana," she hissed without the usual amount of zing in her voice.

Looking back at Sammy, I nodded, smiling. "You aren't the first thing I've touched that was in your mommy's body—"

Vanessa made a choking sound, and I thought her husband might have, too.

She remembered. She remembered that one thing she'd made me hold in my hand that one time when we were twelve.

"But you sure are the best," I finished whispering to him. I propped him up so she could see him and shook my head. "He would have ripped your ass wide open, Vanny. Look at this head. He has your head."

She groaned, and I'd swore on my life The Hulk made a sound that was pretty much considered the closest thing to a laugh I'd ever heard from him.

I felt pretty pleased with myself and winked at her. "I really can't believe you did it. He's amazing."

"Whoever thought, huh, Di?"

"I sure as hell didn't," I agreed, tearing up again, glancing at my best friend looking like shit on the bed. "Remember how after we watched *The Princess Bride*, we used to say we were never going to have boyfriends or get married and have kids unless it was with the actor who played Westley?"

Leaning against the bed, I could see Van glance at her husband, smiling. "I'll never forget."

"We were going to take turns being his wife," I reminded her, taking in her child some more. He was such a miracle.

"You were going to get him ten months out of the year and I could have him two," she informed me. "My mom broke up our fight when we started pulling on each other's hair, screaming. I remember."

"Well yeah, I was going to give you *half* the winter with him. That sounded fair."

"Cheater."

I sniffled. "Cheater? You snooze, you lose. I found him first."

IT WAS EXACTLY FIVE DAYS LATER THAT I FOUND MYSELF IN BED with Vanessa. She was on one side, I was on the other, and Baby Sammy was passed out in the middle. We were watching television; at least that was what we had planned on doing. After spending three days in the hospital following her C-section, she'd been released. I'd taken Van's car back to their house every night, and her husband had stayed at the hospital with her.

Now that she was home, I was helping her with everything possible, trying to enjoy spending time with her and the baby before I had to fly home. I wasn't sure when the next time we'd get to see each other would be, but I'd bet it would be months. A lot of months.

"Enough about me, how's everything with you?" Van whispered from her spot a couple of feet away.

I crossed one ankle over the other and kept my gaze on the rerun we were watching of *The Fresh Prince of Bel-Air*. "Good. Busy. The usual."

"You're a liar," she muttered, rolling her head to the side to look at me since she couldn't roll on to her hip to do it.

"No I'm not."

"You're rubbing your hand on your leg. You know I know you're full of shit when you do that."

My hand was frozen on my leg. Damn it! I hadn't even realized I was doing it.

"Tell me," my best friend whispered. "I know something's up."

Was something up?

Yeah, it was. Just an hour ago, my phone had rung, on the screen Dallas's name had showed up.

The day before, he'd called me, too.

And the day before that.

I just hadn't answered any of his calls. Or called him back. He hadn't left voice mails, and honestly, it was a relief. I was being a wuss.

Did I know I was being immature? Yes, but every time I saw his name, I couldn't help but think about what I had said to him in the restroom after the Christy incident.

I could say it: my feelings were still a little raw at her words. Then I felt dumb for opening my fat mouth and telling Dallas his wife was an idiot and hinting that I liked him. I felt stupid, and I hated feeling stupid unless I was doing it on purpose.

I also hated to admit feeling that way, but who else could I tell if I couldn't tell Vanessa?

"I did something stupid," I told her.

She went "I knew it!" before asking, "What's new?"

"Shut up." I reached over to poke her in the forehead. "Let me make a long story short. There's this guy—this man, really—"

The pillow hit me in the face so fast I didn't get a chance to dodge out of the way, and by some miracle managed to catch it before it hit the baby and woke him up. "What the hell, Van? You trying to wake him?"

"He sleeps like his dad. He's fine. *There's a guy you didn't tell me about?*"

If this wasn't the same person who I used to text **STARTED MY PERIOD. PRAISE JESUS** to, I would tell her that she didn't need to be all in my business. But she was. I didn't feel bad about not telling her everything because this hypocrite hadn't always told me juicy gossip the moment it happened in her love life. She seemed to think I had a big mouth.

And she would be right because I did.

"It's nothing, really," I hissed over at her, eyeing Sammy to make sure he hadn't woken up. "I mean, it shouldn't be anything. He's married—"

"Goddammit, Diana—"

"He's separated. Jesus. Calm down. You know I wouldn't mess around with a married man. He's separated from his wife and has been for a while, either way, there's nothing going on between us. He's Ginny's cousin and Josh's coach. He's really nice to me and the boys because his mom was a single mom…."

"But you like him."

I sighed. "I don't think I've ever met someone more honorable in my life, Vanny. I don't want to like him. I have to tell myself all the time that he's married, and he takes that shit seriously. When we first met, he thought I was trying to flirt with him and he got all weird and defensive on me until I told him I wasn't, but the more I've gotten to know him… the more I like him." I listed off all the things he'd helped me with, except Anita coming over. "And you don't even know how hot he is in his own way. The first few times I saw him, I thought his face was nothing to write home about, but he is. He really is." Unfortunately.

"So?"

I sighed. "So, you bitch, besides the fact that he isn't single and that I know better, we became sort of friends. And I started to trust him." This was the painful part. "And one day at Josh's game, the day I left to come see you, that mom I got into an argument with a while back started saying some really mean shit to me, and I just broke down. I didn't tell her anything back for once in my life. I cried and he gave me a hug to make me feel better, and I basically told him I liked him a lot and that his wife must have brain damage for not being with him."

I paused. "*And I live across the street from him.*"

Vanessa's silence didn't unnerve me. She was either thinking about what to say, or knowing her, counting to ten multiple times. Finally, she went with, "As soon as I'm not dying, I can fly to Austin and do to that mom what we did to your boyfriend junior year."

I had to throw my hand over my mouth so I wouldn't bark out a laugh, remembering exactly what she was talking about. "He deserved that potato in his tail pipe."

"You're damn right he did," she agreed. "We'll do it to that lady this time."

I grinned and she grinned back, looking so tired but just as pretty as always, even with her six-inch roots and the brassy orange left over from her last teal dye job that had faded over time. I needed to find her a hair stylist close by, and soon.

Van reached over and poked me. "You said he's separated and you're not doing anything wrong. There's nothing that says you can't be attracted to someone you have things in common with. He's not the only guy in the world, Di. I know things have been tough for you after Jeremy—"

She's said the name I didn't ever want to hear again.

"But he was an asshole, and you know that. If this guy is as great as you think he is, he won't make it a big deal about you liking him—if he even puts two and two together to figure out that you do—so you shouldn't either. Maybe he won't always be separated. Maybe he will."

Maybe she had a point.

Van kept going. "After Aiden and Sammy, you and Oscar are what I love the most in the world. I want you to be happy, D. You have the biggest heart of anyone I know, buried deep beneath that little bitch shell—"

I had to put my hand over my mouth again to crack up.

"—you stubborn, pain in the ass. If you ever want to date a football player—"

"Nope." I couldn't handle all the women throwing themselves at a football player. Vanessa's husband was an exception. He didn't like anyone but her. The only reason he put up with me in tiny increments was because that's how strongly he cared for her.

"Fine then. One day you'll find some poor idiot to love you." She smiled at me, reaching her hand across the bed, and I took it. "If you don't, we'll pay someone to pretend they do."

THE NEXT WEEK WENT BY IN THE BLINK OF AN EYE. I HADN'T remembered how much work babies were, but good

God, it was a lot. Vanessa's mini-defensive end in the making ate like a teenager going through a growth spurt. I stayed with the two new parents twelve days total, but accepted that I needed to get back home to the boys and a little thing called my job. On the way to San Diego, I had called all my clients and explained to them I had a family emergency—and promised a discount for their next service—so the second I got back to the salon the day my flight arrived, I rescheduled everyone. The next three weeks were going to be busy, balancing all the clients I'd had to fit in from the weeks I'd unexpectedly taken off, while also planning on taking more walk-ins than usual to make extra money.

I was going to be really busy, but I'd make it work. Plus, what could I have done differently? Not been there for Vanessa? The boys and I could live off Ramen for a while and it wouldn't be a big deal.

"*TIA!*" WAS THE SHOUT HEARD FROM AROUND THE FIELD AS this boob-level kid ran full speed toward me.

My first thought was: God, I hoped he didn't trip and fall. An emergency room visit was the last thing I could afford right then.

My second thought was: I missed the hell out of this guy. Louie and I had talked on the phone every single day, but it was different than seeing him in person.

My third and final thought was: I felt stupid for having started to dread coming to baseball practice.

For the earlier part of the day, after I'd agreed with the Larsens to meet them at the ballpark to pick up the boys, I'd started thinking all over again about how I didn't want to see the other parents on the Tornado. How I didn't want to see Dallas.

And I was worried if I saw Christy, I might do something everyone would regret.

But now, as Louie raced toward me and took a running leap with this smile the size of the sun on his adorable face, I hated myself for worrying about those people when I had someone so perfect waiting, happy to see me. It was people like Louie and Josh, like the Larsens—my *family*—who really mattered in life. Everyone else's opinions and perception shouldn't even begin to factor in my day.

And as I caught Louie with an "oomph" that knocked half the wind out of me, I accepted that I'd go through everything with Christy all over again if I had a homecoming like this from my boy.

"I missed you, Buttercup," Louie practically screamed into my ear as his arms went around my neck and he hugged the little bit of breath I had left right out of me. "I missed you. I missed you. I missed you."

"I missed you too, poo-poo face," I said kissing his cheeks. "Oh my God, what have you been doing? Are you planning on hibernating for winter? You weigh like ten pounds more than you did before I left."

Just like when he was a baby, Louie reeled back, smacked his hands—which I was 99 percent sure were dirty—on my cheeks, and jiggled them as he leaned close enough to touch the tip of his nose to mine. "Grandma gave me a lot of pizza and chicken nuggets."

I laughed. "I can smell it on your breath."

His giggle went straight into my heart. "Did you bring me anything?"

"Vanny sent you some toys and clothes."

"Can I have them?"

"When we get home. They're in my suitcase, greedy."

He sighed and let his head drop, his entire body arching backward with the movement, making my arms strain with his weight. "Okay."

"Uh-huh. Let's go see Grandma and Grandpa," I told him, already walking with him in my arms.

Louie started to wiggle and I let him slide to the ground, where he took my hand and led me in the direction of his grandparents.

"Were you waiting for me?" I asked, wondering how he'd seen me when I still had no idea where the Larsens were sitting.

"Yeah. Grandma told me you were on the way, so I was sitting there for you."

This kid. I gave his hand a squeeze and we exchanged a grin. Sure enough, sitting on the first row were the Larsens, their eyes locked on the field. The long, furry white body at their feet made me grin. They'd brought Mac, too.

"Grandma! *Tia's* here!" Louie shouted for half of the parents sitting there during practice to hear. I could see them out of the corner of my eye, trying to see who he was talking about, but I made sure to keep my eyes firmly on the only two adults there I wanted to interact with. Mac's head turned to our direction, his nose twitching, and in the blink of an eye he was up; that white tail slashing through the air violently.

"Diana, honey," Mrs. Larsen greeted me first with a closed-mouth smile as she got to her feet and gave me a hug as Mac squeezed in between us, hopping off his front feet for attention. Kneeling, I wrapped the giant dog in a hug and buried my face in his coat as he tried licking the skin off my face.

Standing again, I hugged Mr. Larsen next. "Thank you so much for watching the boys for me." I'd already told them this exact same thing every time I'd spoken to them, but I really was grateful. When my mom heard that I had left for San Diego and that the Larsens were keeping the boys in the meantime, she had gone on this spiel about how I couldn't just pick up and leave them like that. *¿Que te crees?* Who did I think I was, she'd asked. By the end of the conversation, I'd been torn between crying and screaming.

"Any time you want," Mr. Larsen confirmed, giving my back a pat. "Vanessa and the baby are fine?"

I took a seat on the bleacher beside Mrs. Larsen with Louie taking my left, his hand palming my thigh in a way that had me grinning. "She's great, all things considered." I made a line across my stomach and shuddered. "And the baby is perfect." I set my hand on top of Louie's and wiggled my eyebrows. "Your new cousin is almost as cute as you are."

"He *is* my cousin, huh?" the boy asked.

"Yup." He'd been calling Vanessa his aunt his entire life. "Maybe we can go visit them soon and make a trip to Disneyland out of it." I could already picture grumpy Josh's groans about Disneyland, but he'd have to live with it.

"I always wanted a cousin...," Louie started to say, blinking.

God, he was so cute.

"And a sister."

I coughed. I coughed like I'd come down with emphysema randomly. What the hell did he want a little sister for? What was I supposed to do? Pull one off a tree for him?

What was the best response for that?

There wasn't one, so I pretended not to hear him.

Mrs. Larsen heard him, too, because when I turned to face her, her blue eyes were wide and she had her lips pressed together. I'm glad one of us thought it was funny, because I sure as hell didn't. I peeked at Louie again, making sure not to make eye contact, and wondered where the hell he'd gotten that from. Didn't every kid want to be the baby in the family?

The rattle of the fence protecting the people in the bleachers from the field had me glancing up to find a tall boy I could recognize even with a mask and helmet on, as well as a jersey that covered him from his neck to his hands. "Josh!"

He waved his bat and hand at the same time; I could tell he was smiling even with the black mouthpiece protecting the lower half of his face. I really had missed these kids. I couldn't imagine my life without them.

Josh had just turned around to continue on with practice when I happened to glance to the side and saw *him*. Dallas was standing off by third base with his hands in the pockets of his frayed, ancient jeans, and he was staring over in my direction. He wasn't casually looking; he was definitely staring.

I waved, and I was pretty sure he smiled.

"Goo, are you gonna fall asleep in there, or what?"

"No," Louie answered, two spaceships held up in the air, their noses inches away from each other.

There was no way the bathwater was still warm. He'd been sitting in the tub playing with his spaceships for the last half hour while I was busy trying to sew the knee of a torn pair of his school pants. Usually on nights when Josh had baseball practice, I didn't insist that he bathe, but Josh had admitted to me that neither one of them had taken a bath in two days and that just wasn't going to work for me. While I made a quick dinner of frozen taquitos and a bag of frozen corn in the microwave, the eleven-year-old had showered.

"Then come on. You know you have to go to school tomorrow and you need your beauty rest."

He smiled at me shyly as he climbed to his feet, still completely innocent, not caring that he was naked. A year ago, back when we'd shared one bathroom, I'd accidentally walked in on Josh. He'd been buck naked and had yelled like I'd gone in there to kill him, screaming with two hands covering his privates, "Don't look at my nuggets!"

As if I hadn't seen his little pistachios a thousand times before.

Within the next five minutes, I had Louie dried off and watched as he slipped on his pajamas. The top was Spiderman, the bottom was dinosaurs. After ruffling his hair, I cleaned up the mess we'd made in the bathroom and headed to the laundry room to put a load into the washer. I had just put detergent into the machine when I heard a knock at the front door. I didn't need to look at my watch to know it was damn near ten at night. Who the hell would be coming by so late?

My neighbor, that was who.

Dallas's face was tipped to the side when I peeked through the peephole. Letting out a long breath through my nose, I thought about not answering but then changed my mind. I was going to have to see him again soon anyway. Why the hell not get it over with? Maybe he'd forgotten what I said, and if he hadn't… too fucking bad, I guessed. I couldn't take it back now.

"Hi," I said, opening the door wide. He was still dressed in the clothing I'd seen him in during practice, except he wasn't wearing a baseball cap. I still had his in my car.

"You got a second to talk?" he went right out and asked, his hands loose at his sides.

Was he going to tell me we couldn't be friends anymore? I knew I was bossy and hardheaded. I was well aware I wasn't the easiest person to get along with sometimes either. But he wouldn't be telling me to fuck off now, would he?

Dallas took a step forward, the tips of his worn tennis shoes crossing over into the doorframe, pretty much stopping me from closing the door in his face. His hand went to the back of his neck. He looked tired and tanner than he had before I'd left. "I called you."

Where was he going with this? "I know. I was just… busy. I'm sorry. I was going to call you back, but every time I remembered, it was already late here."

The deep, slow breath he let out seemed to hit my chest. "You didn't come to any of the practices in two weeks. You never answered the door any time I knocked." He paused, his eyes zeroing in on my face. "You left the game that day. I was going to give you some space, but I didn't see you after that and I was worried."

He'd knocked on my door too? "I was out of town, that's all." I blinked, making sure to keep my facial expression even. "We're fine. You didn't do anything to me." It was me who had made an idiot out of myself. "I'm sorry for making you worry."

The relief seemed to punch through the lines of his shoulders. "We're fine?"

If he wasn't going to make this weird, neither was I. "Yeah." Then I said the words that made my throat itch like hell. "Of course we're all right. We're friends. Want to come in? I have beer."

CHAPTER SEVENTEEN

JOSH HAD JUST WALKED UP TO THE MOUND TO PITCH WHEN MY mom decided to lean into me. "He's hitting better?" she asked like he hadn't already been hitting awesome before.

I nodded, keeping my eyes on the eleven-year-old on base. Almost two weeks had passed since I'd gotten home from visiting Vanessa in California. I'd been busier than hell. This was supposed to be my weekend off with the boys, but I'd needed to catch up on appointments I'd had to cancel while I was gone, and the Larsens had offered to pick up Josh and Louie that morning so they could take him to his tournament, leaving me to work. When my last client of the day called and cancelled at the last minute, Sean and I made the executive decision to close the salon an hour early. The tournament Josh's team was playing that weekend was luckily only a half hour drive, and I'd gotten back fast enough so that they had only played—

and won—against two teams after their pool games. This was the first time since I'd gotten back that I'd been able to make it to anything baseball related; I'd been having to stay late to catch up with all the clients I'd had to reschedule.

The Larsens had stayed through the first four games before heading out when I'd shown up, with my parents showing up immediately afterward. This was also the first time I'd gotten to spend more than ten minutes with my parents in over a month, too. Things were still weird between my mom and I. She would never admit she had taken something too far, and I wasn't going to back down from my feelings. I didn't regret or feel bad about going to visit my best friend and her baby, no matter what she said or thought.

"Yeah. His batting coach is great and the coaches have been working with him a lot during practice, too."

The coaches. I couldn't help but kind of glance over at a specific coach standing by third base with his arms over his chest. I hadn't seen much of him since that night he'd come over when I got back. He'd come inside with me and drank the last beer in the fridge while I'd told him about visiting my best friend. He hadn't been able to believe whom she was married to. While I checked on Josh first, Louie had come out of his room and invited Dallas to sit with him while I told him his daily Rodrigo story.

"Who are the coaches again?" my mom asked, dragging me back to the present and away from the mental image of my neighbor sitting on one side of

Louie's bed while I'd been on the other as I told him about the time my brother had thought he'd lost his phone but had left it inside the refrigerator on accident.

I side-eyed her and somehow managed not to shake my head. My parents didn't come to as many of Josh's games like the Larsens and I did, but they had gone to enough so that she should know more. The thing was, when Josh had first started talking about playing sports, both my parents had complained. *Why not soccer?* So I'd said, "Because he doesn't want to play soccer." After so many years, you would figure they'd get over it and accept that he was a natural at baseball, but these stubborn-asses I'd been born to hadn't.

I pointed at Trip first, who was standing by first base and then slowly, more than a little resigned, at the big man standing closest to us.

"Why does he look familiar?"

I eyed her again, not fooled by her question. "You met him at the party." This woman had the memory of an elephant; she didn't forget shit. She still brought up things I'd done when I was a kid that, for some reason or another, still made her mad from time to time.

"Oh."

I didn't like the way she said "oh." So I waited.

"The one with all the tattoos?" she asked in Spanish.

All the tattoos? They only went to his elbow. "*Si.*"

She said it again, "Oh."

If I didn't know my mom the way I knew her, I'd assume she was indifferent about Dallas. But I did know her. And for some reason, her "oh" while referring to him didn't sit well with me.

In front of us, Josh got into position on the base and hit the ball straight between third and second, jetting way into the outfield so far I jumped up to my feet to cheer him on. Vaguely, I noticed my mom raise her hands in the air and start clapping. But it wasn't until I sat down as Josh's feet hit the third base that she finally said what I should have known she would say.

"I don't think all those tattoos are good to have around kids, no?"

I groaned. "Tattoos don't jump out and attack people, *Mamá*."

"*Sí pero... ve lo.*" She huffed, the tip of her chin pointing at Dallas who had his hands on his knees as he talked to Josh. "He looks like a gangbanger."

I hated when my mom did that stereotypical crap, especially while she talked about a man who had been pretty damn kind to me and the boys. It was unfair of him to get judged by his buzz-cut hair and a face he'd been born with. I had to grit down on my teeth to keep from saying something I'd regret. "Ma, he's not in a gang. He's great with the kids. He's great with everyone."

"*Ay.* Maybe, but why does he have to have all those tattoos?"

"Because he wants them," I said in a snappier tone than normal.

Her upper body turned to face me, those black, black eyes narrowing. "Why are you getting mad?"

"I'm not getting mad. I think you're being mean judging him. You don't know him."

She huffed. "*¿Y tú si?*"

"Yeah, I do. He was in the navy for twenty years and he owns his own business. He coaches little boys because he likes to be there for them. He's—" I just about said *almost* but managed to keep it inside "—always been nice to Josh and Louie and me." Before I could stop myself. Before I could think about the people sitting around and consider that they might be listening in, I said, "I think he's great. I like him a lot."

The long and drawn-out inhale that she sucked in seemed to suck up all the air within ten feet of us. "*¿Qué qué?*" What?

"I like him." Was I egging her on? Maybe a little, but I hated, *hated* when she got like this on me.

"Why?"

"Why not?" We seemed to have this argument every time I liked someone who wasn't Mexican.

"Diana, *no me digas eso.*"

"*Te estoy diciendo eso. Me gusta.* He's a good person. He's handsome—" She scoffed. "And he treats everyone well, *Mamá.* You know the day after the party? He came over and helped me and the boys clean for hours." I really hadn't believed him when he'd left my house that night, assuring me that I should leave the mess alone because we could all tackle it the next day.

But he had. Time and time again, he'd done things he didn't have to. We were nothing to him, but he'd done what other people hadn't.

If that wasn't friendship, I didn't know what was.

"Not him, Diana. *Not again.*"

God help me, sometimes I wanted to strangle my mom. "Oh my God, *Ma.* Calm down. I'm not telling you to love him. I'm just telling you I like him. We're not getting married. He doesn't even like me like that. He's just... nice."

The woman who had given birth to me faced forward again. I could see her hands clenching the material of the long skirt she had on. "For now!" she basically whisper-hissed.

Oh hell no.

"You don't know how to pick them," she said, her gaze still forward.

I couldn't look at her either, so I shifted to watch the next batter get a strike. "Mom, I love you, but don't go there right now," I whispered.

"I love you too," she said softly, "but someone has to tell you when you make stupid decisions. Last time I kept my mouth shut and you know what happened."

Of course I knew what happened. I had been there. I had lived through what I lived through. I didn't need a reminder of how dumb I'd been. I would never let myself forget it.

Yet here we were again with her telling me what to do with my life and what to do differently. Sometimes I thought, if she hadn't been so strict with me as a kid, I would take her "suggestions" more seriously, but she had been strict. Too strict. And I wasn't in the mood for it anymore, no matter how much I loved her. "Mom, Rodrigo had tattoos. Don't be a hypocrite."

She acted like I shot her. Her hands went to her chest and her back when ramrod straight. My mom gulped, and I'm pretty sure her hands started shaking.

Jesus. I hated it when she acted like that.

"Don't talk about your brother." I barely heard her.

I sighed and rubbed my eyebrow with the back of my hand. Every single time with her. God. We could never talk about Rodrigo. Ever.

With a sigh, I tried to keep my attention on the game, only paying about half my attention to it while the other half bounced back and forth between thinking about Rodrigo and Dallas. I thought my brother would have liked him. I really did.

The game nearly ended before my mom finally spoke again. "You can be friends, but nothing else." She made this delicate sound in her throat that I don't think I'd ever be able to imitate.

Why could she never let things go? Why could I never let things go and tell her what she needed to hear? Rolling my eyes, I snuck my hand under the cap I'd put on, Dallas's, and scratched at this spot that had been itching for a day or two now at the back of my head near the crown. I hadn't washed my hair in a few days, it was probably time.

"Did you hear me?" she asked quietly.

I slid her a look before focusing on the game again. "Yes. I'm just not going to tell you what you want to hear, *Ma*. Sorry. I love you, but don't be like that."

The breath she let out would have scared me back when I was ten. At twenty-nine, I didn't let it bother me a tiny bit. At the end of the game, my dad showed up with Louie in tow, sweaty and tired from their time at the playground. I didn't exactly go out of my way to give my mom space, but it happened. When the next game started almost an hour later, I made sure to sit beside my dad with Louie on my other side as a buffer between us. The Tornado won that final game of the day—which was always bittersweet because that meant the boys would have a game the next day and I'd have to wake up extra early for it since the salon was closed on Sundays.

We followed my parents out to their car to say bye, and my mom and I just gave each other a quick kiss on the cheek. The tension was so thick my dad and Louie glanced between both of us before they got into the car. On the way to our car, I spotted a red pickup parked five spots down from me. By the bed, busy throwing a bag into it, was an even more familiar sight. Dallas.

Standing a few feet away, talking rapidly, was Christy.

Josh noticed what I was looking at because he asked, "Are you gonna ask him to eat with us?"

It was that obvious to him? I lifted a shoulder. "I was thinking about it. What do you think?"

"I don't care."

Giving him a cross-eyed look, I led our crew over to the pickup just as Dallas closed the lip. He either heard us coming over or sensed us, because he looked over his shoulder and stood there. Christy, who was facing us, scowled just enough for me to notice, but I stopped paying attention to her. Louie was holding on to one hand and Josh was next to me with his bag trailing behind him. The smile that came over Dallas's face as he took us in was genuine.

"I'll get back to you on the fundraising. There's no rush for it," my neighbor told the woman to his right without meeting her eyes. "I'll talk to you later."

Christy's eyes darted from Dallas to me, and she let out a deep breath that I would bet an ovary had some cuss words mixed into it. She said something to the coach, shot me another look, and started walking off.

I waited until she was a decent distance away before lifting my chin at him and asking, "We're having hot dogs for dinner, Lex Luthor. You want some or what?"

∽

"Lou, what's wrong with your head?"

Louie, who was sitting on the couch playing a video game against Josh, had suddenly dropped the controller into his lap and started scratching the shit out of his scalp, wincing. "It itches."

I frowned over at him. "Make sure to wash your hair tonight then, nasty."

He said, "Uh-huh," just as he grabbed the controller again, focused on the fighting game he was currently playing against Josh.

We had finished eating dinner a half hour ago, and since then, the four of us—Dallas included—had rotated playing what I would have called Street Fighter when I was his age. I had no idea what the game was really called. I'd lost the last match against Josh, and Louie had taken my spot.

Adjusting myself on the couch, I pulled up my knee

and accidentally hit Dallas's in the process. His attention had been on the screen until then, and he turned to give me a small smile.

"Do you want another hot dog?" I asked. "We ate all the fries."

He shook his head. "No, I'm stuffed. Thanks."

I wasn't surprised; he'd eaten four already.

Another spot on my head started to itch, and I reached up to scratch at it with my index finger. Louie wasn't the only one who needed to wash his hair. When I glanced back at the man sitting one cushion down on the couch, he raised his eyebrows in question and I raised mine right back.

"Ugh!" Josh shouted out of nowhere, his remote flying across the floor as both of his hands went up to his hair, scratching the hell out of his head. "It itches so bad!"

What the hell was going on?

Out of the corner of my eye, Louie started doing the same, except with only one hand. It looked like they were both trying to get blood. I'd barely thought that when another spot on my scalp started to itch, and I went to town on it.

"What the hell is happening?" I asked, scratching.

The only sound in the room was the sound of us raking our nails across our scalps. Then, Dallas said, "Louie, turn on that lamp."

Louie did what he was told with his free hand.

"Do we have bed bugs or something?" I asked, hoping he might have an idea.

Dallas was too busy bouncing his gaze from one

boy to the other and me; his expression was thoughtful. He gestured at Lou to come toward him and the boy did. I was still scratching as Dallas parted Louie's hair with those big hands, his face dipping forward really close to take a look at his head. He didn't say a word as he drew his hands back and then moved his palms to a different spot, doing the exact same, his nose coming inches away from Louie's scalp. He did it a third time, too.

I glanced at Mac asleep on the floor and asked slowly, "Do we have fleas?" I gave him his flea medication on the same day every month.

Dallas sat up and pinched his lips together, and somehow managed to say calmly, "No. You have l-i-c-e."

"L-i-c-e?" Josh muttered the letters under his breath.

"Li-cee?" That was Louie.

I still had a hand on my head as I wrinkled my nose. "What—Oh my God. No!"

THERE ARE ONLY A HANDFUL OF THINGS IN THE WORLD THAT I'D been embarrassed to buy. When I was a teenager, I'd purposely only buy pads and tampons at stores that had a self-checkout lane. In my early-twenties, I started buying condoms online because I was too embarrassed to buy them at the store. There was also itch relief medicine for that time I had a yeast infection, and lubricant that I had bought for Louie when he'd been a baby and needed to get a thermometer where no thermometer should ever have to go.

And then the lice happened.

Lice. *Lice.* Fucking *lice.*

Vomit crawled up my throat each time I thought about the eggs and little critters covering my head and the boys'.

Buying three boxes of medication and a gallon of bleach at the twenty-four-hour pharmacy went on the list of things I was ashamed to buy. When I was a kid, we had gasped over the nasty kids who'd had lice. And now I had three of them in my house, one of them being me.

"You really don't have to do this," I had told Dallas the second it clicked that I needed to be at the pharmacy five minutes ago and claimed we needed to leave right then.

Standing in front of me and in between two freaked out kids that had yelled, "THERE'S BUGS IN OUR HAIR?" all he had done was blink and stay cool, and then he'd plucked my car keys from my hand. "I'll drive. You look up what you need."

Well, when he put it like that, I swallowed my "I've got this." There were eggs in my hair, in Josh's hair, in Louie's. Oh my God. It was disgusting. Really, really disgusting. I swore my head felt even itchier after Dallas had confirmed what the hell was on us. For one moment, I thought about calling my mom, but after we'd ended the night, the last thing I wanted was for her to find a reason to blame me for the boys getting lice, because she would. Forget that I knew for sure I'd gotten it once in elementary school—my entire fourth grade class had gotten them—but it would be a whole different situation if it happened on my watch.

Like Dallas suggested, I spent the ride looking up what I needed to buy and do. He stayed in the car with the boys while I ran in and bought what was needed, the clerk only side-eyeing me a little when he rang me out.

"You do their treatment and I'll help with the sheets," Dallas said in that crisp, no-nonsense tone of his as we pulled into the house.

"Really, you don't have to do that. It's already almost twelve." Fuck, it was almost midnight? From the instructions I saw online, I was going to be up all night, washing sheets, clothes, and vacuuming. We were going to have to wake up early too, for Josh's next game.

I was going to be sick. I could handle blood. I could handle the boys when they were sick and threw up all over the place. Diarrhea and me were old friends... but this lice thing crossed a line into a territory I couldn't deal with. Bugs and I were not friends meant to have a close, personal relationship together.

I caught him glancing at me briefly before turning his attention forward again, but his hands flexed across the steering wheel. I'd put a grocery bag over the headrest for him because I was paranoid. "I know I don't have to."

"I have fleas!" Louie hollered from the backseat.

"You don't have fleas. You have lice," I corrected him, crying a little on the inside at the reminder.

"I hate lice!"

"Lou, do you even know what lice do?" I asked.

Silence.

I snickered and laughed a little despite it all. It was for the best that he didn't. "Okay, which one of you borrowed someone's hat?"

There was a brief moment of quiet before Josh let out a groan. "I used Jace's hoodie last week."

Son of a bitch. How many times since then had we all spent time on the couch together or had I hugged one of them, pressing our heads together? Louie had slept with me and shared my pillow twice the week before. I knew for sure he had slept with Josh one night also.

"I'm sorry," he blurted out.

"It's okay, J. It happens." I hoped it never happened again, but it wasn't like he'd gone out of his way to get infected, or whatever it was considered.

"I was at sea once when a lot of people got lice," Dallas piped up not two seconds after I finished talking. "I've never seen so many adults cry in my life, Josh. We'll get it all sorted out, don't worry."

Why did he have to be so nice? Why?

"You were in the army?" Josh asked.

"Navy."

The eleven-year-old scoffed. "What? Why didn't I know that?"

I could see Dallas's mouth form a grin even as he kept his attention forward. "I don't know."

"For how long?"

"Twenty-one years," the man answered easily.

The noises that came out Josh's mouth belonged to a kid who couldn't begin to comprehend twenty years. Of course he couldn't. He still had at least seven more years before life started bowling right by him. *"How old are you?"*

"Jesus, Josh!" I laughed.

So did Dallas. "How old do you think I am?"

"Tia Di, how old are you? Thirty-five?" he asked.

I choked. "Twenty-nine, jerk face."

Josh must have been joking to begin with because he started cracking up in the backseat. Without turning around, I was pretty sure Louie was cracking up too.

"Traitor," I called out to the little one. "I'm going to remember that when you want something."

"Mr. Dallas, are you... *fifty*?" Louie blurted out.

Oh my God. I couldn't help but slap my hand over my face. These kids were so embarrassing.

"Thanks for that, Lou. No, I'm not fifty." Dallas chuckled.

"Forty-five?"

The man behind the steering wheel made a noise. "No."

"Forty?"

"Forty-one."

I'd known it!

"How old is Grandpa?" Louie asked.

By the time I confirmed that Grandpa Larsen was seventy-one, Dallas had turned the car into my driveway. We hadn't even made it into the house before our neighbor said, "You three shower, and I'll take care of the sheets." He already had the container

409

of bleach in his hands.

"You're sure?" If I was him, I wasn't sure how I'd feel about being in a house full of people with lice.

Dallas blinked those beautiful hazel eyes as he waved me toward the house. "Yes. Go. I need to grab something from my house, and I'll be right back."

As I unlocked the door and led the boys toward their bathroom, I didn't even think about Dallas going into my bedroom and how I'd left a bra hanging off the doorknob.

I shut the door, with the three of us crammed into their tiny bathroom, and clapped my hands. "I have to put this stuff on you and wait ten minutes before you can shower. So get naked, you dirty monkeys."

Louie groaned, "But I took a bath yesterday."

While the other one—God help me—yelled, "You're a pervert!"

IT WAS THREE IN THE MORNING BY THE TIME WE WERE DONE with the showers... and the picking... and the combing.

Since the boys had been born and especially since they'd come into my life full-time without my brother, I'd been thrown up on, I'd cleaned poop and cleaned up pee off the floor and on underwear more times than I could count. I'd been mentally preparing myself for the day that Josh started balling up his sheets, socks, and underwear. I'd even started taking down notes for what I'd have to say to him the day we had to have the talk about a boy's bodily functions. Somehow, some way, I would survive saying the word "penis" in front of him.

But combing eggs out of a child's hair was almost my breaking point. What kept me from complaining was, when I'd brought the boys into the living room after fighting with them the entire time it had taken me to massage the treatment into their hair and help them rinse it out, how Dallas had come out of the laundry room and asked, "Ready?"

And I'd asked, "For what?"

"To comb the nits out."

I started to open my mouth and tell him he didn't have to do that, but he frowned and gave me an exasperated expression. "I know you can do it by yourself, but I'm here. Let's do it."

So we did it. I shoved Josh, who had shorter hair, to him, and I took Louie to the dining room, the only room in the house that still had seats. Dallas had stripped the cushions off the couch, and I could only assume he was washing those too. I was never going to look at fine-toothed combs the same way again. As I sat in the dining room chair, I saw Dallas reach toward his chest and bring something up to his face.

It was glasses.

He was putting glasses on. Narrow, black, thick-framed glasses. Shit.

He must have sensed me staring because he gave me a goofy face. "Reading glasses. I'm farsighted."

Reading glasses? More like sexy glasses. God help me. I forced myself to look forward as I let out a breath through my mouth.

We were all quiet as we combed and combed and combed, and I snuck a couple more peeks at the man in the chair next to mine.

Eggs. Goddammit. I would take vomit any day.

One blown-up air mattress later, because the sheets hadn't dried and I didn't have extras, the boys were on the bed, and I was falling asleep standing up. My head had started itching even worse over the last couple of hours, but I was pretty sure that was only because of what I saw on the boys' heads. With both of them tucked in, I headed back into the living room to find Dallas shaking out washed, twin-sized sheets in the kitchen.

I couldn't help but let out a big yawn right in front of him, my eyes stinging. "Thank you so much for your help. I don't know what I would've done without you tonight," I said the second I was able to.

He looked so tired, too. There were bags under his eyes. He took his glasses off and rubbed his forearm across his eyes as he said, "Hurry up and shower so I can do your hair."

Oh God. My face must have said what I was thinking because he gave me a yawn, just as big as the one I'd given him, and a head shake.

"Shower, Diana. You're not gonna get any sleep with bugs crawling all over your head."

When he put it like that, how could I not do the treatment? As I washed out the medication and soaped up, I thought, *I could pay him later*. I really didn't know what I could or would have done without him. I'd probably be in tears right now.

By the time I got out, I could barely keep my eyes open. I was yawning every five seconds. Tears were coming into my eyes each time I did it.

I was practically a zombie.

Pouring bleach all over the bathtub and tiled walls because I was paranoid we'd have some mutant lice that could survive without warmth and blood, I opened the bathroom window and closed the door behind me. I'd clean the crap out of it tomorrow. I found Dallas sitting on the same dining room chair he'd used to do Josh's hair with his head propped up on his hand, his eyes closed. I'd barely paused between the living room and the dining room when he sat up and blinked sleepy eyes in my direction and patted his knees. "Let's do it, Eggs."

His nickname was so unexpected, I forgot he'd patted his lap, as I laughed.

Dallas smiled at the same time he spread his thighs and slid the chair back, showing me a folded towel on the floor. "This'll have to be good enough for you to sit on for a while."

"My head is going to be a lot harder than Josh's," I warned him.

He flicked his fingers. "I can do it."

"We have to leave for the boys' games in three hours."

"Don't remind me. Get over here."

I blinked. "Do you do this for all the single parents on the team?"

He smiled weakly, but more than likely it was just

exhaustion. "Only the ones who feed me. Come on before we both fall asleep."

I wanted to fight with him, but I really didn't have it in me. Before I knew it, my butt was on the towel between his feet and my shoulders were wedged between his knees. Soft pressure on the back of my head had me hunching forward.

"I'm going to start in the back and work my way to the front," he let me know in a soft, sleepy voice. "If I stop moving, give me a nudge, okay?"

I giggled, so tired it sounded more like a groan. "If I fall on my face, feel free to leave me there."

His laugh flowed over my shoulders at the same time I felt what could only be his fingers parting my hair in the back, flipping most of it over. "What time did you wake up today?"

I felt something brush over the nape of my neck. "Six. You?"

"Five thirty."

"Ouch." I yawned.

The sides of his fingers brushed against my ears as he continued combing. "I've been through worse in the military."

"Mm-hmm." I leaned forward to prop my head on my hand, elbow on my knee. "You were really in the navy for twenty-one years?"

"Yes."

"How old were you when you enlisted?"

"Eighteen. I shipped out right after I graduated high school," he explained.

"Whoa." I couldn't remember what the hell I'd been

doing at eighteen. Nothing important, obviously. I hadn't gone into beauty school until I was nineteen, once I'd decided going to college wasn't for me and made my mom cry a couple of times. "Why the navy?"

"My dad was in it. My grandfather was too during World War II." He made a low noise in his throat as he parted another section of my hair. "I always knew I'd enlist."

"Did your mom freak out?"

"No. She knew. We lived in a small town in central Texas. There was nothing for me there. Even before I turned eighteen, she was going with me to talk to recruiters. She was excited and proud of me." There was a pause, and then he said, "It was Jackson that lost it. He's never forgiven me for leaving."

"I thought you said you'd had some neighbors or family members that were there for you afterward?"

"They were there. For me. Jack.... They used to take me fishing, camping... my neighbor would take me to work with him for a long time to keep me out of trouble. He did tiling. That's how I learned to do handyman things around the house. Jackson was never interested in going or doing any of those things. Me leaving was a betrayal."

"You couldn't have taken him with you."

"I know." Then why did he sound so sad admitting that?

"Does he try to use you as an excuse for why he got into drugs and all that?" I asked, still looking at the floor.

There was a slight pause and then, "Basically."

"I don't mean to call your brother a little shit—"

Dallas's chuckle was really light. "He's older than you are."

"—but what a little shit. I understand why you help him out so much, I really do, but don't let him make you feel guilty. You were a kid when your dad died. He wasn't the only one who lost his dad, and look at you, you're one of the nicest men I've ever met." I shrugged beneath him. "And I don't know of anyone who hasn't made a stupid fucking decision at some point in their life. You just have to own up to it. He can't blame you for anything."

Dallas made a sharp noise before chuckling. "I used to tell him the same thing: if you fucked up, admit it, learn from it, and move on."

"Exactly. It's embarrassing and it sucks, but it would be worse than being an idiot twice."

He agreed and went on combing through my hair. I could hear both of us breathing deeper, the urge to sleep getting worse and worse until I started taking deep breaths to stay awake.

"I'm falling asleep," I warned him. "So, why did you leave the navy?"

"It's tough moving every few years for half your life." His finger brushed the shell of my ear and I felt a zing go up my spine. "I was ready to settle down. My retirement isn't bad, and I like working with my hands. I always did. It isn't fancy, but I like doing physical labor. It helps me sleep at night and pays the bills. I couldn't handle working in an office. It would drive me nuts. I'm done with uniforms and small spaces."

He likes working with his hands. I wasn't going to make that statement into something more. Nope. No way. I also wasn't going to imagine him in that cute white hat and collared uniform I'd seen men in the navy wear. So I changed the subject. "And you came to Austin because you have family here?"

"Yeah."

"Miss Pearl?"

He hummed his yes. "We've always been close, and it worked out that the house I'm in now went on sale about six years ago, and I got it for a dime."

"I had no idea you were related."

"Forty-one years," he murmured, sounding amused and sleepy. "I never thanked you for cutting her hair and helping her with her water heater a while back."

"You don't have to thank me. It wasn't a big deal." I yawned. "Do you see her often?"

"I'm over there all the time. We have dinner together almost every night."

Shit.

"We watch some TV, I do things for her around the house, play some poker, and I go home at nine most every night we don't have baseball," he explained. "Once a month, I meet up with this guy I work with sometimes at Mayhem, and I go visit my family back home a couple of times a year for the weekend, but that's my exciting life. I like it."

He did things for his grandma around the house, played poker, and watched TV with her. Fuck. My. Life. In. Half. I had to squeeze my eyes closed because I didn't want to watch myself lose my shit on the floor of my dining room.

Didn't he know he wasn't supposed to be this damn... perfect?

I wanted to cry at how unfair the world was. But I already knew that and I didn't have any business being surprised by it.

"Your brother doesn't go over there with you?" I asked him, fully aware he'd already mentioned to me in the past that his nana had had enough of his shit, and how he was the only one left who Jackson still had.

"No. About ten years ago, he got in trouble with some motorcycle club in San Antonio and he..." Dallas blew out a breath like he didn't want to tell me, but he did anyway. "He stole some of Nana's jewelry. She's never forgiven him since."

"Fuck."

"Yeah. Fuck."

No one had a perfect family, but that was something else. All right. I needed to change the topic. "Where does your mom live?" I paused. "I'm so nosey, I'm sorry. I'm falling asleep and just trying to get you to keep talking to me so I don't keel over."

His laugh was soft behind me, more warm air over my neck. "You're keeping us both awake. I don't have secrets. My mom moved to Mexico a couple of years ago. She met this man old enough to be my Pawpaw. They got married and moved there. I see her once every couple of years. More now than when I was in the service."

Something about that made me snicker. "As long as she's happy...."

"She's happy. Believe me. She busted her ass for us. I'm glad she's found somebody. Old as fuck, or not."

"He's really that old?"

"Yeah. His name's Larry. He has a grandson Jackson's age. My ma asks for grandkids from time to time, and I have to remind her she already has a few," he said, amused.

"You don't want to have kids?" I asked before I could stop, immediately wanting to slap myself in the face.

His fingers brushed the shell of my ear again, and I had to fight the urge to scratch my scalp. "I want a few. I like 'em. Can't have them by myself though."

"Your wife didn't want any?" I blurted out.

It was *that* question that had him clearing his throat. Except for the time in the restroom, neither one of us had ever brought up his marriage, but fuck it. He was combing things out of my hair. We were pretty much BFFs by this point. "She already had one when we met."

I waited. I already knew this information courtesy of Trip.

"Her ex had been in the navy, too. I didn't know that when we started seeing each other. She didn't like to talk about him much, but I figured they'd gotten off on bad terms. It turned out he was on the same base as I was." He sighed, moving more of my hair.

Something close to anger flared up in my belly, and I fought the urge to glance at him over my shoulder, but I asked anyway, in practically a whisper, "She cheated on you?"

There was a hesitation. A hum. "No. Not then. We'd met through a mutual navy friend. She worked at the PX on base, and I liked her—"

I would die before I ever admitted to getting jealous that he'd liked the woman he eventually married. But I did.

Oblivious, he kept going. "She was nice. We... fooled around for a while. I was being deployed. About a month before I was set to leave, she told me had found a lump in her breast and that she was worried. She didn't have insurance, her aunt had had breast cancer.... She was scared."

Why did my stomach start hurting all of a sudden when it wasn't jealousy-related?

"I really did like her, and I felt bad for her. I remember what it was like for my dad when he was sick, and nobody needs to go through that alone. I had already been thinking about retiring when my time was up in a year and a half. One night, I told her we could get married and we did. She'd have insurance, and I liked the idea of having someone at home waiting for me. I thought it was fine. I thought we could make it work."

I felt like throwing up. "What happened?"

"She waited about two months before she went to the doctor because she was worried about the insurance not covering her, and it was benign. She was fine."

"And then what?"

"You sound awake again, hmm?" His fingertips tickled the sensitive skin south of my earlobe for one moment in time. "Thing is, Peach, you can shoot the shit with someone and have a good time, and have that be the one and only thing you have in common. That was the same thing with us. She wasn't the great love of my life. I fucked up thinking I knew this person I'd only met a few months before we married. I didn't miss her while I was gone, and she sure as hell didn't miss me while I was away. I'd e-mail her and two weeks would go by before she'd reply. I'd call her phone, she wouldn't answer.

"I found out from one of my COs that she had been all in love with her ex. I'll never forget how he looked at me like he was surprised I hadn't known she was hung up on him when we got together. Everyone who knew her knew that. *He* was the great love of her life. I was just this asshole she had used for insurance who was a fill-in for somebody else whose shoes I could never fill, no matter how hard I tried."

His hands paused in my hair for a moment as he let out a breath. "I'll be honest. I didn't try that hard. Not even close. Absence doesn't make the heart grow fonder if there's nothing there to begin with. By the time I got back, a year later, things were not close to being right. That happens a lot to people in the military when they're deployed, you know. I moved back in to our house on base, with her and her kid, and we made it two months before I packed up and left. She told me out right one day that she didn't love me and never would.

"The last thing I told her was she was going to waste her life away waiting for somebody who didn't love her enough to want to be with her. It was the wrong fucking thing to say to a pissed-off woman." He kind of chuckled almost bitterly. "And she said to me: *You don't know anything about love if you aren't willing to wait for it.* Wait for it. Like I was just killing time for her. I didn't see her again until… a few months ago. Right after you moved in."

Yeah, I knew what he was talking about. I'd overheard that conversation. Awkward.

"You didn't try to divorce her?"

"I've been trying. She wanted half of my shit, and I wasn't going to agree to that. She's been drawing it out for almost three years. When I finally saw her again recently, she asked me to sign the divorce papers, that she didn't want anything from me anymore. I heard from a buddy still in the service that her ex had split from the woman he'd been married to, and that they were getting back together." He let out a disbelieving noise. "I wish them the very fucking best. I hope they're happy together after all the shit they put so many people through. If they wanted each other bad enough, they deserve it—fucked-up love and all."

I tried to imagine all of that and couldn't. It was unbelievable. "Your life sounds like something out a soap opera, you know that?"

Dallas laughed, loud. "Tell me about it."

I smiled, cheek still on my hand. "Can I ask you something?"

"Sure."

"Is that why you were so weird with me there for a while? You thought I was going to do the same?"

"The same? No. I'm not that fucked up. I know my ex was a special case, and if she wasn't, I'll pray for the son of a bitch who gets stuck with another woman just like her. I'm tired of being used, Diana. I don't mind helping somebody out, and I never will, but I don't want to be taken advantage of. It's easier to do things on your terms than on someone else's. I don't want to give anyone the power over my life any more than I've already given her. I should've known better than to do what I did, but I learned my lesson."

"Don't marry someone unless you know you love them a whole lot?" I tried to joke.

He tugged on my hair a little. "Basically. Don't marry somebody unless you're sure they'll push you around in a wheelchair when you're old."

"You should make a questionnaire with that on there for any woman you end up with in the future. Make it an essay question. *How do you feel about wheelchairs? Specifically pushing them around.*"

Dallas tugged again, his laugh loose. "I just don't wanna be with a woman who doesn't care about me."

I ignored the weird sensation in my belly. "I'd hope not. That seems obvious."

"Spend three years of your life married to someone who doesn't know your birthday, and you learn real quick where you fucked up." The knees on the side of my shoulders seemed to close in on me a little. "I'm ready to move on with my life with someone who doesn't want to be with anyone else but me."

I told myself I wasn't going to be that sap who sighed all dreamy, imagining herself being that person.

And I wasn't. *I wasn't.* Instead, I made sure my voice wasn't whispered or anything like that as I told him, "You have a point. I hope you get your divorce settled soon. I'm sure you'll find someone like that eventually."

Saying those words killed a little part of me, but they needed to be said.

Dallas didn't agree or disagree. His hand was gentle in my hair and on my ear as he moved one to the side. "I'm waiting until the divorce is official. I've never gone back on my word or my vows, even with someone who didn't deserve it. I'd want that person I end up with to know they don't ever have to doubt me."

I already hated this imaginary person. With a passion. I was going to pull the plug out of her tires.

His next words didn't make me like his imaginary next wife any more either. "I always figured I'd grow old with someone, so I need to make the next one count since it's for keeps."

My heart started acting weird next.

And he kept going, signing her death warrant without even knowing it. "She wouldn't be my first, but she'd be the only one who ever mattered. I think she could wait for the time to be right. I'd make sure she never regretted it."

There seemed to be this pause in my life and in my thoughts as I processed what he said and what my body was doing.

Was this a fucking joke? Was this really happening to me?

Was my heart saying, *You're perfect, you're amazing, and I love you?*

Or was it saying it was going to kill this bitch before she ever came around?

It sure as hell wasn't saying the first, because I told my stupid heart right then as I sat on the floor with my eyes squeezed shut, *Heart, I'm not playing with your shit today, tomorrow, or a year from now. Quit it.*

Dallas.... Nope. Nope, nope, nope. It wasn't happening.

It wasn't fucking happening.

I wasn't in love. I couldn't be.

I also couldn't be upset over him wanting something wonderful in his life. He deserved it. No one had ever deserved it more.

Somehow I found myself tipping my head back far enough so I could look him in the eye and smile, all wobbly and slightly on the verge of wanting to pull a tantrum even as my heart kept singing it's stupid, delusional song. "I said it before and I'll say it again, your wife is a fucking idiot. I hope you know that, Professor."

CHAPTER EIGHTEEN

WE WERE ALL BUSY LOOKING BACK AND FORTH BETWEEN THE two huge crate-like boxes on the lawn to really say anything. We all knew what was in them.

When Louie claimed that he'd finally saved up enough money to buy a kit that would get him a quarterpipe so he could skateboard at home, I hadn't thought much of it. His other aunt had sent him a hundred dollars for his fifth birthday—I would have given him ten if I was in her shoes—and with the cash he'd collected from everyone else, he'd almost reached his goal. I had offered to cover the last fifty bucks he needed to cover shipping.

Fifty dollars for shipping should have been our first warning of what would be showing up. Now that I was seeing it in person, I was surprised it hadn't been more expensive.

What I hadn't put together was that his quarterpipe would need to be built.

And who would need to build it?

"*Abuelito* can help," Louie croaked almost instantly, wringing his hands from his spot a foot away from his crates.

I glared at him. It wasn't like I *wanted* to build his thing, but I didn't like him assuming I couldn't do it either. Even though we both knew building things wasn't exactly my forté in life. He still hadn't let me live down the bed I'd tried building him when we'd moved into our apartment years ago. "I can do it," I told him, only sounding slightly offended.

He shook his blond head, his attention still focused ahead. "Grandpa. Maybe Grandpa can help."

It was Josh who turned to look at me over his shoulder, grinning wide with his mouth open, like he was way too entertained by Louie shutting me down.

I ignored him. "Fine. We'll figure it out since you don't trust my skills."

All Louie did was glance at me over his shoulder and give me an innocent smile. Traitor.

"Hurry up and go get your jackets if you want to go to the movies," I told them, eyeing the boxes one last time.

They must have immediately forgotten our conversation in the car where we'd agreed to go to the movies, because both boys nodded and headed toward the front door. While they dropped off their backpacks, I let Mac outside even though he could let himself in and out through the doggy door, and refilled his bowl with water and food. Still in my work clothes, I didn't feel like changing. Plus, we were going to the movies to watch the new Marvel movie, not to go husband hunting.

I was tired already. It'd be a miracle if I didn't take a nap halfway through the film, no matter how good it was. But we didn't get chances like these all the time. We probably went to the movies six times in a year with how busy things always were.

On the kitchen stoop, calling out for Mac to come back inside, I heard the loud sound of what could only be a big pickup truck rumbling down the street. It had to be Dallas. That made me smile. With no baseball this weekend, I wondered what he was planning on doing. He'd come home with us a couple of days ago to have dinner as a thank-you for helping out with our lice incident. That was the last time I'd seen him.

Back inside, I rushed the boys out the door, giving Mac a kiss and a promise that we didn't have any plans for the weekend, for once. I couldn't believe how much I was looking forward to just hanging out at home. But as I was locking the front door, I heard the boys yelling. And I heard grown men yelling back at them.

Dallas and Trip were outside, hanging out by the front of Trip's motorcycle. It was the first time I'd seen the shiny Harley. It might have been because he was always lugging around Dean and sports equipment that he didn't drive it to practice, but I figured a man in a motorcycle club would probably ride it often.

"You wanna come with us?" That was Louie hollering.

Hollering and inviting people as always.

"You're going to the movies?" Dallas asked,

diagonally crossing the street.

Louie rattled off the name of the movie we were watching, and our neighbor, still in his work clothes, glanced at his cousin and tipped his chin up. "What do you say? You wanna go, Trip?"

Trip straightened, catching my eye and winking. "Hey, honey. Mind if we tag along?"

I glanced at Dallas and exchanged a smile with him. He was so scruffy looking. I'd swear there was paint all over his forearms. "If you guys want to, we can squeeze into my car."

The "hmm" that went through both men had me frowning. "What movie theater were you planning on going to?" Trip asked, and I answered. "Dean's mom's place is on the way. J, we could pick him up if you want."

Like Josh was ever going to say no to hanging out with Dean. "Okay."

"We won't fit in your car, but we can go in mine," Dallas offered.

I didn't miss Trip's slight wince.

Dallas didn't miss his expression either because he gave him a frown. "What? My truck's clean."

"I don't care what we go in," I told them. "But we should probably go because the movie starts in an hour."

Dallas glanced down at his clothes for a moment, but I waved him on. "You look fine. Let's go."

Trip and Dallas agreed to swap vehicles in the driveway, and in the next few minutes, Louie, Josh, and I loaded into the back, with Trip jumping into the front passenger seat after parking his bike in the driveway. Dean's mom's house really was on the way to the movie theater. Trip called her on the way over and Dean was already waiting outside when we pulled up.

"Diana, come ride up here so he can ride in the back with the boys," Dallas suggested as he put the truck into park.

With another quick swap around of human bodies, I found myself in the center of Dallas's bench seat, admiring how clean he managed to keep his truck. He wasn't lying. Unlike his house, there were no wrappers anywhere and no signs of layers of dust. It was a miracle. The only things he had up front was an air freshener in the shape of a pine tree hanging off his rearview mirror and a pack of yellow Post-it notes sitting on the dashboard.

"It's old, but it works," the man in the driver seat said to me.

I glanced at him. "I didn't say anything. I was just admiring how clean it is."

"You can afford a new one," Trip muttered.

Something about the way Dallas shook his head at the comment told me this was an old argument between them. The hand he had on the steering wheel gave the worn leather a long, gentle rub. "I don't need to get another truck the second a new model comes out."

"You've had this one for… what is this? A 1996?"

"A 1998," came Dallas's response.

I fidgeted in my seat, keeping my legs closed so that

they wouldn't touch either of theirs. "When did you get her?" I asked.

He nodded, his hand back at the top of the steering wheel, his other palm flat on the thigh furthest away from me. "Bought her brand new. She was my first."

"The only reason my car is new is because I couldn't roll around with those two in a Mustang," I offered him up some support. "That was my first brand new car, and I had loved it. I had my mom's old Elantra before that."

It was Trip who squinted over at me. "I can't see you in a Mustang, honey."

I snickered. "I was a different person back then. That Diana drove a red one and got speeding tickets all the time. Me now, drives the speed limit and has better things to do than spend my money on speeding tickets."

Trip's phone started ringing and he answered it. Next to me, Dallas whispered, "How's your head?"

I cringed on the inside. "Fine," I answered. "I have to do the shampoo again in a few days, but I've been keeping an eye on the boys and haven't found any more eggs, so hopefully that'll be the end of them. Are you okay? No itchy head?"

"No itchy head," he confirmed. "But if it comes up, I'll let you know."

"Sure, sign me up for that combing," I mumbled right before laughing and getting one back from him too.

Dallas glanced at me for a second before facing forward again, a smile on his mouth, the sound of Josh and Dean behind us talking, filling the air. "What are those huge boxes on your yard for?"

I snorted. "I figured Louie would have tried wrangling you in to build it for him. He saved up money to buy a quarterpipe. But it's a kit, and it needs to be assembled. I'll probably ask my dad to come over and help me do it when Louie isn't around."

"Why doesn't he want you to build it?"

"A few years ago, I ordered him a bed online and built it for him. *Tried* building it for him. He jumped on it once and it collapsed. He hasn't forgotten about it, and no matter how many times I tried to explain that the bed sucked, he still thinks I did something wrong and that's why it broke," I explained to him quietly, so only he could hear.

"Ahh," he crooned. "I see."

"Yeah, so if you ever hear him make a comment about my building skills, you know why."

"Let me take a look at it. I'm sure I can help you if you want," he offered.

What was I going to do? Tell him no?

FOUR AND A HALF HOURS LATER, THE SIX OF US WERE ELBOWING our way out of the packed movie theater. The showing we'd originally intended to see had been sold out, so we ended up buying tickets for the following screening. To kill time, we'd gone to the nearest burger joint for dinner. When I'd gone for the bill, Dallas had swept my hand to the side and said, "That's cute."

I wasn't even going to reminisce on how his forearm had been pressed against mine the entire length of the movie. Dallas' hazel eyes had met mine the instant our body parts touched and we'd stared at each other. We both wanted the armrest and neither one of us had been willing to give it up.

Actually, I just liked having his arm touching mine. That's why I never moved it. I really couldn't have cared less about the armrest, but I would never admit that out loud.

"Can we go play at the arcade, *Tia*?" Josh asked as we wound our way through the crowd, heading toward the exit after the end of the movie. "Please?"

"Yeah, Dad, can we?" Dean asked Trip.

I wasn't the one driving; I glanced at Dallas who shrugged. "I don't have anywhere to be."

"Are you sure?" I asked.

He blinked down at me.

"All right. Sure, go. But once I run out of money, that's it. I have a bunch of change…." I trailed off as we made our way to the giant arcade by the front doors. The entire movie complex was packed with people going to see the brand-new movie, but there weren't more than maybe fifteen kids hanging around, playing games. Feeling around the bottom of my purse, I scooped out a handful of coins.

"You got a vending machine addiction I don't know about?" Dallas joked.

I crossed my eyes as I picked out the quarters and handed an equal amount to all three of the boys. "I would if any of them carried Pop-Tarts. Hold on a sec, guys. I have more." One more scoop of change from my purse, three five dollar bills from Trip, and a twenty-dollar bill that Dallas gave Dean with the promise that he'd get change and split it between the three of them, and the boys were gone.

"I'm gonna take a piss while we're waiting," Trip announced. "I'll be right back."

"I think Dean's having problems with the change machine, let me go see," Dallas said too, disappearing into the cavern of the arcade.

All right. Keeping an eye toward the front doors, I watched people come inside. I hadn't thought too much about Anita in the last few weeks, but with hundreds of people coming in and out, I couldn't help but remember how she'd shown up to my house unannounced. I had no idea where she was even living now, and a part of me was worried it was Austin. I was looking around when something caught my eye on the other side of the doors by the ticket counter. It was something about the golden-brown hair that triggered a memory in my brain and stole the breath right out of my mouth.

From one instant to the next, my stomach started cramping as the man took a step ahead in the winding line of people waiting to purchase tickets.

My head started pounding. My hands started sweating. I was dizzy.

It had been three years since I'd last seen Jeremy, but it felt like days.

My right hand started shaking.

I dropped my head forward and tried to take a

deep breath. I was fine. I was fine. I was fine.

I glanced back up to process the sight of the man again. He looked shorter... and no, this man had facial hair. Jeremy had never been able to grow facial hair.

And what would he be doing in Austin?

It wasn't him. It couldn't be him, I told myself, but still, I couldn't ease the knot in my stomach or the way my hands were trembling and slick from sweat. *It wasn't him.*

"We got it sorted—Diana, what's wrong?" came Dallas's voice going from his normal voice to a low, distressed one.

I was fine, I repeated to myself, trying to steel my spine, to stand up straight and catch my breath. It wasn't him. On top of that, it had been three years. Three long years, and I wasn't the same person I'd been back then.

"What is it?" Dallas asked again, stopping directly in front of me; his body long and wide, inches away. His voice was low as he noted, "You're pale."

When I raised my head and focused on the triangle of brown ink right above the collar of his faded brown T-shirt, I fisted my hand at my side, even as goose bumps spread out over my arms. "I'm all right," I mostly lied.

"I know you're not. What is it? You feel sick?" He dipped his face closer to mine, those hazel eyes finding my own even though I didn't want them to. His eyelids dipped over his irises and that pale pink mouth formed the shape of a frown. "What's wrong?"

I couldn't help but look away, biting the inside of

my cheek as I let out a breath that was a lot shakier than I would have wanted it to be.

"Someone say something to you?" he asked, his voice getting more worried by the second.

Shit. *Shit.* Reaching up, I scrubbed my hand over my eyes and met his gaze again. I was fine. What happened had been a long time ago. I wasn't that person anymore. *I wasn't.* "I thought I saw my ex," I told him, as my throat burned.

Dallas's expression dropped instantly, and I'd swear his shoulders did too. "Oh."

"No. It's not like that. We—" I glanced to my side to make sure the boys were still in the arcade. All three of them were together, hovering by a big game. "Things didn't end well. I...." God. How could I still feel like such a fucking idiot after so many years? How? I was ashamed of myself for what had happened. How could I tell this man I respected so much that I had been a complete dumbass?

His eyebrows were knit together as he watched me. "You can tell me anything."

I bit my cheek and tried to swallow my giant pride that had gotten in my way so many times in the past. "I'm not proud of myself, okay?" These stupid-ass tears that were becoming way too common in my life lately filled my eyes but didn't go any further. "I was an idiot back then—"

"Diana," he ground out my name, his forehead becoming more lined. Those shoulders that had fallen a second ago came back into position, tight and taut and broad. "You're not an idiot."

"I was back then." I needed him to understand as I glanced toward the doors again, but luckily couldn't see that familiar color of hair anymore. At least for now. "He... hurt me toward the end of our relationship —"

If Dallas was tall every day of his life, on this day, he seemed to grow half a foot taller. His spine extended, his posture turning into one that would belong perfectly on a statue. His Adam's apple bobbed and his nostrils flared. And in the deepest voice I'd ever heard, he asked, "He hit you?" His question was pulled out like each word was its own sentence.

"Yeah—"

Those big hands fisted at his sides, and his neck went pink. "Which one is he?"

"Dallas, stop, it isn't him," I said, reaching for his shirt and grabbing a handful of it. "It was a long time ago."

"A lifetime wouldn't be long enough," he ground out. "Which one is he, Diana?"

"Please don't. I'm not lying. I swear it's not him. He doesn't even live in Austin. That happened back when I lived in Fort Worth."

"Is it the guy over there in the green shirt?"

"No—"

"In the red shirt?"

"Dallas, listen to me—"

Was he shaking?

"Stop being stubborn. *It isn't him*. And even if it was, I pressed charges against him. He went to jail for a few months—"

"Jail?" He turned around slowly to face me. His face… I'd never seen anything like it before, and I hoped I never did again. He *was* shaking. "Tell me what his name is, and I'll put him six feet in the ground."

I sucked in a breath and couldn't help but smile at him, even with my eyes all teary. "It's like you're purposely trying to get me to love you, Dallas. I swear to God. You don't even want me to stick my hand down your pants. You want me to want it all," I laughed, trying to make a joke but failing awfully.

He blinked. Then he blinked again. He grew another two inches it seemed as he stared down at me, that angry face morphing into a serious but somehow slightly softer one.

I smacked him in the stomach with the back of my hand and then reached for his wrist briefly before dropping my hand. "I'm joking. I promise. Just listen to me, all right? I told myself a long time ago I never wanted to see him again, and the boys don't know about that part of my life. They've been through enough shit in their lives. If you don't let it go for me, let it go for them."

He stayed quiet, staring down at me for so long, a shiver shot down my spine. It wasn't until we both seemed to spot Trip about fifteen feet away on a path toward us that he dipped his face closer to mine, his fingers going to my wrist in the same way I had gone for his, but he didn't move away or let go of me. Our eyes were locked on each other, staring, intense, as he said, "Tell me what his name is, and I won't say another word about it."

Trip was even closer.

Shit. I whispered his name. "Jeremy." And then his last name as Trip's voice reached us.

"Goddamn that line was long."

Dallas dropped his hand and took a step back, and if it wasn't for the fists he had at his sides, I wouldn't have thought anything was wrong. But I knew, I knew as he glanced around the movie theater that he was looking for someone. He was looking for the man who I had let get too rough with me. Who had squeezed me a little too hard while he was mad over a story I'd told him about me cutting a male client's hair. The same man who didn't like the way I smiled at our waiter at a restaurant and had reached under the table and squeezed my thigh so tightly it left bruises. The same person who called me a whore and slapped me and punched me when I had gone out with my friends without him.

No matter how much I smiled at the kids when they came back out of the arcade, I still couldn't push aside those memories of Jeremy.

If Trip thought the silence in the cab of Dallas's truck was weird, he didn't say a word. He was too busy typing on his phone's screen as we dropped Dean off and headed home. I didn't know what to say, and I didn't know what Dallas was capable of saying. I didn't think he had it in him to be so mad. Hadn't Trip said something along those words before? How he didn't get mad?

He had barely parked his truck in his driveway,

when he told his cousin, "Help me move those boxes on Diana's lawn into the backyard."

"You guys don't have to do that," I protested.

Trip walked by me. "Take the help, Miss Independent."

I couldn't help it, despite everything going around in my brain, I shook my head at him. "Fine. Help me then."

Between the two of them, and with one, "What the hell is in these? Lead weights?" from Trip, they carried both boxes into the backyard, holding them high above the four-foot fence with only a small amount of grunting to get them over.

The moment the second one was set in the backyard for Mac to bark at later, Trip wiped his hands on his pants. "I'm gonna get going. There's some business at the bar I need to handle before it closes. Di, we'll have a play date again, I'm sure."

"As long as you don't ever say 'play date' again."

He laughed and gave me a hug. "See you later, honey. Tell the boys I said bye. See ya, Dal," he called out, closing the gate behind him with a wave of his fingers as he headed toward his bike.

Josh and Louie had gone straight inside, and it was only us two in the yard with the light outside the kitchen door illuminating the space for us.

There wasn't a specific emotion on Dallas's face; in fact, he looked so detached and unemotional, part of me felt like I'd fucked up telling him about who I'd been to let that happen to me years ago. Maybe he saw me different now. He saw that Diana instead of the one

I was today and didn't like her.

I couldn't blame him. I didn't like that Diana much either, honestly.

He was looking down at the crates when he finally spoke to me for the first time in almost an hour. "I wanna take a look at the inside so I can see what tools you need. You have a hammer by any chance?"

When I had started rubbing my palm on my jeans, I had no idea. "I have tools. I have a hammer. Let me grab it. It's inside."

Dallas still didn't glance up as I went into my kitchen and grabbed my toolbox from one of the cabinets, lugging the colorful, metal container against my leg as I headed outside with it.

"God, this thing is heavy," I told him as I walked down the steps with it. His attention was still on the ground as I dropped it right beside one of the crates, admiring the paint job my best friend had given it.

But as I looked up at the man who I thought was my friend and had just, barely an hour ago, offered to go kill someone for me, I frowned. He was staring, really staring, down at my toolbox. And as furious as his expression had been when I told him about my ex, it was nothing compared to the one that he had right then.

What was wrong with my box?

I toed it, glancing back and forth between it and him, not understanding. "It was my brother's. I kept it after we sold most of his stuff, but it made me too sad and my best friend painted it for me. I thought it was fun. They look like those Giga Pets I used to have when

I was a kid," I explained. "They're puppies. Who doesn't like puppies?"

The exhaled, "Jesus fucking Christ," had me frowning at Dallas.

I watched as both his hands went up to his head and he cupped each side of his skull, interlacing his fingers at the top.

"What is it?" I asked, suddenly getting a little frustrated at his reaction.

He didn't seem to hear me as he sighed, the sound distraught and almost furious.

"What the hell did I do?" I asked him, not understanding but wanting to.

Dallas was still focused on the toolbox when he answered me, his voice thick and strained. "I can't do this tonight, Diana. I can't fucking do this right now."

"Do what?"

"You're—" He closed his eyes and covered them with his palms for a moment before dropping his arms at his sides. He finally raised his gaze to mine, something in those hazel irises looking pained as he said, "I'll help you build it. Don't ask your dad. I just can't do it right now. Okay?"

"That's all right." I took in his stricken features all over again. "Are you okay?"

He lifted a hand but didn't confirm yes or no. "I'll see you tomorrow." He took a step back and eyed my toolbox one more time, his chest taking a big inhale and a bigger exhale. "Night."

"Goodnight," I called out to him as he turned and headed out of the backyard through the gate, closing it behind him. Then he was jogging across the street and disappearing up his pathway to his deck.

What the hell had just happened?

CHAPTER NINETEEN

I KNEW BEFORE I EVEN OPENED MY EYES THAT LOUIE WAS
standing by the side of the bed again. I just fucking
knew, but it didn't scare me any less.

"There's a fire," he whispered immediately before I
could remind him he needed to quit scaring me in the
middle of the night.

And, just like that, at his words, I sat straight up in
bed and took a big inhale. "What?" I asked, knowing
he wouldn't be lying about something like that.

"The house is on fire," he barely had to say before I
threw the covers back, reaching for my phone at the
same time.

"Our house?" I pretty much screeched, my thumb
already hitting 9-1.

"No," he answered. His little hands went to mine
and squeezed. "The granny's house."

"Who?" I blinked.

"The granny. The old lady, *Tia*, remember? Miss

Pearly?"

"Oh shit," came out of my mouth before I could censor myself.

Louie backed up and tugged at my fingers. "Come on."

I went, resisting the urge to finish dialing the emergency number until I saw it. I mean, there could be a fire over there, but it didn't have to mean it was a house fire... didn't it? Not that there would be a reason why anyone would be having a bonfire at a ninety-something-year-old's house. Louie ran down the hallway that led toward the living room, and I followed behind, glued to his grasp. I'd forgotten to close the curtains so I saw the yellows and oranges and reds before I even made it to the window. He hadn't been exaggerating.

Miss Pearl's house was on fire.

At least the back of it was from what I could see. The porch was untouched by the flames licking at the sides by where I knew her bedroom was.

Holy fuck. Her bedroom!

I slapped my phone into Louie's hand as I scanned the houses on either side of Miss Pearl's, but there was nothing there to see. No one was standing outside. No one knew what was happening, and later I'd worry about how and why Louie had been awake at 2:00 a.m. to see that our neighbor's house was on fire.

"Goo, you know our address right?" I asked even as I stepped away from him, my heart beating so fast I couldn't catch my breath.

"Yes," he squeaked, his eyes wide and caught on

the flames.

"Call 911 and tell them there's a fire. I need to go help Miss Pearl, okay?" My voice was quick and panicked, and it was so obvious that Lou turned to look at me, his eyes widening even more.

"You're going in there?" He was scared.

And I understood, I really did, but what was I supposed to do? Sit in my house and do nothing? "I have to. She's old. She might still be in there," I explained quickly, dropping to my knee even though I knew every second counted. "We have to help her, but I need you to call so I can run in there, okay? I'll be as fast as I can, but don't move from here, Louie. *Don't leave the house.*"

I wanted to promise him I would be back, but I couldn't and wouldn't do that.

Even with the lights turned off, I could see his lip trembling, feel the tension and fear rolling off him in waves as his five-year-old brain wrapped around the same possibility mine did. I was going into a burning house, but there was no other choice.

I stood up and nudged at his hands. "Call right now—and don't leave the house. I love you!"

Tears filled those blue eyes I was so in love with, and later on, I could appreciate how mature he was being by not begging me to stay even though I knew it was probably killing him inside. But I had to go.

I blew a kiss at Lou and ran out of the house, only barely managing to stick my feet into the flip-flops I'd kicked off at the door when I got home earlier.

And I ran.

I didn't even bother closing the door behind me; I just sprinted across the street like I'd never sprinted in my life, trusting that Louie knew what he was doing. In hindsight, I should have woken up Josh who wasn't five years old, but there hadn't been any time and... what were the chances that Miss Pearl had gotten out on her own? Maybe she was standing somewhere I couldn't see.

But as I quickly glanced around at the surrounding houses, I saw the harsh reality: I was the only one who knew something was going on despite the crazy amount of smoke already polluting the sky. Dread filled my stomach, as well as this sense of *I don't what to do this, but I have to.*

I had to. I knew I did. I couldn't just pretend.

I shot a quick glance at Dallas's house, but there wasn't time to go bang on his door and try to wake him up. Fires were fast, weren't they? And if it took him or Jackson a while to get up...

My legs pumped even faster as I hit the white picket fence around her front yard, slapping the gate wide open as I vaulted up the three steps leading to her porch in an act I couldn't appreciate.

Like a complete moron, I grabbed the door handle, forgetting everything I'd learned in elementary school about what you were supposed to do during a fire.

The "motherfucking fucker" that came out of me as the metal burned my palm was lost in the night sky and smoke. Cradling my hand to my chest, I thought for a brief second about kicking the door open, but I didn't. Who did I think I was? Leonidas in *300?* I had flip-flops on and there was no way I was strong enough to do that.

After that, everything was a blur.

For the rest of my life, I'd remember breaking Miss Pearl's window with one of her garden gnomes and climbing inside, trying my best not to cut myself. I would never forget the smoke and how strong it was. How it filled everything, every inch of my skin, the surface of every single one of my teeth, the back of my throat, my very fucking heart and my poor lungs. There was no way I could forget how bad my eyes stung and how much I regretted running out in my underwear and a tank top that wasn't long enough for me to at least cover my mouth.

And I would remember finding Miss Pearl crawling across the floor in the kitchen where I'd cut her hair in the past. I could never forget the terror on her face as I helped her up, shouting words I didn't think either one of us knew what they were.

There was no way I would ever forget how hard I was coughing either. How I felt like I couldn't breathe and how I didn't understand how Miss Pearl was still doing it when I'd only been in the house for a second. I carried a lot of her weight on our way out because I knew I was rushing even though she couldn't move very quickly. I'd seen her walk normally and running wasn't an option. But everything stung and I wanted to get the hell out of there before the fire spread or before something else happened. I'd seen *Backdraft* as a kid. There weren't any beams that could fall on us, but I wasn't about to take any chances.

"My cat," the woman somehow managed to tell me. "She's inside."

I couldn't think. I couldn't process what she was saying. I was too worried and scared about getting out of there with her, especially when she couldn't walk fast. I forgot about my hand as I undid the lock and opened the front door, so relieved to be almost out of there.

We made it passed the lawn as we both hacked up our lungs. My back, neck, and cheeks burned and itched. But we kept going across the street where I could spot both boys standing at the doorway with Josh holding the phone to his face.

They ran out as I helped Miss Pearl onto the grass. I'd told Louie not to leave the house, but I wasn't about to remind him he had ignored me.

"Are you okay?" Josh asked as he and Louie barreled into me, throwing their arms around me like spider monkeys, oblivious to the woman by their feet.

"The firefighters are coming," Louie said quickly.

"Diana, my cat is in the house," Miss Pearl's voice pleaded, as something I could only assume was her hand landed on my thigh.

I was coughing, hugging the boys back as her words finally sank in.

"Diana, Mildred is still in there," she repeated herself. "She has bad eyes and can't see good."

I eyed the house over the top of the boys' heads, noticing that it wasn't engulfed in flames yet, despite how smoky everything inside had been.

"Please," Miss Pearl pleaded.

Honestly, I wanted to cry as I got up, disentangling the boys from around me. Did I want to go save her cat? No. But how could I let it die? If it was Mac...

I met Josh's eyes because there was no way I could look at Lou right then. "I'll be right back. I'll be right, right back. Don't go anywhere."

And I ran again, not waiting for either of them to comment or beg me. My burned hand was against my chest as I crossed the street, through the white picket fence that I would forever associate with almost dying. The front door was open as I ducked in, trying to keep closer to the floor because I'd already learned my lesson about the smoke that had gotten worse over the last few minutes it had taken me to get Miss Pearl out of there.

"Mildred!" I yelled, squinting and trying to look around the floor of the living room. "Mildred!" The smoke was horrible, and I coughed up what felt like one of my lungs as I shoved at furniture, trying to find the damn old cat.

I wasn't going to die for it. I couldn't do that to the boys, but I also couldn't live with Miss Pearl's face if I didn't at least try to get her pet back.

"Mildred!" I shrieked with my raw throat.

I barely heard the low *meow*. Barely. It was a miracle I did. With my eyes burning, my skin burning, my hand burning, I couldn't believe I found the old, nearly blind calico hidden in a corner by the door, shaking. I scooped her up, wheezing, crying because my eyes stung so badly. The heat was horrible, and I didn't know then that it would be a long time before I ever took a steaming hot shower again.

I ran out of the front door, coughing, coughing, coughing. I could barely see as I tried to make it down the steps, tripping and missing the bottom one, which sent me flying down the sidewalk, landing hard on my knees. The cat went running away from me and the fire as I hacked up a lung, panicking, knowing I needed to get away. Knowing the neighbors on either side of Miss Pearl needed to get away too.

But my legs weren't working. Neither was my brain. I was too busy trying to get my lungs to breathe.

"You fucking idiot," a voice exploded—angry, so angry—from somewhere nearby.

A split second later, two arms were around me, one under my knees, the other across my shoulders, and then I was up in the air, cradled against a chest as I hacked up coughs so strong my stomach hurt.

"You stupid, stupid idiot," the voice hissed as I felt us moving.

I couldn't even muster up the energy to figure out who the hell was carrying me, much less tell them I wasn't an idiot.

My lungs wouldn't work, and I only coughed harder, my entire body into it.

The male voice right by my head cursed and cursed again, "fuck" and "shit" and "goddammit." The tone as bitter and harsh as the smoke had been. But I couldn't concentrate. I didn't care. My hand was starting to throb unbearably, and I still couldn't catch my breath. There were other things to worry about.

I felt myself being lowered instead of actually

seeing it. I felt the grass under my legs and bare feet— when the hell I lost my shoes, I had no idea. I heard Josh and Louie's voices mixed in with other unfamiliar ones. I heard the wail of a fire truck's siren most importantly, and maybe I heard the ambulance too.

But I was coughing too hard, trying to shield my hand.

Something soft swept over my eyes and mouth—a T-shirt. And still I coughed.

"Josh, get a glass of water," the male voice ordered, low and grumbling against my ear. It was Dallas. It took me a second, but I knew it was him crouched by me, a weight around my back as a supporting gesture. He was the one who had carried me. Of course it was him. Who else would it be?

"Can you tell…" I couldn't catch my breath. The side of my face was pressed against something hard and warm and steady. I closed my eyes, trying to catch my breath. "Miss Pearl… I got her cat, but… she jumped out of my arms?"

"Fuck the fucking cat," the voice by my ear spat out. What had to be his arm around my back moved lower, slinging around my hips. I was pulled in closer to what had to be his body at my side. Something pressed against my cheek, his words almost muffled. "You stupid little idiot. You stupid fucking idiot—"

"I had to," I whispered to him, lifting my head. Had his lips been on my cheek?

"Had to? *Had to?*"

It was Louie, my poor wonderful Louie that explained it to him. "Daddy fell and hit his head, and nobody stopped to see him," he told him, word for word in the same way I'd relayed the story to him in the past, minus a few details. "That's why you gotta help people who need it," he ended, his little chest shaking with emotion at the memories I was sure he was living through right now because of me.

Dallas glanced back and forth between Louie and me, his own body continuing with the tremors I'd originally felt. I was pretty sure he muttered, "Jesus fucking Christ," but I couldn't be positive.

"Dallas?" Miss Pearl's soft, creaky voice managed to tear through my coughs.

"Don't move, Diana," Dallas barked. Something tender pressed against my temple and cheek. Somewhere in the back of my head, I guessed it was his nose to the side of my eye, his mouth at my cheek. "The ambulance will be here in a second. *Don't fucking move*," he told me one last time before his support left me.

In less than two seconds after he moved, he was replaced by a much smaller body. One that was as familiar to me as my own. One that crawled onto my lap and pressed itself against me, whimpering and shivering just like poor Mildred the cat had been when I found her.

"Are you dying?" Louie asked against my ear as he tried to bury himself inside of me, squishing my hand against my stomach, making it hurt even more.

But I couldn't tell him to move.

I shook my head, gritting my teeth at the pain. "I just inhaled... a lot of smoke, Goo." I coughed some more, lowering my forehead until the side of it touched the back of his soft-haired head.

"Are you gonna live?" His voice broke, and that shredded my heart and made me feel like a selfish asshole.

I nodded again as my lungs tried getting rid of more smoke. "I'm gonna live."

He shivered and he shook even more. "Promise?"

"Promise," I rasped out, wiggling my arm out from between us to wrap around his back.

The sirens got louder and louder, and out of the corner of my eye I could see the flashing, bright lights as they stopped in front of Miss Pearl's house. Before I knew it, the firefighters were circling the home, and neighbors from all over the neighborhood suddenly appeared on the streets close by. Josh came back and nudged a glass of water into my hand before promptly coming up behind me and wrapping his arms around my neck, his face pressing against the side opposite of Louie's. He held me tight.

I gulped down the water and watched as the ambulance pulled up a couple of houses down. The paramedics went straight to Miss Pearl, who I barely noticed was right where I'd left her, next to Dallas who was holding one of her hands with Jackson hovering close by. It only took a few minutes for them to put her on a stretcher with a mask over her face, and it was about that time that another ambulance pulled up the street.

"I was so scared," Josh admitted into my ear as Miss Pearl was loaded into the ambulance.

There was no way I could tell him I'd been just as scared as he had been.

I KNEW IT WAS LATE WHEN I FINALLY WOKE UP. TOO MUCH light was coming in through the curtains when my eyes finally cracked open, my hand giving more than a gentle throb at me finally being awake and able to comprehend the pain radiating from it. It wasn't too surprising that I was alone in bed when I remembered all three of us piling on to it in the middle of the night. The paramedics had checked me over to make sure I was going to be fine—making me breathe through a mask that had the boys both crying in a way that I never wanted to see again—and bandaging up my hand after I told them there was no way I was going to the hospital.

It was after four in the morning when we finally trudged inside, and I took a shower, coming out to find Josh and Louie waiting for me in my bed already under the covers. It had been years since Josh slept with me. Years. But now... well, I understood and, honestly, I was more than a little grateful. Last night, I had gone to bed confused about Dallas's reaction to my toolbox, and the next thing I knew, I had run into his grandma's burning house to get her.

I was freaked the fuck out. The entire night before had scared the shit out of me. I could admit it.

If I could go back, I wouldn't *not* do what I'd done, but... I could wish it hadn't come to it. What would the boys do without me?

Sliding out of bed, my shoulders screamed in protest at what I'm sure had been their usage when I'd helped Miss Pearl out of her house. My hand started throbbing even more painfully at the burn gracing its palm. My knees only stung a little as the sheets brushed against them. I hadn't bothered with Band-Aids on them. They were scraped, but I'd had worse.

It took me a few minutes to use the bathroom, dab some honey on my scrapes, and brush my teeth awkwardly with my left hand. My head and throat were achy and raw from the night before.

And it was right then, as I was trying to brush my teeth with the wrong hand, that I realized what the hell I'd done.

I'd burned the hand I used to cut hair.

Flipping my hand over, I looked over the area that was covered by gauze. "Fuck. Fuck!" Most of my fingers were fine, but... "Motherfucker!"

My head throbbed. My eyes got watery. I'd burned myself. What the hell was I supposed to do? I used my right hand for everything. *Everything*. With so much gauze on it, I couldn't cut hair, or even hold a brush for color. I had a feeling that anything that required me to stretch the skin on it was going to cause a world of pain.

"Fuck!" I cussed again, clenching my teeth together for all of a minute before I made myself think of Miss Pearl and what would have happened if I hadn't intervened. My hand for a life. *My hand for a life and the life of a cat*. It hadn't been for nothing.

But, I couldn't believe I had been so stupid to touch the doorknob with my right hand. *Fuck.*

"Aunt Di?" Josh's voice came from the doorway.

I swallowed hard and plastered a smile on my face that wasn't completely fake. He was still in his pajamas from the night before, and he looked like he'd been awake for a while. "Hey. I just woke up."

Josh glanced between the hand I was holding and my face. "Are you okay?"

I nodded, not trusting my words.

"Does it hurt?"

I didn't like to lie to them, so I nodded again.

"A lot?"

"I've had worse," I told him softly, also still not lying. It was the truth. I'd been in worse pain. It hadn't been physical, but that didn't matter.

He didn't look like he entirely believed me, but he let it go.

"Did you eat already?"

"Uh-huh."

"Did Louie?"

"Uh-huh."

"What?"

"Cereal and a banana."

"Good." I gestured toward him, calling myself an idiot for what had happened. "I'm pretty hungry," I said.

Josh walked alongside me toward the kitchen, watching as I put my slippers on and watching even closer as I cradled my hand to my stomach again. But he didn't say anything. Louie smiled at me when I spotted him in the living room sitting on the couch in front of the television playing video games. If he wanted to act like yesterday hadn't happened, so be it. The last thing I'd been thinking about before I'd fallen asleep was what I would tell my parents and the Larsens when they saw my hand. I thought I could just not tell them, but with these two big mouths, it was going to come out at some point.

I was already dreading the comments they'd make.

"Morning, Goo," I greeted him, taking two steps forward before I stopped in place directly in front of the television and glanced back at him.

He'd been sitting pretty high up in the air, but as I gave him another good look I realized why he seemed to be taller on the couch than usual. It was the Iron Man blanket under him that hadn't made me look too closely at the couch, but now that I did... I realized he was sitting on something.

Sitting on *someone*.

It was a long man with short, dark hair, asleep faced down on the couch with a bicep covering the side of his face. And Louie was sitting on what I could only assume was his butt as he played video games.

"Are you sitting on Dallas?"

The five-year-old smiled and nodded, whispering, "Shh," at me. "He's sleeping."

I could see that. When the hell had he gotten into the house? I didn't care that he was over—of course I didn't—but I was confused. I figured I would just ask Josh but told Lou instead, "Get off him, Lou. He's sleeping."

"He told me it was okay," he argued. *"Stop talking so loud."*

Oh my God. Was this kid telling me to be quiet? I opened my mouth and closed it again, taking in the sleeping man beneath him. Shooting Lou a look he didn't see because he'd turned his attention back to his game, I kept going into the kitchen where Josh had disappeared to.

He was already waiting for me, immediately handing me the box of my favorite strawberry cereal and peeled my banana for me as I got out the milk, watching me with those brown eyes so much like Rodrigo's and mine.

"When did Dallas get here?" I asked him in a quiet voice.

Josh hesitated for a second before reaching to take the gallon of milk out of my hands, going to pour it into the bowl for me. "Around eight. Louie woke me up when he heard the knocking."

"Did you check to make sure it was him before you opened it?"

He shot me a look as he put the cap back on the milk. "Yeah. I'm not a baby."

"I'm just making sure," I muttered back. "What did he say?"

"He came inside and asked if you were okay. Then he said he was really tired and was gonna take a nap on the couch." With his back to me as he set the milk back inside the fridge, he asked, "Are you mad he's here?"

Plucking a spoon from the drawer, I stuck it in my

mouth as I moved my bowl of cereal to the edge of the counter. "What? No. I was just surprised... he was here. Did he say anything about Miss Pearl?"

"No." Had Josh's tone gotten husky or was I imagining it? He seemed to think about something for a second before adding in a weird voice, "He called you stupid last night."

With the spoon in my mouth, I realized he was right. He had called me stupid and an idiot. A stupid fucking idiot or something like that. Huh.

"You were dumb," Josh whispered, his words making my head snap around to tell him not to talk to me like that. But the expression on his face made me keep my comments to myself. If rage and grief could have a child, that was what would have been reflected on my nephew's face. It made me want to cry, especially when his eyes went wide as he battled the emotion inside of him. *"You could have died,"* he accused, his eyes going shiny in the time it took me to blink.

The scare from last night seemed to swell up inside of me again, the possibilities fresh and terrifying. My own eyes went a little watery as I shoved the bowl away from the edge of the counter and faced Josh head-on. There was no point in lying to him or attempting to play off the situation as anything less than what it had been. It was easy to forget sometimes how smart he was, how mature and sensitive this eleven-year-old could be.

So I told him the truth, our gazes locked on each other. "I know, J. I'm sorry I scared you. I was scared too, but there was no one else out there—"

"We have neighbors," he declared, his voice uneven and low so that I knew he didn't want to let Louie hear what was going on between us. "They could have gone in so you didn't have to."

"Josh." I reached out and tried to take his hands, but he hid them behind his back, making me sigh in exasperation. "No one else was out there. I didn't want to do it, but I couldn't leave Miss Pearl in there and you know it."

His throat bobbed and he squeezed his eyes closed, killing me a little inside.

"I love you and your bro more than I love anything, J. I would never intentionally leave you," I whispered, watching his face as I pressed my good palm against my thigh. "I'm sorry that I scared you, but there was no other choice for me but to go in there and get her. You can't always wait for someone else to do the right thing when you can do it yourself."

Josh didn't say anything for a long time as he stood there in front of me. His eyes stayed shut. His hands stayed balled at his sides.

But finally, after what felt like forever, he opened them. They weren't glassy. They weren't pained or angry. They looked more resigned, and I wasn't sure how that made me feel.

"Bad things happen all the time, and we can't control them. You'll never know how sorry I am that you've had to learn that the hard way. But I love you, and we can't be scared of shit we can't do anything about. We can just be happy to be alive and enjoy what we have. I don't know if something bad will happen to me now or fifty years from now, but I would do anything to stay with you two." I touched his cheek and watched him let out a shaky exhale. "And like my grandma used to tell me, the devil will probably kick me out of hell the day I die. I won't go anywhere without a fight."

He eyed me quietly for a moment before asking, "You swear?"

"I swear." I touched his head, and he didn't move away from me that time. "I'm sorry, okay?"

"Me too. You're not really dumb."

"Sometimes people say crazy things when they're upset that they don't mean. I get it."

He ducked his chin but kept eye contact with me. "You do that sometimes."

"When?"

"When you're... you know..." His cheeks turned pink. "That time every month."

I was never going to forgive myself for having to break him into the female period so early in his life, but it had happened, and there was nothing I could do to change it. It was him either thinking I was dying, thinking I was a vampire, or knowing the truth. I'd gone with the truth. I'd started making sure I locked the bathroom door after that one incident of him busting in and finding me in the middle of wrapping up a used nighttime pad. It had taken us like two weeks until we were finally able to look each other in the eye again after that.

"Mind your own beeswax. I'm always nice."

That had him snorting.

"What? I am." I smiled at him.

"Sure, *Tia*."

I stuck my tongue out at him, pleased every single time he called me *tia* since he did it so rarely now, and he stuck his out right back.

"Morning." Dallas's voice made us both jump, the sound of it about fifty times raspier than normal.

I turned to look at him, suddenly remembering how angry he'd been hours ago and feeling uncertain. The expression on his face as he moved into the kitchen and rested his hip against the counter didn't help any either. In fact, Dallas looked more pissed than I'd ever seen him. How could someone wake up that mad? Those clear hazel eyes flicked down to Josh's for a moment, a brief smile flashing across his mouth. "Hey, Josh."

"She just woke up," my nephew explained quickly.

Dallas's eyes swung back up to me, the slight smile on his face melting off before he glanced at the forearms I had crossed over my breasts. I'd changed from the night before, and the baggy T-shirt I had on hid everything. "I can tell." He looked back at my face, and I took in the tendons popping out along the column of his neck. Did his jaw jut out more than normal or was I imagining it? "J, can I talk to your aunt alone for a minute?"

The little traitor nodded. "Okay. I'm gonna take Mac for a walk then."

"Don't go far," Dallas and I both said at the same time, watching each other carefully.

Josh gave us a horrified expression, but just like that, he disappeared.

My neighbor tipped his head toward the kitchen door that led to the backyard, and I followed after him, trying to decide whether to tug my shirt down or not. He'd already seen me in just a tank top and underwear the night before, at least I hadn't worn a thong to bed.

Out on the back stoop, Dallas took a step down to give me the top and watched me with that intense gaze, his lips pinched together. Even with him giving me the advantage, he was still taller than me.

I raised my eyebrows at him, remembering briefly that he'd called me things last night that hadn't been okay. "Is Miss Pearl all right?" was the first thing I asked.

"She's fine," he answered in a cool, calm voice. Carefully, he said, "You saved her life."

And risked mine. Just thinking about it sent a shiver up my back. "I couldn't leave her in there. Anyone would have done it."

Dallas bit his lip again, that pink stretch of flesh turning white with pressure. "No, they wouldn't have."

"Any decent person would have."

"No, they wouldn't," he grumbled, his Adam's apple bobbing. "I can never pay you back for that."

I frowned. "You don't have to."

His lips moved but no sound came out, and he took his attention to something above my head. "I went to bed and didn't hear anything until Josh came pounding on the door."

Josh did that?

"I don't know what I would've done if something happened to her..." Dallas kept going, his attention still away from me. "I owe you everything."

Oh God. I was getting uncomfortable. "It's fine, really."

And then, he turned those hazel eyes on me once more and he blinked. But it wasn't a normal blink. It was the kind of blink that changed your life. The kind of blink you noticed enough to earmark this moment in history. It was a preparation. A buffer. It was everything. And then he slashed his hand across the air, angry. "But if you ever do something *so fucking stupid ever again*—"

"Whoa, whoa, whoa," I cut him off, caught off guard by the fury in his tone.

He held up a finger, silencing me. "What you did last night was the stupidest fucking thing anyone has ever done, do you hear me? I get that you went in to get her, but you're a goddamn idiot, and you're a bigger fucking idiot *for going back to get the fucking cat.*"

My bottom lip dropped open for a moment before I shut it. "You wanted me to let the cat die?" I asked, slightly outraged.

The exasperated look he shot me sent the hairs on the back of my neck to standing position. "The cat's sixteen years old and you have two boys and your entire life ahead of you. Are you fucking kidding me? You're going to risk your life for Mildred?"

While I recognized he had a point—and that I'd had that exact same thought when Miss Pearl had pleaded for me to save her beloved cat—I didn't like the brutal honesty in his tone. I wasn't a fan of the accusation and possibility he raised to the forefront of my brain once again either. I did have two boys. It wasn't that they wouldn't be fine without me, but it was… well, I couldn't do that to them. I couldn't be the third person in their lives to leave so unexpectedly. I had never taken a single sociology or psychology class, but my inner guts screamed that chances were, two little sponges so early in their lives couldn't handle those kinds of losses and move on from them very well.

The fact was while nothing had happened to me, something could have. And then what?

Then again… I would have jumped into a burning building for Mac. I understood where Miss Pearl had gotten the balls to ask for a hero.

Regardless, that guilt buried itself deep into the back of my brain, and I sensed my face going warm. Josh had already given me enough shit for only having been awake a few minutes. I'd never handled guilt well. "I'm fine. Mildred is fine. Your grandma is fine. If I could do it all over again—" well, I wasn't positive I would have run in for Mildred again. "It doesn't matter. Everything worked out all right. Miss Pearl is fine. I'm fine. Everything is okay."

My words did nothing for the anger bubbling through his skin, eyes, and mouth. Dallas shook his head and his hands went up to his face in that same exact way they had the night before when he'd asked for my toolbox. Was he red? "If something had happened…." He trailed off, the sound in his throat anguished.

I reached toward his forearm. "You said your nana's fine. You can't think about *what might have happened*—"

"It's not Nana I'm thinking about, Diana!" he exploded, his entire body leaning toward me. "You don't have to save the entire fucking world!"

The breath left my lungs in a sharp inhale and I blinked up at the man radiating so much fucking fury, I didn't know what to say or how to react.

"If something had happened to you—"

I choked. Me? He'd been worried about me too?

The hand connected to the forearm I'd been touching came up to my eye level. His fingers went to my chin, cupping it as he looked directly into my eyes. "If something happened to you, I wouldn't be okay. I would *never* be okay," he practically hissed.

Knowing I was an idiot asking for the pain of a lifetime, I still let myself lean forward into his touch, but I couldn't look him in the eye. Instead, I focused on his nose even as I felt his stare centered on my eyelids. "The good thing is, you're going to be okay because I'm fine."

"Fine?" His snort had me glancing up at him. He raised a brown eyebrow in a completely smart-ass response that seemed so at odds with the calm, mature man I had started getting to know. "Lemme see your hand."

Shit.

I kind of maneuvered it partially behind my butt, as if he hadn't already caught a glimpse of the wrapping around it. "It'll heal," I argued.

He was getting pissed off all over again. I could sense it coming off his body. "Did it happen getting the cat?"

Him and the fucking cat. Jesus. "Why do you hate the cat so much? And no, Dr. Evil, it didn't happen then." During Mildred's rescue, I had almost died from smoke inhalation, or at least that was what it had felt like in the moment. "It happened when I tried opening the door to her house. The knob was hot." Okay that was the understatement of the month. I had a second degree burn from it, and I didn't want to even begin to piece together what I was going to do with a burned hand and my job. How long would it take to heal? How long would I have to take off from work? Could I hold shears in my hand once it got a little better?

I had no idea, and that made me panic a little.

Okay, more than a little.

I didn't have some huge savings account; I'd barely started getting my feet back under me after taking time off to visit Vanessa, and asking my family or Van for money seemed like a horrible fucking idea. I could probably get by without working for a couple of weeks, but that was it—and that was with me counting every penny and not wasting a single cent. There was money in the account I had set aside for the boys from Rodrigo's life insurance policy, but I would never, ever touch it. It was the boys'.

His eyelids hung low over those hazel eyes, and I caught a flash of his teeth as they bit down on the inside of his cheek for a moment. I knew when he didn't comment on me calling him Dr. Evil that he was genuinely really angry. He looked like he was mulling my words over... or talking himself out of yelling at me. From the murderous expression on his face, it could have been both. Then he swallowed hard. "It was stupid. Really goddamn stupid, and I don't think you seem to realize that—"

"I do," I argued.

He shot me this disbelieving look. "You have two boys, Diana—"

Guilt pricked at my chest, and I swallowed at the same time my eyes got teary. "I know, Dallas. *I know.* Josh already—" My voice broke and I dropped my gaze to the bottom of the wrinkled T-shirt he had on. It was a different one than he'd worn to the movies the night before. "He was so mad at me. I feel terrible I did that to him."

The sigh that came out of him wasn't even a slight warning for the hands that came to my shoulders and gave them a squeeze. It didn't prepare me for the arms that went around them afterward, or the chest that came in contact with my forehead. He'd hugged me the night before, hadn't he? I hadn't imagined it? His voice wasn't any less rough or mean as he said, "You scared the hell out of all of us."

I had?

"I thought you were mad at me last night when you left," I told him.

His sigh was so deep, it was choppy on the way out. The arms he had around me tightened, but the rest of his body relaxed. "I wasn't mad at you. I swear. It was other things." He gulped, and I'd swear one of his hands cupped the back of my head. "Look, I have to leave tomorrow for a couple of days."

Why was he telling me this? "Is everything okay?"

"It will be. I have to go. I can't reschedule it," he explained, his breath so deep it made my head move. "Diana—"

A breeze hit the back of my legs as the back door opened and something poked me in the leg while I stood in Dallas's arms. "Can you make me a sandwich?" Louie's voice came from behind. "Please?"

I didn't even freeze at getting caught. "Sure, give me a sec," I answered him quickly.

Lou said nothing; he just stood there, not moving. I could sense him.

I sighed, my mouth inches from Dallas's sternum. "Goo, quit being nosey and give me a second, please."

There was a hum and then, "Can I have a hug too?"

Dallas's arms flexed and I swore I heard him laugh lightly before one of them dropped from around me as he took a step back. "Have at her, buddy."

It was then I finally glanced down at Louie to find he'd moved to stand beside my hip. The kid blinked and edged closer between us. "No, you too," he said so effortlessly it made me want to cry. "Sandwich."

Just like that, Dallas crouched and scooped Louie up. One of those little arms went around my neck, and I would bet my life the other was around Dallas's. The only other thing I knew for sure was that an arm too brawny to belong to a five-year-old wrapped low around my back. The side of my head went to a shoulder and one half of my chest was crushed against a much harder one.

"This is nice," Louie muttered somewhere close to my ear.

I couldn't help it. I laughed, and what I was sure was the hand connected to the arm around my back, stretched wide and covered part of my belly, the tips of long fingers touching my belly button. I sucked in a breath.

"Can we do this more?" Lou continued on.

"We will," the voice above my head agreed.

What was I going to do? Say "no thank you"? I could do this more often. I could do this every day.

But Dallas was married, and we were just friends. I couldn't forget that.

What I couldn't forget either was that he wasn't going to be married forever.

And that didn't necessarily mean anything good for me.

CHAPTER TWENTY

The thing about being neighbors with your nephew's coach and your boss being related to said neighbor/coach was that if something happened to you, everyone they knew was going to find out your business.

And that was exactly what happened to me.

In those couple of days after the fire, Trip called and came by the house. A few of Josh's friends from baseball found out, and their moms dropped off food. I got text messages from other parents on the team who had never given me more than a wave, letting me know that if I needed anything to give them a ring. Doing a good deed didn't go unnoticed. Maybe I wouldn't have money to pay the cable bill, but I'd have people willing to watch the boys or mow the yard. It was an outpouring of love I wasn't familiar with that came at us—this time from people who were practically strangers.

Which was fine, because when I'd called my parents to let them know about how I'd burned myself —because I knew how much worse it would be if they found out another way—my mom had passed off the phone to my dad. I was used to her calling me an idiot, but the silent treatment was worse. The last person who needed to bottle things up was that woman.

I spent those first couple of days going to the salon to reschedule my appointments and talk to Ginny about what she could do while I was out for a while. *A while*. Best-case scenario seemed to be three weeks. Come hell or high water, I was going to be back at work in three weeks. I couldn't afford to take off a week, but I absolutely couldn't take off more than three.

When I wasn't at the salon or moping around at home, holding my burned hand up high and cussing at it, I went to visit Miss Pearl at the hospital, who was being held there because of all the smoke she'd inhaled and she'd gotten a few burns too.

"How are you doing, Miss Pearl?" I asked the elderly woman after I'd set the vase of flowers I'd bought her at the grocery store on the table in front of her bed.

In a faded mint-green hospital gown, and with her hair limp and flat against her scalp, she'd blinked those milky blue eyes at me and sighed. "Half my house burned down, but I'm alive."

Well, that wasn't the positive statement I'd been expecting to get.

But she'd kept going. "You saved my life, Diana,

and I never told you thank you—"

"You don't have to thank me."

She rolled her eyes. "I do. I'm sorry for messing up your name. You're a good girl. Dal says I'm bored and like to push people 'cause of it. I don't mean any harm."

Damn it. Sitting down in the chair beside her bed, I reached up and placed my hand over her cool one. "I know you don't. It's okay. I'm pushy too."

That had the old woman smirking. "I heard."

Before I could ask who she'd heard that from, she continued on. "Dal left, but he'll be back by Wednesday, he said. That's when they're letting me out of this joint."

He'd already warned me of that on Saturday when he'd woken up at my house and then went ahead to spend half the day with the boys and me, hanging around before he took off to visit Miss Pearl at the hospital.

But he hadn't told me where he was going, and so I kind of snuck in, "Is he okay?"

You'd figure I would know you can't bullshit a bullshitter, and Miss Pearl had a lot more experience bullshitting than I did. By the smile she gave me, she knew I was fishing, and the old woman said, "Oh, he's fine. Just great."

And that was all she'd given me. Damn it.

So a couple of days later, when I was lying on the couch with a glass of milk on the table and a smores Pop-Tart in one hand, watching television and wondering how the hell I was going to survive two more weeks without working, I was startled by a lawn mower roaring to life.

It took a couple of seconds for me to realize that the loud sound was coming from close by. Really close by. *Was someone at my house?*

Swinging my legs over the edge of the couch, I peeked over the back of it to look through the window at the side of the house. I saw nothing. I checked my phone as I stood up to make sure my dad hadn't called and said he was coming over, but there were no missed calls.

Pulling up one single blind on the window, looking out toward the front lawn, I paused, let it drop, and then raised it again. At the same time I was doing this, goose bumps broke out along my spine.

Because on my lawn wasn't a stranger, especially since he'd let me just about bawl my eyes out in front of him more than once. It also wasn't *just* Dallas cutting my lawn like it was no big deal.

It was Dallas on my lawn with his shirt off, pushing his lawn mower.

It was Dallas on my lawn with his shirt off.

More goose bumps rose all over my body. He wasn't sweating yet, but even that wouldn't have made him more attractive than he looked in that moment. He didn't need anything to look more attractive than he did right then and there. A thong or nudity was absolutely not necessary.

Because my eyes saw everything they needed to see; what they had last seen months ago. Everything they would *ever* need to see. They took in the faint V-shape of muscle right where the elastic band to his sweat pants rested. They took in those cube-shaped, ridged muscles above his belly button that extended into neatly stacked rectangles. Then there were those shoulders that were just perfect. And those arms and forearms.

I loved forearms. Loved them. Especially his. I could even see the veins lining his from my window.

Most of all though, I took in every single inch of tattooed skin covering him. This was my payment for burning the shit out of my palm from the looks of it.

The brown ink I'd seen by his elbow was part of a wing that wrapped around his entire biceps, stretching out onto his chest. Right between his pectorals was the head and beak of an eagle. Another wing seemed to sweep around his opposite arm, almost a perfect mirror of the first one I'd seen.

God help me. The view was even better the second time around.

Was I going to go out there specifically to catch an up-close look of the details of the eagle's wings? No way in hell.

But was I going to go out there to offer him a glass of water despite the fact he could easily walk across the street to get a drink from his own house? I damn well was.

For one brief moment, I thought about putting on something other than pajamas, but… what was the point? It would be obvious if I did, and despite him being a wonderful friend, person, and neighbor, *he was married*. Getting a divorce. Same thing.

And he'd disappeared for days somewhere.

There was no harm in using my eyeballs on him. Repeatedly. I just wouldn't look at his butt or junk. That was crossing the line. Anything from the waist above was fair game, I reasoned.

Leaving my hair loose around my shoulders, I opened the door and stepped out just as he finished a pass down the lawn away from me, turning the mower at the last minute. I must have caught his attention immediately because he looked up from his focus on the grass to gaze at me, and I waved, smiling too wide at someone who wasn't mine and couldn't be.

When he didn't shut off the machine, I made a drinking gesture toward my mouth and he shook his head.

Okay. What was I supposed to do now?

I watched him for a moment, noticing there was something different about him, but I couldn't figure out what. His lawn mower was bagged, but he had to empty it out. By the time I heard the motor putter to a stop, I had already made it out to the shed to grab a couple of the big, black bags we used for the leaves and opened the gate that led to the front. Dallas was busy taking the bag off the back of the machine when I came up to him.

"What are you doing here?" I asked, telling my eyeballs they better not backstab me right then and there by straying somewhere they had no business going.

"Morning," he said in that low voice. "Did I wake you?"

"No." I used my chin to point toward the bag in my hands. "I can hold it with one hand, can you pour and hold the other side of the bag, too?" He nodded and did it, setting the attachment back to the mower while I shook the clippings so they settled at the bottom. "So, can I ask what exactly you're doing?"

"It's called mowing a lawn," he informed me, his attention still centered on the red-painted machine. "I've seen you do it before."

And people thought of me as a smart-ass. "I'm being serious. What are you doing, Professor X? I was planning on laying a guilt trip on the boys so they would do it on their own."

He eyed me with those golden-brown irises before focusing back on the trash bag in front of him. "*I have hair*, and your lawn needed mowing. Your hand is fucked. I just got back and don't have any work scheduled for today."

"You didn't have to do anything—"

He stood up to his full height and stared me down. "Accept the help, Diana."

I blew out a breath and kept watching him, still trying to see why he looked different.

He crossed his arms over his chest, and it took every single ounce of strength I had to not glance at the eagle head. "Is it everyone or just from me?"

Pinching my lips together, I brought my hand to my chest and watched as he glanced at it. I'd swear a tendon in his neck popped. But I told him the truth. "You, mostly. I don't want to take advantage of you. I'm not shy about asking for things."

"I didn't think you knew how to be shy." He raised an eyebrow. "You're not taking advantage of me. We talked about this already."

"Fine, but I don't want to make you feel weird either."

His reply was low and steady. "I've seen you in your underwear and combed nits out of your hair, baby. I think we're past that."

I focused on one thing and one thing only.

Baby?

Me?

I was still thinking about his word choice when he asked, "How's your hand?"

What hand? There was something wrong with my hand?

"Your burned hand," he said, raising both his eyebrows, a slight smile playing at his lips.

Jesus Christ. I'd lost it. I swallowed. "Same old. It hurts. I'm taking some pain medication when it gets really bad, but not a lot. I have to rubber band a bag around my hand to shower. I cut myself shaving. I haven't shampooed my hair in five days. It takes me longer to do everything with this thing, but I'll live." Poor and in pain, but it could be worse. "Can I help you with anything?"

"Nope."

"Really. I can help. I have one good hand, and I'm bored out of my mind. It's only been a few days, but I don't know how I'm going to make it being stuck at home." That was putting it lightly. I'd gone to help my mom at the store she worked at, but only made it three hours before her comments about my intelligence—because who goes into a burning house?—got to be too much and I left.

Those hazel eyes were on me for a couple of seconds before his mouth twitched. His hands went to his hips and I told myself, *Don't fucking look, Diana. Don't look down.*

The question was out of my mouth before I could stop myself. "Are you really patriotic or do you just like eagles?"

His eyebrows went up and with a straight face, he glanced down at his chest before focusing back on me. "My dad had this tattoo on his arm." Then, like what I'd asked was no big deal, he asked, "You need something to do?"

I nodded, telling myself to let the tattoo go.

"You sure? You'll only use one hand?"

Why was the first thought that popped into my head a dirty one?

And why did my face turn red as I thought that over?

"Cross my heart."

Dallas tipped his head to the side. "You didn't start on Louie's quarterpipe while I was gone, did you?"

There it was. Another reminder he'd gone somewhere. Hmm. "Nope."

"Then you can help me build it."

The "shit" came out of my mouth before I could stop it and he smiled.

"Or I can do it alone." He paused for all of a second before saying, "If you tell me you can do it by yourself

—"

I rolled my eyes. "No," I mumbled. "If you insist on helping, we can do it together, and by together, I mean you're going to be stuck doing most of it because I only have one hand, but I'll try my best." I shrugged. "It would be nice to surprise him tomorrow. He's spending the night with the Larsens today. You think we can get it done?"

The small smile that came over Dallas's mouth was like a roman candle straight to my heart. "We can try our best," he offered with all that patience and easygoing nature that cried out to me.

What I wouldn't do for the best of Dallas Walker. But all I said was, "Okay. I'm ready when you are."

"Give me fifteen so I can finish up here and get this thing across the street," he compromised.

I nodded. "I'll meet you in the backyard."

It didn't take him the full fifteen minutes to make his way over. I'd grabbed my gardening gloves from the shed while I waited and slipped one on, and after thinking about it for a moment, got my toolbox out again too. I still didn't understand what had come over him that other night, but he hadn't brought it up, and I wasn't going to either. The only thing I wanted to talk about was where he had gone to, but I made a promise to myself I wasn't going to ask. *I wasn't.*

Dallas had come prepared too from the looks of it as he opened the gate and closed it behind him, giving Mac—who was outside with me—a rub on the head. Unfortunately, or I guessed fortunately, he'd put on a T-shirt. It was one of his threadbare shirts that he usually worked in from the stains all over random places on it.

"I know they're old."

I raised my eyes to his and frowned. "What?"

"My clothes," he said, giving me his back as he went straight toward one of the crates, his hammer in his hand. He went ahead and pried the lid off with the claw side of the hammer. "I hate shopping."

Straightening up, I kept frowning at him, suddenly embarrassed that he'd caught me looking at what he was wearing. "They're fine," I told him slowly. "The whole purpose is not to be naked, isn't it?"

He "hmmed" as he moved to the corner of the box furthest away from me.

"I don't buy new clothes that often either," I tried to offer him. "If I didn't have to dress up for work, I wouldn't, and I've had all those for years now. The boys grow so fast and tear up their stuff so easily, they're the only ones who get new things regularly in our house."

"Nana's always giving me grief over them," he said, quietly or maybe he was just distracted, I wasn't sure. "She says the ladies like a well-put-together man."

That made me laugh. "Maybe for an idiot. I went on a few dates with this one guy a few years ago who dressed better than I did, and you know what? He lived with his parents and they still paid his car insurance. I know I'm not one to talk because it took me forever to get my shit together—and even now, I don't know what the hell I'm doing half the time—but everyone should have some priorities in life. Trust me when I tell you, clothing isn't everything."

Dallas briefly glanced up at me as he moved to another corner with his hammer. "One of the only things I remember about my dad is that he never matched unless he was in his uniform. Ever. My mom laughed at how much effort he didn't put into his clothes." I could see the corner of his mouth tip into a smile at the memory, and just as quickly as it appeared, it disappeared. "When I tried living with my ex for those two months after I got back on land, she wouldn't let me go anywhere with her unless I changed. She said I made her feel poor."

Now I wasn't just going to have to kill his future wife, I was going to have to kill his ex, too. God. My question came out more gritted than I'd intended. "And did you? Change?"

"For a few days."

"You shouldn't have had to try in the first place," I told him, and he glanced up, a small smile on that bristly face.

"I should have if it really mattered to her that much, but I didn't care enough. I've never been with anyone longer than a year, you know. Long-distance relationships don't usually work, and I never tried one until her, but every couple I know who did it and survived, always compromised. You have to care about the other person's feelings enough to not always be right or have your way. I don't regret not trying to make it work, but if I'd loved her, I should have."

Was it rude for me to think I was glad he hadn't?

Before I could think about that too long, he threw out, "Now I know for next time."

I was not going to sabotage any future relationships of his. I wasn't.

Then what the hell *was I* going to do? I wondered. Move somewhere else? Find a boyfriend to maybe be half the man he was and hopefully he'd keep my mind off the one who lived across the street from me who I had all these... feelings for?

What the hell had I done? Why had I done this to myself? I knew better. *I knew better than to like Dallas.* And yet, I couldn't help but ask, "Have you... had a lot of girlfriends?"

This man glanced over at me with a funny expression on his face before facing the crate again. "I've never been one of those guys with a new girl every week or every month."

That still wasn't an answer, and at the risk of sounding like a crazy person, all I did was mumble, "Hmm." Either I was dying inside or this was what a serial killer felt like when he or she needed to get another fix. It could have been either or.

That was enough for him to look at me again with that weird facial expression. "I'm forty-one, Diana. I've had girlfriends. Except for my ex, I never lived with any of them. Never proposed to any of them. The only girl I've loved was my high school girlfriend, and I haven't heard anything about her since I broke up with her to join the navy. I've never looked any of them up online, talked to them on the phone, and I can't remember most of their names or what they look like. I was at sea a lot."

Of course I knew he'd had other relationships in the past, but him acknowledging them still made my stomach roll in jealousy and maybe a little hatred too. Bitches. Not trusting myself to not call all of his exes sluts, my brilliant fucking response was another "Hmm." And then, as if I was trying to make myself feel better, I told him, "I've only had four real boyfriends in my entire life, my ex not included. If I ever saw any of them again, they would probably run the other way."

How did Dallas respond? With a "Hmm" that had me eyeing him.

Was he using too much force to pry the nail out or was I imagining it?

"Thanks for going to see Nana," he commented suddenly, changing the subject and making me keep looking at him. He walked toward the corner right by me before glancing over in my direction, his eyes going to my pink, puppy toolbox for a brief second. He glanced away from it almost immediately.

I groped for the change in subject. "Yeah, of course. She told me she's going to be staying with you until her house gets fixed."

"Yeah." He positioned his body directly to my side, his butt inches from me. I looked away. "She wants her own place back, but she's gonna be stuck with me for a while, no matter what she says."

"She doesn't want to stay with you?"

"She doesn't want to stay with anyone. She keeps telling me that she hasn't lived under somebody else's roof in over seventy years and she's not gonna do it for any longer than she needs to. She offered to go stay with her sister who lives in a retirement community to 'get out of my hair,' but I'm not gonna let her live with anybody but me until her house gets fixed. She's my grandma. I'm not about to pawn her off."

I did not like this man as more than a friend. A passing acquaintance. He was just a nice guy and it made perfect sense to admire someone with his type of loyalty.

I did not like him. I didn't. And I sure as hell wasn't falling in love with him a little. No way.

While I was busy repeating to myself that, yes, I thought he was super-hot, and yes, his heart might be made of the finest silver in the land, but there were plenty of men like that in the world.

I didn't even believe myself.

Dallas shoved the lid off the top of the crate and took a step back, eyeing me once before glancing back to the contents inside. "The motorcycle club is having a cook-off at the shop where Trip works to raise money for Nana's house this weekend."

Shit. I really had no business spending money on things while I couldn't work. The flowers I'd bought for Miss Pearl had to be my one and only splurge for a long time.

He kept going. "This is the boys' weekend with their grandparents, isn't it?" I nodded and he did the same. "Come. I'll buy you a plate."

"You don't have to—"

That big hand reached over to tap the back of my

hand, his face tipped down and serious. "Are you ever going to accept me trying to be nice without arguing?"

I pressed my lips together for a second. "Probably not."

He smiled. "Come." He touched the back of my hand again. "Trip will be there."

Why was my first thought, *As long as you're there, it's fine with me*? What was *wrong* with me? I was asking for a mess. For pain. For heartbreak. For having to move one day.

And even knowing all of that, like an idiot, I didn't say no, but I did sigh. "If you're paying, Mr. Clean...."

∾

"DIANA! MY HERO!"

Even surrounded by what looked like at least 100 people hanging around the lot of the mechanic shop right by the salon, I still managed to pull that one familiar voice yelling out of the air. Smirking, I glanced around from face to face until I found the one I was looking for in the crowd, pushing his way through. The big smile on Trip's face was obviously the result of being a little drunk.

"Hey." I waved at him, trying to see if I recognized anyone else at the cookout Dallas had invited me to.

Trip tossed an arm over my shoulder as he pulled me into his side, giving me a side hug. "How you holdin' up?"

"Better." I held up my bandaged hand. The blisters had finally started to go away, leaving tight, red skin behind. A couple of days ago, for some reason I was beyond understanding, I'd looked up burns online and almost lost my lunch. Things could have been a lot worse; I wasn't going to complain about my injury after I'd seen that.

"Looks like shit to me," he stated, inspecting my hand but keeping his arm on my shoulder and the other at his side. "What do you wanna eat? I'll get you a plate. Where the boys at?" He was leading me through the people, and I took in the leather vests of the motorcycle club and the other dozens of people who looked like a mash-up of early twenties women to mid-thirties men, to forty, fifty and sixty-year-old people in jeans, layers, and more leather vests.

I thought about asking where Dallas was, but I kept it to myself. I needed to quit with the Dallas thing. "They're with their grandparents. What did you try already?"

He hummed. "Brisket is pretty good. The ribs are pretty good. Steaks aren't as good as yours—"

"Remember arguing with me over making them on the cast iron?"

Trip squeezed me to his side as he chuckled. "Yeah, I 'member. I bought a cast iron skillet last time I ran to the store. I was gonna check up on you during practice on Thursday, but we get so busy with all the parents wanting to talk about how their kid needs more play time." He made a grunting noise.

I snickered. "Don't worry. I know we're friends."

"We sure as fuck are, honey," he confirmed as we came up to three big barbecue pits lined up nearly side by side. "What are you in the mood for?"

I told him what I wanted: brisket and grilled corn on the cob. When the pretty girl helping the thin, elderly gray-haired man at the barbecue pit scooped some potato salad onto my plate, Trip whistled. "You're a doll, Iris."

"Fuck off, Trip," a tall man who had been standing off to the side with a toddler strapped to his back and a baby wrapped in a pink blanket in his arms snarled. I looked once at him and then one more time before glancing away. There were tattoos up to the man's neck and he had the grumpiest frown I'd ever seen on anyone, but that didn't change the fact that his face alone could have impregnated some woman.

"Yeah, yeah." Trip ignored him, winking at the girl helping to serve.

"Trip," the tattooed man barked again.

This blond snorted as his eyes met mine and he whispered, "You ever had someone you just love fuckin' with?"

That man didn't look like someone I'd love to fuck with, but what did I know? Even with two kids in his arms, I didn't want to look at him for too long. I whispered back, "Yeah." That had been my brother for me.

Trip snorted and, with my plate in his hand, led me toward one of the many tables set up along the closed bays of the shop. So many people were standing up, there was more than enough room to sit, and he took the spot across from me, setting the plate down. "I forgot to grab you a drink. What do you want? A beer?"

"I'm driving. Whatever soda you have is fine."

"You got it." He grinned before disappearing on me.

With my fork in my left hand, I took in the meat on my plate and cursed. I should have gotten the ribs instead. Since burning myself, I'd been settling for making food I could eat with one hand safely, which was mostly soups, but I hadn't put two and two together with the meat. There was no way I could use a knife. Hell, I could barely wipe myself with my left hand. So, with my fork on its side, I started trying to break up the meat, but it wasn't going so well.

"That's the saddest thing I've ever seen," a voice said from behind me a moment before someone dropped onto the chair beside mine.

I didn't need to look to know who it was. Only one man had that hoarse, raspy voice. It was Dallas.

And the smile that took over my face to see him inches away had me dropping my fork to pivot in the chair. "I didn't know you were here already," I said, noticing the can of root beer in his hands. In dark jeans and a gray fleece pullover hoodie, he looked great.

"I was busy talking to my uncle when I spotted you getting food," he explained, those long fingers moving the can around in his hand until he had it the way he wanted it. He flipped the tab, opening it for me, and setting it beside my plate before scooting his chair over, leaving him so close his body heat was unavoidable. He leaned over, directly in front of me, blocking my view of my plate as he asked, "You want anything else?"

"No, I'm all right. Are you cutting the meat for me?" I joked, smiling even though he couldn't see it.

"Yes," he said, continuing on with his back inches from my face.

There was something wrong with my heart. There was something seriously wrong with my heart. I stuttered, "You really—"

"Let me do it," was all he said.

I sighed and leaned back, trying to make it seem like it was some kind of bullshit he had the nerve to cut my meat for me when my hand was messed up. I was going to need to go to a heart specialist. Pronto. First, I needed him to stop doing whatever it was he was doing to make this happen to me. "Dallas," I whispered. "You really don't owe me anything. How many times do I have to tell you that?"

"None. Stop wasting your breath."

Did he stop what he was doing? No. He didn't.

"You are so fucking stubborn," I said.

"Pot meet your kettle." He straightened in his chair, propping the knife on the edge of the disposable plate before handing over the fork he'd been using.

My kettle? It didn't escape me he'd cut the meat into perfect square shapes. I sighed again and took the utensil from him. *Quit your shit, heart. Quit it right now,* I tried telling it. *I don't have time or the emotional reserves for this.* "Thank you," I said to Dallas.

His blink was the second most innocent thing I'd ever seen after Louie's. The corners of his mouth went up just a little as he said, "Anything for you."

Oh my God. Why was he doing this to me? Why? *Why?* He wasn't the type of person to string someone else along for the fun of it. I knew that. But why did he have to be so nice? And why did I have to be so fucking dumb?

Fuck me.

If I hadn't been so hungry, I would have taken my time eating, but I was. I'd skipped lunch, expecting to stuff myself this afternoon at the cookout. I'd texted Ginny to find out if she was coming after work, but she'd said she would only get a chance to run by during a break; she had a lot of last minute things to do for her wedding coming up in two weeks. I had honestly completely forgotten about it.

I finished my food silently, meeting Dallas's gaze from time to time as I chewed, but for the most part, I kept my attention focused on my plate and on the people hanging around the mechanic shop. The second I finished wiping my mouth off, I asked him something that had been bothering me for a while now. "Why aren't you in the motorcycle club?"

Dallas set his elbow on the table as he shifted his body in the seat to face me, his temple propped on his closed fist. The side of his knee touched my thigh and didn't go anywhere. "The club's more of a legacy. Father to son kind of thing. My dad wasn't in the MC. I told you he was a navy man." He was watching me with those hazel eyes as he whispered and pointed in the general direction behind him. "But this is a big family at the end of the day. Look at it. They're all here for Nana Walker, and she isn't related by blood to anybody here."

Huh. I guess he had a point.

"You don't mind not being in it?"

Dallas shook his head. "I haven't known any of these guys except my uncle and Trip my entire life. It's different for me. I had a lot of friends in the navy. I'm not missing out on anything."

I narrowed my eyes at him. "You ever had a motorcycle?"

He chuckled deep and shook his head. "No. I like AC just fine."

"You got that right." I grinned.

"Bikes aren't really my thing."

I was not going to give him squinty, flirting eyes, damn it. I wasn't going to do it. I made sure to keep my eyelids normal as I asked, "Do you *have* a thing?"

"I have a thing. I have a big thing—" Dallas immediately closed his mouth. His ears went red.

He blinked at me, and I blinked back at him.

And we both started laughing at the same time.

"Someone's cocky." I cracked up.

"I didn't mean it like that." He chuckled in that low, loose way that sang straight into my crippled heart.

"I know. Me neither. I'm just busting your balls," I told him, reaching over with my bad hand to touch the top of his.

His eyes met mine; we were both smiling at each other. And in that moment, it was the most connected I'd ever felt to anyone. *Anyone ever.*

God help me. *It hit me.* It hit me right then.

I was crazy in love with this motherfucker. I really,

really was.

The realization had just entered my brain when a plate dropped onto the table in front of me, forcing us both to look over, shattering the moment into a dozen pieces. It was Jackson. Jackson who was already partially snarling as he pulled the chair out and dropped into it, carelessly, sloppy. I didn't have to physically see the man next to me to know he had tensed. What I also didn't have to witness with my own eyes was the hand that settled into the space between my shoulder blades, calming and steady. Dallas's entire body shifted from how he'd been sitting facing me to suddenly facing forward, his attention on his brother.

"Where have you been?" was the first thing out Dallas's mouth.

His younger brother picked up the plastic fork that had been on top of his plate of food and pecked at the portion of beans on it, his green-eyed gaze locked on Dallas. He seriously had the face of someone who had definitely been a little shit in his younger years and hadn't outgrown that fucking attitude. "Around," was his vague, muttered response.

The man who had been so at ease with me seconds ago, parked the elbow furthest away from me onto the table. He leaned forward, the palm on my back not moving an inch. His chest filled with a breath before he said, "I tried calling you a dozen times."

"I know."

I could feel Dallas's tension skyrocket. "That's all? You disappeared on me after the fire at Nana's house and you can't even answer your fucking phone?" the normally calm man growled.

I wasn't imagining his face getting redder by the minute. It was definitely getting redder by the second, and it had nothing to do with us joking around.

Jackson stabbed his fork straight into his food, letting it stand, and glared forward. "Why do you act like you give a shit when you don't?"

Dallas's head cocked to the side. I could see him breathing hard; I'd never seen him react that way, but then again, siblings had this way of getting you right where it hurt. "Are you ever going to drop it? Twenty years later, you still can't forgive me? We gotta keep talking about this?"

Oh no.

Jackson shook his head, his attention going down to the plate below him. When his attention was up again, he watched his brother as he angrily scooped food into his mouth, chewing with a mouth half open. He was trying to be an asshole. Really trying. What the hell was wrong with this man? As I looked through my peripheral vision at Dallas, I could see the muscles in the forearm resting on the table were flexed. I could see how tight his jaw was, and I hated it. This was the nicest man I'd ever met, and he lived with this stupid sense of guilt for no reason, all because of this prick in front of us.

Sensing me judging him, Jackson flicked his eyes in my direction, his expression an ornery one that drew his eyebrows low. "What? You got something to say?"

The palm between my shoulders slid up to drape

over the shoulder furthest away from Dallas. He gave it a squeeze, and I knew it was a warning. The problem was I didn't give a shit. "Yeah. You're acting like a prick."

Jack reared back like he was caught off guard or offended at what I'd said. "Fuck you. You don't know me."

Dallas squeezed my shoulder tight, his entire body going tense—more tense. "Don't fucking talk to her like that—"

I cut him off, my gaze stuck on his brother. "Fuck you too. I'm glad I don't know you. You're a grown-ass man acting like a little kid."

When Jackson dropped his fork and leaned forward onto the table, his hands grabbing hold of the sides, I didn't flinch.

"Jackson, back up *now*," Dallas growled, already shoving his chair back.

He didn't move and neither did I.

"Jack," Dallas repeated in that bossy voice of his, getting to his feet.

The youngest Walker didn't move an inch, the expression on his face said that he wanted to hit me. I'd seen it on another man's face before, and I knew it for what it was. Violence. Anger. The difference was that I wasn't the same person I'd been before. The difference was that I cared about the person this jackass was constantly hurting. Maybe Dallas felt so guilty he wouldn't tell it to his brother like it needed to be, but I wasn't afraid to.

"You don't know shit, you Mexican bitch," the man

spat, staring at me with those eyes somehow so much like Dallas's and so different at the same time.

"Say one more fucking word, and I'm gonna beat the shit out of you." Dallas's voice was so low, so purred that I couldn't catch my thoughts for a second.

But once I did, I raised an eyebrow at Jackson and tipped my chin down in an "oh really" face, my hand going to rest on Dallas's forearm. "My brother died two years ago. I know that I would do anything to have him back in my life, and you have one in yours who loves you and puts up with your bullshit even though you don't deserve it with the way you act, jackass. I miss mine every single day of my life, and I hope one day you don't regret pushing yours away for something he did twenty years ago that doesn't require forgiveness."

The leer on his face should have warned me he was going to take his assholeness to a different level. I really should have known. But I wasn't prepared for Jackson snorting as he dropped into the chair and leaned against the back, his expression a horrible one.

"Get the hell outta here," Dallas told him. "Now."

But like most younger siblings, he didn't listen.

The younger Walker snarled. "What'd your brother do? Kill himself eating too many tacos?"

It was easy to remember when you weren't angry that people say things they don't mean when their feelings are hurt. It wasn't so easy when you were a breath away from taking a butter knife and using it to stab someone. Somewhere in the back of my head, I realized that Jack didn't know anything about me and my life, or me and my family.

By some miracle, out of the corner of my eye, I caught two big hands gripping the edge of the table, I caught a *"Jack"* out of Dallas's mouth that didn't sound human. It didn't take a stretch of the imagination to figure that Dallas was on the verge of flipping it. It could only be that extreme love you could have for someone who had come out of the same womb as you —or been born from someone who had—that could persevere in a situation like this. I couldn't blame him. He loved this jackoff, asshole or not.

But I'd learned over the last few years that the only person who could fight my battles was me. And even though I was sure I would later regret him not defending my honor and taking this matter into my own hands, I brushed Dallas's forearm with the back of my burned hand before reaching over to grab a cup of something red with ice that Jackson had brought to the table. Dallas's eyes met mine even as this sickening feeling filled my belly at his brother's thoughtlessness.

His hands loosened a moment before I faced Jack again and tossed the liquid inside the cup at his face, watching the red go everywhere—his face, ears, neck, and shirt. His mouth dropped open like he couldn't fucking believe it.

Good.

"He had a traumatic brain injury, you insensitive, immature asshole," I spat out, wishing there was another cup of red liquid to throw at his stupid face again. "He slipped on some ice, fell, and hit his head. That's how he died. There weren't any tacos involved, you prick."

Fuck it, I wish there was a Slushie so I could toss that at him instead.

Angrier than I'd been in a long time, the muscles in my arms and neck were tight and my stomach hurt.

"Oh, hey, Diana, let's go see what Ginny's doing, what do you think?" a voice asked from behind me as two hands settled on my shoulders and literally yanked me back. "I got her. Dallas, deal with him." Trip's voice was right by my ear.

I was mostly numb as Trip steered me through the crowd that had been watching what had happened so quickly. I didn't like being the center of attention, but if I'd had to do it again, I would. Damn it, I wanted to do it all over again.

It wasn't until we were halfway to the salon that my poor hand gave a dull throb, reminding me that I'd used it to grab the cup. "Damn it," I hissed, shaking it, like that would do something to help the pain.

"You all right, honey?" he asked, looking down at my hand.

"I used the wrong hand." I shook it again and gave that wrist a squeeze with my good hand. "Oww." It had been getting better, but I had gripped the cup too hard.

"What the hell happened?" he asked. "One minute, I saw you sitting there with Dal, gigglin' like a girl, and the next, you're both standing up, you start yelling at Jackson and throw Hawaiian Punch at his face."

"What happened is that he's a spoiled little bitch. That's what happened."

Trip laughed that laugh that made me do the same. "Spoiled little bitch. Got it."

"Dallas's brother or not, he's the worst. I don't understand how two people can be so different," I grumbled as we made it to the door of Shear Dialogue. Trip opened the door for me, and I went in first. "He's lucky I didn't grab a chair and go WWE on his ass."

Trip laughed even louder.

At her station, Ginny had her back to us as she cut a client's hair, tossing over her shoulder, "We'll be with you in a minute!"

"It's just me," I called out. "And Trip."

Over at my station, there was a woman I'd met a couple of times in the past who had worked with us before when someone went on vacation. She was a nice lady who was a stay-at-home mom who took jobs here and there. Recognizing me, she waved and I waved back. In the seat in between my station and Ginny's was Sean. I settled for holding up a hand, and he did the same right back. According to Ginny, he was mad I had taken three weeks off work. Like I could control how quickly I healed.

Ginny didn't reply as she kept up what she was doing. By the time she finished blow drying her customer's hair, I had led Trip into the break room and we'd taken seats at the table. I was calm again. She took one look at me and asked, "What happened?"

"Your cousin happened," Trip snickered as he took a sip of Pepsi.

"What did Dallas do?" she asked, confused.

"Not Dallas," Trip replied before I could.

Her features dropped into a blank mask. "Oh. *Him*."

Cradling my hand on my thigh, I leaned back on the chair and watched my boss. "I should have asked why you always made faces every time his name was brought up. Now I know."

"He said something stupid?"

How did she know? "Uh-huh."

Ginny shook her head before making her way to the fridge and pulling out a glass bottle of water, taking a slow drink. "It's what he does best. I don't think there's a woman he's related to he hasn't insulted at some point or another, even Miss Pearl. What he say?"

"Something about my brother," I told her, not in the mood to replay what the hell had come out of his mouth exactly.

She winced. "He called me a slut when I was pregnant with number two because I wasn't married. And maybe about six years ago, he said I was an old bitch." Ginny's smile was grim. "Good times."

That asshole. "Now I definitely won't feel bad about throwing Hawaiian Punch at his face."

Ginny howled, settling her bottle of water on the counter, which made me smirk. "What happened? Where's Dallas?"

"At the shop," I told her.

"My best guess is that he's telling Jackson to fuck right off," was Trip's input.

"He should," Ginny scoffed, her gaze meeting Trip's as they exchanged a look I didn't understand.

"What was that about?" I asked.

She was trying to be innocent, but it wasn't working. We'd known each other too long, witnessed each other want to kill people while plastering smiles on our faces. "What?"

"That face you made at each other. What is it?"

"Nothing—"

The chime of the front door opening had, by instinct, Gin and I both glancing at the television in the corners where images of the security camera were shown. On the screen, the body I would always recognize as Dallas's appeared.

"He's not here looking for me," Gin commented.

Getting to my feet, I shook off the rest of my bad mood and made my way out of the break room toward the front, leaving the two cousins inside to go over whatever little secret they were harboring between each other. When Dallas's eyes landed on me, I was torn with what to say or how to act. He tipped his head in the direction of the door behind him and I nodded, following him outside.

The door had barely closed when he said, with his attention aimed at the sidewalk, "Diana, I'm sorry."

Sorry? I couldn't help but poke him in the chest, right in the center of his pecs. "What do you have to be sorry about? You didn't do anything."

"Jack—"

I poked him again, waiting until his gaze was drawn from the ground and landed on me. Those brown and gold eyes looking ashamed and remorseful made me feel awful. "What he does is not your fault. I'm not mad or hurt by you."

His irises moved back and forth from one of mine to the other, as if trying to search for the truth I had just said out loud.

"I'm sorry I'm not sorry for butting into a conversation that wasn't mine to get into, and I'm not sorry for throwing that drink on him, either," I whispered for no real reason at all. "You don't deserve that, and neither did I."

That handsome, handsome face didn't crack with the seriousness burned into every line of it. "I'm sorry for what he said," he whispered back.

I raised my eyebrows. "You didn't say it or make him say it. I'm not mad, and I hope you aren't mad at me either."

"Why would I be?" The corners of his mouth drew up into a smile I wasn't positive he even knew he made.

"He's your brother. I don't want to come between you two, but I can't sit there and let him talk to you like that either." I blinked. "Was everything okay after I left?"

In the blink of an eye, Dallas's entire body language went back to an angry one. "We had some words and he left. I don't care what he does right now, but I've had it."

I couldn't help *but* feel a little guilty. I didn't want to come between his family.

He tipped his chin toward me, those pretty eyes focused on my face. "You and me are good then?" He used the same words I'd used on him so many months ago.

"We're good, Lord Voldemort." He made a snickering sound that had me smiling. There was something about him standing so close to me, looking down that touched me in a way I wasn't willing to put words to. "You want to hug this out or is it against the rules? No one's watching." Except maybe Ginny and Trip, I realized after I said it.

Dallas was still looking down at me as his arms went around my head without another word, pulling me into his warm, tall body. My cheek found a spot between his pectorals as I wrapped my arms around the middle of his back, feeling long, hard muscles under his clothes. As much as I didn't want to accept it or believe it, the truth was, I was in love with him. Completely. It was pointless to want to think otherwise.

And, as if he could read my mind, the arms around me tightened and he hugged me like... I wasn't sure what. Like he'd missed me. Like he didn't want to let me go, now or ever.

Like he felt the same thing for me that I felt for him.

Before I could stop my big mouth from running, I told him the truth bouncing around in every cell of my body. "This is nice."

CHAPTER TWENTY-ONE

"OH MY GOD, JOSHUA! WOULD YOU HURRY UP FOR THE LOVE of all that is holy in this world?" I called out from the living room where I was pacing. I'd already been hollering for him for at least ten minutes, and he still hadn't come out.

What the hell would make an eleven-year-old take so long to get ready for a tournament? He didn't have to shave or put on makeup. He didn't even have to shower. His stuff was already packed because I'd made sure he did it the night before. I didn't understand how hard it was to put on his clothes and shoes.

"Five minutes!" he yelled back.

I groaned and eyed the clock on the wall. We were going to be late. There was no avoiding it now, much less five minutes from now. I didn't know what it was about these kids that had them thinking we could teleport places, or maybe they thought I drove NASCAR on the weekends I didn't have them and could go 200 miles an hour to get from point A to point B.

The thought had just entered my brain when I realized what I had thought. My mom had said those exact same words to me in the past when I was a kid, except I thought she'd referred to *Knight Rider* instead of NASCAR.

Jesus.

If that wasn't bad enough, the night before, I'd had the same thing happen. Josh had been on the couch while I'd been folding clothes next to him, and after listening to him moan for half an hour about "how bored he was" I'd finally given him the stink eye and said, "Then start cleaning, homeboy."

It was official. I was turning into my mom. How many times had she told me back when I was younger and had whined about not having anything to do, *"ponte a limpiar"*?

It was horrifying.

Pinching the bridge of my nose, I cast a glance at the kid who was leaning against the wall with his tablet and sighed. He already had his backpack on the floor and his jacket on. The weather was supposed to be chilly today, and when I'd gone outside to load the cooler into the car, I confirmed it was definitely jacket weather and told both boys to be prepared. At least one of them had listened to me. "Louie—I mean, Josh, we'll wait for you outside! Hurry up! I'm not getting a ticket because of you, and if you don't warm up, they're not going to let you play!"

All he bellowed back was "Fine!"

"Josh—damn—darn it, Louie, I'm sorry. Let's wait for him outside. Maybe we'll drive a few houses down and make him run after the car," I told him.

The five-year-old grinned and nodded. "Yeah!"

That was way too enthusiastic and it made me laugh. "Hey, don't forget to tell Dallas thank you for building your quarterpipe for you."

I'd helped him, but with only one hand, I had been more like moral support. Plus, I didn't care if he was going to give Dallas all the credit or not. He might not trust using it if he thought I had too much to do with it.

"Okay," he agreed.

Tipping my head toward the door, we made our way outside. Thankfully, Josh was out soon afterward and was settled in by the time Louie finished buckling himself into his booster seat. I didn't say a word for a long time as I backed out of the driveway and drove five miles over the speed limit, already imagining myself blaming Josh for why I was speeding to the cop that might pull us over.

"Can you drive faster?" the eleven-year-old asked.

Through the rearview mirror, I shot Josh a look I hoped would make him look away.

It worked.

Decked out in his Tornado uniform and surrounded by his bag and all his stuff, he was ready to go for the game that was supposed to be started in… twenty minutes. We were running so late that Trip called ten minutes after we were supposed to get there to make sure everything was fine.

By the time I pulled into the lot, Josh was flying out

of the car before I'd even put it into park and yanking his bag out, running to the field like he was on fire. I couldn't see where the boys were warming up but didn't worry; Josh would find them. Louie and I had just made it to the field when the game started. We were the last ones to arrive, despite half the bleachers being empty because no one went to an early game unless they had to. The people who were there were all huddled in their jackets and blankets. The cold front was kicking everyone's ass.

I was honestly not surprised to find that Josh wasn't playing catcher. They'd stuck him in the outfield. A part of me was relieved Dallas and Trip had done that. Hopefully it would teach him a lesson since me yelling at him almost daily did nothing to make him rush. The Tornados barely scraped by with a win.

With an hour break between games, Louie and I waited on the bleachers for Josh, partially watching the other game going on in the field next to the one the boys had just played on. There were eight teams in this tournament from what I could remember. I wasn't paying attention until Josh was standing in front of me, shivering and asking for a dollar.

I blinked at him. "Where's your jacket?"

He had the nerve to look sheepish. "I left it at home. Can I have a dollar for hot chocolate?" Silence. "Please."

"You forgot your jacket even though I told you twice to get it?" I asked, looking at him while I stuck one hand in my bag for the pocket I kept all my small bills from tips at.

"*Yes.*"

"You didn't bring your long-sleeved undershirt I bought you for cold weather either?"

I was pretty sure Louie, who was leg to leg beside me, let out a "heh" as he tried to make it seem like he was paying more attention to the show he was watching on his tablet than our conversation, but I let it go.

"I'm sorry," Josh whisper-hissed. He shivered again. "Can I have a dollar, please?"

Why did this always happen to me and why wasn't I prepared enough to leave two jackets in my car for occasions like this?

A small part of me wanted to cry as I began pulling one arm out of my sleeve and then the other, eyeing Josh the whole time. The good thing was, I'd put on a sweater beneath my black fleece jacket that was a size too large—a present courtesy of my mom.

Josh rolled his eyes. "I don't need it. I'll be fine."

"Until you get pneumonia." I handed the fleece zip-up to him in one hand and two one-dollar bills in the other. "Wear it. If one of us is going to get sick, it's going to be me. Stop looking at me like that. It isn't pink and it doesn't look like a girl jacket. Nobody will know it's mine."

He huffed as he took the jacket from me first, casting a look around to make sure no one was watching him, and then put it on faster than I'd ever seen him put on anything in his life.

"Take your brother with you and get him a hot chocolate too."

To give him credit, he only frowned a little before he nodded. "You want one?"

I shook my head. "I'm good."

He shrugged, pulling the zipper up. "Butt face, come on."

The nosey child at my side was ready and pushed his backpack toward me before jumping off the bleacher and following Josh. The boys had barely turned their backs to me when I finally let myself shiver and crossed my arms over my chest, like that would help. Fuck, it was cold.

"It's chilly, huh?"

Shifting in my spot, I watched as the divorced dad, who sometimes sat by me and always mentioned that he wasn't seeing anyone, took a step down from the bench he was on to the one below it, the first one. The same one as me. If that wasn't bad enough, he sat one body length distance away, his jacket zipped up, hands stuffed into the pockets.

I smiled at him, trying to be polite. "Very."

"I might have a blanket in my car…," he offered.

"You forgot your jacket?" an extremely familiar voice asked from my left. I knew it was Dallas without needing proof, but I still swiveled to take him in, shivering again.

In a worn leather jacket that looked like it had some kind of shearling on the inside, he had his usual Tornado collared shirt on and at the V-shape there, he had something white beneath it. But it wasn't what was on his body that captivated me. "I did have a jacket. Someone else is wearing it now," I told him, eyeing the green knit cap that was molded to his head.

The scowl on his face disappeared instantly.

"Do you want me to check and see if I have that blanket?" the dad asked, reminding me where he was.

"Oh, that's okay. You don't have to do that," I told him even though, if he'd been just about anyone else, I would have taken it. I didn't want him to get the wrong idea after I'd spent so much time keeping things casual between us.

Dallas was standing in front of me by the time I finished talking, so tall I had to tip my head back as I wondered why he was standing so close.

Before I could ask, or figure it out, he pulled one arm behind his back and peeled a sleeve off and then followed that up by drawing his arm out of the second sleeve. In the time it took me to ask myself why he was taking his jacket off, he crouched in front of me and drew one of my arms away from my chest, then slid my hand into the sleeve he'd just vacated, all while I watched him like a total idiot.

He was putting his jacket on me.

My mouth had to be slightly gaped as he slipped my arm fully into the warm cocoon, drew the leather around my back, and then, his face and chest inches from mine, those hazel eyes catching my brown ones and keeping them there, he pulled my other wrist away from me and guided it into the other sleeve.

In a rare moment of my life, I didn't know what to say.

I definitely had no idea what the hell to say when his fingers went to the bottom of the jacket resting on top of my thighs and engaged the zipper, pulling the tab up straight between the valley between my breasts, up until it notched right below where my throat started.

Dallas smiled at me a little as he leaned toward me —and for one stupid second, I don't know why, I thought he was going to kiss me—but all I felt was a tug at the back of my hair and I knew he'd pulled my loose hair out of the collar. He narrowed his eyes and I narrowed mine right back, and the next thing I knew, he reached behind me again and tucked the rope of hair he was holding back inside his jacket.

And he still smiled at me, just a little, little, little thing, as he said, "Better." His hand went to the red baseball cap on my head, and he pulled the brim down a half-inch on my forehead. "Nice hat."

It was that, that had me smirking at him as I soaked in the heat his body had left in the soft material of the inside of the jacket. "It came broken in to the shape of my head." I huddled into the jacket. "I don't ever give things back. You've just learned that the hard way."

He smiled, slowly coming to his feet from the crouch he'd been in.

"I like your cap," I told him honestly. The emerald green made his hazel eyes pop like crazy. Plus, it was just fucking cute. "Did Miss Pearl make it for you?"

"I made it," he said with a twist to his mouth. "She taught me how."

The stupid smile that came over my face had me staring at him in awe. I even slapped my hand right over the left side of my chest. "Are you real?"

Dallas tapped my chin. "I'll knit you one, Peach."

"I could have given you my jacket," the poor, poor dad beside me piped in, breaking my trance of love.

Dallas's attention instantly moved toward the man, and as the words "She's fine" came out of his mouth, he turned that tall, muscular body and parked himself in the tight space between both of us. He didn't fit. Not at all. His elbow pretty much landed on my lap and most of his thigh and calf were pressed and aligned to my matching body parts.

I shifted to my left an inch and the length of his leg followed me, his elbow staying exactly where it was.

What the hell was happening?

"How's it going, Kev?" Dallas asked the dad, still smothering me but somehow his attention elsewhere.

Hmm. Shoving my hands into the pockets of his jacket, the back of my left hand hit something crumpled. Paper. Making sure he wasn't looking at me, I pulled what I figured were balled-up receipts out, being nosey and wondering what the hell he'd bought.

But it wasn't recycled white paper I pulled out.

They looked like Post-it notes. Plain, yellow Post-it notes like I'd seen in his truck. That just made me more curious.

Both men were talking as I started opening the notes as quietly as possible, really not caring if he caught me in the act by that point. But he didn't turn to look at me. He was too busy talking about who he thought the Texas Rebels were going to try and recruit next season.

The ball of paper was really two square-shaped

notes stacked together.

I read one and then I read the other.

Then I went back and read the top one and followed it up by reading the bottom one.

I did it a third time. And then I balled them back up and stuffed them where I'd found them.

I didn't need to look at them again to remember what was on each.

The first one, in small, neat handwriting that was crossed out with hard dashes across the letters, like he'd changed his mind, had said: **YOU ARE THE LIGHT OF MY LIFE.**

The second one... I sucked in a breath through my nose and made sure not to glance at Dallas even out of the corner of my eye.

It was the second one that had me feeling like a twitchy crackhead. The words hadn't been crossed out like the first one, and there was a smudge on the corner of the Post-it that went straight to my heart. It was a smudge like the ones I always spotted on his neck and arms.

I CAN'T LIVE WITHOUT YOU.

I can't live without you.

The first time I read it, I wondered who the hell he couldn't live without. But I wasn't that stupid and naïve, even though my insides felt like they were on the verge of exploding.

He wasn't... there was no way....

What exactly was it that I had told him and Trip in my kitchen during Josh's sleepover what felt like forever ago?

"Tia!"

I sat up and looked around, recognizing Louie's voice instantly. Dallas must have too, because he shot to his feet and scanned the area. But I found the blond head instantly; beside him was Josh. It was the woman in front of them that had me zeroing in like an eagle on the hunt for an innocent mouse for breakfast. Of all the women it could have been, it was Christy.

Fucking Christy.

The notes forgotten for now, I swiped my bag off the bleacher and left the rest of my shit where it was, that second of hesitation giving Dallas a head start on the route toward the boys. He made it before I did, and that was when I noticed that Josh had his arm around his brother's shoulder. The last time he'd made that kind of protective gesture had been at Rodrigo's funeral.

Which meant someone was about to die because Josh and Louie should never feel threatened by anything.

"What happened?" Dallas asked immediately, his hand reaching out toward Louie. I didn't miss how Lou took his hand instantly.

"She called me a brat," Louie blurted out, his other little hand coming up to meet with the one already clutching our neighbor's.

I blinked and told myself I was not going to look at Christy until I had the full story.

"Why?" Dallas was the one who asked.

"He spilled some of his hot chocolate on her purse," it was Josh who explained. "He said sorry, but she called him a brat. I told her not to talk to my brother like that, and she told me I should have learned to respect my elders."

For the second time around this woman, I went to ten. Straight through ten, past Go, and collected two hundred dollars.

"I tried to wipe it up," Louie offered, those big blue eyes going back and forth between Dallas and me for support.

"You should teach these boys to watch where they're going," Christy piped up, taking a step back.

Be an adult. Be a role model, I tried telling myself. "It was an accident," I choked out. "He said he was sorry… and your purse is leather and black, and it'll be fine," I managed to grind out like this whole thirty-second conversation was jabbing me in the kidneys with sharp knives.

"I'd like an apology," the woman, who had gotten me suspended and made me cry, added quickly.

I stared at her long face. "For what?"

"From Josh, for being so rude."

My hand started moving around the outside of my purse, trying to find the inner compartment when Louie suddenly yelled, "Mr. Dallas, don't let her get her pepper spray!"

The fuck?

Oh my God. I glared at Louie. "I was looking for a baby wipe to offer her one, Lou. I wasn't getting my pepper spray."

"Nuh-uh," he argued, and out of the corner of my eye, I noticed Christy take a step back. "I heard you on the phone with Vanny. You said, *you said* if she made you mad again you were gonna pepper spray her and her mom and her mom's mom in the—"

"Holy sh—oot, Louie!" My face went red, and I opened my mouth to argue that he hadn't heard me correctly. But... I had said those words. They had been a joke, but I'd said them. I glanced at Dallas, the serious, easygoing man who happened to look in that instant like he was holding back a fart but was hopefully just a laugh, and finally peeked at the woman who I'd like to think brought this upon herself. "Christy, I would never do that—"

The pain in my ass had some balls to her because, even though she had one foot set to the side like she was prepared to take off, she still managed to clear her throat and bring her attention to Dallas, her mouth pursed. "Dallas, I feel like that's grounds for kicking them off the team. It isn't sportsmanlike."

"Neither is making someone cry, and we already addressed that, didn't we, Christy?" he replied to her in that cool voice that now had me imagining him in his dress whites. "Drop it. It was an accident, he apologized, and we can move on from this."

She blinked so fast, it was like she was fluttering her eyelashes. Seeing her up close again, Christy wasn't ugly. She had to be in her mid-thirties, she was in good shape, and when she wasn't making ugly faces, she wouldn't be horrible to look at. A memory from the tryout nudged at my brain... had those moms said something about Christy liking Dallas?

"Drop it?" she asked in a squeaky voice.

"Drop it," he confirmed.

"If this was anyone else, you'd at least suspend them—"

I knew she had a point, and suddenly I sucked in a breath, expecting the worse.

But all Dallas said was, "You're right. But I'm not going to. You've been starting this mess with them, Christy, and we all know it. You and I already talked about this, didn't we? I don't want to suspend anyone, but if I do, it isn't going to be them."

Yeah, I could tell from the look on her face, she liked Dallas. And she liked Dallas a lot. "But you're playing favorites!"

"I'm always going to be fair with the boys, but I will play favorites with everyone else who isn't an active member of the team. Don't put me into that position, because I know she"—he tipped his head toward me—"only bites when she has to, and I will always take her side. Are we clear on that?"

He would?

Christy's cheeks puffed up with so much indignation, she literally squawked. Everything from her forehead down was red. "This is unbelievable. Fine! But don't think Jonathan is going to be on this team much longer." Her gaze stayed on Dallas for a moment, a dozen emotions flashing across her face before, just like that, she turned on her heel and disappeared into the crowd.

Why did I suddenly feel bad for her?

It wasn't until then that I noticed half the parents of the team were sitting on the tables around the concession stand. What was probably half the parents of every other team playing in the tournament that weekend were, too. Great.

I cleared my throat and popped my lips. "Well, that was awkward."

"I'm not a brat." Louie was still hung up and outraged.

I pointed my finger at him. "You're a tattletale, that's what you are. Nosey Rosie. What did I tell you about snitches?"

"You love them?"

It was Dallas who laughed first, one of his hands already sliding into his back pocket where he pulled out his wallet and a bill. "Lou, go buy another hot chocolate."

Louie nodded and took the five, heading back into the line as Josh, who was at my side, said, "I'm gonna go find my friends."

"All right," I said. "Careful."

Josh nodded and disappeared.

Dallas looked down at me with a serious expression on his face, and I raised my eyebrows back at him. A sense of being overwhelmed filled my chest as I snuggled in deeper into the warm jacket, the backs of my fingers brushed against the Post-it notes in the pocket.

What exactly was going on?

"You're always going to take my side, Professor?" I pretty much whispered the question.

He took a step toward me, his gaze still centered directly on my face. And he nodded.

"What did you guys talk about?" I asked him, still so low only he could hear.

Dallas took another step forward, the tips of his tennis shoes touching the tips of my boots. His chin was down to his collar as he took me in. And in a voice that was a lot louder than mine had been, he said, "I suspended her for two weeks after what happened, you know."

I didn't know. I was actually pretty damn shocked no one had told me.

The surprise must have been apparent on my face—or maybe he knew me too well, because he dipped his chin down even further in a partial nod. "I did. And I apologized to her if I'd given her the wrong impression that I was interested in her, informing her that I wasn't and we needed to keep things professional."

"I thought she liked you."

He shrugged, the corners of his mouth indenting just slightly. "It isn't the first time it's happened."

"What? Getting hit on by moms on the team?"

"Yeah."

I snickered. "Are you sure you weren't imagining it?"

Dallas made a face before this giant, beaming grin took over his mouth, so potent I could have taken his jacket off and been warm the rest of the day. "I'm sure, baby."

Baby again? All I could say was "Uh-huh," so that I wouldn't sound like an idiot.

"I wanna ask if you really said you'd pepper spray her, but I already know the answer."

Pressing my lips together, I shrugged.

He reached up toward me and brushed the backs of his fingers over my cheek, still smiling wide, and pinched my chin. "You're fucking nuts."

All I did was shrug again. "You know that, but you're still here, aren't you?"

His smile melted into a smaller one, and the deep breath he let out made it seem like it had weighed a thousand pounds. Then his fingers brushed over my cheek again, and Dallas moved to tuck a strand of her behind my ear. His voice was soft. "I'm still here, Peach."

CHAPTER TWENTY-TWO

I NEVER THOUGHT THE DAY WOULD COME WHERE I WOULD BE excited to go to work, but after almost three weeks of taking time off, my body was so ready. I had tried picking up shears twice in the last week, and it was a little iffy and painful, but I couldn't take being home any longer. My bank account couldn't either. So, hand hurting or not, that Wednesday morning, I was pumped beyond belief.

So pumped Josh was steadily scowling at me through the reflection in the rearview mirror.

"Why are you so happy?" grumpy britches muttered his question.

"Because I'm going back to work," I sang back to him, earning a bigger scowl. I really enjoyed my job on a normal basis, but after so long, I was ready to love it again in a way that only time and space was capable of.

"I'll be happy next week when we get off from school for Thanksgiving," the grump muttered.

Shit. I'd forgotten about Thanksgiving. "Did you guys decide what you want to do?" The Larsens were going to Louisiana and my family was staying in San Antonio, so I'd given the boys the option to choose whom they wanted to spend it with. Last year, we'd all stayed together at my parents, but I couldn't be greedy and keep them if they wanted to see the other side of the family. Either way, I had to work the day before, half the day of, and the following day, too.

"No," was the same reply they'd given me when I first brought up them going to Louisiana.

I sighed. "Well, you better decide soon or," I sang, "you're stuck with me."

"Stop, please," Josh pleaded.

"I like the way you sing," Louie piped up, earning a dirty look from his brother. "You sound like a cute kitty."

I didn't think that was as much of a compliment as he meant for it to be, but I'd take it.

"If we stay, will Mr. Dallas eat turkey with us?" the five-year-old asked.

I glanced at him through the rearview mirror, letting myself think about how nice he'd been this past weekend at Josh's game and how he'd given me a hug while he walked us to our car that night at the end of the tournament. He'd even apologized for having to skip dinner, but he'd left Miss Pearl alone at home all day and thought he should spend some time with her since she was staying with him and all.

I'd accepted it. I was madly, crazy, stupid in love with this guy.

The problem was that I didn't know what to do with it. With him being more affectionate and saying the things that he said... but not doing much else. I mean, he could kiss me and that would make a statement. Or tell me he liked me... if he did. It seemed like he was dropping hints, or I don't know what, but I wasn't sure whether to interpret his messages or let them go.

So I was going to let them go for now and settle for what he'd been willingly giving me.

"I don't know, Goo. He has family too. He might have plans to spend it with them. I haven't asked him," I explained.

"I'll ask him," he offered.

"Can I get a new game this weekend?" Josh asked out of the blue, making that the second time this week he'd tried.

I told him the same answer he'd already heard. I could applaud his effort, but that's all he was getting from me. "Not anytime soon, J. Maybe for Christmas."

"Why?"

"Why? Because I don't have the money right now." I'd barely been able to pay the mortgage and the water; I'd put the light bill on my credit card along with the cable bill.

"Why?"

"Why don't I have money? Because I haven't worked in weeks, J. I know you guys think I'm pouring money out of my ears, but I'm not. Sorry."

He grumbled so much I shot him a dirty look through the rearview mirror that had him stopping the moment he saw it. "Okay," he muttered.

"That's what I thought," I whispered to myself, trying to hold on to my optimism and excitement about getting back to work with two hands. I'd gone in to the salon the day before to try and start arranging my schedule again, and managed to get most of the day booked up.

"*Tia*, do you think Santa will give me a bike for Christmas?" Louie asked.

"As long as he doesn't hear about all your criminal activity over the year, I think he might," I told him, laughing when he let out a disgruntled noise as I pulled the car up to the school. "All right, have a good day at school, you menaces to society. I love you."

Louie slipped out of his car seat just as Josh pecked me on the side of the forehead with a kiss that was more of a brush of lips—the end was coming one day for that, but it hadn't yet. Lou did the same on my cheek, hollering, "Bye!" right before slamming the door shut.

For one moment, I glanced at my hand again, the skin pink and tight and a lot more tender than I wished it would be, but it was going to have to be good enough. I needed to work.

"D, we got a walk-in asking for you," Ginny informed me with a sly smile as I closed the door to the break room.

A walk-in asking for me? I didn't have enough time between clients to do a color job, but I could squeeze another cut in. My palm was only hurting about a five on a scale from one to ten from holding shears. I couldn't afford to say no. The day had been busy, busy. I had to go slower than I was used to because closing the shears quickly bothered the freshly healed new flesh too much, but I'd been doing all right. The salon was only open for two more hours. I'd make it.

I walked toward the front desk and stopped when I caught sight of a familiar brown head tipped down at the floor. Sitting there with his elbows on his widespread knees, hands centered between them with a cell phone in his hand, wearing his usual outfit of vintage jeans and a T-shirt that he had worn to work based on the shade of gray it was covered with, was Dallas. I'd seen him at practices over the last week and a half, but besides that, we hadn't seen each other around the neighborhood. I knew Miss Pearl was staying with him, and I couldn't say I didn't think it was sweet he wasn't leaving her home alone... even if I did miss having him come around the house.

The sound of my wedges on the smooth concrete floor had him glancing up from whatever he'd been looking at, and he smiled, wide, so beautiful I felt like an idiot for ever thinking the most attractive part of him was his body. "Hey."

"Hey, Professor," I said, even though in my head I was really asking: *what are you doing here?*

"Busy?" he asked, smiling a little and coming to a stand.

"Not for you." Why did I say that and why was my heart beating so fast in my chest?

"Someone told me you don't take new clients, but I was wondering if you'd make an exception for a friend," he said, running a hand through what had obviously grown out to be about an inch-long hair where he usually kept it at half an inch.

Cut his hair? Get close enough to cut his hair? The tiniest bit of unease settled right in my chest, but just meeting his gaze reminded me of who he was. My friend. My neighbor. The man who had been almost nothing but kind to me, time after time. There was nothing to worry about.

Well, at least not physically. My heart was a different story.

The smile that came on my face was as easy and natural as it should have been. "Of course I can. Come on."

He smiled and I turned into a puddle of goo, but by some miracle, I managed not to get all moony-eyed over him. That was the plan at least. "How's your day been?" he asked as I waited for him to walk up to me.

"Pretty good. I get off in two hours." I met those murky brown-green eyes. "You?"

"I finished a big tiling job. It was a good day," he answered, brushing the back of his hand against mine.

This couldn't be happening to me. Not with my neighbor. Not with this man who was technically still married and was Josh's coach. It couldn't be. I wouldn't let it.

"One day when I have the money, I'll ask you to give me a quote on redoing the floors in my house, but that isn't going to be any time soon," I told him.

"All you have to do is ask, Diana." He looked down at me from over his shoulder. "We can do it together when you have the time off."

"Together?"

"Together," he repeated.

I hummed and eyed him. "All right. For free?"

That had him smirking. "Yeah. You get a special discount."

"What? The single parent who feeds you discount?"

Dallas shook his head and smiled, but didn't say anything.

All right.

"We're going for a Mohawk then or what?" I made myself ask.

The expression on his face was that playful one that squeezed the shit out of my ovaries every single time he brought it out. "Maybe next time."

He winked.

He winked right at me.

He had never done that before.

What the fuck was going on?

"Okay," I practically choked out, awkward and weird and instantly internally cringing at how I should have kept the joke going but didn't. Damn it. "Let me get my clippers real quick and lower your chair. I don't get anyone over six feet tall in front of me very often."

"Okay," he replied.

"Same cut as always?" Pulling the drawer open, I kept my gaze down as I took out the clippers and set of attachments I had in there.

His voice was low. "Whatever you think looks

good."

Grabbing a cape, I slipped it over his shoulders and made the Velcro parts meet together. "You sure?"

"Sure," he answered back, all raspy and hoarse. "I trust you."

Why did he do this to me?

I turned my body away from him to let out a deep breath. Those hazel-colored eyes were on me through the mirror. I could see them out of my peripheral vision as I moved around him to plug the clippers in to the extension cord I had hidden beneath my station. "You're the one looking at me more than anyone, do what you want."

I sucked in a breath. "Okay."

Our eyes met as I stood up again and walked around to take in the cut of his hair. I could do it with my eyes closed and one hand behind my back. I reached up to touch my thumb against the hollow at the base of his head and moved the clippers around to where they needed to be. His face was peaceful as I shaved from the front to the back of his head, over that gentle curve of his skull, gentle, gentle, gentle not to cut him. I slowly moved my way around him until I stood in front. His knees hit my upper thighs as I paused where I was, and he let me move his head around without any resistance to get the spots I needed to reach.

I'd be lying if I said I didn't let my fingers linger just a split second longer than necessary over the smooth skin of his forehead and his temple and that ultra-soft skin right behind his earlobe. I could feel his stare on me as I worked, but only let myself look him in the eye a couple of times, smiling each time like this was no big deal, when it felt like anything but. The clippers were loud between us, a distraction to the tension I felt in the pit of my stomach in reaction to how close we were.

"Sorry if I stink," he apologized in that near-whisper voice.

"You don't smell at all," I said to him, forcing myself to keep my gaze on the very center of his newly trimmed hair. "I'm almost done. I just need to use my shears on a couple of spots." Did my voice sound hoarse or was I just imagining it?

"I'm not rushing you. You doing this for me is a hell of a lot better than my usual barber." God, how could a voice be so attractive? "I might have to start coming in every two weeks if you're gonna be rubbing the back of my neck like that, Buttercup."

I smiled, but it was off and my stomach was fluttering, and I'm sure my face was turning pink.

"Why you blushing?" he asked in that croon that sang straight to my ovaries.

"Because." I laughed again, awkward and stupid, and why the hell was I doing this to myself? *You know better, Diana.* "You reminded me of something I heard. That's all," I said, rubbing my hand on my pants before moving around him.

He hummed. "You can tell me. I can keep a secret," he said. "I don't share."

"Me neither," I kind of mumbled before shuffling over to stand behind him, trading one tool for the other to catch a couple of super fine hairs right by his ears that I hadn't been able to get. "It's stupid. I'll tell you another day."

I spotted his Adam's apple moving. I wouldn't be surprised if he could hear my heart racing inside my chest. It only took a couple of minutes to finish up, to make sure the lines and edges along the nape of his neck were clean and straight. After brushing his bare skin off, I pulled the cape off him. I slowly shook it out as he got to his feet, avoiding the small pools of rich brown hair on the floor.

"How much do I owe you?" he asked.

I gestured toward the front desk area with my head, conscious that Sean and Ginny were nosey as fuck and still not done with their clients. "How about ten bucks?"

He touched the back of my hand again with his, and I knew without a single doubt, for one split second, his pinky finger hooked around mine before letting it go. "That's how much I pay my old guy to cut me behind the ears and shove his sweaty armpit in my face. How much?"

He sounded just like Miss Pearl.

I kept myself from coughing and from glancing down at his hands, and somehow even rolled my eyes, trying to keep this light and playful even though it felt like something more. "Ten bucks. That took me fifteen minutes, tops, Dallas. It's a friend discount, and don't think about tipping me. I'll sneak the money back in your bag during practice."

"Yeah?"

"Yeah. You help me all the time. I can avoid shoving a stinky pit in your face and make sure I leave you without any cuts."

"You sure? I know you charge like a hundred bucks for a haircut."

I'd do it for free at my house if he wanted, but in that moment, that seemed like a dangerous idea. "I don't charge a hundred dollars for a haircut. It's like eighty, and it takes me over an hour to do that usually. Ten bucks. Cough 'em up, Captain."

That slow smile crossed his harsh features, lighting up my gut. "As you wish."

I started grinning before I stopped. What did he just say?

Before I could ask myself if he'd really just said what I thought he said, Dallas added, "And it's Senior Chief, Peach. Not Captain."

Was I having hot flashes? Was I imagining things? I tugged at the collar of my shirt with my good hand and replied, "You got it, Senior Chief."

He snickered and shook his head. As he handed over a ten-dollar bill from a scuffed leather wallet, he asked, "You putting me down for two weeks from now?"

I blinked and even my hands stopped moving. "You're serious?"

He was dead serious. I could tell from the expression on his face. I'd seen it before. And he confirmed it. "I'm serious. Put me down."

"Why don't you just come over to my house and have me cut your hair there?" I offered, whispering. I could do it. I could keep my hands to myself.

"I like having an excuse to come see you," he replied in a low voice that went straight to my chest.

I eyed him and nodded, slipping the cash into the register before reaching over to take the computer off sleep mode. "Is Monday fine?" I managed not to croak.

"Sure, baby."

I was not going to make a big deal about the "B" word. And I didn't. Words were just words sometimes, with no special meaning at all, and Dallas and I had been through some stuff together. Trip called me "honey" all the time too. Maybe Dallas was just practicing terms of endearment on me? Yuck. "All right."

"You got me down?" he asked before I'd even saved the date.

"I'm about to."

"Good. Make me your six o'clock from now on. Any day you want, I'll make it work."

My index finger hovered over the mouse for a moment and I held my breath. There was something about this that felt different. Heavy. "For how long?" I asked slowly.

"For as long as that calendar will let you."

"THAT WHORE."

Ginny let out a laugh from her spot across the salon where she was cleaning out the sinks we used to wash customers' hair. "Your tip was that bad?"

The fact she knew why the insult was called for didn't even register to me. We'd been working together for so long doing this, we were both well aware that there were only a handful of reasons we would call our customers names. It was either they missed an appointment, complained about a haircut they specifically requested even though we tried to talk them out of it, or we were tipped like shit. Under normal circumstances, we didn't usually complain about our tips. I mean, shit happens; sometimes people have less money than they do at other times, but in this case...

"She just finished telling me she got promoted at her law firm. She left me five dollars, Gin. *Five dollars.* It took me half an hour to blow out her hair after I cut it. My hand hurts like a son of a bitch from holding the dryer."

Her laugh exploded out of her, because that kind of shit happened to all of us on a semi-regular basis. Some weeks were better than others. It was why I never tipped waiters badly. While Ginny paid us based off a fair commission structure compared to other salon owners I'd worked for in the past, every penny still counted, especially when you had bills and kids. Today alone I'd had six stingy customers. On the other hand, I'd had to cancel her original appointment because of my hand. Her roots had been pretty brutal.

"Ugh," I groaned. "It's just been one of those days."

"Aww, Di."

I sighed and dropped my head back before shoving the five-dollar bill into my wallet. "I need a drink."

"I don't have the kids today," she mentioned slyly, earning a look from me.

"You don't?"

"No. Their dad called last minute and said he'd keep them for the weekend." She glanced up from her work at the sink and raised her eyebrows repeatedly. "Mayhem isn't that expensive."

"I probably shouldn't be spending money when I have a perfectly good bottle of wine at home," I said. I hadn't been back at work long and my checking account was still crippled.

"I'll buy you two drinks. One of my guys left me an extra good tip as a wedding gift, and I'm not having a bachelorette party. Let's do it. You and me, one last time before I become a married woman again."

I knew where she was going with this and I approved. "Two drinks, no more?"

"Only two," she confirmed.

To give us credit, we were both straight-faced as we recited the greatest lie ever told.

~

"ONE MORE!"

"No!"

"One more!"

"No!"

"Come on!"

My face was hot and I'd hit the giggly level two drinks ago. "One more, and that's it! I'm not kidding this time!" I finally agreed, such a total fucking sucker.

What was this? Drink number four? Number five? I had no clue.

Watching as Ginny leaned over the bar and asked the bartender, who had been very attentive to us tonight, for two more whiskey sours, I wiggled out of the soft button-down shirt I'd put on over a lacey camisole for work that morning. I was hot. So damn hot considering the November temperatures had dropped. The bar was packed. It was Friday night after all, and we'd fought for our two spots at the counter, smashed in between two burly men with motorcycle club vests on and two guys we'd learned a drink ago who worked at Ginny's uncle's garage.

What happened to our two-drink limit? Ginny's uncle happened. The most weathered-looking man I had ever seen in my life had come straight for us the second we sat down and told the bartender the drinks were on him tonight. The man, I learned moments later, was named Luther, put a hand on the back of the chair I was sitting on and said to me, "I heard what you did for Miss Pearl. You're good here anytime you want."

"You really don't have to do that," I told this man I'd never even seen before.

His intense attention didn't budge for a second. "My grandson is in love with you. You're good," he decided.

Oh my God. Dean.

The man named Luther continued on, "Ginny, I can't afford your drunk ass. Consider tonight a wedding gift," he drawled, patting his niece's shoulder as she choked on a laugh.

And then, just like that, the Alcohol Fairy was gone. And Ginny and I silently said "fuck it" and decided to take advantage of it, which was why and how I found myself five drinks in to an evening at a biker bar, laughing my ass off with someone I loved.

I was fanning myself when Ginny turned with two glasses of the yellowish concoction. Reaching back, I started tying my hair up. "Is it hot or is just me?" I asked.

"It's hot," she confirmed, sliding the drink over the counter in my direction. "Last one and we'll go home."

I nodded, smiling at her, my facial muscles feeling pretty tingly. "Last one. Seriously."

"Serious," she promised.

The much older man to my right, the big biker Ginny and I talked to for half an hour earlier, turned in his seat to look down at me. His bushy gray beard was long and in definite need of a trim. "What'cha drinking now?"

"A whiskey sour," I replied, taking a sip.

He scrunched up his nose and looked back and forth between Gin and me. "That's an awful lot of liquor you've had for being so small."

"I'm okay," I told him, taking another sip. "I'm just going to call a cab."

He looked horrified. "Honey, that sounds like a bad idea."

"Why?" Ginny piped up from her spot next to me. She'd been talking to him too over the course of the last couple hours we'd been at the bar.

"Two drunk girls in the car with a stranger?"

Well, when he put it that way.... We'd taken a cab the last time and it was fine. Plus, how many other times in the past had I done the same thing?

"Ginny, have Trip drive you two home. I know his ass hasn't drunk that much tonight. He's upstairs dealing with club shit. I'll go get him for you, or shit, call Wheels. He'll come get you. No problem."

She shook her head. "He's asleep. I don't want to wake him up."

"I can take y'all home," a man sitting on the other side of Ginny, one of the two mechanics, offered.

I didn't need to look at my boss and friend to know that, though the guy seemed nice enough, we weren't idiots. We'd learned not to get into cars with strangers. Shit, we'd taught our kids not to get into cars with strangers.

"No. I'm taking you both home," a new voice claimed from somewhere behind me unexpectedly.

I felt the two arms come down on either side of my chair before I saw the twin columns of heavily muscled forearms cage me in. It was the beautiful brown and black lines of a bird's wing stamped onto the inside of the biceps by my face that told me who was in my space. I didn't have to look up to know who was talking. It was Dallas.

I'd like to think it was all the alcohol that led me to drop my head back as far as I could. "Hi."

Dallas tipped his face down to look at me, his expression harsh, no-nonsense even through my hazy brain. "Diana," he said my name solidly without a single trace of the familiar affection we'd grown for each other.

"I didn't know you were here," I said, still looking at him upside down.

He might have blinked, but his mouth was drawn so tight I couldn't look past it. "I've been here the entire time."

I swallowed and only managed to nod, my face getting hot all over again. Even in that position, I could see his eyes flick over my face and my throat and some other place I couldn't confirm. "You could have come said hi. We're friends. We can sit next to each other in public." And that was how I would later on know I was drunk. What the hell was I thinking saying that?

"You've been busy," he stated in that same detached, almost mean voice.

"What?"

"You've had enough to drink," Dallas said. "I'm taking you both home."

"But we just got this drink!" Ginny protested.

"I'll give you the ten bucks. Let's go, now," he demanded. Without warning, the arms on either side of me moved, his hands going to the handles of the stool I was on right before he jerked it away from the bar, making it scrape against the floor.

Some reasonable part of Ginny's and my brains must have recognized that we'd overdone the drinking, because neither one of us grumbled much at his order. Out of the corner of my eye, I noticed my boss pushing her chair back, not forced out of it like I had been. Turning the stool around so I could get out and grabbing my purse at the same time, I came face-to-face with Dallas's body standing centimeters from my knees. Glancing up at his face, ready to ask him to back up so I could get down, I couldn't help but smile at the scowl on his face.

"Hi," I said again like I hadn't just greeted him two minutes ago.

He wasn't amused. In fact, I'm pretty sure he sounded more pissed than he had a minute ago when he spoke next. "Let's go."

I thought I narrowed my eyes at him. "Why do you sound so mad?"

"We'll talk about it in the truck," he said and gestured me forward, his tone still low, even.

"You sure you don't want me to drive you?" the mechanic guy asked as Ginny slid out of her chair and came to stand next to Dallas.

Dallas didn't tear his eyes away from me as he beat us to answer, "No."

I'm pretty sure I heard the biker in the seat beside mine laugh.

My ankles betrayed me as I took a step forward and wobbled, my chest hitting Dallas's, and I craned my neck back to give him a funny look. There were more lines at his forehead and beneath his eyes than I'd ever seen. What was up his ass?

"Bye, Diana," the older biker called out.

Tilting my head to the side, forcing myself to look away from my neighbor—Josh's coach—I waved at my new biker friend. "Bye. Be careful getting home," I told him.

But before I could say anything else, a big, warm hand slipped into mine; the long fingers meshing through my smaller ones, and I lost my train of thought in less than a second. I knew those fingers. All I managed to do was look up at Dallas with a confused and shocked expression on my face before he was tugging me forward and through the bar and the mass of people inside of it. Distractedly, I looked over my shoulder to make sure Ginny was following, and she was. Shit. Taking her in right then, I noticed how flushed her face was.

We really had drank too much.

The night air was chilly, and I suddenly realized I hadn't grabbed my shirt after I'd taken it off. "Wait!" I started to say before Dallas held up the hand not holding mine.

"I've got your shirt," he said, taking a quick glance over his shoulder that landed directly on my chest.

I was a little drunk but not drunk enough to not notice how the tendons along his neck flexed. I was also pretty sure he muttered "Jesus" under his breath as he pulled me along behind him.

Could I have let go of his hand?

I flexed my fingers inside of his, linked together tightly, and decided probably not.

Not that I even wanted to, even though I knew I had no right. I knew this didn't mean anything. Couldn't mean anything. How many times had he made it apparent he wasn't interested in me other than us being friends and because he'd had a single mom and related to me on that level?

Friends held hands when they'd had too much to drink.

This was nothing. Just one friend watching out for another. It wasn't the first time I'd been around him in a bad mood. I had no reason to think too much about it. He probably just thought I was stupid for drinking too much and he'd be right. I was.

None of us said a word as we headed toward the double cab truck parked a block over at the same lot where I'd left my car. I had this strange urge to reach out and touch my beloved CRV, but the grip on my hand was too secure and I was steered right to Dallas's passenger side door. I watched him shove his key into the lock and turn it, pulling the door open, and without meeting my eyes, he grabbed me by the hips and lifted me in—so quick I didn't even have time to register his action until it was over.

I'd had too much to drink, but I could have gotten into his truck on my own. Couldn't I? I'd definitely had way too much in the past and had never had a problem getting into a car... at least from what I could remember.

"Scoot over," Dallas's rough voice ordered.

He didn't have to tell me twice. I moved over to the middle, watching as he crossed the front of his pickup, leaving Ginny to get into his truck on her own. His entire body looked strung tight, his jaw a straight line that reminded me of my mom's when I'd piss her off as a kid and she was planning on putting me in my place the second we had some privacy. I looked around the inside of the cab and appreciated again that, while he didn't take care of his house that well, he treated his truck like a baby.

"Why did you talk me into that third drink?" Ginny muttered as she settled in next to me, the side of her jean-covered leg and shoulder touching mine.

"What? You talked me into it," I argued with her in a whisper.

All she did was shake her head.

"I'm never going out with you again."

"We had fun. Don't even try to pretend we didn't." I bumped my thigh against hers.

She giggled as the driver side door opened and, a second later, Dallas's big body slid in behind the wheel, taking up all of the remaining space and more. So much more he was practically sealed to my side, gluing me to him like a conjoined twin I'd be stuck with forever. Just as I started to scoot over toward Ginny, he slid me a look at the same time his key went into the ignition, the low sound of country music cutting into the stinging silence. And there was something in that hard, uncompromising gaze that stopped me in midmovement.

His eyes, still somehow light-colored even in the dark cab, centered right onto me. "Seat belt."

Dropping my eyes, I looked at my sides for the strap. I hadn't been searching for it but maybe five seconds when that arm I'd become so familiar with over the course of the last few months reached over my lap—the palm of his hand cupping my hip for one brief moment in history—and grabbed it from where it was wedged beneath the seats almost like he'd planted it there. And slowly, with the backs of his fingers grazing across the band of my pants, going just above the zipper of my jeans, from one pelvic bone to the other, he clipped it in for me.

I held my breath the entire time.

And I wasn't going to deny that I couldn't help but glance at his face immediately afterward, feeling that electric heat from him searing every inch of exposed skin my tank top left out in the open.

What did I do? I smiled.

And for one rare occasion out of so many in the last few months, he didn't smile back. Without breaking eye contact, he reached under the seat and handed me a bottle of water.

Okay.

"Where do you live?" he asked Ginny.

My boss and friend rattled off the address and directions with it.

None of us said anything as Dallas drove and I sipped on the water he'd given me, offering it to Ginny after each time. There were some country songs on the radio I vaguely recognized in the twenty minutes it took to drive to the opposite side of town where we lived. When he pulled in to the driveway of the new house in a new subdivision Ginny had bought a year ago, I hugged her before she got out and then watched as Dallas got out of the truck and walked her to her front door.

As he made his way back, I pulled my phone out of my purse and checked the screen, thankful that the Larsens had taken the boys to their lake house and I hadn't missed Louie's nightly phone call. I was just in the middle of putting my phone back into my purse when the door opened and my neighbor slid into the driver seat of the still-running truck. His hand went to the gear shift just as I reached to release the latch on the seat belt...

He covered my hand with his, stopping me.

"Are you okay?" I asked, keeping my hand where it was even as he reversed out of the short driveway, his chin over his shoulder as he looked out the back window.

His answer was cool and calm. "You're asking me if I'm okay?"

I blinked. "Yeah."

Moving his hand off mine and making me forget that I'd been about to move over, he put his truck into drive, his attention now focused outside the windshield. "You"—he still sounded normal, collected —"had too much to drink and spent the last three hours talking to men you don't know."

I wasn't sure if it was the drinks or just that small part of me that hadn't been able to come to terms with what I felt for him that led me to voice just about the stupidest thing I could have said. At least in hindsight, I realized how dumb it was. "So?"

That wasn't something I hadn't done a hundred times before. I knew the difference between being friendly and being a flirt, and I hadn't been flirting with any of those guys at the bar.

But I learned pretty quickly that "So?" was obviously not the kind of answer that Dallas was looking for. I accepted that a moment later when he slammed his brakes, sending me rocking forward—his arm shooting out across my chest to keep me from smashing my face against the dashboard.

"What the hell!" I cried at the same time he shouted, "*So?*"

My heart was beating in my damn throat from thinking I was about to have to get reconstructive surgery to my face, but somehow I managed to pant out, "What is wrong with you?" I was awake then, the tipsiness disappearing as I tried to catch my breath.

"You don't know those fucking guys, Diana!" he yelled. "One of them got accused of rape a couple of years ago, and you were sitting there becoming BFFs with him."

I was that angry and upset that I let him using "BFF" go.

"The only reason I was there was because I was meeting up with my friend I told you about. I sat there watching you the entire time. Waiting for you to turn around and come sit with me so I could introduce you to him, but you're so fucking unobservant—"

"I am not unobservant," I argued.

"Then how the fuck did you not see me ten feet away from you for hours?"

"I..." Well, what the hell was I supposed to say? There wasn't a good excuse or explanation for that. He had a point. I just wasn't going to admit it. Ever. "Well, I don't know. But I wouldn't have gone home with them. Are you crazy?"

The way he glared at me almost had me checking

my eyebrows to make sure they hadn't been burned off. He bared his teeth in an expression that was nowhere near a smile. "You're damn right you wouldn't have gone home with them."

He was breathing hard and it had taken me too long to notice that he was just as riled up as me. This normally calm, patient man was resembling a dragon hell-bent on destroying a town. That town being me.

"I would have dragged you out by the ear if you had tried, just like my mom used to do to me. And God help me, if you'd taken a fucking cab—"

"What's wrong with a cab?"

I would swear on my life this sweet, passive man snarled at me, so I sat back in the seat. "Don't ask me stupid questions right now, Diana. I'm not in the mood for it."

I blinked at him, suddenly feeling overwhelmed. "Why are you being so mean to me?"

He blinked. "You think I'm being mean to you?"

"Yes! I had too much to drink. I didn't do anything wrong. That wasn't my first time going out, you know. I wasn't going to do anything wrong, but you're here, yelling at me—"

The hand he had closest to the window went up to scrub at his short hair. "Because you worried me! You think I want something to happen to you? I can't read your mind. I don't know what the hell you're planning on doing," he explained, at least it seemed like he was trying to explain, but there was still so much anger in his voice, it didn't totally seem that way.

For the second time in such a short amount of time,

I said something else stupid that I didn't realize until hours later. "Look, I appreciate you looking out for me, but I'm a grown woman. I can take care of myself."

"Maybe you can take care of yourself, but have you thought for one single fucking second that maybe somebody else might *want* to take care of you too?" he growled.

And in that split second, every thought, every emotion, left my body. Just *poof*. Disappeared.

"You... what?" Was I drunk enough to not understand what was coming out of his mouth? It wouldn't be the first time, but I didn't think I was on that level yet.

He reared back, his expression all "are you fucking kidding me?" "Being your friend has been the hardest fucking thing I've ever had to do."

Wait. "It has?" I asked, torn between his comment a moment before and the one that had just come out of his mouth. I'd thought he was trying to say he wanted to take care of me, but now...

"You are the most ridiculous fucking woman I have ever met in my entire life, Diana. Half the time I want to shake you and the other half of the time...." He trailed off, glaring right into my eyes.

In the second that followed that fraction of time, that muscular arm that had slashed across my chest to keep me in place moved. His hand, that long-fingered, callused hand, slid behind my neck, and Dallas kissed me. His lips touched mine, gentle, barely a brush, a whisper of a warm mouth and breath over my own.

And then he went for it. There was no hesitation, no

warning peck. That fuller upper lip went over the top of mine, those blunt, white teeth caught my bottom one... and then he was kissing me.

Over and over again. Softer, then softly, then just soft.

Then I didn't hesitate. I opened my mouth and caught his top lip the instant my brain caught up with what was happening. His mouth slanted over mine, his tongue sliding into the slight opening I'd given him. One tongue against the other, one hand covering the back of my neck while the other clutched at my hip. My hands? They might have been on his ribs, or they might have been on his thighs, I had no idea. All I could think about was Dallas. *Dallas, Dallas, Dallas.* How much I wanted this. How much I wanted this more than I'd ever wanted just about anything.

My hands kneaded. His hands kneaded.

His lips drifted away from mine, skirting my jaw, sucking an earlobe briefly before he trailed his damp, warm mouth down my neck like he was hungry, like the world was going to end if he didn't kiss me everywhere with everything in him. His tongue grazed the skin on my throat, his lips skimming before his teeth made contact. And God help me, all I could do was move closer to him, almost climbing on to his lap. I started leaning forward when it hit me.

What the fuck was I doing? He was married. Separated. Same shit.

"Oh my God," I hissed, rearing back so fast, he was still where I'd left him when his hooded eyes opened. I pointed at him, the blood I usually had in my head going down. "You're married."

Dallas blinked slowly. His Adam's apple bobbed and the hand he had on my thigh stayed exactly where it was as he focused those amazing eyes on me, looking only slightly dazed. "Diana," he said my name like he'd never said it before as his thumb slipped over my knee. "My divorce was finalized."

CHAPTER TWENTY-THREE

"HE'S FINALLY DIVORCED?" VANESSA'S VOICE WAS AS CLOSE TO excited as her normally pretty even-temperament allowed her to be. "Since when?"

"Yes!" I, on the other hand, was not so even tempered. I'd been dying to tell her what the hell I'd found out two days ago, but the instant I was up the next morning, I went straight to making breakfast, feeling more than a little like shit from how much I'd drank the night before, and headed right to the salon. By the time I got off work, all I wanted to do was pass out on the couch. I'd fallen asleep two hours after getting home. "A few weeks."

A few weeks. I still couldn't wrap my head around that. *Weeks.* Since right after the fire. When he'd left for a few days.

"What did he say after that?" Van asked.

How could I explain the look he'd given me after he said he wasn't married anymore? Or how his hand had slid further up my thigh and squeezed my leg like he owned it? There wasn't a way to. All I had managed to do was sit there looking at him while my heart ran a marathon inside my chest.

"Nothing, I just sat there and stared at him and he stared back at me, and then he drove us home. He parked his truck at his house, walked me home, and all he said was 'Goodnight, Diana,'" I relayed the information back to her.

"Did you say something to him?"

"I told him thank you for the ride and goodnight?" It hadn't been my finest moment. I hadn't even looked him in the eye, but I didn't tell Van that.

Either way, she still went with "What a chicken."

"Chicken? Coming from you? Really?"

Vanessa scoffed. "What are you talking about?"

Did I really need to remind her about her non-relationship with her now-husband years ago? *I like him. I don't know what to do, wah, boohoo,* I recapped.

Her response was a grunt. "Shut up."

"It's all right, Chicken Little. Don't give shit if you can't take it. At least I told him I sort of liked him before."

"Now that you mention it, I seem to remember you telling me to quit being a pussy."

"That was a completely different situation, you idiot."

"How?"

"You were married!"

She thought about it for a second before huffing. "Whatever. Eat shit. What I want to know is what are you going to do about it?"

Wasn't that the question of the century? What was I going to do? Dallas had kissed me. Really kissed me. Not this peck on the side of the mouth that you gave someone you were fond of… unless I'd gotten him totally wrong and maybe now that he was divorced, he was planning on making up for not dating for years.

That single thought left a huge lump of rotting crap in my belly.

Was that what was happening? He was taking his brand-new freedom card and using it on me?

He had to know it wouldn't work. He had to. The more I thought about it, the more convinced I was that he wouldn't do that to me. I'd made it clear to him time and time again that I was a crazy person. Plus, I had the boys. I couldn't be doing that "getting around" crap. Plus-*plus*, we were neighbors. If he wanted to hit it and quit it, I was the worst option in the world, and he had to know that.

He had to.

I wasn't going to believe otherwise. But that was the problem, what was I supposed to believe?

"Di?" Van's voice came over the line, worried.

"Sorry, I spaced," I apologized, shoving the thought of his reasoning aside. "I don't know. He just got divorced. Does he want to date around? Does he want to date me? Did he only want to kiss me? *I don't know*. We never talked about it. It always just seemed like this far-off thing that was never going to happen." This felt like high school all over again. "We see each other too much for this to be something that will end badly. I like him too much for that to happen, too, I guess."

"Okay, Negative Nancy. Ask him, or give it some time. I don't know. You're the one with all the boyfriend experience."

All the boyfriend experience? This bitch. "I was almost nineteen when I lost my virginity, asshole, and I've had four boyfriends. I'm not exactly an expert here. I don't know what the hell is happening. I don't know what his plan is."

The silence on the other end of the line said exactly what I knew was true. I was a serial monogamist. I'd been in four relationships my entire life and, with the exception of Jeremy, they had all been long-term. Jeremy would have been if he hadn't been a piece of shit who needed to get stabbed in the kidneys repeatedly. I'd liked plenty of boys and men in my life, but I wasn't big on dating around and playing the field.

And considering how much I liked Dallas—and felt even more than that toward him—my heart couldn't handle disappointment, and at this point in my life, it wasn't just me I was looking after. It was the boys too. They liked him and he was Josh's coach. I wasn't about to ruin a positive male influence for them by dating Dallas who had just gotten divorced after so many years.

He was going to date around.

And his neighbor across the street with two boys, who was always all up in his business and stuff, couldn't be his first choice.

I lived across the street from him.

If Jeremy moved in across the street from me now, I would key his car and throw eggs at his house until he got a clue and moved.

There was no way I could be a revolving door. I wanted to be settled. I needed it. I knew he cared about me, but what were the chances he wasn't thinking straight?

Shit. I wasn't going to risk it. We could be friends and that was all he had ever given me the impression he wanted, with the exception of him rubbing his mouth all over my neck...

And the notes I'd found in his pocket that might not have anything to do with me.

I couldn't think about that, or ever again, if I was supposed to survive this.

"Well, you can look but not touch if you want to do that, D."

"That's real useful advice," I grumbled.

"What do you want me to tell you? You're the one who's never had a problem saying whatever is on your mind. You always do what you want to do, and everyone else can go to hell. The Di I know—the Diana I know *now*—doesn't chicken out on things. So do whatever you want to do."

I let out another grumble. How the hell was that supposed to help me?

"We'll change the subject, chicken," Vanessa went with when I didn't say a word. "Did I tell you how Aiden makes Trevor call me when he's gone, once every hour to make sure I'm fine? Can you believe that?"

"Nope." Because I couldn't. I knew how much Van hated her husband's manager, and for him to have to call her all the time because Aiden was practicing was pretty damn hilarious. So I laughed because I was sure it must have been killing her inside a little too. "Sucker."

My best friend snickered. "He's the suck-up. I know for sure I never told you about how he bought us this baby stroller, and I looked it up. It costs four thousand dollars. For a baby stroller! I tried to return it, but he won't tell me where he got it from. He should have used that money to buy things for someone who can't afford the basics. I want to find a charity for pregnant women and donate money or items to them in exchange. It makes me feel guilty to get all this stuff."

"Rich girl problems," I teased her.

"Screw you."

"Donate the money, or you can donate the money to me—"

That made her laugh. She knew there was no way I would ever ask her for money.

"You're making me hurt, and I need to get back to work while Sammy is still napping," the workaholic announced in a watery voice. "Text me later."

"I will. Love you."

"Love you too. Be my Diana and take what you want!" she shouted before the call ended.

Hanging up, I gripped my phone, took another swallow of the coffee I'd been drinking all morning, and headed back out onto the floor.

Take what I want.

I didn't have to figure out what it was that I wanted. I knew what it was. Exactly what it was.

And that was Dallas.

But what the hell was I going to do about it? I wondered as I left the break room and headed into the main section of the salon for my next appointment.

Sean had his client in his chair doing what looked like a keratin treatment, and Ginny was sitting at her station, texting on her phone. She looked like as much shit as I did. There were bags under her eyes and she looked pale. She'd come in to work after I did, and all we'd done was wave at each other. I wanted to tell her about what happened with her cousin two nights ago, but...

Well, they were family. Distant family, but family nonetheless. You didn't talk about matters of the heart with people who were related.

But I could ask her what had been bugging me on and off for months.

Making my way to her station, I leaned over and took a peek at her roots as she finished typing whatever it was she was sending.

Self-consciously, she lifted a hand to her ruby red hair. "I know. It's about time you did my roots."

Continuing on to the counter of her station, I leaned my butt against it and took in her clear, stressed but happy face. "Tell me when and I'll do it for you."

My boss nodded and raised her eyebrows, eyeing me closely. "How you feeling?'

"Like shit. You?"

"Like shit."

I laughed and Ginny grinned. "How'd you get your car yesterday?"

"I made the kids drop me off. You?"

"The Larsens drove me."

We both looked at each other for a moment before I finally blurted out, "Hey, is there something I should know about you and Dallas?"

She tipped her head to the side. "What do you mean?"

"Why don't you like him?"

Her mouth formed an *O* shape before she closed it and sighed. "It isn't that I don't like him. We've never... hit it off. You know what I mean? When we were kids, he was serious and uptight. When we were older, like teens, it was always like he thought he was better than the rest of us. There's nothing *wrong* with him. I guess I just never really gave him a chance. I didn't know I was still doing that, but he can't be that much of a stuck-up if he hangs out with Trip, I guess."

It was my turn for my mouth to form an *O*. Just as quickly as Ginny had, I closed my mouth too. I could definitely picture Dallas being this mountain of judgmental black and white as a kid. He was still like that.

The difference was, I liked it.

Ginny kept going. "Now, Jackson on the other hand, what a waste of a human being."

～

I AM NOT GOING TO LOOK AT DALLAS'S BUTT.

I am not going to look at Dallas's butt.

Nope. Not doing it.

Not doing it.

As if tempting me, Dallas walked by in front of me, all of his attention on the boy beside him during practice. Deep in the outfield was Josh, running drills with Trip and some of the other boys. But as terrible of a person as it made me, it was Dallas I was busy looking at.

Dallas and the skintight, long-sleeve thermal shirt he had on and jeans I was not going to be focusing on. I was too busy not thinking about Dallas to notice when someone took the seat right next to me. It was the divorced dad.

"Hey, Diana," he greeted me, his hair combed neatly, hands on his lap.

I smiled at him. "Hi."

The man, who had to be in his late thirties or early forties, gestured toward my hand, his gaze was wide. "How's your hand doing?"

"Much better," I told him, mostly honestly. I was better. Way better. But that didn't mean it didn't ache like hell after a few hours of working. I'd been putting vitamin E oil on it every night before bed, but the skin still hadn't completely healed.

He hissed, craning his neck to eye my hand closer. "Sheesh."

I pressed my lips together and smiled. "It'll get even better."

The man tipped his head to the side, still eyeing me. When he didn't immediately say anything, I thought he'd let it go. Most of practice had gone by, and the coaches had the boys in a huddle, talking to them before he finally spoke up again.

"I think I told you already I'm divorced." He'd only told me about ten times since we'd met. "I'm not dating anyone seriously."

But he was dating someone, and trying to weasel in some flirting. Great.

"If you ever need any help, you could give me a call. I'd be more than willing to help out with anything you might need," he said softly, obviously fully aware of how nosey the rest of the parents were and how everyone eavesdropped on everyone else.

I felt uncomfortable. Even though I didn't want to, I tore my eyes away from the boys on the field and turned to look at this guy, knowing exactly what I needed to do even though I really didn't want to do it. "That's really nice of you to offer, but my dad helps me out a ton, and between the boys and me, we're usually pretty good with most stuff, but I appreciate the offer."

This poor, attractive man by most women's standards wasn't stopping. "It doesn't have to be help. Our boys are friends." I wouldn't call Josh his son's friend, at all, but I'd keep my mouth closed. "We could do something with them, if you're interested." He blinked. "Or by ourselves."

Shit.

I barely opened my mouth to tell him something along the lines that I was flattered he was offering but that I was really busy and not interested in dating anyone when a shadow came over me. A big hand reached across my face to take the bag I had sitting between the dad and I. Before I even looked, I knew there was no way it was Josh. He was tall but not that tall, and the hand that I'd briefly seen was bigger than mine by a lot. But I guess… well, I wasn't sure what I guessed, but I sure as hell didn't really expect to find Dallas at my side, looking down at me, with Josh beside him glaring at the dad.

"Hey, guys," I greeted them quickly, frowning at the faces they were both making. I understood Josh's, he always gave that specific dad dirty looks every time he sat by me, but Dallas? What was up his butt?

Those warm hazel eyes stayed locked on my face. He didn't once look at the man beside me. "You ready?"

To leave? "Yeah." I glanced at Josh and tipped my chin up.

He was too busy glaring at the dad to notice me.

As I got to my feet, I started to reach for my purse in Dallas's hands but he pulled it in closer to his body, eyeing me the entire time. "Let's go."

No part of me was putting the pieces together. Not one single bit. All I did was nod before turning around to face the dad still sitting on the bench, watching and listening. I smiled at him. "I'll see you later. Thank you for the offer."

The dad's gaze bounced from me to Dallas and back again before he nodded, slowly. "Yeah, sure," he said, going back to Dallas who suddenly seemed to be standing inches away from me. I could feel his body heat.

I didn't even freeze a little when what was obviously his hand landed on my shoulder, gently turning me in the direction where everyone was headed. I only partially eyed his hand as I dropped my own for a low-five from Josh, who gave it to me easily.

"Good practice, J-Money?" I asked, completely conscious of the weight on me and of the man beside me.

The eleven-year-old smacked my hand again with a smirk. "Good practice. Did you have fun talking to your friend?"

Did I give my eleven-year-old the stink eye? Damn right I did.

The problem was, I'd learned the stink eye from the best: him.

I stuck my tongue out at him and he stuck his right back.

"That's why I have to follow you two home," came the voice that seemed right by my ear.

I stared at Josh a second longer before I winked at him, and he winked at me right back.

"Do you want to have dinner with us, Mr. Dallas?" Josh asked as he continued to watch me.

Since when did Josh invite people over for dinner? That was Louie's job.

"J, I'm sure he has better things to do than see your face longer than he needs to," I said jokingly, still watching that face I knew too well. It *felt* like he was up to something, but what? "Plus, I'm sure he wants to spend some time with his grandma."

"There's nothing better I could be doing," came the

reply right by my shoulder a moment before the hand on the opposite side gave me a squeeze before dropping. "And Nana's probably asleep by now."

With my heart up in my throat and this sneaky shit with Josh going on, I managed to keep my attention forward.

"All right, I just have to go pick up Louie first," I said, mostly to my shoulder.

There wasn't a single doubt in my mind that what had to be a hand touched the small of my back. "I'm good at waiting," he replied.

I nodded, and as I raised my gaze to start making our way toward the parking lot, I noticed it. A good chunk of the moms, waiting around for the kids or talking, were watching us. Why did that surprise me? And why didn't it bother me?

"We should start carpooling."

That comment had my head swinging to the side and up. Dallas was looking down at me, his expression clear. The hand on my lower back made a circle even through the material of my jacket, and his thick, dark eyebrows rose a millimeter, like he was trying to challenge me.

But why would he do that?

I didn't narrow my eyes, but I wanted to. "That would save gas…" I cleared my throat. "Maybe not on the days Louie doesn't come though."

And this man, this man of my dreams who I didn't know I even wanted, stitched back up a whole inch of that part of my heart that hadn't been the same since my brother. "I don't mind picking up Lou." There was a pause and he blinked those beautiful eyes. His voice was hesitant. "Unless you don't want me to?"

Didn't want him to? What a dumbass.

I smiled at him, trying to tell him with my eyes that I wanted him to love me back. To kiss me again. To tell me what he wanted from me. "What did I tell you about stupid questions, Mr. Clean?"

I HAD JUST FINISHED SETTING THE LAST CLEAN DISH ON THE rack when my phone rang from wherever I'd left it.

"Aunt Di! It's *abuelita!*" Josh shouted from the living room a moment before the slapping of his feet on the floor warned me he was coming.

Sure enough, he had my phone outstretched in his hand; his practice uniform still on. Before I'd gone into the kitchen to wash dishes, he, Lou, and Dallas had all been sitting in front of the television, taking turns playing video games. It was too much. So I'd gotten up and decided to wash dishes while I collected my thoughts.

"Thanks, J," I told him, taking the phone from his hand. "Hey, you and Lou need to go ahead and get ready for bed, all right? It's past ten."

The entire time I'd been talking, his lip started to snarl a little but he nodded, reluctant and shit. "You want me to tell Mr. Dallas to go?"

No, I didn't want him to kick out the neighbor, but I couldn't exactly say that. "Don't worry about it. You and Louie get ready for bed. Dallas can leave when he's ready."

Josh nodded and turned to walk out of the kitchen as I brought the phone to my face.

"*¿Bueno?*"

There was silence before my mom's voice came over the line, slow and crawling. "Who is at your house?" she asked in Spanish.

I hated rolling my eyes seconds into our conversation, but I couldn't help it. "My neighbor."

"*You have a man at your house?*"

She was hissing. Fantastic. "Yes, *Mamá.*"

"It's ten o'clock at night!"

"I know," I told her, drawing the letters out in frustration. "Did you need something?"

"Is he alone with the boys right now?" She was still speaking in quick, angry Spanish.

Fuck. "*Ma*, did you need something?"

"*¿Qué piensas? Qué estás haciendo?*"

"I know what I'm doing, Mom," I told her as calmly as possible even though the reality was, I never had any idea what I was doing. Ever. "What do you need?"

"Diana," she grumbled. "*Is he going to spend the night?*"

"Oh my God," I muttered, rolling my eyes. "*Mom*, tell me why you're calling. I still need to put the boys to sleep and I have to go to sleep."

"*Que Dios me bendiga. ¿Donde te fallé?*"

I rolled my eyes and shook my head in exasperation. She had just asked where she had failed me. God help me.

"It's the man with the tattoos?"

I sighed and pinched the bridge of my nose, already deciding I needed to find my Pop-Tarts and stick two of them in my mouth at once. "*Si*. What do you need?"

The most dramatic noise ever made in the history of bodily sounds came through the phone and my eyes tried to go find my brain again.

"Mom, I like him and you're going to have to live with that. So tell me why you called, please."

She started mumbling words in Spanish that I was pretty sure made up a prayer I hadn't heard in decades, since my First Communion. There was something about God helping her and something after that about paying for her sins. Planting one hand on the kitchen counter, with the other one holding the phone to my face, I dropped my head back and fake sobbed.

"*Mom.*"

She wasn't listening to me. Like always.

I only fake sobbed more.

Then I heard the soft laugh behind me. It was Dallas with his hip to the counter, those muscular arms crossed over his chest. He looked way too amused.

Had he heard me say I liked him?

"Mom, *Mom*, just call me later, okay? You're not paying attention anymore. I love you, tell God I said hi." I waited a second, and when she still hadn't acknowledged me, I sighed and hit the red button on my screen.

"Mom troubles?" Dallas asked.

"Like always."

"The boys went to get ready for bed just now," he

said, taking a step forward.

"Okay." Why did I feel shy all of a sudden? "Are you leaving?"

"Not yet." He took another step. "I've missed seeing you."

He missed me?

I gulped. "I live across the street."

"I know, Di," he replied with a smirk on his pink mouth. "I've been trying to give you some space to think about things."

"Think about what?" I gulped again, watching him slowly creep closer to me.

"What happened in my truck."

Luckily, I knew that the wrong thing to ask was "What happened in the truck?" Instead, I had this deer-caught-in-the-headlights look on my face and muttered, "Oh. That."

His eyebrow went up. "That?"

"Yeah. That." *Stupid, stupid, stupid, Diana.*

Dallas took two more striding steps forward until he stopped directly in front of me, so close the upper part of his stomach brushed against my breasts. One of those big hands came up to my face and he pet my cheek again with the backs of his fingers, his voice low and steady. "I'm gonna kiss you again."

I sucked in a breath as he dipped his head closer to mine. There were a million things I should tell him. Maybe even two million things. But instead of telling him I wasn't sure where his mind was at or what he wanted from me or telling him that I thought he'd hung the Milky Way, all I did was nod.

I didn't even ask him why he liked me or since when. *When?*

What I did do was stand there as his hands curled over my hips and his breath hit my skin.

His lips brushed across my forehead from one temple to the next and back again. I swallowed hard.

The soft skin of Dallas's mouth went from my temple down along my ear and halfway across my jaw. Gentle. Barely a touch. I held my breath.

When he went up the path he'd come down, back across my forehead and down the same route along my ear on the other side, I closed my eyes and still didn't breathe.

The hands on my hips tightened, and either Dallas took a step closer or he pulled me to him because our lower bodies were suddenly pressed against each other. And then, *and then*, his lips hovered over mine for all of a heartbeat before they covered my own. From one instant to the next, his mouth slanted over mine and the gentleness was nowhere to be found because it had gotten replaced by something I could only call hunger. Starving, I-can't-get-enough-now-and-it-feels-like-I-might-never-get-enough hunger.

Dallas's tongue dueled mine, and I wasn't about to let him win. I couldn't remember the last time I'd taken a breath, but I didn't give a shit.

It was me who pressed my hips against his, a rock, a roll. But it was Dallas with the hard thing between us, hot and like a pipe against me, right above my belly button.

"I love the way you kiss," he whispered when he

drew his mouth away from mine just an inch.

I said it. I told him. "I like everything about you." Because it was the truth.

This choking, groaned noise bubbled in Dallas's mouth and I could feel the heat of his stare on my face, but I could only talk myself into looking at his mouth. His slightly parted, swollen lips inches away. And it was only because I was looking at his mouth that I knew it was being redirected to my cheeks, to my jaw, to two spots on my neck, and then I couldn't see at all as his hips rocked into my stomach again, his cock harder and so warm through my clothes. Dallas pressed that soft mouth to my collarbone as his hands slid up from my hips to my waist to just directly below my breasts, so that the undersides rested on the curve of his hand between his thumb and index finger.

"I knew it would be like this," he murmured into my collarbone, nipping at it with those flat, white teeth.

I was panting. I couldn't talk.

One of his thumbs took a detour from my ribs and went up, swiping over my nipple, which I wasn't surprised at all was hard. Dallas was breathing roughly as his thumb did it again. His mouth kissed the patch of skin my button-down shirt couldn't cover and he whispered, directly into my damn heart, "I've thought about doing this with you in here a hundred times—a thousand times—"

"Buttercup! Are you gonna tuck me in?" came a shout that had me jerking back to reality.

But it didn't have Dallas going anywhere. It didn't have his hands moving from where they'd taken residence. And that thick shaft across my stomach didn't go anywhere either.

It was only Dallas's head that rose until his face hovered just above mine, that beautiful pink mouth brushing my own. He focused those green-brown-gold eyes in on me and kissed my lips, just a peck, one, two, three, four, five times. Then he touched his mouth to one of my cheeks and then the other, pausing right in front of me as his gaze bounced from one of my eyes to the second and back.

"Buttercup!" Louie yelled again.

His hands moved over to my arms and down to my wrists before cupping each of my hands in his palms. He brought them up between us and against his hard, flat belly. "I'll let you put the boys to bed, but we'll talk tomorrow. I'm not gonna keep putting this off, Diana."

And I answered with the only word my stupid, stunned brain could come up with. "Okay."

"*Buttercup!*"

"Poo face! Give me a second!" I hollered, shaking my head as I held Dallas's gaze.

"Bring Mr. Dallas!" the little boy shouted back.

This beautiful, perfect man who had just finished kissing me smiled softly at Louie's request. "You mind?" he had the nerve to ask.

"You know I don't." I waved him toward me. "Come on."

Dallas nodded and took a step forward as I turned my back on him. I managed to take maybe a couple of steps before two arms wrapped around my shoulders from behind in a hug that lasted all of a squeeze and what I could only assume was a kiss to the back of my head. I stood there and took it.

A giant part of me wished he would do it again and again.

It wasn't until he dropped his hold on me way too soon, that I reached back without looking at him and took his hand. I laced my fingers through his and felt his pads curl over the fine bones below the outside of my wrist. We walked the fifteen feet to Louie's room holding hands, not saying a word. Sure enough, his blond head was the only thing peeking out from over the top of his Iron Man covers and he was grinning that grin that lit my entire world up.

"I like this," Louie confirmed as I took a seat on the bed furthest away from the door and Dallas took the opposite spot as we let go of each other's hand.

Snorting, I started tucking his comforter in around his legs and let his comment go. "Did you brush your teeth?"

"Yes."

"What story do you want to hear today?" I asked, still tucking him in.

The little boy made a humming noise as his eyes bounced to Dallas. "What do you think, Mr. Dallas?"

"What do you usually hear? Only stories about your dad?"

"Yeah," he answered like he was saying "duh."

Dallas made his own thoughtful noise. His hand went to the top of where Louie's foot was and he gave it a squeeze. "What about one of your mom?"

The cowardly part of me said "Shit." The part of me

that knew this was a conversation I'd continued to push aside even though I shouldn't thought that it was about time someone had brought this up. Louie, on the other hand, didn't say a word but I could sense his gaze on me. I could feel his tension.

Dallas knew Louie's mom wasn't alive. I'd mentioned Mandy and Rodrigo's wills before, but I still hadn't told him what happened. Guilt was a painful son of a bitch no one liked to remember.

"My mom died."

The statement out of Louie's mouth had me glancing up at him as sneakily as possible. That sweet, innocent face wasn't exactly blank, but it was his eyes that said it all. He looked as hurt as he had two years ago, and that ate me up inside. *I should have handled this better.*

"My dad died when I was a kid," Dallas told him gently. "I still miss him a lot. My mom used to tell me stories about him too sometimes but not like your Buttercup does. You're really lucky, you know that?"

"Your dad died too?"

Dallas nodded. "I was ten. He was the best man in the whole world. I wanted to be just like him. I still wanna be just like him."

I kept my mouth shut and watched Louie's face as he said, "My daddy was a policeman. I wanna be like him too."

"You can be whatever you want to be, Lou," our neighbor said. The hand he had on Louie's foot moved and his fingers plucked at one of Louie's toes.

"That's what *Tia* Di says."

"She knows what she's talking about."

Louie smiled. His eyes flashed over to mine and his smile grew even wider. "Yeah." Just as quickly as it had arrived, the curves of his mouth disappeared and he glanced once more at Dallas. "I only like stories about my dad."

"You might like stories about your mom, too, buddy. I'm sure she had to be pretty special to have such a nice son like you."

This guy was killing me. "She was pretty special, Goo," I let him know, my voice just a little unsteady. I had to take advantage of this opportunity Dallas was giving me. "Where do you think you get how sweet and cute you are from? Everyone loved your mom."

He blinked and his fingers peeked out from over the top of the comforter, curling over the edge of it. I'd swear his eyes narrowed just a little. "They did?" From the tone of his voice, it confirmed he didn't believe it. Had my parents said something in front of him to make him think otherwise? I doubted the Larsens had, but what did I know?

A lump settled into my chest, and I had to force myself to ignore it. "Oh yeah. Ask Josh." I wanted to ask him if he didn't remember her but that seemed almost cruel. "She was always happy and she never had a mean thing to say about anyone." I smiled at him.

Those blue eyes jumped between me to Dallas and then to his comforter. I glanced at Dallas and reached out to put my hand over the one he had on Louie's feet. His fingers spread wide and took mine between his.

"Did she..." Louie hesitated. "What did she say when I was born?"

I wasn't going to cry in front of him. I wasn't going to cry in front of him.

The last time we'd talked about Mandy had been right after she died, weeks, maybe a couple of months maximum. Louie had cried. He'd been a toddler back then but his hurt over how his mom had rejected him in the long weeks after Rodrigo passed away had been unavoidable. It had taken long enough for him to understand my brother wasn't coming back. Death wasn't something a three-year-old could really process. For the longest time he'd thought he was at work, and it wasn't until one random day that he accepted never meant never. His daddy—my brother—was never coming back. Not that day or the next, or a year from then.

What he hadn't been able to accept or comprehend was why his mom hadn't been there afterward.

I could remember the tears and the questions. *"Where's Mommy?"* and *"Why doesn't Mommy play?"* There's no way I could forget how confused Louie, more than Josh, had been back then. I didn't doubt Josh had loved Mandy, but she wasn't all he'd ever known. Josh had always been aware of the situation with Anita. The only thing that had worked out in that time period was that Louie had always been close to me and hadn't rejected my love and attention back then. He hadn't understood what was going on with his mom but he'd jumped into what I had been more than willing to give him.

I think he'd been too busy grieving my brother to really let him feel anything other than anger at his mom after she was gone, and after a while, he'd just stopped talking about her. Like he didn't want to remember she existed. No matter how much I tried bringing her up, he refused.

Until today.

"She cried a lot," I told him softly, forcing myself to smile. "Happy tears. Like when Santa brought Josh his baseball bat and he cried, remember that? She kept saying you were the most beautiful thing she'd ever seen, and how she couldn't believe she could love anything as much as she loved you. She didn't let me hug you for two days after you were born, can you believe that? She didn't want to share you with anybody, only your dad."

Louie watched me the entire time. A smile never crossed his face. It was only the fingers he had at the top of his covers that tapped along the material as he listened.

Dallas's fingers tightened around my own. "That sounds like she loved you a lot," he said to my Lou.

All the little boy said was "Hmm." That was it.

I was going to take it. For now. Not wanting to force him to talk about her any more for now, I told him, "Your brother has tons of stories about her. You should ask him to tell you some of them one day. He loved her a lot. I loved her, too."

Louie's eyes were glassier than normal when he glanced at me and nodded his head quickly. Way too quickly. His mouth twitched sadly and he swallowed.

Then he swallowed again, and I felt like he'd come to a decision about something. "Like you love me?" the sneaky booger asked in his normal voice.

I had to accept we had gotten somewhere tonight by at least bringing her up. I winked at him. "Don't get crazy. Not that much."

That made him smile.

"Why don't you tell me a story about your dad tonight, Lou, hmm?" Dallas asked.

CHAPTER TWENTY-FOUR

"I'LL BE OUTSIDE WAITING FOR YOU, JOSH!" I YELLED THAT following morning when I noticed we had exactly five minutes before we needed to leave for school so the boys could make it in time.

"Okay!" he hollered back from the kitchen where he was finishing his cereal.

Louie stood right next to me with his backpack on and a toasted piece of bread with honey on it in his hand. I could already imagine the crusts stuffed into his seat or thrown on the floor of my car. "I'm ready," he said, those blue eyes completely innocent, as if he wasn't capable of doing anything remotely bad in his life.

I gave him a tired smile, and tilted my head toward the door. I was exhausted. After putting the boys to bed, I'd stayed awake, replaying every single conversation I'd had with Dallas since we'd met. And there had been a lot of them.

How many times had he told me that he was going to stay faithful to his wife until they got divorced? Every single time she was brought up?

How many times did he mention something about his imaginary future girlfriend having to wait for him?

He knew me. I know he knew me. And mostly, he wasn't some asshole who might say a bunch of things and not mean a single one of them.

And then, I thought about Vanessa's words and how she'd told me not to be a chicken. How she'd reminded me of who I was *now*. It had taken me a lot of years, but I knew who I was and I knew what I was willing to do for the people I loved and the things I wanted.

And that was everything. I would do everything and anything.

So where the hell did that leave me?

Busy thinking about all things Dallas-related, I turned around with my bag to head down the pathway when I spotted a motorcycle across the street in Dallas's driveway.

It was Jackson's.

It had been weeks since our confrontation at the barbecue. Weeks since I'd seen his bike on the street. Just the day before, while I'd been making dinner after practice, I asked Dallas if he'd seen or heard from his brother, and he'd said no. But it was his face when he answered that had really dug deep into my gut.

It was only with family that you could be so fucking angry, and yet still worry and love them. I understood. His brother was a piece of shit, but he was still his brother.

I sighed and glanced at Louie who was already heading toward the back passenger door of my car. "Goo, I'll be right back. I think I see Dallas's brother, and I want to ask him something. I'll be back in a second."

"Okay."

Did I want to go across the street and talk with this motherfucker again? No, I didn't. But this adulting thing was a lot harder and more complicated than anyone had ever warned me, and I had never known how to mind my own business. This whole loving-the-wrong-person thing also wasn't easy either.

I jogged across the street, ready to say my two cents and hopefully not get smacked in the face in the process because I'd seen the urge in Jackson's eyes at the barbecue.

Sure enough, standing beside the beefy motorcycle was the blond with the thick beard who was obviously not going to the tournament this weekend if the bags he had on the back of his bike said anything. As I came up to him, he looked up and blinked in a way I'd seen his brother do countless times by that point.

I came to a stop, leaving close to ten feet between us, and raised my hands in a peaceful gesture, watching that face that really did look older than Dallas's. "Look, I just came to tell you that you shouldn't punish Dallas for what I said and did to you, all right?"

He snickered and shook his head, moving around to tighten down a strap on the other side. "You're not here to apologize?" he scoffed, so full of sarcasm I wanted to smack him in the face or throw some more Hawaiian Punch at him.

"Why would I? You deserved it." I watched him to make sure he didn't start to get all bent out of shape, but he didn't even glance in my direction again. "I just don't want my big mouth to make things worse than they already are between you two. That's all." I paused and watched him for a second before this tiny amount of dread filled my stomach. "Look, I'll shut up after this and never say anything to you again, but if you disappear on him like this... he already feels guilty enough about what happened when you were kids—"

"I'm not *disappearing*," he grumbled. "I can't stay here when Nana Pearl is here. She already gave me enough shit in the five minutes I was—" Jackass Jackson let out a frustrated breath. "Forget it. I'm packing up my shit like he asked me to weeks ago."

Weeks ago? As in at the barbecue?

He'd kicked his brother out?

I didn't even think Louie or Josh had been this much of a pain in the ass at any point in their lives. This was cranky kid behavior, and my gut said it was pointless. I'd sensed the stubborn-ass in him the first time we'd met, and I could still sense the stubborn-ass in him right then.

Rolling my eyes, I took a step back and sighed. I almost told him good luck, but then again, this was the person who had called me a bitch and made rude comments about my brother after what I'd done for him. Ungrateful asshole.

Luckily, I hadn't been expecting an apology because I sure as hell didn't get one as I ran back across the street just as Josh came hustling out of the house, running down the steps of the deck before I pointed back at the door so he could lock it. By the time we pulled out of the driveway, we were running more than five minutes late.

And Jackson hadn't left yet.

I wondered what would happen to him and Dallas, and part of me hoped they somehow managed to work it out. But who knew. Sometimes self-destructive people didn't know how to ever turn that button off. My *abuela* had always said you can't help people who don't want to help themselves.

I MADE IT ALL THE WAY THROUGH MY FIRST TWO APPOINTMENTS before I realized that Dallas's appointment was that evening.

It was no big deal.

It was no big deal that the more I thought about our situation—with him kissing me and writing notes that he hadn't given me and telling me "as you wish"—the more I wanted it—him. I wanted something with Dallas if he did, and I was pretty sure that was the case.

So I knew what I was going to do, and I wasn't going to back down.

When my appointment right before his ran late because the client showed up twenty minutes after she was supposed to—and she was one of my regulars who showed up religiously for her roots to get redone —I might have been rushing to finish. Just a little.

I'd caught his eyes in the reflection as I drew the straightener through my client's hair and took in an eyeful of his slow smile as he paced around the waiting room with his attention on his phone.

"What's *American History X* doing here?" my client sneered. We joked around with each other, that was nothing new, but in this case, I froze.

"What'd you say?" I asked playfully, thinking I'd heard wrong.

"The skinhead. Since when do y'all do fades?" She kind of laughed at the end of her question.

I cleared my throat and clamped her hair between the ceramic. "We'll do anyone's hair," I answered her slowly, reaching for another piece of hair even as I felt my neck get hot.

She made a dismissive noise in her throat, but as the minutes rolled by, I got angrier and angrier. Who was she to judge Dallas? And to assume he was a skinhead? *American History X?* Really?

I stared at her head as she walked in front of me toward the front desk, and I was gritting my teeth as I swiped her card. My head started hurting in the five minutes it took to do all of that, and when she asked, "When can you schedule me in for four weeks from now?" in a cheery voice, I just about lost it.

Dallas had gotten off his phone and was sitting on one of the chairs, looking at me. I let out a shaky breath as I took in those beautiful hazel eyes that had done so much for me. Then I glanced back at my client. "Trish, I don't think I can schedule you in for a month from now. Sean's gotten pretty good with doing color. He can definitely do what you need. I'll put you with him if you want to keep coming back here, but it's completely up to you."

The expression on her face melted off in a split second. "I don't understand. What do you mean you can't schedule me in?"

"I can't schedule you in. Thanks for coming to me for so long now, but I don't feel comfortable with it anymore."

Her face paled. "Did I do something wrong?"

"The 'skinhead,'"—I used my fingers as quotation marks—"is my really good friend." I dropped my hands. "Actually, I think he's going to marry me one day."

I said it. I owned it.

And she, my client, went pink from the roots of her hair down her chest.

"You can call in to schedule an appointment if you want to come back, I don't mind. I'd ask for Sean though."

She cleared her throat, nodded, and ducked her head. Then she spun on her heel and, with her attention still on the ground, rushed out of the salon. I could sense my own face getting hot and uncomfortable, but I knew it was either that or living with that layer of guilt that would saturate my thoughts and bones for days if I didn't do something. It wasn't until after you had a major regret that you understood the importance of not putting things off or being scared to do something about your problems. I could live with my client thinking I was a dick for saying something. I could live with never coloring or cutting her hair again.

What I couldn't live with was not standing up for someone who was so much more than his looks and his skin color and his fucking haircut. Someone who was worth so much more than two hundred dollars a month.

"You ready?" I called out as I went around the front desk, my head still pounding with my not-really altercation.

He already had those amazing eyes narrowed on me as he stood up, making me think of how he'd pressed his boner into my stomach the night before. Shit.

"Yeah." He took me in again and raised his chin. "What's wrong?"

"Stupid people. They're what's wrong with me," I answered him honestly, too frustrated about what had just happened to be thinking about other things. Things like kissing.

His grin was a wary one. "Stupid people will do that to anybody," he replied.

I nodded and blew out a breath, willing myself to chill out and forget about Trish. "Come on. You don't look like you need a haircut, but I can take my time so you think you're getting your money's worth."

The smile crept over his features slowly and easily, like he didn't have a single worry in the world, like this thing between us didn't make him lose any sleep at all. God, he was handsome. "Do what you did to my neck last time, and I'll pay you double."

I snickered and gestured toward my station. "Stop."

Dallas walked ahead of me saying, "Or right at the spot where my hair and ear meet. Triple."

That had me laughing like everything was fine and there hadn't been any kisses between us. "Get in the chair. I don't promise those kind of happy endings."

He chuckled as he sank into the chair, his forearms resting on the arms. I shook out a cape and draped it over his chest when he asked, "What kind of places are you going to that give people happy endings, huh?"

"The same kind of places you do, since you know what I'm talking about." I couldn't help but laugh.

My fingers were on the nape of his neck, attaching the separate pieces of Velcro together to hold the cape to him when he tipped his head back just enough for me to mostly see his eyes. "I don't go to those kinds of places."

Dear Jesus. I coughed. "Oh?"

He was still watching me as he whispered just loud enough for me to hear, "My hand is just as good as any other."

God help me. God help me. God help me. *God help me.*

He'd just said what I thought he'd said. His hand. On him. Once the mental image of Dallas naked on his bed with his hand on himself—long and thick, because I'd felt that thing against me and there had been no mistaking it for anything except what it was—filled my head, picturing him stroking over and over again, up and down, a twist here and there, squeezing and pulling... there was no going back. There was absolutely no going back. Not now, not ever.

There was no way that my thoughts weren't written all over my face. I could *feel* it go hot. I could *feel* myself get all bent out of shape into so many loops and spirals there was no straightening me out.

Dallas jerking was going to be in my head tonight and every night for a really long time.

Or always, a little voice in my head warned.

A big hand reached out to wrap its fingers around my wrist, and he pulled on it gently. "How can I miss you so much when I just saw you yesterday?"

I sucked in a breath and darted my eyes up to his face to find him watching me carefully, that gentle, soft smile of his aimed right at me with so much honesty and openness I forgot how to think.

But the second I was able to, I remembered Vanessa's words. And I remembered what I had stayed up all night thinking about. And I remembered what I had decided.

Life could be brutally short, and happiness was never guaranteed.

There were so many things I wish I could have told my brother before he died—how much he'd meant to me, how much I loved him, and how I would try to be someone he could be proud of. I had made plenty of mistakes in my life; I just didn't want to continue making choices that would lead to regrets.

And it was with that knowledge—with thinking

about Rodrigo's short and brilliant life and how much he had loved me and his sons—that I went for it. I asked him, "Do you like me?"

It sounded just as middle school as it should have, but I didn't give a single shit. How the hell else could I have asked?

Dallas blinked and his teeth went to bite his bottom lip. His eyebrows went up a millimeter, and he let out a slow breath through his mouth. "I wouldn't call it 'like.'" The fingers he had around my wrist loosened and trailed down to my hand. Spreading those fingers apart, he linked those long, strong digits through mine.

Dallas was holding my hand.

He was holding my hand as he said, "You told me you were a little in love with me, do you remember?"

How could I forget?

"But I wouldn't use 'little' to describe what I feel for you, Diana. I think you know that already."

It was my turn to blink. I squeezed our palms together. "So I'm not imagining it?" I pretty much whispered.

"No, baby, you're not." Dallas squeezed my fingers between his.

I dropped about four F-bombs in my head as I stood there, not trusting my words. Or his.

And he must have known that because he didn't wait for me to open my mouth. "I'm your poor bastard and you know it." He kept tugging on my arm until I stood in front of him, the front of one of my thighs touching his kneecap.

There went another dozen S-bombs and M-bombs

as every nerve in my spine lit up like a pinball machine.

Without thinking about what would be the best thing to say next, I made my gaze meet his, like I had every other time we discussed things, and I asked, "Are you sure?"

Dallas was the most constant man I had ever met in my life. His patience, steadfastness, and determination covered every inch of his entire being as he smiled at me. "Positive." His eyes went from one of mine to the other, even and patient. "Of all the houses you could've bought, you got the one across the street from me. Of all the sports Josh might have played, it was baseball and I happened to coach his age group. You were meant to be in my life."

Those hazel irises went so tender my heart hurt. His whisper didn't help any. "I know you love me."

It was one thing to admit it to myself but a completely different thing to say the words out loud. But I said them anyway. "Yeah, I do." I breathed. "But —"

"No buts."

I couldn't help but smile a little even though it felt like my entire future—my life—depended on what happened right now. But I couldn't stop as I looked over Dallas's weathered, serious face. "Yes buts. You can love me, but that doesn't have to mean anything, Dallas. What do you want from me?"

"Everything."

I sucked in a breath and blinked. Out of all the ways he could have answered, that wasn't what I was expecting. I thought it would be more of a "let's date" or "be my girlfriend" or... something.

In that way that was all him, like he knew what I was thinking and feeling, the corners of his mouth came up. But he didn't say anything.

"Everything. All right. Okay."

The corners of his mouth curled slightly, and I'd swear on my life he looked just a little nervous. Just a little. "I want you. I want your smile. Your hugs. Your love. I want your happiness." He paused. "Every single thing."

Was this what being shot in the heart was supposed to feel like?

I looked right into his eyes and I asked him, "Are you sure you know what you're getting yourself into?"

His mouth stayed in the same smirking smile and he nodded. "One hundred percent."

"You know I'm crazy."

"You're my best friend. I know you're crazy."

Why that felt like the best compliment I'd ever been given, I had no idea. But I gave him a serious look. "I'm a jealous bitch, Dallas. Do you understand that? I'm not saying you can't talk to women or other parents on the team or anything, but if you cheated on me—why are you smiling?"

"If I cheated on you, you and Josh would kill me and bury the body somewhere no one would ever find." He kept my story going, smiling so wide, his face had to hurt.

I blinked at him and shrugged. "Pretty much."

"I would never cheat on you. We live across the

street from each other, so you'd never have to get jealous wondering where the hell I am or who I'm with. Coaching Josh, we'd get to spend our weekends together. See? That sounds perfect to me."

I was dying, slowly. Why did it feel like I was picking at threads that didn't exist?

His mouth perked up even more, so much he was practically beaming.

"I have the boys, Dallas—"

"So?"

I hated when he used my words and tactics against me. He said the word like it was nothing. Like my worry about Josh and Lou wasn't even a consideration into our relationship or whatever it was he wanted to have with me, and that unsettled me more than anything else he'd said before.

As I took a step back, he let my wrist go and I turned my back to him, reaching for the clippers in one of the drawers. This was happening. This was really happening.

"You told me you trusted me," he reminded me.

I was sure my face was pink as I turned to him, the device in my hand. It wasn't until I was right in front of him again that he spoke up once more, his fingers reaching out to touch a spot just above my knee.

"You can tell me anything."

That was what scared me. It was the truth. I'd always felt like I could tell him anything. Now more than ever that seemed terrifying.

Like it could make me or break me.

So I told him, looking him in the eye before I took a

step that brought me so close his breath hit my forearm as I leaned over him. I started with the clippers, going over the rounded surface of his head. "You just got divorced. I know you already said you wouldn't cheat on me and that you know exactly what you're doing, but... I don't... this is serious to me. I don't like or love just anyone, Dallas. I know you can't promise you won't break my heart someday, but—"

"This is serious to me too. I won't break your heart, Diana. I've never been scared to work for things or wait for them. *I know you*, and I know that you're it. I just had to wait to get divorced so I could do this right for you. Life is so fucking short, Peach, and I'm too old to not know and go for what I want. And you know what I want. What I've wanted. For a long, long time." He paused. "You."

Shit, shit, *shit*. There was only one more thing I needed to tell him before I forgot. And it was the most important one. "Okay. I want to get married someday. I'm not saying tomorrow or six months from now, all right? And I'm not sure I want to have kids anytime soon. Can you deal with that?"

Something nudged at my thigh. I could see the back of his hand, feel him rub his knuckles up and down. His hand drifted up another inch. He wedged his hand in more so that his palm gripped the back of my thigh. Those eyes I was more than a little in love with burned my retinas. "I'd be happy with just two boys."

Was I tearing up? Was that why my eyes were watery? I blinked and the tears didn't go anywhere.

And Dallas's sweet expression didn't help any.

"You are the toughest person I've ever met, Diana, but you're also the most vulnerable, and that drives me fucking crazy," he said to me. He squeezed my thigh, his voice low and almost feverish. "I know you can take care of yourself, but I want to be there to help you out. I need you more than you need me, and that's okay," he told me.

This man was going to be the death of me. For the seventh or eighth time in my life, I had no idea what to say or even where to start.

That big hand squeezed. "Just like I tell the boys, we don't play for one single run, we play to win the whole game. And I'm in it to win it."

I clenched my hand around the clippers. "But there're so many other teams to play against."

The corners of his mouth curled, and one of the fingers on my thigh did a caressing little line. "The only team I'm ever going to worry about is the best one. I've never been so sure of anything in my life."

It wasn't until closing time, after Sean and I had cleaned up, while he was busy counting out the register at the end of the night because he claimed he was faster than me at it, that I went to my tip jar. But it wasn't the bills in the blue Mason jar that caught my eye. It was what looked like a few folded pieces of paper inside that had me reaching for it.

If someone had left me an IOU or a business card, I was going to scream.

Turning the jar upside down, everything came out. There were dozens of papers inside, each about three inches long and one inch wide, I opened one genuinely wondering what the hell someone had put in there.

But I knew the instant I unfolded the first one who had done it.

Everything about you makes me smile. -Uncle Fester.

I laughed out loud and picked up another one the instant I read the last letter of the first. *Uncle Fester.* Fucking Dallas. *Fucking Dallas.* He had no idea what he did to me. I only made it through another three before I started tearing up.

Really. I love you. Love, Professor Xavier Before He Lost His Hair

In all the ways that matter, you can be my #1 – (infinity). Deal? Love always, your poor bastard

I love you. —Your born-again virgin Catholic convert, Dallas

I WAS SITTING ON THE EDGE OF THE COUCH, SLIPPING MY HEELS on when I zeroed in on Louie, who was sitting beside me on the couch dressed up in an outfit I'd found on sale around Labor Day. But it wasn't the navy blue pants or vest he had on that caught my eye, or the fact he was matching for once in his life when he wasn't wearing his school uniform. It was the red spot on the collar of his white shirt that had me reaching to pinch the tip of my nose.

"Louie."

"Huh?" he asked, his body hunched over with a tablet on his lap as he played whatever it was he was playing.

"Did you eat something after you changed?" I'd specifically told him not to eat anything because I knew him.

"No," he answered quickly, his attention still below him.

Sliding my heel down into my nude shoe, I gave my toes a wiggle to make sure my foot was in there as deep as it would go, telling myself not to freak out over his shirt. It had been inevitable, hadn't it? Hadn't I known this was going to happen and tried to prevent it? With a deep breath, I glanced back at his shirt and stood up, tugging on the skirt part of my dress. "Gooey, did you get something from the fridge?"

"Apple juice."

I pinched the tip of my nose again. "Did you grab the ketchup bottle by any chance?"

He stopped playing his game to glance up and give me a curious expression. "How'd you know?"

"Because there's a big red stain on your shirt, Goo."

Louie's hands immediately went to his chest and started patting around as he tried to find the spot. "I didn't eat anything!"

"I believe you," I moaned, trying to think if he had any other dress shirts that he hadn't out grown.

He didn't, and we didn't have time to wash this one. Ginny's wedding was in half an hour.

"I'm sorry," he apologized.

It was just a shirt and he was just a kid. It wasn't the end of the world. "It's fine."

"I promise! I didn't eat anything!"

"I believe you. You probably just held the ketchup bottle too close to you, you sloppy mess." I stared at him for a moment longer before telling him, "Come here. Maybe I can wipe off the worst of it with a napkin."

He tipped his chin down to try and see his collar.

Without a warning, he poked at the button closest to his neck, tugged the material away from him and stuck his tongue out. He licked at the ketchup spot. Over and over again.

"Louie! Oh my God, give me a towel. Don't lick it off, Jesus." I laughed, knowing I shouldn't but not being able to stop myself.

One blue eye peeked at me as he licked it again. "Why? I'm saving water. I'm saving the Earth."

Saving the Earth. If I hadn't just spent twenty minutes putting on makeup, I would have smacked myself in the forehead. "Stop. *Stop*. Leave it alone. It's fine. You can save the Earth another way."

"Are you sure? I can lick more."

That really made me laugh. "Yes, *stop*. Put your tongue back in your mouth, nasty." I laughed even harder as the tip of it peeked out between his lips.

Louie cracked up as he inched his face closer to the spot, as if daring me.

"*Stop*. Just pretend there's nothing there now," I ordered him, right before he gave the ketchup stain one more lick. "Oh my God, look at that! There's no stain anymore!"

"What are you doing, ding-dong?" came Josh's voice from behind where I was standing. "Why are you licking your shirt?"

"Ketchup," was the boy's reply.

I looked at Josh as he muttered, "What a weirdo."

Dressed in black pants my mom made him wear when they went to church, a blue long-sleeved shirt, and a black vest, my little Josh looked so much like my earliest memory of Drigo it nearly took my breath away. I had to bite my lip to keep from saying anything. "Looking good, J-Money."

He rolled his eyes. "I look stupid."

"And if by stupid you mean really handsome, you're right."

He rolled his eyes so far back I was surprised they managed to make their way forward again.

"Ready to go?"

"Yes." He paused. "Do I have to go?" he asked for the fourth time since I'd told him we were all going to Ginny's wedding.

I told him the same thing I had when he'd argued that he could stay with his grandparents, or that he could stay with my parents. "Nope." But I did tell him something I hadn't before. "Dean is going to be there."

That wiped the frown off his face just enough. "He is?"

"Yes. Trip texted me and asked if you were going."

His response was a grunt that I chose to ignore.

"All right, let's go, gangsters."

Louie hopped to his feet. "Okay, gangster."

Grabbing my purse and Ginny's gift, I corralled the boys outside, trying to balance everything under my armpits as I made Louie lock the door behind us. Josh was already at the back passenger door of the SUV when I heard, "Diana!"

I couldn't help but smile as I turned in the direction of the person yelling. Not "the person." Dallas. Sure enough, striding across the street in the way that only someone so tall with his kind of confidence was capable of, was my neighbor looking better than ever. And that was saying something since I'd seen him shirtless. In charcoal gray dress pants, a white shirt, and lavender tie, he was the best-looking man I'd ever seen.

Coming toward me.

Smiling.

Who said he was in love with me.

And looking at me with this focus that almost made me break out in a sweat. He'd shaved recently, his facial hair more of a five o'clock shadow than the neat beard he usually kept.

"Hi, Professor" I called out to him as he took a step onto the sidewalk directly in front of my house.

"You mean Coach," Josh suggested.

I shook my head, still watching my neighbor. "No, I meant Professor."

Dallas must have heard us because I spotted him smirking and shaking his head.

Louie immediately asked, "Are you coming with us?"

Dallas touched Josh on the back of the shoulder as he approached us, one of his hands extended out toward me. He took the gift from under my arm as he answered, "If you guys don't mind."

Like I would ever mind.

"Come with us!" Louie agreed.

"I don't care," Josh added.

I swallowed the knot in my throat as Dallas leaned forward and kissed my cheek for one brief moment that would be etched into my memory forever and ever even as Josh made a gagging noise. "Of course you can." I gave the keys a jiggle. "Want to drive?"

He looked me right in the eye as he took the keys. "Tell me how to get there, Peach."

~

I'D BEEN TO A LOT OF WEDDINGS IN MY LIFE—MY PARENTS USED to drag me to every single one they ever went to when I was a kid—but even if I hadn't known Ginny, I would have thought it was the most beautiful wedding I'd ever been to. There was a reason why she'd been so tight with money for so long. She'd splurged. A lot. But as I sat in the banquet hall following the ceremony, which had taken place in another section of the facility, I had a feeling she was going to have zero regrets about all the struggling she'd put herself through. Gin was beaming. Her happiness was like a light at the end of a dark tunnel.

It made my heart swell. I hadn't known Ginny back when she'd been with her ex, but I'd heard why they split up. They'd both been young, and by the time they decided to go their own way, they were completely different people. No shit. You weren't the same person you were at seventeen that you were at thirty-three.

I thought about Trip and Dallas's dislike of her new husband—of why they felt the way that they felt—but all I could think to myself was that, if she could be so happy with someone who had "been around the block" a few times, what did it matter what someone had done before you? No one ever succeeded at anything on the first try.

"Saving your first dance for me?"

I blinked from the empty plate of food in front of me and gazed at the man standing beside my chair. I smiled at Trip. "You dance?"

"You bet your ass I do. Come on." He flexed his fingers at me in an invitation. There was a slow country song playing through the speakers, following the couple's first dance.

He didn't have to tell me twice. I got up and followed him, setting one arm on his shoulder and letting him take my other hand in his. He grinned as he took a mini step away from me with a wink.

"I don't feel like dying tonight," he explained, like that made any sense.

"Who's going to kill you?"

"Dal." He peeked over his shoulder for a moment before glancing back at me with a smile that reminded me of a little boy who knew he was doing something bad. "I give him two minutes before he's over here."

"He's with one of your relatives right now. They were asking him about Miss Pearl," I explained.

I'd gone over to Dallas's house two days before to give the old woman a haircut. She'd acted like normal, didn't call me Miss Cruz once, and then all of a sudden, in the middle of trimming her hair, she'd announced, "I've thought about it, and I wouldn't mind some tan great-grandchildren someday."

What the hell did I respond with? "Okay?"

Tan grandchildren. Oh my God.

My white-haired neighbor turned in her chair just

enough to see me with one of those rheumy eyes and then said, "He looks out the window to check on you every night. I tell him to call you and quit being a stalker, but he thinks I'm going to listen in on his conversations." She huffed. "I have better things to do with my time."

All I'd managed to do after that was just nod. Obviously, Miss Pearl was doing just fine after losing a lot of her things in the fire.

"I still give him two minutes." Trip raised his eyebrows at me as he turned us, bringing my attention back to the present. "So you two finally, huh?"

"Finally?"

"Yeah, finally. It's only been, what? Three months?"

"No." I narrowed my eyes. "Really?"

"You sweet, sweet, blind child." He chuckled. "I told him he was an idiot for waiting until his shit had been settled, but he 'wanted to do it right' —"

"Go find your own girl to dance with," came a voice from behind me.

I'd bet my life that Trip's easy acceptance was a sign of how much he cared for his cousin and that was why he backed away so quickly. He still winked at me before telling the man behind me, "Just warmin' yours up for you, brother."

"I bet you were," Dallas said. He came around me and slipped so fluidly in front of me, placing my hands where they needed to go, I didn't react until his chest was an inch or two away from mine. Those brown-green-gold eyes hovered above my own. I didn't even watch in what direction Trip had gone I was so sucked in to the man in front of me. "There's my one and only."

I blushed and pinched my lips together. How was it that I had no idea how to act around him anymore? It was dumb. "Your one and only," I muttered. "There're lots of pretty girls here to dance with too," I said like a complete idiot, even though my stomach started hurting immediately afterward.

His eyebrow arched upward as his hand curled over my shoulder, touchy, touchy, touchy. "Are there?"

"Yeah."

"That's nice for everybody else," he said, drawing me toward him.

The sigh that came out of me was long and probably showed how confused I felt.

"What's that sigh for? They don't do me any good." That broad palm of his went to the small of my spine, the other led our hands to the corner of his chest and shoulder, settling there as he dipped his face closer to mine. His eyes were steady and even, staring right into my own. "I already have the one I want right here," he said.

"Dallas," I groaned, ducking my head. What was I doing?

"What?"

Our talk at the salon a couple of days ago hadn't eased my worries much. Talk was talk. Anyone could say they were Batman, but not everyone could *be* Batman. "There're a million other women in the world who would love to be with you—"

"You want me to go find them?" he asked with way too much humor in his voice.

I glanced up at him. "No, but I can't do casual. I don't think you get that."

His mouth went to my ear. "What gave you the idea that's what this would be? The last thing I feel for you is casual, Diana."

I groaned, feeling a warm sensation fill my belly. "Look, I just... I've really been trying hard to be an adult, and an adult would want someone like you to be happy. I care about you so much, and I'm a mess, you know that."

"I know, baby." He pulled me in closer to him with the hand on my spine. "It's one of my favorite things about you."

Heaven help me. *Heaven help me.*

I groaned again, trying to put my thoughts together. "You have a thing for single parents, huh?"

The hand on my back lowered, going over the curve before sweeping back up, teasing. "I got a soft spot for single parents. It's tough. But I got this thing— you might know what it is, it's red and it's in the center of your chest—and that has more than a soft spot for hot aunts who raise their nephews. You can't even call it a spot, really."

I choked and felt his chin rest on the top of my head. "How big is this... spot?"

"It's big enough so where I'd do anything for an aunt like that," he told me.

"Anything?"

"Anything," he confirmed.

I gulped and let myself swallow up the feel of his arms and hands around and on me. "Huh."

"You can't go around giving something that big and important to just anybody."

I glanced at him, watching his face. "You're going to give it?"

Dallas only cuddled me closer to his chest so that I couldn't look at his face. "I gave it to you a long time ago, Diana. In little pieces and then bigger pieces, and the next thing I knew, I didn't have anything left in me, so I hope it's enough."

I drew back and glanced up at him, and I swallowed. "I hope you know what you're doing."

"I do, baby. Trust me. I know exactly what I'm doing. You three feel like *my* family. It isn't every day you look at your friend and two kids and know this is where you were supposed to be. Do you believe me?"

I didn't even have to think about the answer. "Yeah, I do." I shook my head at myself, trying to remind my brain that we trusted this person. That everything would be all right. "You're never getting your big red thing back if I have anything to say about it. I want you to think about that. I want you to know what the hell you're signing yourself up for, because nice Catholic girls who only go to church twice a year don't believe in divorce." I blinked. "You know, when the time comes."

He smiled at me and I smiled back. Before I could take my next breath, Dallas dipped his head and pressed his mouth, closed and sweet, to mine. He pulled back and then pressed it again.

"God, you guys are gross," came a voice I'd be able to distinguish in a crowd. It was Josh. "When can we go home?"

∽

I WAS SMILING AND MORE THAN A LITTLE SLEEPY AS WE DROVE home hours later. Going against Josh's wishes of bailing an hour into the reception, I sent him back to hang out with Dean and play, or do whatever it was eleven-year-olds did at weddings when there was a playground and an adult in charge of watching the kids. Luckily, they must have gotten into something interesting because it wasn't until I went to check on the boys once every hour that I found them still alive and in one piece, sitting at a picnic table looking at videos on Dean's phone.

Meanwhile inside, I'd laughed my butt off with friends and family of Trip and Dallas, who filled up the rest of the table I'd been sitting at, and danced one song after another with one of the two of them, and even once with Trip's dad. All those clubs I had gone to in my early twenties had really paid off. Mostly though, I'd spent the night either beside Dallas or in front of him. I wasn't going to complain even a little bit.

With Louie passed out in the backseat in his chair and Josh playing a game on the tablet his brother was obviously not using, it had been a good night. I was ready to get home, change, and kick off my shoes though.

"Tired?" Dallas whispered the question.

"Little bit," I answered him. Shifting how I was sitting, I watched his profile in the darkness of the car, taking in that almost long nose, his full bottom lip, square jawline, and the notch of his Adam's apple. I loved him and it wasn't even a little bit. It was a lotta bit. "You?"

"I'm fine."

Hesitating for one second, I reached across the center console to grab his right hand, the one he didn't use to drive. I didn't know what it was about doing that that made me feel like an insecure kid again. The nerves, the wonder. The *I hope he likes me as much as I like him*. But Dallas didn't pause as he flipped his hand up and linked his long, cool fingers through mine, holding them tight.

I smiled at him and he smiled right back.

Before I knew it, he was turning the car into my driveway. I was too busy looking at him to notice the car parked directly across the street.

I was moving slower than usual as Dallas got out and opened the back passenger door, his hands going to unbuckle the straps of Louie's seat, gathering him into his arms before I could tell him I'd carry him. He was halfway to the door, and I had just finished closing the door with my hip as Josh got out, too. We were rounding the back of the SUV with me ruffling his hair when it happened.

"Josh!"

I stopped walking so fast, I turned my ankle in my heels. I knew immediately that voice could only belong to one person.

The one person who Josh spotted before I did. Anita was crossing the street.

"It's me," she called out to the boy who was frozen in place at my side.

Without thinking, as I straightened up, not giving a single shit about an ankle I had for sure either twisted or sprained, I set my hand on his shoulder. And I panicked a little. I didn't tell him anything in the time it took his biological mom to cross the street and end up four feet away from us on the driveway.

What was she doing here again?

"You're so big," she said before I snapped out of it and took a step forward to block her from seeing him, a sharp pain shooting up my foot.

"Anita, this isn't the time or the place," I told her as calmly as possible.

She didn't even glance at me. Tenting her hands under her chin, the woman who was almost my age but looked so much older tried to peek around me. "You look just like your dad, baby boy. I can't believe it."

My hands fisted and I took another sidestep over, faintly hearing the sound of the front door closing. I hoped Dallas had taken Louie inside so he wouldn't wake up and witness this. As well as Louie had adjusted to all of the changes in his life since he'd lost both his parents, I'd never fooled myself into thinking that one day it wouldn't catch up to him. I just really didn't want that day to be anytime soon.

"Anita, focus. You're not supposed to be here. You

can't drop by like this," I told her as nicely as possible, fighting the growl in my throat as a hand touched my back, a hand that could only belong to Josh.

"He's my son," she finally spoke to me, her gaze going to mine.

I opened my mouth to tell her that he was mine too, but Josh beat me to it.

"Leave me alone," he whispered.

Anita's head jerked back, her gaze going to the boy behind me. "Josh, I'm your mom."

That was the worst thing she could have said to him, and I wasn't surprised how he reacted.

"You're not my mom!" he shouted all of a sudden.

Shit. With one hand going to the back of his neck, I started leading him toward the front door, careful to keep my body between him and the woman neither one of us wanted to see. At least *I* didn't want to see her. Not like this.

"Josh!" she called out to this boy I wasn't convinced we both loved equally.

I kept moving him forward, pointing my index finger at her as I stared her down. "Go. *Go.*"

"You can't keep me from him!"

"I don't want to see you!" Josh shouted again, suddenly turning around and moving aside so he could look at the woman who had given birth to him. "I never want to see you again! You're not my mom today. You're not my mom tomorrow. You're never going to be my mom!"

"Josh—"

"No! You didn't want me! You can't change your

mind!" he yelled at her, his chest puffing.

Fucking shit. I placed my hand on Josh's shoulder and turned him around, quickly leading him up the pathway to our house just as Dallas came storming out of the front door, his eyes going from Josh, to me, and finally to Anita. It seemed to click. He remembered her. "Take him inside. I'll deal with this," he told me firmly as he walked by us.

The last thing I heard as the door closed behind us was his low voice spitting, "Do I need to—"

Josh shrugged my arm off almost instantly, and before I could stop him, he took off running toward his room. The door slammed to a close, and all I could do was stand there, trying to figure out what the hell had just happened. Jesus Christ.

Pinching the bridge of my nose, I let out a breath for a minute, kicked off my heels, and went straight for Josh's room. Partially expecting the door to be locked, I was surprised when the knob turned. I didn't ask if I could come in. I was going to whether he wanted me to or not. I found Mac on the floor by the bed, his ears pinned back and his expression anxious and focused on Josh, who didn't even glance in my direction as he plopped down on the carpet and reached for the controller to his game console. His fingers pressed hard into the buttons.

I swallowed. "J, do you want to talk about it?"

He was staring at the television screen, sure, and his fingers were moving across the controller of his game, but I could tell he wasn't paying attention. I knew him too well to be able to ignore the anger and the hurt radiating off him. This kid was never the crying kind; he usually went straight into getting angry, and that was exactly what he was doing right then.

With that in mind, I wasn't surprised when he snapped out a "No."

I sighed and walked further into his room, taking a seat on the floor by the television, my dress forcing me to tuck my legs under me. "All right. Let me rephrase that: let's talk about it."

He didn't look at me as he repeated himself. "No."

"Joshua." I moved my head to the side to block his view of the screen. I raised my eyebrows. "We're going to talk about it. Now. Save your game. You're not even going to play well right now anyway."

Those little fingers hammered at the keys of his controller a moment before he sent it flying behind his head, the innocent remote hitting the wall before it crashed to the ground. His chest started expanding in and out, and he was breathing hard, his face turning red.

It was times like these I had no idea what the hell I was supposed to do with him. What was the right thing to say? How was I supposed to soothe him? I didn't fool myself into thinking that it wasn't these moments that would shape how he handled bad things for the rest of his life. I *knew* it was. I knew that however I taught him to deal with shit would be the route he would most likely take from now on. And throwing shit was not something I wanted him to continue with.

"I get that you're pissed off, J, and I don't blame you." I couldn't tell him I understood he was hurt; it would immediately put him on edge and defensive. He didn't get hurt. "But throwing your shit around is not all right. You want to deal with your anger? Do something productive. Scream your anger into a pillow to get it out of your system, but don't bottle your shit, don't break things, and don't take it out on someone else. If your remote is broken, I'm not buying you another one."

"I didn't ask you to buy me another one."

"Cut the attitude, Josh. Now. Talk to me."

"I don't want to."

"Too bad," I told him as I watched him avert his eyes to the wall at his right. Fucking Anita. I couldn't believe it. I wanted to kick her ass, mother of my nephew or not. But I couldn't and I wouldn't. I had to be a role model and role models didn't go around tasering people. "You can tell me anything, you know that."

He said nothing.

"If you don't want to talk, then listen. No one is perfect, J. No one. We've all made stupid mistakes in our lives, and when you get older, you're going to make a ton of them yourself, but that's what I want you to understand—you have to learn from what you do, the good and the bad. I will never forgive Anita for what she did when you were a baby, but I don't know what it must have been like to be so young and get pregnant either, okay? Neither one of us will ever understand that. And God knows, every time I see her,

I want to smack her in the face for getting into so much trouble after you were born, but that's the thing: I remember your dad telling me she wasn't close to her parents. She didn't have anyone to love her the way that *Abuelito* and *Abuelita* loved me, much less the way that I love you and Louie. *You know I would do anything for you.* I'm going to be here for you for the rest of my life, J. You'll always have options in your life, and I won't let you fuck up, do you understand me?

"I've told you before, you don't ever have to do anything with her if you don't want to, but maybe one day you will. I've told her before that, if she wants a chance of getting to know you, she'd have to get her life together."

"I don't want to know her!" he screamed, high and sounding so young the sound was like acid to my soul. "Not today! Not tomorrow! Never! She's a bitch!" Before I knew it, he was off the carpet and throwing himself on his bed. He yanked his pillow from where it had been sitting and smashed it against his face, screaming into it for several long seconds until he tapered off. His chest started doing that puffing thing again, and I was 99 percent sure he was crying. It killed me. And what he finally said next, slid the knife in even deeper. "Don't make me go with her. Please. You promised me—you promised me you would always take care of me."

"Don't call her a bitch," I told him calmly, even though I felt anything but that. One of the worst things in the world was watching someone you love fall apart. "I told you, if you don't want to see her, that's fine. I'm not going to force you to, but maybe one day when you're older you might want to. *Maybe*. I don't blame you, but I want you to understand that you're mine. You're not going anywhere. I didn't carry you around inside of me for nine months, but that doesn't mean anything to me. You're mine, Josh. You're my Joshy Poo and you always will be. I'll fight anybody for you who tries to say otherwise. But just because you're mine doesn't mean one day—*if you want*—she can't be in your life, too. Some people don't have even one person who cares about them, and you've had Mandy, too."

He was silent. His back was bowed over his pillow, and he was shaking. I had never, ever wanted to kill a person more than I did in that moment. This was what Anita had done to unbendable, resilient Josh. I'd never forgive her for it. His question came out like a croak, muffled and raw. "You promise I'm yours?"

"Josh, you really believe you're not?" I asked him as I got to my feet and sat on the edge of the bed with him, scooting back until I was lying alongside him, my head resting next to his chest. "I've wiped your butt. You've thrown up on me. I've spent my weekends at your games screaming my voice sore. I've hugged you and loved you even when you haven't been very nice. You're my d-o-double-g. You're the peanut butter to my jelly. The pain to my ass—"

I was pretty sure he snorted even with the pillow covering his mouth, but it sounded watered down and hurt.

My own eyes started to get teary. "One day when

you're way older, you're going to get a girlfriend and I'm going to want to kill the little b-i-t-c-h. I'm going to hate her guts. But you know what? I know at the end of the day, I'm still going to be your number one girl."

"Why?" he asked.

"Because she will never know what it's like to have put a thermometer in your butt."

That time, his laugh reached his chest.

"Josh, I love you and Louie, and nothing and no one will ever replace you two losers. I swear on my life. I will lie, cheat, and steal for you, and I always, *always* will." I scooted my head closer to him, so the side of my face rested on his rib cage. "You hear me?"

His face was still covered. "Yeah, I guess."

I'd have to take it. "You better."

Neither one of us said anything for a while, but eventually the pillow on top of his face fell away, and his hand went to my hair. "Promise, we'll always be family?"

"Kid, you couldn't get rid of me if you tried."

"Even if you have kids one day?"

I wasn't stupid. I knew where this was coming from, and I'd messed up by not addressing it with him. So I made sure to wrap my arm around his forearm and kiss the soft skin there. "If I ever decide to pop out a baby, he or she is going to be your brother or sister. If you think of them as your cousins, it would break my heart and I'd give you a wedgie until you said otherwise. We're family. There's nothing tighter than blood." I paused, needing to make him laugh. "And vomit. There's no going back once you've been thrown up on."

He sniffled, and I could sense him nod his agreement.

I swallowed and decided to take advantage of the moment. "I need to tell you something that has nothing to do about what just happened, but about our family, okay?"

"What?" he croaked suspiciously.

"Dallas—"

"*Oh.*"

"Oh, what?"

"I know about Mr. Dallas already," he announced.

I sat up and set an elbow under me, watching his puffy, red face as he stared up at the ceiling. "What do you know?"

"He loves you. You love him," he muttered with an eye roll, glancing down at me briefly before focusing up again. "You know, first comes love, then comes marriage, then comes Aunt Di with a baby carriage."

Uhh, where the hell had that come from? "How... did you know?"

"I have eyes?"

This fucking smart-ass.

"And he told me."

"What did he tell you?"

He glanced at me from his spot still lying flat on the mattress. "Remember when Jonathan's mom yelled at you during the tournament and you cried?" How could I forget? "He told me."

What the hell? "What did he say?"

Josh rolled his eyes, sliding his elbows underneath

his shoulders to sit up, bored with this conversation. "I don't know. He said he liked you—yuck." I blinked at him. "One day during practice when we saw that dad talking to you, I told him I didn't like you talking to him, and he said he didn't either. So I asked him what we should do, and he said nothing because you were never gonna do anything with him and that one day soon, between me and him, none of those jackasses— he said it, not me, don't get mad—would never bother you again."

Was my heart about to burst or was I imagining it? "And what did you tell him?"

"I told him okay as long as he didn't make me go live with Grandma and Grandpa—"

"I would never make you go live somewhere else!"

"That's what he said! Jeez. He said he knew I already have a dad, and he told me that his dad died too and that he knew that if his mom had got married again when he was young, that he would never call anybody else Dad. So, he said we could be friends and he could show me how to do stuff and we could be a family, that I didn't have to call him anything but Dallas if I didn't want to."

I was not going to cry. I was not going to cry. "And what did you tell him?"

"I said okay."

"Okay? That's it?"

He grinned. "What did you want me to do? Ask him for money?"

I burst out laughing. "You're the man of the house. You can't just give me up like that."

He shrugged and said, "You know how many Xbox games he has?"

My mouth fell open and I shook my head at him. "You traded me for Xbox games. I cannot believe it."

"Believe it."

Where the hell had this monster come from? Had I created this?

I had. I really had.

"Just don't kiss in front of me. That's gross," he added with a shudder.

"Your face is gross."

"Not as gross as yours."

I grinned at him, and he grinned right back.

"You really don't care if I..." What word was I supposed to use? Date? It seemed like so much more than that already. "See Dallas all the time? If he comes over a lot and stuff?"

Josh shrugged as he sat up completely, wiping at his eyes with the back of his hands. "I don't care, Aunt Di. I like him, and Louie likes him, and he likes you a lot. That's why he's always doing stuff for us. Just... don't kiss, and close the door to your room. I don't wanna see anything. Dean told me about stuff he's seen his dad do, and that's nasty."

His words made me pause. *That's why he's always doing stuff for us.* Had Josh seen this before me?

And what the hell was Dean telling him? I needed to talk to Trip.

He pushed his knee against mine, grabbing my attention. "Are you gonna tell *Abuelita* you have a boyfriend?" he asked.

Shit. "I have to. One day."

Josh smirked. "She's gonna be mad."

"Too bad for her, huh?" I smiled at him and reached over to pinch his nose. "Are you going to be all right?"

"Yeah," he said a little softer than a moment before, his expression turning just slightly grim.

"Good." I dropped my legs off the bed. "Let me know if you need anything, okay?"

"I'm just..." He patted his pillow. "I'm gonna play some games and go to bed."

Standing up, I nodded. "Okay. I love you with all my heart."

"I know. Love you too."

With two exchanged smiles, I left his room, closing the door behind me just as he called for Mac to join him on the bed. I could see the light in the living room on, the sound of voices from the TV drifting down the hall, but first, I headed to Louie's room. The door had been left cracked, and I peeked in to find the small body face down under the covers.

I sure as hell wasn't going to wake him up to get him into pajamas. He wasn't going to die sleeping in his clothes. From how much he'd played with the other kids on the playground, he was going to sleep all night.

Backing out, I headed the few feet down the hall, keeping weight off my ankle that was all of a sudden reminding me that I'd twisted it. When I got to the living room, I found Dallas on the couch with the television on. His thighs were spread wide and he had a hand on one, the other was draped across the back of the sofa.

"Hey," I whispered to him, limping over.

"What happened?" he asked, watching me carefully.

"I rolled my ankle outside. It hurts."

He frowned as I stopped beside his knees on the couch and plopped down. Before I could even sit back, he leaned over and swung my legs onto his lap, my knees bent over the middle of him, feet on the couch on his other side.

"Josh okay?" he asked as his hand went straight for my foot, his thumb sweeping gently over the bone.

"He was pretty upset, but he'll be fine," I explained, watching his fingers move over me. "She left I'm guessing?"

He hummed. "She's gone, I made sure."

"Thanks."

His palm went down to cup my heel. "Will you tell me about the situation with the boys' moms? I get that Louie and Josh don't share the same one."

I scooted my butt over on the couch until my hip came in contact with his, where I was basically one move away from sitting on his lap. My dress had hiked up pretty high, but I didn't worry about it. He'd seen more of my legs than this the day of the fire. "My brother was married to Louie's mom. She's like you—"

"Tall?"

I snickered and grinned. "No, ding-a-ling. Your skin color. Where do you think he gets his blue eyes from?" I moved over a little more. "When my brother died, Louie's mom lost her shit. She wasn't eating, drinking, or sleeping. I had to take the boys because it was obvious she didn't know she was the one alive and my brother was the one who wasn't."

When I sighed, the arm he had over the back of the couch was lowered to rest against my shoulders, his hand going to palm my upper arm.

"She wasn't dealing with it. We should have—we should have done something about it. We all knew she wasn't doing well, but..." Oh man, the guilt hit me hard in the solar plexus. "She fell down the stairs, which I think about now and I'm pretty sure she did it on purpose to have an excuse to take painkillers... and six weeks after my brother died, she overdosed."

There was something stuck in my throat, and for the second time in minutes, I felt my eyes tear up. "I'll never forgive myself for not saying or doing something. Getting her help. I don't know. *Something.* You know, I expected somebody else to do something or maybe thought she would eventually just get it together, but that's not the way it works."

"You couldn't have known," he said softly.

I shrugged under his arm. "I don't know. Maybe not. But now Lou's stuck with *me* forever. He doesn't ever want to talk about her or acknowledge she even existed. You saw how he gets when we bring her up. That night in his room was the first time he'd said anything about her in forever. Even Josh, every once in a while, says something about her, but Lou refuses to. The only person he ever wants to talk about is his dad."

"She's the lady in the pictures around the house?"

"Uh-huh."

"That's better than nothing."

I shrugged again and the arm over me tightened, pulling me in closer to him.

"It didn't click until now that the Larsens aren't Josh's real grandparents."

"Yeah. Only Louie is biologically related. But they met Josh when he was three. They love him so much. I know Mandy, that's Louie's mom, loved him, too. She was great with him. I think that's why they're so helpful. I like to think she would have wanted them to stick around in his life, and they have."

"He's an easy kid to love," he said. "If I didn't know he was your brother's, I'd think he was yours. You two are exactly alike."

I scoffed. "We are not."

"You are. Trip and I have talked about it."

"You talk about me behind my back?"

"All the time." He smiled. "You two are... savage. You're honest, and you're loyal and love the shit out of things. Both of you give everything to what you care about. I love it."

I pulled my head back and smiled at him. "That's probably the nicest thing anyone has ever said about me."

"When you were about to kick Christy's ass—"

"I was not going to kick her ass."

"That's when I knew, this girl has lost her fucking mind. For a week afterward, all I could think about was how you weren't going to let anybody—even me —do the wrong thing for Josh, like you'd fight to the death for him. It made me think I'd want someone to feel that way about me."

This knot formed in my throat, and I couldn't help but lean forward to kiss his neck as his hand slid up my calf from my foot and settled on the sensitive skin behind my knee. "I threw Hawaiian Punch at your brother, that's a start."

Dallas bit his lips and smiled, kissing my cheek once and jawline another.

I tipped my head back to let him trail his mouth down to my neck, his lips warm and soft as they pressed closed and then opened, his breath damp on my skin. "I would never let anyone talk about you."

"I know, baby. I know," he said, kissing the hollow part on the right side of my throat. "I heard what you told your client that day at the salon."

"You did?" I asked, staying where I was with my head back as he leaned over to kiss the other side of my neck, making me squirm.

"Mm-hmm," he answered. "If you wouldn't have been at work, I would have kissed the hell out of you."

I moaned in my throat when his mouth latched on to my earlobe and gave it a suck. Shivers spread throughout my upper body, my nipples hardening. "You can make up for it now if you insist," I told him in a whisper.

"I'm going to," he said, sounding husky and raw right before he dipped his face lower and kissed me over and over again between my jaw and collarbone.

Shifting on to a hip, his hands roamed as my head stayed where it was, lulled backward to give him all the room he wanted. Those big palms went from my lower back to tangling his fingers in my loose hair, cupping my skull gently. I tried to keep myself from making noises, settling only for low pants as that wonderful mouth opened from time to time for his tongue to swipe at the skin over one tendon or another. He moved me, maneuvered me however he wanted, to get to whatever spot he wanted.

When his lips went low to kiss from the hollow at my throat, down, down, down a straight line to where the V-shape of my dress ended, I arched my back. I was turned-on. More turned-on than I'd been in my entire life. It was like drowning in pudding. I didn't want it to end, ever.

And when his low voice spoke right into my ear as his nose drew a line over the shell of it, I was pretty much in a trance. "We don't have to do anything tonight."

"You don't want to?"

His chuckle had me pressing myself closer to him. "What did you tell me about stupid questions?"

Somehow I managed to smile.

"Can I take you to your room?" he asked, pressing his lips just below the corner of my mouth.

He could take me to Mars for all I cared, but I couldn't speak. All I could do was nod as I swayed into him, needing his mouth on my throat again. His husky laugh hit the sensitive damp skin he'd just had his mouth on. His hand went to my hip, curling those long fingers over my side.

"Yes?" he asked, drawing his mouth back up to kiss

my cheeks, my nose, the sliver of skin just above my upper lip, everywhere but my mouth.

I was panting. *Panting.* "Uh-huh" was all I could get out.

Slowly, without breaking our closeness, he pulled me up to my feet, his mouth still everywhere, his hands going everywhere else—up and down my back, one hip, two hips, my shoulders, upper arms, lower arms, even my hands. Mapping me out. It wasn't until he pulled me closer to him that I remembered we weren't alone in the house.

"The front door," I whispered, out of breath from just letting him use those lips on me.

"It's already locked," he told me as both those big palms slid from where they'd been at my waist, down, over the hem of my dress, before making a return trip upward, inside the skirt that time. Those rough, callused fingers and palms scratched my skin in the two heartbeats it took for Dallas to reach my ass, cupping the bare skin there in those big hands, gripping and molding them together as his breath hit my ear. "I always thought you looked like mine, but you sure do fucking feel like you're mine, too," he said, drawing a circle around my pulse point with his tongue.

Without a word of warning, he suddenly boosted me up, my dress straining as the material slid up to rest around my hips. Somewhere in the back of my head, I prayed he'd get us to my room fast—really, really fast—before Josh decided he needed to go to the bathroom and found me with my butt hanging out of my clothes, wrapped around Dallas like a spider monkey. Because that was exactly what it had to look like. The instant I was up in his arms, my legs had wrapped around his waist, my arms twining behind his neck. Face-to-face, my mouth hovered inches away from his. Millimeters, really.

And without kissing me, his forehead to mine, his eyes locked on my own, he started walking us down the hall.

One of my hands loosened around his neck to go up to the back of his head, running my fingers through the super soft short hair on his head. Neither one of us said anything as he kept walking, and eventually, I knew we were in my room even with all the lights being off. He kicked the door closed and took a step back, one of the hands he had supporting me disappearing for a brief moment before the low click of the lock being engaged filled the only other sound in my bedroom other than our breathing.

He didn't turn on the lights and I didn't bother to either.

Days later, I liked to think we were so quiet because there was nothing that could be said that would have made the moment better or more meaningful. There really wasn't. Every time his hands touched me, it was like a sentence was being spoken. And I hoped that every time I set my hands on him, he could feel every single thing I thought of him, everything I felt for him.

He was wonderful and I loved him. I loved him more than I thought I was capable of. If I really put it into perspective, how could anything I had ever felt for anyone before him even be close to the "L" word when what we had was ten—twenty, thirty, forty, fifty—times brighter and more real than any man I'd ever met before him?

It couldn't. It just couldn't.

Because no one else was as kind or selfless, as giving or as patient, as loving in all the little and the big ways, as he was.

I'd never really known what I wanted most of my life, but this—him—was it.

And as he set me down on my feet in my bedroom, with only the faintest light coming in through the window from outside, his hands went to the bottom of my dress. In one quick move, the dress was up and over my head, gone to another dimension for all I cared. Those cool, scratchy palms went to my waist, and as I stood there in my underwear and a strapless bra, he pulled me into him, pressing my front to his. He sealed us together from the chest down just as his mouth finally decided to meet mine.

Mouth tilted, it opened over mine. Our tongues clashed and stroked. I was faint and dizzy as he kissed me, his mouth slanting from one side to the other as we ate at each other, like it was the end of the world and there was nowhere else either one of us would rather be.

It was the truth.

As he kissed me and kissed me and kissed me—his body warm and fully clothed pressed flushed to my chest, breasts, belly, and even my thighs—all I wanted was to be wrapped around him again. I was so busy sliding my tongue against his that it took me a while to notice him fumbling with the snaps on my bra with one hand. If that wasn't my cue to get him out of his clothes, I didn't know what was.

I sucked in a breath as I tore my mouth away finally, going up to the tips of my toes to kiss that warm, almost salty skin at his neck, tiny hairs prickling my lips and chin. Dallas's hands kept fumbling at my back, and it took me a moment in the dark for my hands to slide up the hard, bulky muscles of his abs, up over his pectorals until my fingers found the buttons near his throat. I got his tie off and threw it before going back.

He got my bra off as I was about halfway down, unbuttoning his dress shirt. His hands stroked over my shoulders and the back of my neck as I finished and started pushing his shirt away, feeling him help me get it off, fast, almost desperately. With only his thin undershirt between me and all those rippled, hot muscles, I sucked in a breath as Dallas leaned down to kiss my upper lip before pulling away. From the sound and the feel of it, he took his shirt off, because the next thing I knew, a bare, smooth shoulder brushed across my cheek.

In the dark, everything felt so much more intense. His thumbs tucked into the scrap of lace at my hips as he tugged my thong down my legs. The kisses he fluttered on the trip down, at the side of my collarbone, my upper breast, the swift suck he gave my nipple once and only once as he kept lowering his body. Another kiss at my ribs and my bare hip. The sound of his knees hitting the crappy carpet told me where he'd ended up.

When he kissed my thigh and followed that up by pressing his warm breath and mouth to the crease where my thigh met the place my underwear had uncovered, I sucked in a breath, loud, so loud. And when he drew a moist line of kisses down and over, before pressing to the cleft at my seam, I swallowed hard and reached for his head for balance or to get him not to go anywhere, I had no idea.

He kissed me there and kissed me there again. He didn't part me as the tip of his tongue tapped the outer skin and he gave me another kiss. His sigh was deep and rattled as his hands cupped the back of my thighs, gripping them hard, keeping me in place. Then Dallas parted my seam with his tongue, tasting that little knot of nerves that had come alive with the first kiss he'd given me.

His forehead pressed low against my belly, his nose at the skin I'd luckily shaved before the wedding, Dallas kissed me, sucking and licking those lower lips like I wasn't already dying and ready for him. He made out with me like he had when we'd both been standing up.

Slowly, the hands on my thighs tugged and led me down until I kneeled in front of him. I kissed him, tasting myself on his lips as I moved my hands all over that chest I'd only seen twice in person, then slid them over those rippled abs that shouldn't belong on someone over thirty. His own hands were at my breasts, pinching my nipples between his index finger and thumb before he cupped them. Dallas's mouth dropped to take one and then the other between his lips, over and over again.

I squirmed and moved in front of him, dragging my hands up and down his abs again, over the hair trailing to the button and zipper of his dress pants. In no time, I had him unzipped and slipped my hand inside, my palm toward me. The back of my fingers grazed over his short, wiry hair before I felt that thick, hot root at the center of his body. Dallas's body jerked as I kept sliding my hand inside, feeling his length tucked to the left, nestled against his thigh, and I still couldn't reach the tip.

Flipping my hand over, I wrapped my palm and fingers around his thick width, and as gently as possible, I pulled him up enough until the tip faced the ceiling. Dallas stopped what he was doing, with his lips parted around my nipple, as I gave him a squeeze. He was just as thick as I'd imagined, and as I slid my palm up and up and up, he was just as long, too, eight or nine inches of swollen cock. His hips jerked and he sucked in a breath as I tightened my grip back up around him and pulled on the excess, super soft skin. Up and down, up and down.

In a quick movement, Dallas pushed me onto my back on the carpet, and before I even managed to let out a breath, he was over me. Covering me like a human blanket, but so much bigger, heavier, and warmer. I didn't need the light to know the blunt, hard thing poking at my seam was him, ready, ready, ready. "I'm on birth control," I whispered almost shyly. I wasn't ovulating either, but I wouldn't tell him that. Not yet at least.

He exhaled and I did the same as I slipped my arms under his armpits, leaving my forearms on his shoulder blades, my hands curling over the muscles of his trapezius muscles. "Diana," he said from just above me.

I wrapped my legs around his hips, my ankles resting against his dress pants which were still covering everything except that big organ slowly pressing against me, trying to find that place we both wanted.

"I love you, Dallas," I whispered as I tipped my hips up so he could ease in an inch.

His mouth and entire body came down on me, heavy, like he was trying to consume me into him. His weight was what pushed him in deeper, another inch, and another inch and another, pushing through my wet muscles that were protesting his thickness, protesting him period.

But Dallas kept going, kissing me over and over again until he was settled completely over me and in me, skewering my body with his.

The only sound he made before he started throbbing inside of me was a gasp, then a groan, and he jerked and swelled, shoved deep to the root in me. Dallas came and came, so much cum that when he retreated an inch before thrusting back in me, his cum trickled out from around his cock and down my skin.

"Fuck," he muttered, all raspy onto my cheek as he held himself as deep as he could get in me. "I didn't mean to cum that fast."

"It's okay."

His mouth moved over my cheek, from one spot to another, softly. "I'm not done. I promise." Dallas pulled that thick organ out, slowly and rolled his hips forward, stuffing me one more time. "You couldn't feel more like mine if you tried," he told me, punctuating each word with a hard thrust that had me scooting across the carpet a few inches.

My back burned just a little as he kept his speed slow, and the last inch of his push into me a slap, a pound. He kissed me like he was making love to me, slowly, angling his mouth from one side to the other as his tongue caressed mine. His hips moved in a circle, like he was trying to get deeper.

I sucked in one breath after another, trying to keep from making a bunch of noise because the boys were just down the hall, but I kept moving my hips, trying to adjust the angle until he moved his body just enough so that his pubic bone started grinding down on me perfectly.

His chest brushed against mine, both of us sweaty and breathing hard, and he kept rolling his hips, building me up and up until I came around him. I had to toss my head back, bite my lip, and arch my back to keep from making a noise as he held himself still inside of me until I caught my breath. One hard thrust followed by another harder one, and then one more hard pull and push of his cock had us moving across the carpet again. Dallas shoved that thick girth in deep and he groaned, long and low, coming again, pulsing more and more, his length twitching and jerking.

Slowly, his weight went slack on top of me. He was heavy and it was harder to breathe, but I didn't move my arms from around his back and shoulders, and I kept my legs around him tight, as all those fine muscles pulsed on top of me and in me. He was breathing just as hard as I was, it was like neither one of us could catch our breath.

After what could have been ten minutes or thirty, he got up to his hands and knees, and I could hear him swallow hard, his breathing shallow and choppy. With my eyes slightly more used to the dark room, I could see him reach toward my face. His hand cupped my cheek as I lay there on the carpet sprawled out, still not able to catch my breath.

I moved my head to kiss the pad of skin below his thumb, and just like that, Dallas was lowering himself back down to lay on the floor beside me. His arm slipped under my neck and he curled me into his side. He was damp from sweat, and when I rolled onto my side and draped my leg over his thigh, I felt what had to be both of us on his inner thighs. Sticky and wet. I loved it.

With my head on his shoulder, I slung my arm across the middle of his chest and hugged him.

When he started chuckling, I tipped my face up but could only catch the faint outline of his jaw. "What are you laughing at?"

The hand furthest away from me settled high on the thigh I had on him. He stroked further up, touching my hip with his palm and the side of my butt with his fingertips. He did that twice before he said in that awesome, hoarse, totally worn-out voice, "You know that hug of yours started all of this."

What? "What do you mean?"

He moved his hand in a circle on my thigh, slowly kneading. "I saw you outside your house a few weeks after you moved in. The Larsens must have been dropping the kids off because you were all outside. You'd been standing on the deck waiting for them, and Josh came out of their car. When he came up to you, he wasn't even paying attention, but you hugged him with this huge smile on your face. You were laughing. I don't know what you told him, but then he started hugging you back and you shook him until he finally laughed too.

"And every single fucking time I saw you after that, you were always hugging somebody. Kissing somebody. Telling them you loved them. I'd go to bed thinking about you and wondering why you were always doing that," he said to me in that low voice, hugging me closer.

"Because I love them and life is short."

"I know that now, Diana. I learned that every time I was around you. You can see how much you love your family, and it's the thing I love the most about you. I wanted someone to love me like that. I wanted you to love me like that." The hand he had on my side found my own hand, and he linked our fingers together. "I'm not rich and I'm not good-looking, but I could make you happy. We could make our own patched-up family."

My heart broke in half. "Of course you could make me happy. You already do. And you are so good-looking, what are you talking about?"

"No, I'm not. You told me I wasn't your type, remember?" he reminded me in a tone that didn't sound sad or disappointed.

"You were being an idiot. What was I supposed to tell you? *My, what big arms you have*? Then what? Please let me snuggle in your lap, my friend?" I laughed, squeezing my fingers in his. "You were married and you took it seriously. I would never do that. *And* it wasn't like you were really nice to me for a while anyway."

"What did you want me to tell you? That I wanted you to snuggle on my lap?" He chuckled back. "Baby, I took being married to someone I didn't even love seriously. I never once cheated on my ex, even after we split up. What kind of man would I show you I was if I'd changed my mind about how I should act after I'd met you?"

He had a point and he knew it.

"I thought you were crazy at first, and then I got to know you and I liked you—you were my friend and you were nice just because that's how you are, not because you wanted anything from me. And then that day I was taking lice out of your hair, you looked up at me while we were laughing and I knew I was done," he said.

His hand went to my cheek again. "If I can respect being in a relationship with someone who I won't remember years from now—someone I don't ever think about—I wanted you to see how seriously I would take spending the next fifty years with the girl who's keeping my heart for herself."

This man. This man was going to stitch me together with industrial strength thread. How? How could I live a day without him? A week, a month, a lifetime?

As if sensing I was losing my shit, but not in the way he thought, Dallas lifted himself up onto a forearm to look down at me. "Diana, I love you, and every bone in my body tells me that I'm gonna love you every day of my life, even when we want to kill each other."

I sniffled, and what did he do? He laughed.

"When you're old, I'll hold your hand when we cross the street. I'll help you put on your socks," he promised.

I started laughing, even as tears came into my eyes. "What if I have to help *you* put on socks?"

"Then you'll help me put on socks. And if I'm in a wheelchair and you're not, I'll give you a ride."

My tears spilled over as I laughed, and I couldn't help but put my forehead to his shoulder. "You can't promise me you'll always be there. You know that's not the way it works."

"While I still have breath in my body, I won't go anywhere, Peach." He kissed my temple. "You never know what will happen an hour from now, a minute from now, but I won't make you regret any of it too bad, even when I get on your nerves and we bicker because we've been together forever and know everything about each other. That time could be a month, or could be until we're both in diapers, but I'll be there."

"Diapers?"

"Diapers," he confirmed, leaning down to kiss my face three times. "I promise."

CHAPTER TWENTY-SIX

"TELL HER," JOSH WHISPERED AS HE PASSED BY ME IN THE kitchen to refill his cup with apple juice from the fridge.

I ground my teeth and made my eyes go wide in his direction while going back to keeping an eye on my mom who happened to be standing at the stove in the kitchen, giving the rice she was making a stir. "I will. Give me a second," I hissed at him, glancing in my mom's direction one more time to make sure she was oblivious.

My eleven-year-old mouthed "Wuss" to me over his shoulder as he left the room with his glass full.

Sadly, I knew he was right. I needed to tell my mom who was coming over for Christmas dinner. Well, more specifically, *why* someone was coming over for dinner with Miss Pearl in tow.

Shit.

Grabbing a clean kitchen towel from a drawer, I'd

barely dipped it under the running tap when I finally said, "*Mamá*, Miss Pearl and Dallas are coming over for dinner."

"Miss Pearl? *¿La vecina?*"

"Yes, the neighbor. The one whose house burned down."

"And who else?" she asked distractedly, her back still to me.

"Dallas. My neighbor. Josh's coach." It wasn't like we hadn't talked about him a dozen times before. Knowing my mom though, she was just playing dumb, possibly hoping I'd mysteriously come up with someone else with the same name.

"The one with all the tattoos?"

Jesus Christ. "He doesn't even have that many tattoos," I groaned.

"Enough," she mocked back.

When I squeezed the excess water off the towel, I told myself that I wasn't imagining it being my mom's neck. "Please stop with the comments. You're going to have to get used to them. You're going to be seeing a lot of him." There. I'd done it. I'd told her.

"*¿Cómo?*"

I turned to look at the woman who had carried me around for nine months, who fought me more than anyone else, criticized and judged me five times as much, and gave me more headaches than any person in the world. But she meant the world to me. Nuts and all. "You know *como*."

One of her eyes went a little squinty, and I saw her let out a deep breath. "He's your boyfriend?" she asked in Spanish, drawn out and in nearly a shocked breath.

I couldn't disrespect her by lying, so I told her the truth. "You can say that."

This dramatic woman, who had given birth to me almost thirty years ago, reached straight for her heart.

"I love him, Mom."

She turned away, giving me her cheek. Jesus Christ. Slightly scared of her even though I was taller than she was, I took a step closer and lowered my voice, trying my best to be understanding. It didn't work well, but I tried. "He's the best man I've ever known, Mom. I'm lucky. Stop looking like you're going to die, come on. *Es un güero,* he has tattoos. Rodrigo married Mandy who wasn't even Catholic, much less Mexican, and he had tattoos. Stop with the face."

"How can you even—" She gasped dramatically.

Here it was. "How can I what? The boys really like him. Louie is half in love with him. He has a steady job. His grandma lives with him. He was married and he didn't want to have anything to do with me until he got divorced—"

"He was married!"

I blinked at her, almost at my end with her shit. So I threw down the one card I had to trump this freak out: "You were married before Dad. Remember that guy?"

She sucked in a breath that had me raising my eyebrows.

"You thought I didn't know? Mom, *I've always known.* Dad told me a long time ago. Who cares?"

Her face went about as red as someone so brown was capable of. "Diana…."

I cracked a smile at her and took a step forward, trying to put my hand on her shoulder, only to have her move out of the way at the last minute. It hurt my feelings a lot more than it should. "What is it? I don't care that you were married to someone before. You don't have to be embarrassed. Obviously, we all struck out with our first relationships. It happens. Rodrigo did too, but look, you met dad and had us. It's fine."

My mom's back went to me, and I could see her dipping her head, her shoulders hunching as she bent over the kitchen countertop. "Stop talking about Rodrigo, Diana."

We were back to this? "Mom—"

"No, *no*. This has nothing to do with me and what happened before you were even born."

All right, so she was ashamed I knew her secret from years ago. Fine. I understood. I would probably feel the same way too if I'd lied to someone for almost thirty years.

Then she shook her head dramatically, clutching her chest again, and my sympathy disappeared. "How can you bring another man into your life? Into the lives of the *boys*? They already had a father. A great one—"

"What are you talking about? I'm not getting them another dad. I love him, and I know he feels the same way, and even if we got married one day in the distant future—" I scoffed, not believing what my mom was trying to imply. "—no one could ever replace, Rodrigo, Mom. How could you think that from me just finding someone I like? I thought you were going to freak out because you hate everyone I've ever dated, but this one is different. It's so different. He's wonderful. He's probably too good for me. But he has nothing to do with Rodrigo."

I could see her shake her head, see her shoulders shake, and I came up behind her and wrapped my arms around her neck.

"I think about him all the time. I talk to the boys about him. None of us have forgotten him, and we never could. But don't you think he'd want us to be happy?"

She didn't say a word and my stomach turned.

"Mom, I love you. What is it?"

Her chin lowered until it touched my forearm, and she said nothing for a long time. "I'm sorry, *amor*. You're right. You're right," she finally admitted.

"I know I'm always right."

She sniffled, wet sounding and reluctant. "*No te creas.*" Her palm went to one of my hands, interlocking our fingers. "I miss your brother," she whispered softly, like saying the words too loudly would cut her. "I caught myself buying him a Christmas present twice this year."

I wanted to ask her for more, to tell me more about when she thought about him. But I kept the question in my mouth. I loved to push and push for more, but with something like this…. What she gave me was more than enough. It was a start. Or maybe if it wasn't a start, it was something.

"I only want the best for you. That's all I've ever wanted. I've made so many mistakes, Diana. I know I have, and I don't want you to repeat them. I haven't always been the person you wanted me to be, and I'm sorry."

Ugh. "Mom, you're fine. I know I haven't always been the person you wanted me to be either, but you're kind of stuck with me and I'm stuck with you." I gave her a squeeze. "I love you anyway."

"*Te quiero mucho, amor.*" Her small fingers gave mine a squeeze that was a lot stronger than someone so little should be capable of. "Not everyone can marry a man like your cousin, I understand."

I rolled my eyes so far back I wasn't sure how they found their way forward again. God. I should have expected this from her. I wasn't sure why I let her continue to shock me.

When she released my fingers and gave the back of my hand a pat, I decided to just let it go. "Okay, I'm fine now." She didn't turn around to look at me as she acted like nothing had happened. "You could have told me earlier there were more people coming. I could have worn a nicer dress."

I gave her shoulders, not her neck, a squeeze as I took a step back. "Who are you trying to impress? You're already married."

That had her peeking one teary eye at me over her shoulder. "I don't know where I went wrong with you."

A knock came from the front door just as I said, "Me neither."

I was 99 percent sure as I walked out of the kitchen that my mom threatened me with her shoe, but I was too relieved that we'd gotten that conversation over with to do anything but smile at the person standing on the other side of the door. Miss Pearl's hair was a pale halo around her head and she'd put on a turtleneck with Christmas trees on it and cute dangling earrings with snowmen on them.

"Merry Christmas, Miss Pearl."

The older woman gave me a smug smile. "It's Christmas Eve, Diana, but Merry early Christmas."

God help me. I laughed as I leaned forward to give her a gentle hug. "Come in. Come in," I told her as I backed up to let her pass.

And that was when I finally took in the man who had been standing right behind her. In a soft gray flannel shirt with the top button undone was Dallas. He took a step forward. "Hello, light of my life."

I scrunched up my nose. My heart was racing instantly from one beat to the next, from one blink of my eyes to the following one. Was this ever going to get old? I sure as hell hoped not. "Hi, Professor." I reached up on my tippy-toes and felt him press his mouth against me, the kiss slow and sweet, a reminder to my heart of what we'd done in my bedroom three nights this last week. Of what I hoped we'd do in my bedroom, with the doors locked, tonight, too. He'd left to help Trip with something the day before so he hadn't come over last night. I trusted him—both of them, really. I didn't need to ask what they were up to.

"Thanks for having us."

Rolling my eyes, I pecked his mouth again. "Don't thank me."

"Okay, you can thank me," he said, reaching into

his pocket and pulling out something pink. Dallas reached up over my head so quickly, I couldn't get a good look at it until his fingers grazed the sides of my face and something came down over my hair. His eyes flicked down to mine as he settled the pink material over the hair I'd left down and curled. "I made you a cap."

And he smiled as he said it, his palms curving downward to cup my cheeks.

All I could do was blink.

"Pink like Princess Peach."

I swallowed, hard. "If you're trying to get laid, we have to wait until everyone leaves," I whispered.

Dallas grinned and I did too.

"Thank you," I told him. "I can't believe you knit me one."

"I told you I would."

He had. He really had told me that. I took his hands from my face watching as he winced at the contact and looked down at the big palms and long fingers I was holding between us. The knuckles were a purple-ish red and two had the skin broken. I blinked. *What the hell did you do?*

There was no hesitation in his answer. "Stuff."

I peered up at him, narrowing my eyes and ignoring the sneaky smile creeping at his cheeks. "Did you guys beat someone up?"

Trip, I could see getting into a fight for whatever reason. Dallas? It had to be a damn good reason. Maybe Trip had gotten into a fight and Dallas had stepped in—

His nonbruised hand came up to my cheek again and he flat-out grinned. "Yes. He deserved it." Before I could react, he leaned forward and kissed my mouth softly.

Had he... Jeremy...? With his lips hovering just above mine, I asked slowly, "Where did you go?"

"Fort Worth."

Holy shit.

Dallas pressed his lips to mine again. "It's better if you don't ask any more questions, hmm? Consider it one of your Christmas presents, baby."

My heart seemed to swell about ten sizes larger than it originally was and in one of the rare occasions in my life, I didn't know what to say. All I could do was draw his injured hand to my mouth and kiss the knuckles, snickering and laughing as his eyes met mine. I must have done something fucking awesome in another lifetime to deserve this man. And it was pretty damn easy to not ask any more questions about where he'd been and what he'd done. I was still grinning at him as I asked, "Are you still off the day after tomorrow?"

Dallas nodded, those green-brown-gold eyes focused in on mine.

I wasn't surprised by how much my chest didn't tighten or how my stomach didn't ache as the question came out of my mouth. I'd thought about it last night while I lay in bed and decided to go for it. "Could you watch the boys for me for half the day? I have clients —"

"Sure," he cut me off.

Did he look relieved or was I imagining it?

"You asked me for help."

This funny feeling rolled around in my belly and I smirked at him. "So?"

"You really do love me." His mouth was gaping. Ugh.

"Shut up," I groaned. "You better get used to it. I'm not letting you get out of this one day because you get tired of me asking for help."

Dallas shook his head. This giant smile that seemed like the greatest Christmas present in the world took over his mouth. "I won't. Ever."

I couldn't help but eye him a little. "You said it."

"I'll get it to you in writing one day."

"Uh-huh." My face went hot so I changed the subject. There was only so much my heart could take in a day. Maybe one day I'd get used to him, but I hoped I didn't. You stop appreciating things the moment they become a routine. "Did you get in touch with your brother by any chance?"

He shrugged a shoulder. "No. I left him a voice mail. Trip said he thought he saw him last week, but I don't know."

I scrunched up my nose. "I'm sorry. I hope he calls you back."

"Me too." He kissed my cheek. "The good news is that Nana's trying to play it cool, but she's excited to be here," he said, his mouth inches from mine when he pulled back.

"Good. I made sure we have lots of Mexican food she can stuff her face with." I smiled at him. "Has she said anything else about… you know, us?"

His hands came back up to my cheeks. "She was awake a few nights ago and caught me sneaking in. All she said was *about time*."

My face went red and I couldn't help but crack up from how embarrassing that was. God. "Okay. Now I have to sit through dinner knowing she knows you *come over*."

"I came over right now."

"That's a whole different kind of coming over." I laughed. "It's more like crossing the street, if you know what I mean."

Dallas shrugged, easy, easy, one of his thumbs going to my bottom lip to tug it down a little. "One day we can have Christmas and I won't have to cross the street, hmm?"

"I'd like that. I'd like that a lot." I looked him right in the eyes. "All I care is that this is the first of many. I hope."

His smile grew wider, his forehead going to mine, and he sighed, "You're damn right it's the first of many."

EPILOGUE

"ARE YOU SURE YOU WANT TO DO THIS?"

Louie nodded quickly—excited—he was so damn excited it made a knot form in my throat for about the thousandth time since he'd brought up his idea to me months ago. It had been all him. I couldn't take credit for what he was about to do.

All I wanted was to make sure no one's feelings would get hurt.

"Lou, you're positive?" I asked him, knowing we'd gone over this each and every single time in the thousand times since he'd mentioned it.

He had the same answer each time: Yes, *Tia*.

"You can't go back from this."

He blinked those beautiful blue eyes at me as he moved away from the breakfast table and went toward the birthday cake I'd just pulled out of the fridge. The white and blue sheet cake we'd bought from the grocery store on the way home said HAPPY 80TH

BIRTHDAY, DALASS on the top of it in red icing. Josh and I had fist-bumped each other at least three times at how funny we were.

Louie shrugged as his hands gripped the edge of the kitchen counter. He was so tall now it made my heart hurt a little. Josh had left me in the dark height-wise about three years ago, but I thought I'd had more time with Louie before he grew up. I'd give him another year before he shot up like a rocket, and I knew eventually that would make me cry over the baby he no longer was.

"I know, *Tia*." His mouth twitched and he smiled down at the cake. "I really want to." He eyed me. "You're sure Dad wouldn't mind?"

Oh, my fucking brother. A day hadn't gone by that I didn't think about him and not wanted to cry, but especially while talking about this... it got to me every single time.

It didn't help that I was four months pregnant.

Me. Four months pregnant. I still couldn't pinpoint how or when Dallas had talked me into it, but my guess was he'd convinced me about a year ago. He never brought up having kids outright, but had gone about it the same way he'd made me fall in love with him. Slowly, unexpectedly, and completely.

I also blamed Vanessa for how it happened. If the four of us hadn't gone to visit her, and I hadn't seen Dallas playing with her youngest baby, my ovaries might have never been lit on fire. The next thing I knew, we were in the middle of baby-making fever, and I was sure as hell never going to complain about that.

Now I was paying for it with horrible morning sickness and mood swings that had me crying half the day over the dumbest stuff. I'd walk by a picture of my brother randomly? I'd cry. Josh needed a new pair of pants because he'd outgrown his? I'd cry. Dallas left me a Post-It note on the mirror of our bathroom? I'd cry.

It was a little pathetic.

And I wouldn't change it for anything. Dallas had lit up like a firecracker—like I'd given him the world—and the boys had been more excited than I ever could have imagined when they found out I was expecting the newest member of our family. I now had three over protective males that nagged at me when I carried groceries, took the trash out, and worked too many hours.

Fast-forward to two months after I'd found out I was carrying someone new to love. We were celebrating Dallas's forty-sixth birthday, just the four of us. One of my distant aunts had died, and my parents were out of town attending the funeral.

When Louie had first asked me if I thought my brother would be fine with what he wanted to do, I hadn't been sure what to tell him. I wanted to think he'd be okay with it, but how could I *really* know? But the more I thought about Louie and Dallas's relationship, taking in how close they were after five years, how much Dallas genuinely loved this boy who had always been my heart...

I had my answer.

"Nothing will ever take him away from you. Your dad would want you to do what makes you happy, Gooey Louie. He'd understand, and I know he would have really liked Dallas."

Louie nodded slowly, thinking about it, and then nodded with more determination. "Yeah, me too. I wanna do it. I really wanna do it."

I'm not going to cry. I'm not going to cry. "I know you do, but I want to make sure you understand this isn't something light. This is a huge decision. Like if I ever get tired of him, we could get a divorce—"

"Over my dead body," came the reply from behind me.

Shit. How much had he heard?

Dallas came up behind me, his chin coming to a rest on the top of my head as his arm went around to my front to palm my stomach, instantly going to the exact spot where my tiny peanut of life was still hiding. "I'd never let you go anywhere," he said, and I could already imagine him smiling at Louie from over the top of my head.

I leaned back into him and squeezed the hand that he'd just placed at my hip. "I'd like to see you try to stop me if I wanted to."

"You wouldn't make it down the block. You love us too much."

I laughed. "Us?"

"J and Lou wouldn't leave me."

Honestly, he was right. They wouldn't. I'd been the star of the show until this man came into it and set this space for himself that no one else could ever fill. The boys loved him almost as much as me. I wasn't even a little upset about it.

That was a lie. Maybe a little. I'd always had problems sharing, but I figured, if they were going to love anybody new, it might as well be him.

Dallas's chin moved down the side of my head, rubbing the bristles against my temple. "Why are you talking about something that's never gonna happen?" he asked.

Of course it was never going to happen. If I'd thought I loved Dallas back when he first divorced She Who Was Never Mentioned Again, it was nothing compared to now. He was honest to God, the love of my life, and he told me at least once a week I was the love of his. Via Post-It note, whispered into my ear when we were in bed together at night, said out loud when he gave me a hug....

I eyed Louie and watched him smile as I lied. "We were talking about what to name the baby and how we have to pick something good because it isn't like we can change it later on. If it's a girl, I think we're both still thinking Pearl would be a good name."

He made a thoughtful noise against my ear. Almost immediately after Dallas moved in with us, we had asked her if she wanted to come live with us instead of staying in her remodeled house all by herself, but we had never talked her into it. She was happy alone and seemed perfectly fine with us going over there to help with things or invite her to dinner. There hadn't been anything wrong with her. So two years ago, when Dallas found her not breathing, sitting on her couch, we had all been shocked as shit to find out she'd passed away.

Her funeral happened to be the last time we saw Jackson, too. Dallas told me he called him from time to time, but that was all there was between the two of them. It broke my heart a little because I knew Dallas still held out hope that his brother would come around and quit being an asshole, but it hadn't happened.

Louie cleared his throat way too loudly, and it made me grin and shove away thinking about Miss Pearl and Jackson. I knew exactly who he had picked up that habit from. "Dal, want your present?" he asked him.

"You didn't need to get me anything, Lou," the man behind me said.

Louie's face brightened. "I wanted to," he said as he grabbed the slim, eight-by-ten-inch package he'd wrapped all on his own a couple of days ago.

I watched as Dallas stepped around me and paused at my side. He took the gift with one hand. If he thought it was weird that the part he wasn't touching bent toward him, flexible and paper-like, he didn't comment. He reached forward with his free arm and threw it around Louie's back, hugging him with a pat as the ten-year-old wrapped both arms around the man who had come to mean so much to him.

"You're doing presents and you weren't going to tell me?" Josh's voice came from behind all of us.

At nearly six feet tall and sixteen years old, he looked a lot older than he was. My Josh. He still hadn't filled out his height yet, but I knew it was coming; his was all long muscles and a face that was still boyish enough. Still the face of my Joshy Poo. He elbowed Dallas as he went between me and the man who had stopped being his Select coach two years ago, and put an arm over my shoulders. "What'd you get?" he asked him, knowing damn well what his little brother was giving him.

That was the second thing I'd asked Louie to do when he'd come to me: talk to his brother and let him know what he was planning. I thought Josh had been hurt for maybe a day once he found out, but we'd talked about it, and he'd come to peace with it. He got it.

The other person I had told Louie to talk to was my mom. Over the years, she had warmed up to Dallas a lot which wasn't surprising. He was perfect, why wouldn't she grow to love him once she gave him a chance? But what Louie wanted to do had the potential to send my mom over the tipping point. I wasn't positive what exactly was said between the two of them during their conversation, but whatever it was, Louie was still going through with his plans. I figured it couldn't have gone that badly.

Dallas elbowed him back as he flipped the gift over, his fingers going to the creased, taped edges and plucked at them. "I don't know."

I pinched my lips together and looked back and forth between Louie and Dallas as he opened his gift. This was going to change both of their lives, but for me, nothing at all would be different.

I watched as Dallas frowned a little as he tore the

paper off the stack of papers Louie had wrapped up. He flipped them over, right side up, and his forehead scrunched up as he read the print.

Seconds later, he glanced over at Louie and his throat bobbed. Seconds after that, he turned to me with those hazel eyes wide, and his throat bobbed again. Then he turned his attention back to the papers and mouthed the words he was reading before he brought his hands down to his hips, papers clutched in one hand, and let out a deep, deep breath.

His eyes were watery. He blinked a whole bunch of times. The tip of his tongue went to his upper lip and he let out another deep breath.

Dallas glanced at me and raised his eyebrows again before facing Louie once more and stated in a broken voice, "Lou, I would adopt you a thousand times over, bud. Nothing would make me happier."

I'd blame the hormones for how I burst into tears the second Louie rushed into Dallas's arms, but honestly, it wasn't the hormones at all.

All I could think about as I stood there was that sometimes life gave you a tragedy that burned everything you knew to the ground and changed you completely. But somehow, if you really wanted to, you could learn how to hold your breath as you made your way through the smoke left in its wake, and you could keep going. And sometimes, *sometimes*, you could grow something beautiful from the ashes that were left behind. If you were lucky.

And I was a really, really lucky bitch.

AUTHOR'S NOTE

I took some liberties with adoption laws. In my fantasy world, Dallas adopting Louie could happen.

ACKNOWLEDGMENTS

To the greatest readers in this universe and the next (and my Slow Burners!)—every time I release a new book, I think that you all can't get more amazing, but you do. Thank you for all your support and love, whether you've been with me from the beginning or just found my work, I am so grateful. I couldn't be here writing this for my sixth book if it wasn't for you.

A massive thank you to my friend Eva. Eva, oh Eva, where would this story be without you? You put up with me whining, freaking out, and stressing. You read my drafts when they're awful and advise me so well. You're a wonderful friend, and I'm so thankful that you put up with me.

Thank you to Letitia Hasser at RBA Design for the amazing cover. Jeff at Indie Formatting Services, thank you for your excellent formatting. Virginia and Becky at Hot Tree Editing for never breaking my heart when I go through edits. Lauren Abramo at Dystel & Goderich for getting my books into a format I never envisioned.

To my friends and pre-readers, thank you for your help!

A giant thank you to Kaitlyn AKA Pickles for answering my thousand and one questions about all things baseball related.

A great big thank you the people who mean the world to me: Mom and Dad, Ale, Eddie, Raul, Isaac, my Letchford family, and the rest of my Zapata/Navarro family. And last but never least, my three loves: Chris, Dor and Kai who remind me of what's important at the end of the day.

ABOUT THE AUTHOR

Mariana Zapata lives in a small town in Colorado with her husband and two oversized children—her beloved Great Danes, Dorian and Kaiser. When she's not writing, she's reading, spending time outside, forcing kisses on her boys, harassing her family, or pretending to write.

Mailing List (New Release Information Only)
Twitter: www.twitter.com/marianazapata_
Facebook: www.facebook.com/marianazapatawrites
Instagram: www.instagrame.com/marianazapata
Website: www.marianazapata.com
Email: marianazapata@live.com

ALSO BY MARIANA ZAPATA

Lingus

Under Locke

Kulti

Rhythm, Chord & Malykhin

The Wall of Winnipeg and Me

Printed in Great Britain
by Amazon

24403745R00378